**The full story of the legendary wizard Merlin—
revealed at last!**

The Lost Years of Merlin

"Wonderful." —Madeleine L'Engle

The Seven Songs of Merlin

"Full of action and excitement. . . . A tale of the heart."
—*Kirkus Reviews*

The Fires of Merlin

"Young readers with a taste for mythical adventures will devour Barron's books." —*BookPage*

The Mirror of Merlin

"With lots of surprises and some laugh-out-loud humor, this should be eagerly devoured by the saga's fans."

—*Booklist*

The Wings of Merlin

"Barron brings his epic story to an exciting and satisfying conclusion." —*The Horn Book Magazine*

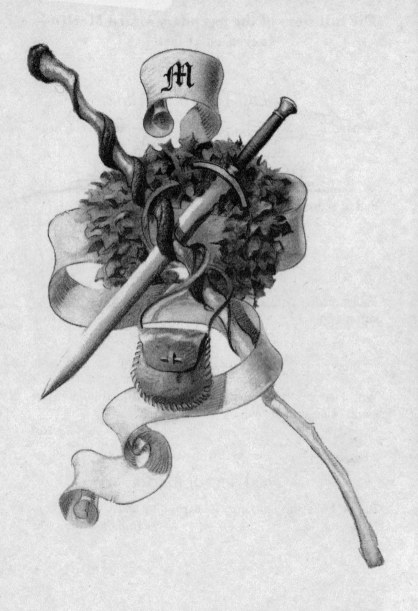

	DATE DUE	
AUG - 4 2004		
AUG - 9 2004		
AUG 3 1 2004		

This is a work of fiction. Names, characters, places, and incidents either are the
product of the author's imagination or are used fictitiously, and any resemblance to
actual persons, living or dead, business establishments, events, or locales is
entirely coincidental.

THE WINGS OF MERLIN

An Ace Book / published by arrangement with
the author

PRINTING HISTORY
Philomel Books hardcover edition / October 2000
Ace mass-market edition / November 2002
Ace digest edition / February 2003

Copyright © 2000 by Thomas Archibald Barron.
Cover art by Mike Wimmer.
Cover design by Rita Frangie.

Visit our website at
www.penguinputnam.com
Check out the ACE Science Fiction & Fantasy newsletter!

ISBN: 0-441-01024-5

ACE®
Ace Books are published by The Berkley Publishing Group,
a division of Penguin Putnam Inc.,
375 Hudson Street, New York, New York 10014.
ACE and the "A" design
are trademarks belonging to Penguin Putnam Inc.

PRINTED IN THE UNITED STATES OF AMERICA

10 9 8 7 6 5 4 3 2 1

*This book is dedicated to
the elusive wizard himself—
and to all those who have gathered to hear him
reveal, at last, the secrets of his lost years*

W   E

S

L
O
S

T H E

Ruins of Varigal

be there giants?

Lake of the Face

dwarves last seen here

living stones   Tuatha's Grave

crossing

Crystal Cave of the Grand Elusa

orchard

THE MISTED HILLS

Cobblers' Rowan

Arbassa, Home of Rhia

The River Unceas

DRUMA WOOD

Forgotten Island

The Last Shomorra

Trellings once lived here

shore of the speaking shells

Trouble found here

dunes

Emrys' Landing

I. SCHOENHERR MCMXCVI

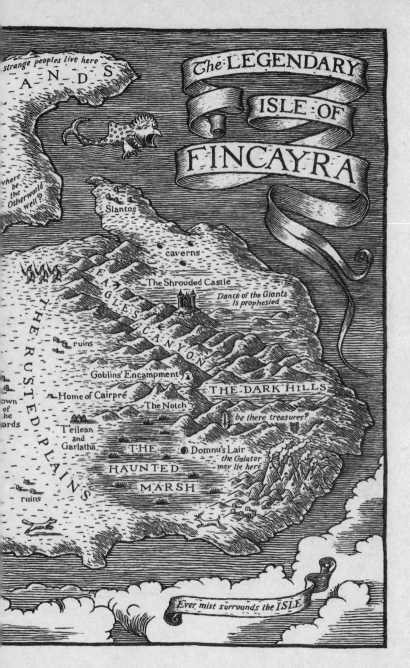

The LEGENDARY ISLE OF FINCAYRA

strange peoples live here

...ANDS

where be the Otherworld well?

Slantos

caverns

The Shrouded Castle

Dance of the Giants is prophesied

EAGLES' CANYON

ruins

THE RUSTED PLAINS

Goblins' Encampment

THE DARK HILLS

own of he ards

Home of Cairpré

The Notch

be there treasures?

T'eilean and Garlatha

THE HAUNTED MARSH

Domnu's Lair
the Galator may lie here

ruins

Ever mist surrounds the ISLE

THE·FORGOTTEN·ISLAND

here be treasures

People of the Mer
dwell here

The Forgotten
Island
"So it shall remain...
cursed and condemned."

SEAS

Main·Isle·of·FINCAYRA

IAN SCHOENHERR 2000

Voyagers:
Beware the
Web of Spells

To the Circle
of Stones

As·it·appeared·just·before

Winter's·Longest·Night

contents

PART ONE

PART TWO

PART THREE

AUTHOR'S NOTE

Almost a decade ago, I had a dream—strikingly vivid, deeply mysterious. In it a boy, nearly drowned, washed ashore on a strange, rugged coast. He had no memory at all of his childhood, not even his own name. And he certainly had no idea of the glorious destiny that awaited him.

Nor did I, in truth. For I hadn't yet realized that this lone, bedraggled boy was really the wizard Merlin. He bore no resemblance whatsoever to the legendary mentor of King Arthur, the mage of Camelot, the greatest enchanter of all times. No, that discovery would be the first of Merlin's many surprises.

But only the first. As those who have read the first four volumes of this epic already know, this wizard is full of surprises. He startled me, as his scribe, with the true nature of his sight, his family, and his heritage. Then he went on to introduce us all to the mysterious isle of Fincayra, unknown except to the ancient Celtic poets who called it an island beneath the waves, a bridge between the mortal Earth and the immortal Otherworld.

Fincayra has become Merlin's home. The people he loves most are there: Rhia, Shim, Elen, Cairpré, and Hallia, the deer-woman who has taught him how to run like a stag, hearing not just with his ears but with his very bones. The brave hawk, Trouble, along with the spirit lords Dagda and Rhita Gawr, may not be physically present, but they are never very far distant.

This mythic isle was best described by Merlin's mother, who saw Fincayra with a Druid's eyes, as a place much like the mist swirling about its shores. She called the island *an in between place*. Like the mist—which was neither quite water nor quite air, something of both and yet something else entirely—Fincayra is both mortal and immortal, dark and light, fragile and everlasting. Just how fragile it truly is, young Merlin will discover in this book, which concludes *The Lost Years of Merlin* epic.

In this volume, Merlin will also discover some new aspects of his own spirit—aspects that are, themselves, truly in between. For the wizard he is destined to become is not really a man, yet not really a god; not fully shadowed, yet not fully luminous. When he becomes Arthur's mentor, his greatest wisdom will spring from his essential humanity, his understanding of both our frailties and our highest possibilities. And his greatest power will arise from those elusive meeting places of nature and culture, masculinity and femininity, consciousness and dreams.

Much of Merlin's depth as a character, I am convinced, stems from these very qualities. And something more: They make him the perfect mentor for a young and idealistic king, a king whose vision of a just society would fail in his own realm, but would lodge firmly in the realm of the heart—so firmly that Merlin's pupil would ultimately be celebrated as the Once and Future King. Small wonder that Merlin himself, in tales stretching back fifteen centuries, has long been seen as a bridge builder, a unifier, a wizard of many worlds and many times.

The scope of his bridge building is astonishing. The very same Merlin who gives counsel to a great ruler may well, a moment later, ask advice from a homeless wanderer—or from an ancient, green-eyed wolf roaming the mountainside. The same Merlin who urges his companions to seek the Holy Grail, with its abundant Christian symbolism, often speaks as a Druid master with the spirits of rivers and trees. The same Merlin who, in traditional tales, was fathered by a demon was also mothered by a near-saint. Most remarkable of all, the same Merlin who inspired so many tales hundreds and hundreds of years ago remains wholly present in our lives today. At the dawn of the twenty-first century, he is more alive than ever.

That half-drowned boy, spat out by the sea in the opening scene of *The Lost Years of Merlin*, could not have foreseen his remarkable destiny. Indeed, looking back on that day, the elder wizard intones:

> *If I close my eyes, and breathe to the rolling rhythm of the sea, I can still remember that long ago day. Harsh, cold, and lifeless it was, as empty of promise as my lungs were empty of air. . . .*
>
> *Perhaps I remember it so clearly because the pain, like a scar on my soul, will not disappear. Or because it marked the ending of so much. Or, perhaps, because it marked a beginning as well as an ending: the beginning of my lost years.*

In time, I came to understand Merlin's greatest surprise. The lad who washed ashore on that fateful day was more than a boy, more even than a mythic figure. He was, himself, a metaphor.

Perhaps, like that boy, each of us harbors some hidden gifts. Gifts that are invisible to everyone, even ourselves, and yet remain there, waiting to be discovered. And who knows? Perhaps, like that boy, we harbor a bit of magic as well—magic that just might hold the makings of a wizard.

As with the prior volumes, I am most grateful to my wife, Currie, and my editor, Patricia Lee Gauch. All the other people I have thanked before, including Jennifer Herron, and each of my children, I thank once again. But one more source of inspiration deserves to be thanked above all: Merlin himself.

T. A. B.

Ay, wingëd as the summer wind,
I left the haunts of men behind:
By waters dire, through forests dark,
Under the white moon's silver arc;
O'er hill, down valley, far away.
Toward the sunset gathering gray,
I, Merlin, fled.

—From "Merlin and the White Death,"
a ballad by Robert Williams Buchanan

PROLOGUE

Wings, take me back! How often have I dreamed, in the centuries since that day, of returning to that place and time, of facing once again the choice that changed everything.

Such longing, though, is useless. An idea that is lost may yet be reborn, but a day that is lost is gone forever. And even if I could return, would I choose any differently? Probably not. Yet how can I be certain? Even after all these years, I know so very little.

But there is one thing I do know, a gift of that long ago day: Wings are far more than feathered arms. They are part mystery—and also part miracle. For what bears high the body may also give flight to the soul.

Bare feet in the water, the boy sat alone.

Though his sandy hair spun in jovial curls, his eyes, as brown as the muddy tarn before him, seemed strangely sad. Not that he minded being alone. As far back as he could recall—most of his eight or nine years—he'd lived that way. Even when others welcomed him at their meal table, offered him a pallet of straw for a night's rest, or shared their games with him, he knew his only real companion was solitude.

His life was simple—just like his name, Lleu. Whether the name had come from his parents before they died, or from someone else he'd met in his travels, he didn't know. And why should it matter? His name was just a word. A sound. Nothing more.

He plucked a reed, ran his finger down the shaft as if it were a tiny spear, and tossed it at a dead leaf floating in the water. A perfect hit: The leaf sank under the weight, sending rings of tiny ripples across the tarn. As the water lapped at his toes, the boy almost smiled.

Then, seeing that his spear had dislodged a small, lavender-backed beetle, he leaned forward. The little insect flailed, trying without success to work its sopping wings in the water. In a few seconds, it would drown. The boy stretched out his leg, caught the beetle on his toe, and brought it safely to shore.

"There ye be, friend." Taking the tiny creature in his hand, he blew gently on its wings. "Jest a bit o' sunshine an' ye'll be flyin' again."

Almost in answer, the beetle shivered and lifted into the air, flying haphazardly. It veered toward the boy's head. With a moist tap, it landed on top of his ear, then crawled onto one of his dangling curls.

"Likes me, do ye?"

Chuckling, the boy turned back to the tarn. This was one of his favorite places to camp, whenever his wanderings brought him to this part of Fincayra. Even now, as the days shortened and ice choked many streams, the water here still burbled freely. More than once, he'd caught a pheasant here, or made supper from the brambleberries lining the water's edge. And it was quiet, far from any roads, and the rascally knaves he sometimes met there.

Met—though not for long. He could outrun any of them. He could run for a whole day without stopping if necessary. Lifting one foot out of the water, he studied its calluses, as thick and rough as the leather on an old boot. But even better. These soles wouldn't wear out. All they needed was a tarn like this, for soaking after a long day's trek.

Lleu's face tightened. He scanned the wintry sky, watching the gray, leaden clouds slide above the leafless trees on the far side of the tarn. Turning back to his foot, he knew he'd really welcome a pair of boots, or sandals at least, in the colder days to come. Days when he might need to cross long stretches of snow to find his next meal.

To be sure, being an orphan had some advantages. He could roam wherever he pleased, sleep wherever he liked. The sky above was his ceiling, often brightly painted. Meals came at odd times, but at least they usually came. He expected little, and normally got it. And yet . . . he longed for something more. Placing his foot back in the cool, dark waters of the tarn, tinted red from the leaves still clinging to the bramble bushes, he thought about another place and time—a time too distant for memory, yet impossible to forget.

He couldn't recall her name. Nor even her face. The color of her eyes, the shape of her mouth, the length of her hair—all lay hidden, buried deeper than his dreams. He didn't know her name, or the sound of her voice. He wasn't even sure she was his mother.

But he remembered her smell. Earthy, like fallen leaves; tangy, like rose hips in summer; zesty, more than meadowsweet.

She had held him, that much he knew. Every so often, sitting by a tarn like this one, he might hear a blackbird warbling, and the wind humming through the reeds. And then he'd feel sure that she had sung to him, too. Yes, she had! What sort of song, in what sort of tones, he couldn't say. Yet he knew she'd held him close, singing softly, surrounding him with her fragrant skin.

He shuddered. Probably, he told himself, it was just a sudden chill in the air. Sunlight felt weaker at this time of the year, and the wind harsher. Already a tracery of ice lined the far side of the tarn. The longest nights of the year, he knew, lay just ahead.

But he'd survived other winters, at least five or six, and he'd survive this one, as well. Tomorrow he'd move farther south, closer to the coast. Meadows there stayed mostly unfrozen, and if snow fell, it rarely lasted for more than a day or two. As long as he didn't venture too close to the sea, and that shoreline where the dark mist swirled endlessly, forming twisted shapes and scary faces, he'd be fine.

A fire. That's what he needed now. He reached into the pocket of his tunic, squeezing some shavings of dry bark, as well as the pair of iron stones that never failed to spark a flame. He would warm himself, as well as the strip of dried beef a man had kindly tossed him that morning, and make camp for the night.

Lleu stood, scanning the bank as he slapped his feet on the mud. He knew from experience the weight and thickness of the sticks he needed for a good fire: several as thin as his smallest finger, a load or two of larger ones, and at least one about the size of his leg. Dry kindling was more tricky to find, especially at this time of year, which was why he always carried some. Otherwise he might have to use a strip of cloth from his tunic. And burning his tunic was burning his blanket.

Behind the brambles, he spied the largest branch he would need, ripped from a hawthorn tree by some heavy wind. He ran over. But the branch weighed more than he'd thought—too heavy to carry, or even drag. Nonetheless, he tried, tugging on it with all his weight. Still it wouldn't budge.

"All right then," he muttered aloud, "I'll bust ye! All I'm needin' is 'nuf to burn."

Bracing his foot against a cracked portion of the branch, he grabbed the upper end. Hard as he could, he pulled. The branch wriggled, creaking slightly, but didn't break. Again he tried, without success.

"Jest break now, will ye?"

As the boy set his hands to try again, a sword suddenly slashed through the air. The blade severed the branch, as if it were nothing more than a twig. A section just the right size to carry rolled on the muddy ground.

Grateful as well as startled, the boy whirled around. But his words of thanks caught in his throat. There, facing him, stood the most fearsome warrior he had ever seen—a man, immensely tall and sturdy, wearing a horned skull as a mask. Behind the mask shone wrathful eyes. And worse, the warrior carried two massive swords, each strapped to one of his arms.

Strange, thought the boy. *Those swords . . .* He sucked in his breath. They weren't, he suddenly realized, strapped to the man's arms. Rather, they were his arms, bound somehow to the warrior's powerful shoulders.

The masked man stared down at him. In a deep but hollow voice that seemed to echo from somewhere faraway, he commanded, "Tell me your name, boy."

"Ah, 'tis . . . Lleu, m-master." He tried to swallow, but his throat only made the sound of a whimper. "Least that's what I be mostly called."

"Have you no home?"

"N-no, master."

"Have you no parents?"

"N-no, master."

The warrior laughed mirthlessly, even as one of his swordlike arms lifted. "Then, young whelp, you shall be my first victim."

PART ONE

1

ᴛHREADS

This wasn't just a familiar stroll down a wooded path. No, this was something far different: more like a flight.

Luminous threads of light wove through the loom of branches, making the forest floor sparkle. The springy turf, softened by centuries of fallen leaves, seemed to lift me higher with every step. I felt I could leap into the trees, or sail like the golden butterflies among their branches. I had taken this woodland path many times before, to be sure. But it had never seemed at once so bright and so dark, so full of clarity as well as mystery.

Hallia, her hand in mine, walked with the same lilt in her step—and something more, the added grace of a deer. She knew, with every curl of her toe and sweep of her arm, the simple glory of motion. Truly, she *was* motion, as fluid as the falling leaf that spun downward from the highest boughs, as gentle as the forest breeze that stroked her auburn hair.

I smiled, thinking of the many such walks we had taken in the past few months. When she had first invited me to live among her people and learn their ways, several of the elders of her clan had objected. Long councils and fierce debates ensued. I was, after all, not a member of the Mellwyn-bri-Meath. And worse, I was a man. How could they possibly trust me with some of their most precious secrets, when my kind had so often hunted and killed their own, for no better reason than hunger for a slab of venison?

Hallia, in the end, had prevailed. The tales of how I'd saved her life didn't sway the elders, nor even the things I'd accomplished for the land of Fincayra. No, it was something far more simple, and powerful: Hallia's love for me. Faced with that, even the most skeptical members of her clan finally gave way. And so, in the time since, I'd learned how to drink water from the rill without disturbing its flow, how to feel the ground as if it were part of my own body, and how to hear with the openness of the air itself.

Such walks we had taken! Hallia guided me through meadows where ancient trails lay hidden, through tall stands of eelgrass that could be woven into baskets or clothing, and through secret glades where many a fawn-child had been born. Often we strode upright, as we did now. Just as often, we ran side by side as doe and stag, our bodies sailing above the soil more than treading upon it.

Yet on this day and on this trail, I felt closer to her than ever before. Tonight, when we reached the far side of the forest, I would show her a secret of my own—my stargazing stone. And there I would give her the present I'd been saving. I tapped my leather satchel in anticipation, knowing that in many ways the gift belonged to her already.

Seeing a stream just ahead, I lifted my staff so it wouldn't catch on the gooseberry brambles along the bank. Then, without a word, we leaped into the air, our four legs springing in unison as if they belonged to a single person. Beneath us, the water sparkled, its surface alive with light, even where it passed under a branch or over a moss-splattered stone. We landed gently on the opposite side and continued down the path.

I gazed about, my second sight—now sharper and truer than my lost eyesight had ever been—overwhelmed by the wide array of highlights and colors. Even the etchings on my staff seemed to glimmer with the magic surrounding us. Dew glistened on rain-washed limbs, while the forest floor shone orange, scarlet, and brown. Above our heads, a pair of squirrels, their eyes nearly as large as their bulging cheeks, scurried over a branch, chattering ceaselessly. Beech trees' smooth bark reflected the sun like mirrors, and linden leaves trembled like running streams. Clumps of moss, deep green flecked with red, nestled among the burly roots of oaks and pines, often joined by parades of yellow toadstools.

Resins wafted everywhere—from the needles of fir trees, sweeter than honeysuckle; from rainwater cupped in palmate leaves, as rich in smells as marshland pools; and from fallen branches already more soil than wood. I could smell, not far away, the gamey scent of a fox's den. And I knew that the fox itself could smell us approaching.

The sound of the stream behind us merged with the undulating whisper of wind among the branches. And, as always, I heard in the forest wind many distinct voices: the deep sighing of oak, the crackling of ash, the rhythmic whooshing of pine. Many voices, yes—and one above all, the unified breath of the living forest.

A place of many wonders. Those words, the first description I'd ever heard of Fincayra, never felt so true as today. Especially here, in the depths of Druma Wood. Even the harsh winds of winter, which had already brought snow and frost to much of the rest of Fincayra, seemed unable to penetrate here. Though some forest animals had retreated to their burrows and hollow logs, and many trees had changed to brown and tan, the Druma still pulsed with life.

And that wasn't all that set this forest apart. Much of Fincayra still suffered from the long years of suspicion, even hatred, that divided its many races and kept them separate from one another—and especially from the race of men and women. But not here. Even during Stangmar's Blight, when creatures in other parts of the island feared to show themselves in daylight, this place remained at peace. Here, someone's good fortune also gave strength to others; one creature's loss brought widespread grief. It was truly a community.

Hallia squeezed my hand, halting us both. Following her gaze, I spied an extraordinary bird perched on a branch above our heads. There was no mistaking the bright purple crest on its head, nor the flaming scarlet feathers along its tail. An alleah bird! For a breathless moment, the creature watched us in silence, cocking its head pensively. Then, with a dazzling flash of iridescence, it flew off into the forest and disappeared.

"The long-tailed alleah bird," whispered Hallia. "A sign of good luck."

At that instant, something slammed into my back, sending me sprawling into a stand of hip-high ferns. I tumbled through the stalks, finally smacking into a boulder. Head spinning, I crawled free of the ferns. With effort, I straightened my leather satchel, which had wrapped itself around my neck, retrieved my staff, and started to regain my feet.

"Greetings, Brother." Rhia, dressed in a suit of tightly woven vines, placed her hands upon her hips and laughed heartily. "You're still my favorite place to land."

"Sure," I groaned. "But great seasons! Need you always land so hard?"

She reached down and tugged on my arm to help me stand. "Well, you might not notice me otherwise." She paused to give Hallia a knowing wink. "Occupied as you are with the world of romance."

Hallia's face flushed as red as the leaves of wild geranium by her feet. "Rhia!"

"Haka-haka-tikky-tichhh," cackled a tiny creature who had poked his head out of the leafy pocket on Rhia's sleeve. His small, furred head bobbed with laughter, causing his long ears to flap against the sides of his face. Meanwhile, his lopsided grin opened wide, revealing only three teeth, all of them as green as his eyes.

"Haka-haka-tichhh. Poor lover manman!" cried the beast, speaking in a rapid, squeaky voice, almost too fast for me to catch his words. "Lost his wittywits, he has. Now his balance, too! Haaa-ha-haka-tch."

I glowered at him. "Quiet there, skinny ears! Or I'll—"

Hallia stepped over and touched her finger to my lips. "Hush, now. He's just a scullyrumpus, and they're all endless pranksters. He can't help himself, young hawk."

Hearing her use my familiar name, I suddenly relaxed. As I looked into her wide brown eyes, as deep as magical pools, I forgot my anger. All I could think of was the woman beside me, the woman I loved. Slowly, I leaned closer, ready to . . .

"Kissiesnug! Kissiesnug!" exclaimed the beast, flapping his oversized ears. "No more words for clumsy manman. Just kissies! Haka-haka-hakakakak."

Straightening myself, I glared at Rhia. "Why do you keep that little pest around?"

She watched me with amusement, even as she scratched his furry neck. "Scully? Oh, we have lots in common. He's part of the forest, like me. And a tree dweller, like me."

"And totally disrespectful," I added.

She nodded. "Also like me."

Despite myself, I grinned. "All right. But can't you stop landing on me like that?"

"Why? It keeps you humble."

To my dismay, Hallia herself smiled.

"Keeps me bruised and broken!" I roared.

"Oo-cha-oooo-cha," squeaked the beast, waving his paws in mock terror. "Now clumsy man veryveryvery angry." To Rhia, he cried, "Better go now. Next time he fallfalls, could be on us!"

He clutched his sides, cackling so merrily he almost fell out of the pocket. "You too, deersister," he called to Hallia. "Run away fast, ha-chhh-ha-chhh. Fast as hoofyfeet will carry you!"

This was too much for me. "Enough, Scullyrumpus." I brandished my staff. "One more insult and I'll turn you into the worm you really are."

Instead of shrinking back into the pocket in fear, as I'd expected, he simply scowled back at me. "Scullyrumpus Eiber y Findalair to you," he piped. "Think you cannycan use first name only? A cheeky little manman you are."

"Cheeky!" I exclaimed, my temples pounding. "You dare call *me* cheeky?"

Rhia raised her hand. "Hold, Merlin." She glanced down at the beast on her sleeve. "And you, Scully. It's too lovely a day for this." To emphasize the point, she gave her head a shake, tossing her brown curls. "Come now, Brother. You can join me."

"Join you?"

"Yes. I'm learning to fly."

I glared at her. "You'll have to sprout wings first."

"Not that way, you fool." She rubbed her hands on her leafy thighs, wiping away any moisture. Then she secured to her belt the small orange globe that sometimes, as now, showed no light, but other times glowed without any warning: the Orb of Fire. Her care, I knew, was justified, for like the other legendary Treasures of Fincayra, the

Orb held great power—and even greater mystery. Ready at last, she reached for one of the thick vines dangling nearby. Then she announced, with great confidence, "This way."

Her furry companion nodded, ears flapping. At the same time, he shrank deeper into the pocket.

Wrapping her hands and feet around the vine, Rhia uttered something in the low, rustling tongue of a hemlock. Instantly, the tree behind her straightened its trunk, lifting the vine and her with it. Again she spoke a command, and the vine whipped suddenly, hurling her through the canopy of branches. Hallia and I gasped in unison as she let go, spun twice through the air, then grabbed hold of another vine. This time she swung a wide arc, showering us with needles and twigs. Again she released, flipped over, and spread her arms outward like a pair of wings. For a split second, she hung there, resting on nothing but air.

Hallia clutched my arm. "She's going to fall!"

I stiffened, my mind racing. Should I make a gust of wind? Another vine?

Before I could do anything, the hemlock tree swept itself around. A long, wide-limbed branch reached out and caught Rhia bodily, bouncing with her weight. Swiftly, the tree lowered her. Just above the ground, she rolled free, twirled in the air, and landed gently on her feet, smiling broadly. She stood before us, stroking the bulge on her sleeve where Scullyrumpus had withdrawn.

Hallia sighed. "Rhia, you are truly a herd of one."

"Thanks," she replied, working back into her hair the dressing of leaves that had come loose. "Care to try?"

Hallia's round eyes shone with amusement. "No, no. Unlike those of you who crave those wings you lost so long ago, we deer-folk have no need to fly."

"Once you took a ride on the back of your dragon friend," Rhia reminded her.

"That was Gwynnia's idea, not mine! I jumped off the first instant I could."

Rhia faced me. "How about you then, Merlin? Are you willing to try?" Sensing my hesitation, she added, "Or will that stubble on your chin have to grow into a full-length beard before you have enough courage?"

Hallia glanced at me worriedly. "Don't, young hawk."

"I've no lack of courage," I declared, rubbing my chin.

"Justjust intelligence," said a muffled voice in Rhia's sleeve.

"Quiet, now," barked Rhia. "Let him try." Turning back to me, she said, "Now, here's how you—"

Ignoring her, I tossed aside my staff, unbuckled my sword, and reached for the vine. Brusquely, I spoke my own rustling phrase. To my own surprise, the vine jumped upward, carrying me aloft. Wind rushed by my face, streaming my black locks of hair, fluttering the sleeves of my tunic. Feeling my confidence swell, I spoke again, and the vine swung around the hemlock's trunk, slicing graceful curves through the air. Over limbs and under I sailed, as free as a soaring hawk.

Flush with the joy of flight, I called once more to the tree. A new vine whipped to my side. At the highest point of my arc, I cast the old vine aside and leaped to grasp the new one. For several heartbeats I floated high above the ground, feeling like a creature of the wind itself. Even as I reached for the vine, its supple length wrapped around my hands and feet.

Holding tight to the vine, I plummeted downward, ready for the sudden tensing that I knew would hurl me high into the boughs again. Lack of courage, indeed! Rhia should know better by now. Down, down, down, I sped, watching the whirl of green and brown.

Craaack! My back rammed into a spiky lower branch, snapping it off completely. A rustling howl arose from the tree. My vine jerked violently, shaking me loose. I hurtled through open air, flying straight into the same patch of ferns where I'd landed when Rhia first arrived. With a thud, I hit the ground, rolling through the ferns and smacking into the boulder again.

It was all I could do to lift my head, and then only for a moment. I slumped back into the stalks. My entire body ached, especially the tender spot between my shoulder blades. With supreme effort, I tried to stand, but a new spell of dizziness struck and I collapsed again.

Hallia and Rhia rushed over. Together, they dragged me out of the ferns and helped me stretch out on the soft turf of the path. Pulling a mass of torn fronds from my mouth, I could only sputter, "What . . . happened?"

Hallia merely shook her head. Rhia, for once, said nothing. Even the little terror in her pocket remained silent, probably because he knew he was within my reach.

"I guess flying," I said groggily, "takes more than courage."

At that, the hemlock twitched abruptly. From high among its branches, a single cone fell, plunking me on the forehead.

As I groaned, Rhia bobbed her head. "Right," she agreed. "Much more."

2

TREASURES

When at last I felt steady enough to rise, I stumbled over to a nearby stream and plunged in my whole head. The frigid water slapped my cheeks and chilled my tongue, and soon I felt revived. Even then, it took me several minutes before I could walk without tripping over roots or branches. And several more before I could find my leather satchel, torn off during my attempt to ride the vines.

It was Rhia who spied it. High above our heads, it dangled in the arching branches of the hemlock. She made a sharp, creaking sound, and the tree stirred. The satchel broke loose, but snagged on a lower branch. This time it tipped upside down, dropping its contents to the forest floor. Down came my supply of healing herbs—mostly willow-root, rosemary, sprite's balm, and the white-tipped mushroom called Loth's bane—along with three more precious items: a seed, a string, and a feather.

The seed, no bigger than a rounded pebble, hit the ground first, bouncing on the springy turf and rolling to a stop not far from my feet. I picked it up, holding the little sphere in the palm of my hand. As I had many times before, I felt its magical pulsing, almost like a beating heart. And I recalled the words that had been spoken when it was entrusted to my care: *If you succeed in finding just the right place for the planting, this seed will bear fruit more magnificent than you can possibly guess.*

My brow furrowed. *Just the right place for the planting . . .* Where could that be? How would I know?

Then, draped over a root covered with purple moss, I saw my piece of string, charred and twisted by fire. As I reached for it, Hallia's gaze met mine, and the understanding in her doelike eyes cheered me. For she knew, as did I, that this tarnished old string was all that remained of a musical instrument—the psaltery I'd made myself at the fabled tree called the Cobbler's Rowan. And she also knew, as did I, that it held a surprising power.

As I gathered up the string, I scanned the area, searching for any sign of my third small treasure. Finding none on the ground, I looked upward, following the shafts of light across the hemlock's tangled boughs. There it was! My feather rested lightly on a branch just beneath my satchel. Streaked with silver and brown, it reminded me of its original owner: the feisty hawk, Trouble, who had given his life to spare my own.

A gentle waft of wind caught the feather, dislodging it. Gracefully it drifted downward, playing with the currents, spinning and weaving even as Trouble himself had once so enjoyed doing. At last, the feather approached, brushing softly against my shoulder before falling into my open hand.

"Nice catchycatch, clumsy man," Scullyrumpus rasped, poking out of his niche on Rhia's sleeve. "Too bad your sacksack still up there! Maybe try ride again on viny rope? Haka, haka-hachhhh-hach-ch-ch." He clutched the ends of his ears, laughing mirthfully.

Clumsy man. He said it so fast it sounded like a single word. My anger rose, but I didn't let it show. With a slight turn of my wrist, I beckoned to the satchel. Instantly, it started quivering. The branch shook, sprinkling us with needles, as the leather cord gracefully unwound, untangling itself. A few seconds later, the satchel pulled free, sailed around several more limbs, and dropped to the ground beside me.

The beast's eyes narrowed considerably, and he released a squeaky version of a growl.

I retrieved the satchel. "No viny ropes necessary."

Another growl, louder this time.

"Be fair, now," admonished Rhia, planting a finger on her companion's tiny black nose. "That was nicely done." She considered me. "You've honed your Leaping skills, haven't you?"

"A little," I replied, tying a knot in the satchel's severed cord. "But I still have a long way—a *very* long way—to go. Making small objects go where I want is one thing. Making myself go where I want is quite another, believe me."

Hallia started combing her hair with her slender fingers. "I believe you! The last time you tried to send someone by Leaping, the two of us ended up in the middle of the Haunted Marsh."

"Hecha-hecha-hech-ch-ch," cackled Scullyrumpus. "A lovely placeyplace, that is."

I frowned. "Perhaps you'd like to go there now?"

For the first time, I saw a genuine glimmer of fear in his face. The lopsided grin vanished, and his ears wiggled nervously. He looked so frightened that I almost felt sorry for the little fellow. Then, without warning, he burst into howls of laughter. "Hakacha-cha-cha, cheechee. Clumsy manman fooled again! Haka, haka, ho-ho-hee, ho-ho-hee, hoo hoo."

Seething, I started to speak, when Hallia cut me off. "Shouldn't we be going, young hawk?" Her eyes gleamed, as she shook her hair playfully. "You said you had something to show me."

"That's right," I replied, sending a sharp glance at the bothersome beast. Then, turning back to Hallia, I added, "And something to give you, as well."

"Where are you going?" asked Rhia.

"To the stargazing stone. You know the place—on the hill north of the old stringfruit tree."

She nodded. "Perfect place to camp, I agree."

My face fell. "You mean . . . you're coming?" I waved at her sharp-tongued passenger. "Him, too?"

Rhia leaned closer, placing her hand on the gnarled top of my staff. "A little company will do you good. You two have been spending so much time by yourselves recently, the trees are full of whispers."

Hallia cocked her head to one side. "Really? What do they say?"

"Oh, just whispers."

"What do they say?" pressed Hallia.

Rhia almost grinned. "Well . . . that you two are as close as honey on a leaf."

Scullyrumpus rolled his eyes. "Lovesicky whispers. *Aagghh!* Makes me want to stuff ears with mud."

"Good idea," I suggested. "You should try it."

"Anyway," Rhia went on, "we're heading that direction. We're meeting Mother the day after tomorrow. She's traveling with Cairpré, as you know, and invited me to join them for a night." With more than a touch of mischief, she added, "Care to come along?"

"Er, no. Much as I miss her, and also Cairpré, these days I have . . . other plans."

"So I noticed," she said knowingly. "Oh well. It looks like tonight will be my last chance to see you for a while."

I blew a sigh and turned to Hallia. "It seems we're stuck."

Gently, she brushed the back of my hand. "Like honey on a leaf."

The branches above us stirred, slapping themselves together as if they were applauding. Beams of light shimmered on the roots, leaves, and strips of bark that lined the forest floor. A round hedgehog, nestled at the base of a scarlet maple, lifted its head at the touch of warm light. Its small, black eyes examined us, calmly passing from one face to the next, until it apparently concluded that we weren't worth interrupting a nap for. Replacing its head upon its bristly back, the creature closed its eyes and returned to slumber.

Rhia tapped the head of my staff. "In case you're worried, I'll be taking the faster route to the stargazing stone. That will give you two a little more time for, well, whatever." She lifted an eyebrow. "Just remember, the trees are watching."

I shifted, suddenly feeling rather warm in my tunic.

Clearly enjoying my discomfort, she whispered in my ear, "You two deserve some time alone."

In her sleeve, Scullyrumpus snorted. "Clumsy manman not know what to do, anyway."

Before I could respond, Rhia reached up and seized the lowest branch of the hemlock towering above us. Swinging herself onto the limb, she waved down at us. "See you there for supper."

"Wait," I protested. "There *isn't* any faster route to the stargazing stone. This path is the way."

"It's one way," she called back, "but not the fastest."

With that, she swished three times in succession. The hemlock's limb bent low, almost down to the ground. Rhia, her face alight, gave her curls a shake. Scullyrumpus did the same, flapping his ears against his furry cheeks. Another swishing sound—and the branch whipped upward, hurling them high into the air.

"Whee-hee-heeee," cried Rhia, spreading her arms and legs wide. Before she even started to descend, an oak branch, completely bare of leaves, reached out to catch her. That branch cradled her momentarily, carried her higher, then pitched her across the canopy to the waiting boughs of a cedar. Spraying cones in all directions, the cedar tossed her affectionately several times before finally flinging her onward. Seconds later, Rhia's cries of delight had faded into the whispering and clacking of the trees around us.

Watching her disappear, I smiled. "She is part eagle, part tree."

"Yes," agreed Hallia. "And she loves you as much as she loves this forest."

"What makes you say that?"

She merely bent down to gather a few sap-dusted cones in her hands. Bringing them to her face, she inhaled deeply. After a moment, she offered them to me. Like her, I savored their aromas, so fresh and full.

"Because Rhia knows," she said softly, "that for us, a little time alone is the best gift of all."

3
RASPBERRY SYRUP

Before we reached the edge of the forest, the smell of Rhia's cooking fire reached us. Wrapping around Hallia and me like a long scarf, the savory smoke drew us out of the intertwining boughs and into a grassy clearing. A small but steep hill lifted above us, crowned with the great flat boulder that was my stargazing stone. From atop the stone, smoke curled upward, branching out like a wispy tree before merging with the twilight sky.

We paused in the knee-high grasses, a few more seconds with only ourselves. She watched me as I watched her, the two of us breathing in unison. I reached over and stroked her chin with my finger. Shyly, she turned away, though not completely. Leaning closer, I turned her face back toward mine, and gently kissed her on the lips.

"He knew," she whispered. "My brother, Eremon, knew. Do you remember what he said before he left us for the Otherworld of the spirits?"

I nodded. "That a day would come when you would be happy again."

She swallowed, and brushed the moistness from her cheek. "When I would overflow with joy, he said, *as the river in spring overflows with water.*" After a long pause, she said quietly, "I can't imagine living without you, young hawk."

"Nor I without you, Eo-Lahallia." I cleared my throat. "There's something I've been wanting to give you. I planned to do it tonight, under the stars, but I'd rather give it to you now, while we're still alone."

"What more could you give me?"

"This." Without looking away, I reached into my leather satchel. Slowly, I drew out my psaltery string, bent and blackened. "It's for you."

Her doe's eyes blinked. Slowly, a smile spread across her face. I knew she was remembering how this very string had once saved our lives—as well as the life of her friend, the dragon Gwynnia.

"For me?" she asked.

"For you." I placed the string in her hand. Despite its charred exterior, it bent with surprising suppleness, curling easily inside her palm.

She swallowed. "I shall never look at this without thinking of how much your power has grown."

Softly, I replied, "Even as something else has grown."

"Do you remember the old riddle? About the origins of music—and magic?"

I studied her open hand, and the precious item that it held. "How could I not? *So where, indeed, does the source of music lie?*"

She nodded, then completed the passage: *"Is it in the strings themselves? Or in the hand that plucks them?"*

I placed my hand over hers, covering the gift. "It lies in both places, but in your hand most of all."

"No," she replied. "The greater music lies in the place where both our hands are touching."

I could only smile.

In time, our hands released. With care, she started to place the precious item into the pocket of her purple robe.

I caught her arm. "Wait. I have a better idea." Swiftly, I wrapped the string around her wrist and tied the ends together with a wizard's knot. "There now. A bracelet."

She studied the gift, then me. "Thank you," she whispered.

"You're welcome, my love."

Hand in hand, we walked up the slope, stiff stalks of grass brushing against our legs. As we advanced, the smell of smoke grew stronger—along with traces of other smells, both tangy and sweet. Near to the top, we halted, huffing from the climb. For a moment we looked at each other's faces, darkened by the onset of evening, which came so early at this time of year. Then, wordlessly, we started climbing again.

Just as we topped the hill, a cloud of smoke blew over us, so dense it seared our eyes and throats. We darted to the side, waving away the dark cloud, coughing uncontrollably. When, at last, the air cleared and I could breathe normally, I spotted Rhia, looking down on us from the stargazing stone. She sat cross-legged, tending a snapping fire.

"Welcome," she said placidly, tossing another branch onto the flames.

"Some welcome," I replied, coughing again to clear my throat. "You know just how to make someone feel at home."

Scullyrumpus hopped nearer to the fire and added a twig of his own. In his usual rapid delivery, he piped, "In my home clumsy man not asked for supper, nonono."

My eyes narrowed. "In my home, you'd be *eaten* for supper."

"Stop, you two," said Hallia, wiping her eyes. "It's just a little smoke, that's all."

Together, we climbed up the side of the boulder—Hallia much more gracefully than I. When we reached the flat surface on top, she reached into the folds of her robe and pulled out a long, slender fruit that glowed pink in the firelight. She offered it to Rhia. "Here. The very last stringfruit from the tree over there. Are we too late to cook it?"

"Not at all." Rhia took it, peeled its skin quickly, and plucked out several triangular seeds. Handing the seeds back to Hallia, she dropped the milky white flesh into a pot made from an immense black nutshell. "There's plenty more cooking right now."

Plenty, indeed. Surrounding her on the stone were the husks of four different types of beans; remnants of sweet sassafras, beetroot, and turnip; cracked shells of walnuts, chestnuts, and almonds; as well as dicings of onion shoots, mushrooms yellow and brown, fir cones, pepperbulb, and a few late sprigs of mint. From the three interlocking sticks that served as her tripod over the fire, Rhia had dangled the simmering pot, as well as some strips of linden bark, frosted with resins. On a mat of woven rye grass behind her sat a thick slab of honeycomb, an assortment of herbs and spices, plus a cupped leaf that I knew contained sweet butterfly milk.

Hallia sat down and started cracking the seeds, using an almond shell and a stick as her mortar and pestle. Soon, she had ground them into a fine, pink-tinted powder. With care, she sprinkled the powder into the pot. Rhia gave a grateful nod as she continued to stir the contents, now bubbling vigorously.

Rich aromas filled the air, especially since the smoke had died down substantially. Glowing pine branches, sizzling with sap, popped and hissed beneath the pot. Seating myself between the others, I reached for Rhia's flask, made from goat's bladder and embroidered with a web of vines that seemed as fresh and vibrant as those on her gown. Using two halves of walnut shells as miniature cups, I poured some deep purple liquid into each.

"Raspberry syrup, anyone?" I asked, offering the tiny cups to Rhia and Hallia.

"Wonderful," said Hallia with a sigh, as she leaned back against an outcropping of stone. "It's truly a gift to have a little taste of spring even now, more than a month after the first frost."

"Mmm," agreed Rhia with a smack of her lips. "I'm so glad, Merlin, you remembered. I got so caught up with supper that I forgot the flask was there."

I nudged her. "If you're there, something sweet to drink is also there. I've learned that by now."

"Notnot learned how to count, though," groused the furry fellow on her thigh. His bright green eyes watched me expectantly.

Grudgingly, I poured him a shell of his own. As I handed it to him, his little paws snatched it away and lifted the contents to his face. Whiskers trembling, he swallowed it speedily, not even pausing to take a breath. When finally he lowered the cup, his three teeth had been stained purple.

I knew better than to wait for a word of thanks. Pouring myself a cup, I capped the flask and set it aside. My first sip exploded with flavor, filling my mouth with the sweetness of spring—and my heart with gratitude for the fields and forests and shores of Fincayra, where every taste seemed sharper, every scent stronger, and every color richer.

"I'm wishing," I said wistfully, "that we could stay here, in this time and place, forever."

Hallia glanced at me, her expression as warm as the fire.

"As long as we don't run out of raspberry syrup," replied Rhia. She reached for some thick, waxy leaves that she had molded into bowls and dipped out some stew for each of us. She set Scullyrumpus' bowl on the ground, since it was too heavy for him to hold. Grumpily, he crawled down from her leg and started lapping at the steaming contents. Meanwhile, Rhia handed Hallia and me each a strip of linden bark for use as a spoon (or, if crunched into bits, as additional seasoning).

As we savored the rich, nutty flavor of the stew, the last touches of daylight, lavender as the petals of flowers, vanished from the sweeping forest that stretched outward from the base of our hill. Though the light had dimmed, no stars had yet appeared. I looked upward, appraising our chances for stargazing later on. To my dismay, lumbering clouds were massing to the north. Already, they were starting to spread across the darkening sky, like ships of war sailing into a tranquil harbor.

In time, Rhia produced a pair of golden biscuits apiece. Topped with cream from the butterfly milk, and a scattering of mint, they made the perfect dessert—if, that is, Rhia hadn't already had another dessert in mind. In fact, she had two. First, she passed around fresh slices of honeycomb for us all, flavored with the subtle tartness of rose-hip blossoms. Then, from underneath the coals of the fire, she retrieved the very last apple of the season, the gift of one of the Druma's late-blooming fruit trees, baked with lavish amounts of honey and cinnamon.

As we split the steaming, juicy bits of apple among ourselves, Rhia removed the tripod and cooking pot, then threw a few more pine boughs on the fire. Instantly, the flames spurted higher. I noticed my shadow swaying in the flickering light, and it gave me an idea. Tapping the shadow lightly with my finger, I nodded at the flames.

Instantly, my shadow leaped closer to the fire. Throwing itself upon the shelf of rock behind Rhia, it started to dance, spinning and twirling wildly. Seeing this, Scullyrumpus shrieked in fear, dropped his apple slice, and scurried up Rhia's arm to his hiding place. As the rest of us grinned, my shadow continued to cavort in the light of the fire, showing its best leaps and twists, rolls and spins.

Rhia's bell-like laughter rose into the night air. "It looks like a fledgling jumping around in the nest, trying to find some way to fly."

"No," I answered. "More like *you* jumping around, trying to find some way to fly."

At that, we all laughed. Except, of course, for Scullyrumpus, who remained buried in Rhia's leafy pocket.

Finally, I motioned to the shadow with my hand. The antics ceased abruptly. "Excellent, most excellent. All right now, come back to me."

But the shadow did not follow my command. Sulkily, it placed its hands upon its hips, glared at me for a moment, and sat down at the opposite side of the fire. Knowing my shadow well, I merely shook my head.

"As you can see," I muttered, "it's still as obedient as ever."

"Actually," said Hallia, licking some honey off her wrist, "it's just about as obedient as its master."

"Right," chimed in Rhia. "And besides, maybe it simply loves to dance. How can you blame it for that?"

"I can't." Looking upward again, I scowled at the thick clouds moving over us, already obscuring Pegasus, the first constellation to show. "Fumblefeathers!" I exclaimed. "We may not have any stargazing at all tonight."

Hallia placed her hand on my knee. "Don't fret, young hawk. It's still been a beautiful evening." She touched her bracelet, glittering in the firelight. "Truly beautiful."

A chill wind, driving the clouds overhead, swept through the trees below us, making them moan and clatter. Dead leaves swirled in the night air as the wind rushed across our hilltop. Quickly, Rhia reached to catch a walnut shell and two linden strips before they blew over the edge of the stone. The fire sputtered, and Hallia slid closer to my side for warmth. Defiantly, I threw another branch onto the coals. But the wind blew stronger, and the wood barely smoldered.

Slapping her hands against her sides, Rhia said, "Feels like winter all of a sudden."

"It does," agreed Hallia. "But the truth is, winter's been with us for a while already. Even the Druma is much less lively now. No amount of baked apples and raspberry syrup can change that. The longest night of the year is just two weeks away."

I nodded, feeling more glum than I could explain. "Summer doesn't last forever," I mused. "Nothing does—not even our time in Fincayra."

At my words, Hallia tensed and withdrew her hand. "Please, not now. I don't want to think about that."

"Sorry. I only meant . . ."

She frowned. "And I don't give a hoofprint about that sword of yours, either."

"I'm not talking about the sword," I grumbled.

"Well then, it's that young king, from the place called Britannia. The one you promised would carry the sword one day."

"It's not about him, either—though I do see his face often enough in my dreams." I sucked in my breath. "No, it's the fact we all know: that someday Rhia and I, being part human, will have to leave."

"Why?" asked Rhia, trying to poke some life into the fire. "Maybe Dagda, great spirit that he is, will just change that ridiculous old law."

I shook my head, even as the wind howled anew.

"He can do whatever he wants. Besides, it's just a silly rule."

"But it's not! You know that. It's part of what keeps all the worlds separated, and in balance—Earth, Otherworld, and Fincayra somewhere in between."

"I know, I know," she replied. "But Dagda himself might be surprised. Like he was when you, just a boy, overthrew Stangmar."

Stangmar. The name itself blew more frigid than the wind. How could a man, entrusted to rule all Fincayra, have become so corrupted, so twisted? He had utterly destroyed that trust—and so much more besides. The anguish of his Blighted Years still lay thick upon the land.

Whatever troubles had existed among the races before Stangmar's reign, they were far worse now. I thought of Hallia's own people, so reluctant to allow a stranger in their midst. And the canyon eagles, who rarely showed themselves at all anymore. The dwarves never even spoke to the giants, once their allies; any man or woman foolish enough to enter the dwarves' territory would probably never leave it alive. The examples went on and on.

To be sure, Stangmar didn't deserve all the blame. Rhita Gawr had played a terrible part in all this. It was he, warlord of the spirit world and Dagda's eternal foe, who corrupted Stangmar and bullied him into fostering rage and mistrust among others, so Rhita Gawr himself could ultimately rule. The balance between the worlds meant nothing to him—only his craving for power.

Even so, Stangmar should have resisted. Known better! Closing my hand into a fist, I imagined him now, imprisoned in the lightless cavern where he would remain until his bones finally rotted away. Good riddance! No one—except perhaps Dinatius, the fool who tried long ago to kill both me and my mother—had ever made me feel so much anger as that man Stangmar. Why, I wondered? Why couldn't I move beyond that anger?

Because Stangmar was more than a wicked ruler. More, even, than a warrior who had tried to strike me down when I stood against him. He was, beneath all those things, one thing more. He was my father.

Ever so lightly, Hallia's hand touched my brow. "Come, young hawk. Let's forget about all that for now. This day has been ours, and nothing can ever take that away from us."

I nodded, though deep within myself I didn't feel so sure.

4
A DISTANT DOORWAY

That night, to shelter ourselves from the wind, we slid off the stargazing stone and hiked down the steep slope to the base of the hill. Even among the thick grasses, howling gusts whipped past, raking us with icy fingers. The constant rattling and groaning of limbs in the surrounding forest made sleeping all the more difficult.

In time, the others drifted off—Hallia curled snugly in the manner of a deer, and Rhia stretched out as if she were resting in the boughs of a tree, her fingers twirling the vines of her gown. Scullyrumpus joined them in slumber, snoring in high-pitched whistles within Rhia's pocket. Only I lay awake, rolling from side to side, rearranging my pillow of grasses to find a comfortable position. All the while, dark clouds scudded overhead. Whenever a glimpse of starlight broke through, the clouds swiftly erased it. Some stargazing night this had turned out to be!

Knowing I needed to relax, I thought back over the day, hoping to find some memory that could calm the churning waters of my mind. There was the bracelet, and Hallia's smile upon receiving it; the vine, and the momentary thrill of flight—before it ended all too suddenly; the little hedgehog lazily scrutinizing us. At last, I hit upon the vision I'd been searching for: the sight of Trouble's silver-brown feather, drifting slowly to the ground. In my mind I watched its fall, riding the air with ease and grace, over and over again. In time, I began to relax. And finally, to sleep.

I dreamed, not surprisingly, of the feather, floating gracefully. Yet this time the feather was enormous, at least in comparison to me. For I was seated on it, riding the currents of air.

Once, long before, I had ridden on Trouble's back as he soared through the night. He had carried me effortlessly then, and did so again now, though this time nothing more than his feather supported me. Chilled air flowed over my face, enough to make my sightless eyes water, and I nestled deeper into the bristling quills to stay warm. The feather quivered, as did I, with every new gust, both of us moving as one with the wind.

Freedom. That's what I felt, more than anything else. The freedom to float aloft, following the currents wherever they chose to bear me. I didn't need to know where I was going. Nor did I care.

Without warning, the world darkened. The feather's bands of silver and brown turned to dull, uniform gray. A new rush of air, colder than before, tore over me. I grasped at the quills, trying not to fall off.

From out of the dark clouds above came an immense arm, girded with metal bands for battle. No—not an arm, but a sword, flashing menacingly. But wait! It was something worse yet: a fearsome sword that was also an arm! I shrank down on my feather.

Down came the blade, slashing through the clouds. In another instant, it would slice apart the feather, and me with it. I was helpless to stop it, helpless to prevent my own destruction. Closer came the sword, and closer, its edge turning the color of blood. Fresh blood! Just as the sword struck my own arm, biting deep into my skin—

I awoke. Shivering, panting rapidly, I grasped at my arm. Through my tunic, soaked with perspiration, I could feel my own skin. My own arm. As my heart pounded, I told myself it was only a dream. Yet it had felt so terribly true.

Rolling over, I stared up at the clouds, peering with my second sight. I found no sword, no deadly arm. Nor any stars at all. Just clouds, ominous and thickening.

I sat up, my back arched, feeling a strange new tension in the air. The hairs on my neck prickled. Darker grew the clouds, and darker, piling on top of each other, leaving no space at all for light. Soon I could see no trace of movement, no hint of shape or substance. This was a sky like none I'd seen before, the home of utter darkness, the final night of night.

My sword started buzzing in its scabbard. I put my hand on the hilt and felt the growing vibrations run up my arm and into my chest. Then, in the distance, I heard a faint rumbling—like thunder, or waves bashing against some faraway shore. Without knowing why, I sensed something was calling to me, beckoning to me.

As quietly as possible, I rose. With barely a glance at my slumbering companions, I started climbing the steep hillside. Driven by a yearning I couldn't begin to name, I moved swiftly higher, clutching bunches of grass to help me go faster. Before long, I reached the top of the hill, panting hoarsely. I pulled myself over the edge of rock and stood alone atop the stargazing stone, the wind tearing at my tunic.

The rumbling deepened, even as the air around me crackled with tension. Suddenly the clouds directly above my head shifted, lightening in places, parting a little. Driven by the skirling wind, the patches of light swelled and arranged themselves into shapes. No—into one particular shape. A face. *A man's face.*

"Young Merlin," the face in the clouds intoned, its voice rolling across the forest and distant hills.

"Dagda," I whispered in awe. I hadn't seen the spirit lord since we stood together years before, under the glistening boughs of the Tree of Soul, wrapped in the eternal mists of the Otherworld. Then, as now, he chose to appear as a man, frail and silver haired. But now, somehow, he seemed much older.

"I come with woeful tidings," he announced, his words buffeted by the wind. "The time of greatest peril has arrived."

"Peril?" I asked. "For who?"

Dark clouds sped past his luminous visage, casting shadows on the silvery lines of his face. "Peril for you, Merlin, and for those you love. But most of all, for the world that has been your home, the place called Fincayra."

I glanced over my shoulder into the darkness below where Rhia and Hallia lay sleeping. Turning back to the sky, I demanded, "How, great spirit? When will this danger arrive?"

"Already it has," he declared, his resonant voice echoing through the night. "The greatest struggle, and greatest sorrow, I fear, lie just ahead."

A massive cloud slid over his eyes, and he waited in silence until it passed. "On the longest night of the year, less than one full moon away, the cosmos will complete a shift that began ages and ages ago. When that happens, the world of Fincayra and the Otherworld will move perilously close together. So close, in truth, that their terrains will nearly touch."

"And that will bring the peril?"

"Yes indeed! For at the moment of sunset, a doorway will open between the worlds—a doorway that must not be crossed from either side, or much more than I can say will be lost."

More clouds, thin and wraithlike, flew past his glowing face. "The passage will appear at a spot you well remember: the circle of stones where the Dance of the Giants took place years ago." He waited, as if the words weighed heavily upon him. "And it is through that doorway that Rhita Gawr and his army shall come."

Dagda's brow, streaked with silver, knotted. "Even now, in the Otherworld, I am trying to ward him off, to prevent him from crossing over. But even with the help of many brave spirits, I cannot contain him. I fear he will succeed, sending his own deathless troops into Fincayra as soon as the doorway opens. He covets your world, for it is the very bridge between Earth and Heaven."

I stood rigid on the stone. "But can't you pursue him after he comes here?"

The luminous eyebrows drew together. "That I cannot do, even at the risk of losing Fincayra. You see, Rhita Gawr expects me to follow him, leaving the Otherworld unprotected. I have learned he will take only part of his army into Fincayra, leaving the rest behind, so he can seize the chance to conquer the spirit world as well."

"But if Rhita Gawr can have troops in both places, why can't you?"

"Because," came the solemn reply, "our numbers are too few. And I have other reasons as well—reasons that even Rhita Gawr cannot comprehend."

"Can't you do *anything* to stop him?" I beseeched.

His face grew stern. "I am doing all I can." His shining eyes dimmed slightly. "And there is also this: If I were to send spirits through the doorway, I would be violating one of the most basic principles of the cosmos. The worlds must stay apart, or cease to exist."

"But Fincayra will cease to exist!" I shook my head, as the wind whipped my cheeks and brow. "Dagda, forgive me. It's just . . . so much."

His voice rolled again over the hills, though it sounded somehow closer, almost at my side. "I forgive you, my young friend."

Taking an unsteady breath, I asked, "Why didn't you tell me sooner?"

"I had hoped to prevail without your help, to halt Rhita Gawr before he ever reached your world. But that hope has failed."

"And now there is no other."

"No," he corrected, "there is still one hope, though it is frail indeed. If enough Fincayran creatures, not just men and women but many more besides, amass at the stone circle in time, they might find some way to turn back his invasion. Many lives may be lost, with much suffering, but that is our only chance."

"Then we're doomed," I lamented. "Even if there were two years, instead of two weeks, to gather everyone in Fincayra, it couldn't be done! Don't you know how much bitterness and suspicion there is here? Ever since the days of Stangmar, most races live in fear of each other." I thumped my chest. "And of my race most of all."

"This I know well," answered Dagda ruefully. "And it began long before the days of your father's rule. Long before, in days now forgotten . . . but that does not concern us now."

He paused, and I felt that his vaporous eyes were peering right through me. "Only someone who is known to all those races can possibly rally them—someone who has labored with dwarves, walked with marsh ghouls, spoken with talking trees and living stones. Someone who has swum with mer folk, flown with wind sisters, and stood upon the shoulders of giants."

I stepped backward, right to the edge of the stone. "You can't mean . . . No, I can't. No."

The glowing face, rippled with streaming clouds, watched me impassively.

"It's not possible!" I knelt on the boulder, clasping my hands.

"Even if I could assemble an army, I wouldn't know how to lead them. I can fight, sure, but I'm still not a warrior. No, no, I'm something else—a seer, maybe, though not with my eyes. Or a healer, or some sort of bard."

"Or a wizard," declared Dagda. "And a man who loves peace far better than war. But there are times, I must tell you, when even a peaceful man must stand in the path of harm to the land he loves. And yes, to the people he cherishes."

I wrung my hands together, lowering my head. After a long moment, I lifted my face again. "Only two weeks? That's next to nothing."

"It is all we have," declared the visage on high. "To prevail on winter's longest night, you will need to defeat your greatest foe, nothing less."

"But tell me," I pleaded, "is there any real chance of winning? Any chance at all?"

Dagda studied me long before answering. "Yes, there is a chance. But all Fincayra's threads, in all their colors, must bind together in a sturdy rope. And for that to happen, the rarest of seeds must find a home at last."

Perplexed, I shook my head. "The rarest of seeds?" I tapped my leather satchel. "You mean this one in here?"

"Perhaps, though a seed may take many forms." All at once, the silver lines of his face brightened, even as his voice grew deeper, so that every word echoed in the night air. "Heed well these words, young wizard: Fincayra's fate has never been more in doubt. You may find unity in separation, strength in weakness, and rebirth in death, but even that may not be enough to save your world. For in certain turns of time, when all is truly gained, all is truly lost."

Wind swept past the hillside, howling in the trees below. Gradually, the clouds overhead started to thin and pull apart. As I watched, the face of Dagda faded, until at last it vanished completely. Only his words remained, throbbing like a fever in my head.

Then I heard something else—a strange, ominous creaking. It sounded, vaguely, like a distant doorway starting to open.

5

RADIANT SPIRIT

Dawn came at last, so slowly and dimly that it seemed merely an extension of the lingering night. Gray-washed clouds streaked the sky, shrouding the forest lands and the grassy hillside where we had camped. The air, while calmer than last night, felt colder still. No whispers stirred the trees; no songbirds heralded the start of day.

Pulling the collar of my tunic over my face, I shivered. And not just from the chill of morning. Whether I had slept or not after seeing the vision of Dagda, I wasn't sure. I could only recall stumbling down the hillside, trying not to fall in the darkness. But the vision itself, and the words Dagda had spoken, were carved upon my mind as sharply as the seven symbols of wisdom were carved upon my staff. I vaguely remembered having had some sort of dream before his face appeared, etched on the clouds—something about flying, or falling. But the harsh reality of his words had thrust that memory aside. *Fincayra's fate has never been more in doubt.*

Feeling Hallia's warm breath on the back of my neck, I rolled over. Her eyes, as deep as the deepest pools, watched me soulfully. I sat up and caressed her lightly on the cheek.

She pushed some stray hair off her brow. "You slept poorly, didn't you?"

"Yes. How did you know?"

"I just knew. Your face—it's strangely clouded."

I stiffened at her choice of words.

Her eyes lowered briefly. "I, too, slept poorly. Oh, young hawk, I had a terrible dream."

Gently, I wrapped my arm around her. "Can you tell me what it was?"

"About . . ." She bit her lower lip. "About losing someone I love."

I pulled her close to my shoulder. How could I tell her that Dagda's old law was now the least of our troubles? And that the future she ought to fear was not my going to live in the realm of Britannia, but going to die in battle with Rhita Gawr?

I wove my fingers deep into her unbraided hair. Tenderly, I spoke the only words that came to me. "Nothing can separate us, you know. Not distance, not time, not even . . ."

"*Shhh,*" she said softly, placing her forefinger on my lips. "Speak not of such things, nor even of the future. Let us just rejoice in the present, in the days we have together now."

Though I wished I could have felt comforted by her words, or confident enough to comfort her in turn, I felt nothing of the kind. Turning aside, I merely kept working my hand through her locks, studying the reddish glints that reminded me of a fire's dying embers.

"Ah, so you're awake," called Rhia's voice from above us. She stood at the crest of the hill, waving vigorously. "Come soon to breakfast if you want any."

Silently, Hallia and I walked through the bristling stalks of grass, climbing the slope together, pausing now and then to catch our breath. Moments later, we stood on top of the hill, and in a few more seconds, on the flat surface of the stargazing stone. Rhia sat there, cross-legged as before, surrounded by assorted leftovers from last night's repast. Perched on her shoulder was the furry form of Scullyrumpus, busily chewing on a slice of beetroot.

"Come," she beckoned, her mouth full of honeycomb. "Before Scully eats it all."

"Get awayway," snapped the little beast. "Clumsy man no steal breakyfast!"

Rhia held up two wedges of honeycomb. "Never mind him. He's just grumpy in the morning."

"How can you tell?" I asked. Oblivious to the creature's glare, I set down my staff and sat upon the stone. Hallia joined me, and in short order we were feasting on almonds with cinnamon cream, sweetberries, tangy strips of linden bark, and rose-hip jelly on biscuits, all washed down with the remains of Rhia's raspberry syrup.

Still feeling chilled, I flapped my arms against my ribs.

"Trying to fly again?" asked Rhia mischievously. "It's easier with vines."

"No," I said flatly, not responding to her jest. "I'm just cold, that's all." I glanced at the place on the stone charred by last night's fire coals. "Too bad the wind scattered all our embers. A fire would be nice."

"Not necessary." Rhia reached down and unraveled the vine that held the Orb of Fire to her belt. "I still don't know how to use this yet, at least in the way it's supposed to be used. But I have learned something."

She placed the orange sphere on the stone. Then she held her hand above it, so that her fingers nearly touched its shining surface, and closed her eyes. Seconds passed. With a sudden flash, the sphere erupted with light, glowing like a small sun.

Hallia gasped, while my back straightened in surprise. We looked at each other, and at Rhia, in amazement. Scullyrumpus ignored us, sliding down Rhia's arm so he could warm his paws.

My sister smiled, coaxing us to move closer. "I know the Orb is really for healing—broken spirits, not broken bones. Until I figure out how to do that, though, it makes a fine little fireplace. Don't you agree?"

"Oh yes," answered Hallia, tugging me nearer to the glowing sphere. "And all aglow like that, it's as pretty as the spots on a fawn."

"Moremore useful than a fawn, it is," squeaked Scullyrumpus.

"Or you, friend furball." I ignored his chattered protest and stretched my palms toward the Orb. It felt as warm as any hearth. Like Fincayra's other legendary Treasures—such as the Flowering Harp that could bring the barest hillside to life, or the Caller of Dreams that could make someone's wish a reality—this object held incalculable power. Right now, though, a little warmth was power enough. Turning to Rhia, I asked, "Have you tried to bake bread on it?"

"Several times." She tossed her brown curls. "Doesn't work too well, though. This heat is of a strange kind, better for spirits, somehow, than for bodies—or muffins."

"It feels good, in any case," I replied. "You're right, though, about this heat. I feel it more, well, *under* my skin than on it."

She nodded. "Remember how you first described it to me? Less like a radiant torch than a radiant spirit."

"That's right. And the spirit I was referring to, I also recall, was you."

Rhia's face glowed a bit brighter, though it might have been just the reflection from the Orb. "And Dagda's description of it, remember that? If used wisely, its flame can rekindle hope, or even the will to live." She pursed her lips. "Someday I'd like to do that."

I didn't respond. The mention of Dagda's name chilled me again. All at once, I felt as distracted as before. Hallia, sensing my change of heart, looked at me with concern. I felt strongly tempted to tell her about Dagda's warning, but couldn't quite bring myself to do it. Not yet anyway. Just thinking about it was hard enough; speaking about it would be harder still.

Nor was I ready to tell Rhia, though that, too, was tempting. Glumly, I watched her finishing her last crumbs of honeycomb. She cared about Fincayra, too. But if I told her, she'd only feel as powerless as I. And for good reason! Even if I could somehow convince the giants, the dwarves, the canyon eagles, and all the others to join forces with one another—and, more difficult, with the race of men and women—how could I possibly cover enough territory to reach all of them in so little time?

Rhia reached over and tugged my legging. "Merlin, what is it? You're not thinking about the Orb anymore, are you?"

My throat tightened. "I'm just thinking about . . . well, Leaping. How useful it would be, say, for travel. Why, I could get around this whole island in an instant! But no . . . that's impossible—for me, anyway. That sort of Leaping takes at least a hundred years to learn."

Scullyrumpus snorted. "A thousand years for youyou."

Hallia shook her head. "Why should it take so long, young hawk?

Since you can already move objects—your staff or your satchel—why can't you move yourself?"

For a moment I gazed into the glowing sphere. "Because Leaping one's own self requires all the levels of magic working together, as a complete whole. And to do that, the wizard must also be . . . well, a complete whole."

"Notnot a complete fool," piped Scullyrumpus. "Heka, heka, hee-hee-ho."

Ignoring him, Hallia cocked her head in doubt. "You mean having mind, body, and spirit—with no gaps? That's a lot to ask."

"Definitely," I replied. "And if any gaps exist, the magic goes awry. With terrible results."

Rhia waved her hand dismissively. "Forget the whole idea, Merlin. That's not the way to travel, even if you could manage it."

"What do you suggest, then?"

"Wings! That's right, real wings. The kind Fincayran men and women had long ago before they were lost."

"If that old story is true," I began, "then—"

"It's true," she declared.

"Well, whether it's true or not, Leaping's far superior. Much faster, and more direct."

A serene, contented look passed over her face. "Oh, flying is much more than speed. So much more." She closed her eyes, and spoke as if dreaming. "Imagine . . . feeling your wings moving, and the air supporting your weight. Having all your senses come fully alive. Taking time to rise above the lands below, your spirit along with your body."

For an instant, as she spoke, I felt myself remembering something. A dream of my own, perhaps, though I couldn't be sure.

Her eyes opened. "If you could fly, Merlin, *really* fly, you'd see the difference. Right away. And you'd never go back to Leaping. You just don't know!"

"Really?" I picked up a walnut shell and tossed it at her. "In case you've forgotten, I have flown already—twice, in fact. To Stangmar's castle, and with Aylah, the wind sister."

"But that wasn't really flying on your own power. Trouble carried you to the castle, and Aylah, on the wind."

I raised a skeptical eyebrow. "What's the difference?"

Rhia sighed. "You're going to have to figure that out for yourself."

All I could do was scowl, to the delight of Scullyrumpus. Seated once more on Rhia's shoulder, he half cackled, half chirped, wiggling his long ears in mirth.

Finally, Rhia raised her hand to silence him. "Just think of the possibilities, Merlin. If you could fly, you could go anywhere you choose—even, say, across the western waters, all the way to the Forgotten Island." Her eyes took on a sly gleam. "You did promise me once you'd go there. Remember?"

"I remember. And I catch your hint, as well! Don't deny it. You're thinking about that old rumor that the Forgotten Island has something to do with the lost wings."

"I don't deny it. I just thought you might go there and find out what happened."

"And, while I'm at it, bring you back a nice big pair?"

She shrugged carelessly, trying not to grin. "If you like."

I shook my head. "You're obsessed, Rhia! Even if that rumor is true, there's a small matter you're forgetting: that thick web of spells that surrounds the whole island, keeping everyone out. Why, no one's been there since, since . . ."

"The wings were lost," she finished. "Think about it, Merlin. Having wings would also help you get around faster."

I could only grimace. If only she understood why I needed to travel fast! And if only I had some idea—any idea—what to do next.

"It could also solve the ache between our shoulders," she pressed. "You can't deny that exists, can you?"

"No." I worked my shoulders, then lay down on my side, resting my elbow on the rock. "No one knows for sure, though, whether the ache really comes from lost wings, or something else entirely. Maybe it's just part of being Fincayran."

"*Hmfff,*" she replied. "Everyone knows it's true, except maybe young wizards."

Scullyrumpus broke into such wild cackles that he nearly fell off her shoulder.

"The one thing no one knows," Rhia went on, "is *why* the wings were lost."

"That's right," offered Hallia, gracefully sweeping her legs around to move closer to the warm globe. "I've heard your friend Cairpré say he'd gladly give half his library to find the answer to that question."

I nodded, remembering my old mentor saying something similar to me. "Cairpré's theory is that Dagda, long ago, gave people wings. Then something happened that made him take them back forever."

"Only Dagda himself knows why," said Rhia, frowning. "The people must have done something really horrible to deserve such a punishment."

"Really horrible," echoed Hallia.

Rhia reached out and took the last two sweetberries. She plunked one in her mouth, then tossed the other into the air. Scullyrumpus' tiny jaws snapped closed, and he grinned crookedly before swallowing.

"Well," said Rhia, "I think we'll be going now. I have a little time before heading off to join Mother, and there's something I need to do first."

"What?" I asked.

"Oh, something."

"You have that look of a mischievous fawn," observed Hallia.

"Do I?" she replied innocently. "Can't say why."

Rhia grasped the magical Orb, which instantly stopped radiating heat. As she tied it to her belt, she nodded to her little companion. He chattered something unintelligible while wrapping his paws around her shoulder. Watching them, I thought of how Trouble used to ride on my own shoulder, clasping me tightly with his talons. And how I still carried him with me in a way, just as I still carried the name he inspired.

With a wave to Hallia and me, Rhia leaped down from the rock and quickly strode down the hill. I nearly called after her. But no—I couldn't do it. I merely watched her make her way through the tall grasses. A few seconds later, she disappeared into the trees, the Orb of Fire bouncing at her side.

6

ESCAPE

Hallia took my hand, and her touch somehow warmed me even more than the Orb. "Tell me what it is, young hawk."

I sat up, unsure of what to say, or whether to say anything at all. My boots twisted uneasily on the grainy surface of the stargazing stone. The brisk morning air gusted slightly, causing the surrounding forest to creak and clatter. I felt as if the hill where we sat was an island in the middle of a turbulent sea, and that any moment the waves would rise up and overwhelm us.

"Something is troubling you," she continued. "Something more than you've been saying. Is it . . . about us?"

"N-no, not us."

"Tell me, then. What is it?"

I forced myself to swallow. "It will upset you."

"It will upset me more to watch you suffer inside." Her brown eyes, ever welcoming, watched me. "If telling me would help, then do it. Please."

I drew a breath. "All right then." I glanced upward at the gray, shadowed sky. "Last night, I saw a vision. A face in the clouds. It was—"

A sudden pounding, rolling out of the distance, arrested me. I listened as it swelled steadily, like a thunderstorm fast approaching.

Unlike the rumbling I had heard last night, the sound that had called me to Dagda, this sound had no subtlety. It simply pounded. Before long the boulder beneath us began to shake, vibrating to the incessant rhythm. Hallia squeezed my whole arm as the trees at the base of the hill started swaying dangerously. An enormous limb tore away from an old, leafless elm and crashed to the ground near the spot where we'd slept just a short while before.

I grabbed my staff so it wouldn't slide off the edge of the stone. The pounding continued to rattle the hillside, more so by the second. Hallia's expression told me she wanted to bolt, to become a deer and bound away into the forest. But I shook my head, urging her to stay. For I had heard this sound before, many times. It was a sound that had stirred the land of Fincayra for ages beyond memory, for seasons beyond count.

The footsteps of a giant.

Out of the mist-shrouded forest, a shape gradually appeared. Like a hillside itself, it rose above the trees. In time, I could make out the giant's wild hair, enormous shoulders, and gangly arms, though I couldn't yet discern any features of the face. All the while, the pounding, pounding, swelled louder. Now I could see enough to know it was a male, wearing a baggy yellow vest and wide brown leggings, in the custom of the residents of Varigal. He lumbered toward us, wading through the forest much as a man would stride through a field of wheat.

At last, I saw his eyes, wide and reddish pink. And a cavernous mouth full of misshapen teeth. Above that hung a nose that bulged like a swollen potato—a nose I couldn't help but recognize.

"It's all right," I assured Hallia, clasping her shoulder. "It's my friend Shim."

"Young hawk, what about that vision?"

"I'll tell you everything, I promise."

With a few more enormous strides, Shim reached the base of the hillside. Bending a pine tree aside with his huge hand, he stepped out of the forest. As he released the tree, cones and needles rained down, bouncing through the branches. He took another step closer, planting his massive foot on the slope, and his weight caused the stargazing stone to shift. My staff nearly rolled off again, but I seized it just in time. At last, the giant (as well as the hillside) stood still.

Gingerly, Hallia and I rose to our feet. We found ourselves facing the tip of his bulbous nose. "Well met, old friend," I declared, swaying from the force of warm air from his nostrils. "It's good you found us atop this hill, so we can look you in the face, instead of staring up at your hairy toes."

To my surprise, he didn't laugh at the joke. Nor did he even so much as grin. Rather, his whole face twisted into an uncharacteristic frown. He blinked once, nearly brushing Hallia with lashes as big as oak saplings. Then, in a voice that bellowed hoarsely, he spoke.

"I is, this oncely time, not happily to see you, Merlin. Or you, missly maiden Hallia."

At my feet, my shadow stirred, waving one of its arms.

Understanding, the giant nodded. "Or you, wizardly shadow."

The dark form assumed a dignified pose, holding its chin out with pride.

Ignoring the shadow, I demanded, "Why? What's wrong?"

Shim's eyebrows, as thick as forested knolls, drew together. "The wickedly king, the one you calls Stangmar, escapes this morning! Nobodily knows where he is gone."

My knees suddenly weakened. I stumbled, almost stepping off the edge of the boulder. Hallia caught my arm, then directed her own disbelief at the giant. "Are you sure? Wasn't he held in one of those caverns in the far north? No one's ever escaped from there."

"I is sure," Shim answered. "Certainly, definitely, absolutely. With his barely hands, he kills two prison guards, maybily three, gettings out."

I slapped myself on the forehead. How could all this be happening? *Stangmar—free.* What would he try to do? Join forces with Rhita Gawr once again? Or, wait. Was he already part of the wicked spirit's plans?

Shim scrunched his nose, clearly finding the whole business distasteful. "I hears more badly news, Merlin. The guard who still survives said Stangmar's bent on findings somebodily. Yes, and that somebodily now is in gravely danger."

My fist clenched. "You mean me."

"No," countered Shim. "I means someone else. Your motherly, Elen."

"Mother!" I cried, my heart pounding. "You're certain?"

Shim nodded glumly. "The guard says Stangmar didn't know she'd returned to Fincayra till yesterdaily. Then, when he finds out she's here, he gets angrily—very angrily."

I groaned. "He thinks she betrayed him. Helped his enemies, including me. He'll be out for revenge. We must find her!"

Hallia's bare foot stamped on the rock. "Wait, young hawk. Rhia knows where she is, remember? If we can just find her, she'll take us straight to Elen."

"Rhia, the woodly woman?" asked Shim. "I sees her while I comings here—not fars away." His massive lower lip protruded thoughtfully. "She is draggings something heavily, a greatly bird maybe, just over theres."

Bewildered, I followed the line of his pointing arm. "A bird? What could she be doing?"

"I will takes you theres," offered the giant, his whole frame swaying like a huge tree. "That's the quickliest way."

Hallia tilted her head skeptically. "I'd rather run, thank you." Before I could protest, she cut me off. "It can't be far. I'll follow you."

"Then I'll run with you," I declared. "Shim! Show us the way."

He answered by swinging himself around. His elbow struck the stargazing stone, nearly dislodging it and sending several smaller rocks tumbling down the hillside. The forest below shook as he took his first heavy step. Then another, and another. Somehow, Hallia and I kept our balance. We started to run after him, plunging down the slope, our legs slicing through the stiff grasses.

As if we weren't two creatures running over the land, but one connected being that flowed like a wave across a pond, we loped faster and faster. Our bodies leaned forward, our arms reached the ground, our neck muscles lengthened. Hallia's robe and my tunic melted away, replaced by glistening fur the same color as the grass. Arms became legs, while feet transformed into hooves, moving with the land as much as upon it.

My head, crowned with a rack of antlers with five points on each side, turned toward my companion. She moved effortlessly, springing through the air with every step. She was still Hallia, to be sure—the wide eyes told me that—but she was, in some irrefutable way, more herself now than she could ever be in her woman's form. Like the wind she ran, the most graceful creature I had ever known. And despite the lingering dread I felt over Shim's news as well as last night's vision, I was deeply glad, once again, to run beside her.

We followed Shim into the trees, leaping over the branches that his enormous legs had broken loose. The ground rocked beneath us, but I never felt imperiled, for my stag's legs tensed and flexed with ease, treating the land as an extension of my body. Once again I noticed the Druma's vitality, as if it refused to accept the onset of winter. Even amidst its leafless branches, bright mosses bloomed; among patches of ice, fresh water flowed. As I ran, I heard a dragonfly's whirring wings, smelled a sprig of scented fern, and felt the hidden passage-ways under the soil where tiny animals burrowed and ancient roots stood secure, as they had for centuries upon centuries.

We entered a clearing, wet with the spray of rushing water. Shim's bare feet, covered with curly hair, stopped just before us. Hallia and I slowed, first trotting and then walking. Our backs narrowed and lifted upright; our chins withdrew. We stepped forward, walking on two legs once again.

Before us, the clearing fell away sharply, making a cliff that over-looked a loudly splattering stream. There, at the edge of the cliff, stood Rhia. She seemed in deep concentration, giving barely a glance to the giant towering above her, and no notice at all to the two people standing by his ankles. It looked as if she was, as Shim had said, holding a sizable bird upon her back. Then I realized that it wasn't a bird at all.

It was a pair of wings! Made from the broad, reddish-brown leaves of marshland cabbage, woven into a frame of flexible willow shoots, the wings had clearly taken a substantial amount of work. Her crafts-manship was evident, too, in the frilled strips of lichen that dangled from the outer rims like colorful flags. Right now, she was busily tying the whole thing to her back, using some of the same bright green vines that served as the threads of her gown.

I shook my head. How many days (or weeks) had she spent building her contraption? No doubt she'd chosen this cliff carefully to try it out, storing it nearby while she worked on it. And she probably would have tried it out yesterday if she hadn't taken so much time to prepare our dinner.

But for the steady rumble of Shim's breathing, we watched in silence. I chewed my lip. Did she really know what she was doing? Yet I knew better than to try to stop her. She was, after all, Rhia.

Her jaw firmly set, she backed away from the cliff. Meanwhile, Scullyrumpus, wearing an expression of self-importance, scurried down her leg and placed himself at the edge of the precipice. As Rhia came to a halt, she quickly untied the Orb of Fire from her belt and set it down on the grass. Then she stood alert, her eyes fierce with determination. Slowly, she spread her arms out wide, extending the wings to their fullest. The frills of lichen fluttered in the breeze.

Scullyrumpus, his ears standing erect, glanced behind himself at the churning waters below. All of a sudden, he waved his paws. "Start flyfly! Start flyfly!"

Rhia leaned forward. She started running and flapping her makeshift wings, causing a loud rustling. As she reached the edge, she leaped upward, floating in glorious freedom above the stream, her wings sweeping the air. She was aloft! Joyous, she released a cry of exhilaration and flapped again—when a hole suddenly burst open in one wing. Several willow shoots sprang loose, tearing the fabric of leaves. In midair, she careened wildly to one side and plummeted downward, disappearing behind the cliff. Scullyrumpus started jumping up and down, shrieking.

"Rhia!" shouted Hallia and I simultaneously. We ran to the spot where she had vanished. Scullyrumpus stood peering over the edge, his little brow furrowed.

Below us lay a twisted mass of leaves, sticks, and vines, sprawled in a pool at a bend of the stream. Several torn cabbage leaves drifted through the air and fell on the heap. Instantly, I started scrambling down the steep bank, joined by my shadow, whose arms were waving wildly. Then a much larger shadow fell over us. Down reached Shim's great hand. With surprising delicacy, he plucked the crumpled, winged form. He hauled the dripping tangle up to the clearing and laid it gently beside us.

Scullyrumpus scampered over, tugging on Rhia's soaked hair. To my relief, she lifted her face and weakly rubbed noses with the little beast. She twisted on the grass, groaning miserably. Though too weak to stand, she gave the drenched leaves on her arms a disgusted shake, then tore off the harness and threw off the whole contraption.

"What's the point of having wings," she groused while rubbing her forehead, "unless they hold together?"

I laid my hand on her sopping shoulder. "I'm glad *you* held together."

"As am I," added Hallia, examining a cut on her neck.

"I also," boomed Shim, bending low to examine the wreckage of the wings. "You is full of madness, Rhia, just likes your brotherly."

"Oh no," she replied, pulling a broken willow shoot out of her curls. "He's much worse than me."

I started to grin, when Scullyrumpus added in his squeaky voice: "Much worse, he is. So muchymuch worse! But Rhia clumsy, too! Hoo-hoo-hoo, clumsy woman! Heka-chika-chhha-ha-ha."

Still chortling, he started to climb up her sleeve, using the vines of her gown as a ladder. Rhia flicked some water on his face. "Don't get sassy with me, Scully. I'm still your favorite ride, remember."

"Unless you wearing wings!" he replied in his lightning-fast delivery. "Better you stick to viny ropes for flying, I saysay." Ears flapping, he ducked into her sleeve pocket before she could spray him again.

I knelt by her side. "Anything broken?"

"No. Just a few cuts and bruises." Her gaze moved to the ruined contraption beside her. "I really hoped it would work."

Determinedly, she pushed herself to her feet. As she reached for the Orb and affixed it to her woven belt, she said gratefully, "At least I remembered to take this off. If I'd broken it . . . well, that would have been a *real* disaster."

I squeezed her arm. "Rhia, there's been a different disaster. Mother's in trouble." She stiffened, watching me severely as I continued. "Stangmar—he's escaped! And he's looking for her."

Her whole body shuddered. "We planned to meet tomorrow night at Caer Aranon, that village east of here, by the great river. Cairpré's going to read a poem when they open their village theater." She took a deep breath. "Stangmar! We must warn her."

"Yes," I agreed. With a glance at Hallia, and another at Shim, I cleared my throat. "But first, there's something more I must tell you. All of you."

The wind gusted, showering the clearing with crisp dead leaves from a linden tree. As the leaves settled on the wet grass, I began to describe my vision from the night before. I spoke of the heavy clouds, the tension in the air, the anguish on Dagda's face, and his warning about winter's longest night. And I recalled his parting, ominous words: *Fincayra's fate has never been more in doubt. You may find unity in separation, strength in weakness, and rebirth in death, but even that may not be enough to save your world. For in certain turns of time, when all is truly gained, all is truly lost.*

"In certain turns of time . . ." repeated Hallia, her voice somber. "It's a terrible, terrible dream."

"And a perplexing one," added Rhia, as a dead leaf twirled down from the branches and landed on her shoulder.

I stomped my boot on the wet turf. "It was no dream at all! The whole thing was as real as Shim right here."

"Rightly now I wishes I is a dream," muttered the giant, his breath blowing down some more leaves. "What is we goings to do?"

I paced over to the cliff's edge. Twisting the base of my staff into the mud, I surveyed the briskly flowing stream, as full of light and song as springtime, as magical as the land through which it flowed. Turning back to my friends, I declared, "We're going to save what we love, that's what! Rhia, I want you to come with me to the village, where we can warn Mother. And I'll tell Cairpré about the vision. Learned as he is, he might know something about Dagda's prophecy, something that could help us."

I angled my face upward, gazing at the gargantuan figure who stood higher than the trees. "You, Shim, will return to Varigal. Try to convince the others there to help. Our whole world is at stake! If Rhita Gawr's forces overrun Fincayra, even the giants won't be safe for long."

Shim scowled, twisting his prominent nose. "That's impossibly," he grumbled. "Lots of giants won't even speak to mens and womenses, let alonely fight alongsides them."

"Try to win them over," I insisted.

"And worsely, some of thems won't even listens to me. They thinks I is a traitorly spy for the dwarves, or really ones of them, since I lived with dwarves when I is small."

I nodded, peering up into his massive eyes. "You're not small now, my friend."

"No," he replied with an emphatic shake of his head. Lowering his face almost to my own, he spoke in his version of a whisper, which sounded like a thrashing windstorm. "I is big now, as big as the high-lyest tree. But Merlin . . . I is still afraid."

I bit my lip. "So am I."

Shim straightened up. "I will try, my verily hardest." He added under his breath, "But I thinks somelyhow I won't succeed."

"Remember now, no one thought the Dance of the Giants would succeed either. And today all that remains of Stangmar's castle is the circle of stones your people call *Estonahenj*. Let us meet there, on the day before the longest night."

"Meets there we will," promised Shim. "Even if I is all alonely." He lifted a huge foot and started off, slamming the ground with every step.

Turning to Hallia, I tried to keep my voice from cracking. "You, I don't want to leave."

"You don't have to," she answered, her voice as gentle as the breath of a fawn. "You never have to."

"But I do. You, too, have a task—one even more important than staying by my side."

She stared at me, unconvinced. "I'm going with you and Rhia."

"No." I took her hand, feeling the slender fingers that had so recently been a hoof bounding next to my own. "You must go to the dragon lands, far in the north. Find Gwynnia, convince her however you can. She'll only listen to you, Hallia. And we'll need her to pre-vail! Fincayra's last dragon must help us."

Shadows darkened her eyes. "She's not a fighter, young hawk. You know that! Why, she hasn't even learned how to breathe fire. She's a peaceful dragon."

"And I am a peaceful wizard. Yet even above peace, I cherish life."

Hallia stamped her bare foot on the muddy soil. "I won't leave you."

I moved closer, gazing at her. "If Fincayra is lost, then our future together is also lost."

She swallowed. "I might not find her at all. What if I get all the way to her lair and discover she's gone off somewhere? It could take me longer than the two weeks we have left just to locate her."

Softly, I said, "Do your best."

She frowned, and her hand shook inside my own. "That I will, but I'll feel no joy until we're running with each other again."

I opened my mouth, but no words came.

She kissed my cheek. "May green meadows find you, young hawk. Remember always . . . I am with you."

I tapped the charred bracelet, tied with a wizard's knot around her wrist. "Like honey on a leaf," I said hoarsely.

Briefly, she embraced Rhia, then spun around to go. In a blur of tan, a magnificent deer sprang from the clearing. I watched her depart, wondering how her journey would end. And how swiftly our lives, our futures, had pulled apart.

"Rhia," I said at last. Then the two of us began an uncertain journey of our own.

7

CAER ARANON

All the rest of that day, Rhia and I ran eastward through the forest. A frigid wind blew in our faces, rattling the trees and stinging our cheeks. The hand clasping my staff felt stiff with cold. Yet for both of us, a colder wind blew upon our thoughts, rasping like the breath of Rhita Gawr himself.

As usual, my vine-clad sister outdistanced me, hurtling over tumbled trees and racing up hillsides slick with frost. Atop each hill, she would wait for me to catch up, her face uncharacteristically grim. On her shoulder sat Scullyrumpus, watching me with a disapproving eye while I climbed after them, panting heavily, my breath making white clouds. Though Rhia never spoke a word, I knew that now, more than ever, she was wishing she could truly fly—just as I was wishing I could tap the power of Leaping. Why did that particular magic have to be so difficult?

The temperature dropped as we reached the banks of the River Unceasing. Black clouds rolled overhead, sending down a sprinkling of snowflakes that melted into the water and frosted our backs and shoulders. Rhia plunged straight into the rushing river, and I followed. The incessant current lifted my boots, as if urging me onward.

But it didn't last long. As soon as I reached the other side, my sopping boots slapped the ground, feeling heavier than before.

By the time we reached the village of Caer Aranon, the sunset was seeping across the sky like blood soaking through a cloth. The village gate, like the leafless tree by its side, took on the same reddish-brown color, while a lone thrush, rounder than a gourd, watched us from the tree's lowest branch. Beyond the gates stood a collection of square-shaped hovels, made from mud brick and thickly woven thatch. Each of them seemed to be leaning, though in different directions, like an assembly of drunkards. Atop one, a rooster sat alone; two or three scraggly goats milled about. All in all, it reminded me of the squalid village in Britannia where I'd spent so much of my childhood—and lost forever the use of my eyes.

Two dozen people, of all ages, clustered around a raised floor of uneven planks that rested on the dirt common between the huts. This was, no doubt, the theater. And this little throng could have turned out to hear Cairpré's reading. That man could read poetry like no one I'd ever heard.

At one side of the stage stood a flagpole, flying a banner marked with the image of a black quill pen. At the base of the pole lay a pile of old robes, along with one tattered gray wig and a couple of roughly carved masks. At the other side, the stage planks ended abruptly, as if the builders had simply run out of wood before they could make any railing. Nearby, a pair of upright timbers suspended a brown sheet that would, during any production, allow the performers to change costume (or perhaps hide from thrown objects).

"Lovely placeyplace," piped Scullyrumpus. He shook his head, causing his long ears to slap his cheeks. "Need a good strong flood, they do, not a stage."

"Hush, Scully," came Rhia's stern command. "We'll get back to our forest home soon enough."

"Promise, youyou do?"

"Hush, I said. Merlin, do you see Mother in that crowd?"

"Not yet. Let's—"

I stopped as a loud whinnying echoed across the common. A great black horse, his broad back glistening, came trotting toward us.

"Ionn!" I cried, stretching out my arms to greet the stallion who had borne me so often since childhood. To Rhia I said, "Mother must be here. Weeks ago she asked if she could ride Ionn in her travels with Cairpré."

The horse approached, crunching the dirt beneath his hooves. I reached to rub his nose, to feel his warm breath on my hand. But he turned sharply away. Instead of nuzzling me in greeting, he whinnied shrilly.

"Something's wrong," Rhia declared.

"Very wrong," I agreed. "Ionn, take us to our mother."

The stallion tossed his mane and trotted over to the mass of people surrounding the theater. Pushing our way past all of them was made more difficult because everyone else, it seemed, wanted to get closer to the stage. Hearing their gossipy whispers, I realized they weren't gathered for any performance. No, this was the kind of crowd that assembled to gawk at someone who'd been injured—or worse. Ionn's sturdy neck pushed others aside, clearing us a path. Yet my temples pounded. Were we already too late?

At last, Rhia and I broke through. With relief, I saw our mother, kneeling on the planks near the middle of the stage. Her long hair, as radiant as the sun, fell over the shoulders of her dark blue robe. She was bending low, scrutinizing something intently—so intently she didn't even look up when I called her name.

Then I saw what occupied her: A boy, dressed in a tattered tunic, lay on the boards beside her. He was shivering, staring open-eyed. Elen was dabbing a cloth against the side of his face, trying to clean a wound. I caught the smell of lemon balm, a sure sign she was trying to ease his pain. As she lifted her hand to reach for a bowl of herbs, I stiffened. For this boy's wound was something I had never seen before.

His ear was gone—sliced off completely. Nothing but a blackened stub of skin remained.

"Mother!" cried Rhia, shouldering past me.

She turned our way, her sapphire eyes not so bright as usual. "My children." Setting down her cloth, she reached out a hand to each of us, drawing us nearer. She leaned over, kissed our foreheads, then gazed at us somberly. "I have wicked tidings for you."

"As do we," I declared, "for you."

"How could any be worse than what I have seen, but cannot heal?" She retrieved her cloth, dipped it in the bowl filled with water and herbs, and went back to work. The boy winced at her touch, but didn't make any sound other than his ragged breathing. Without looking up, she continued, "This dear boy was attacked, for no apparent reason, at a tarn not far from here."

"His ear . . . ," I began.

"Was cut off." Elen herself shivered. "A farmer, bringing his cow for a drink, saw it happen, though he arrived too late to help the poor lad."

I clenched my fist, convinced that this was the latest example of Stangmar's cruelty. "How could he have done such a monstrous thing?"

"Because he is just that: a monster." Her face twitched in rage. "To prey on an innocent child like this!"

I sucked in my breath. "It could have been you, Mother."

She started, dropping her cloth. "What?"

Grimly, I nodded. "When he escaped from his prison, he said he was coming after you."

"Me?"

"Yes, you. And he killed two prison guards when they tried to stop him."

She stared at me, aghast. "Killed them?"

"With his bare hands."

Suddenly her face relaxed a little. "Then whoever you're talking about didn't attack this boy."

"What do you mean?"

"The farmer," she explained, "said it was a warrior, an immense man."

"Yes! That's—"

"Wait," she commanded. "Let me finish. He said it was a warrior who had . . ." She stopped, her expression bewildered. "No hands. He had sword blades attached to his shoulders. Sword blades—instead of arms."

I shook my head in disbelief. Stangmar wasn't responsible for this? Who was, then? All at once, I remembered my dream just before the vision of Dagda had appeared. A warrior with swords instead of arms! My thoughts whirled. Rhita Gawr's plot. Stangmar's escape. And now this.

"But why?" Rhia demanded, bending over the boy. "It's so utterly cruel."

Our mother ran a hand through her shimmering hair. "No one knows. The warrior, whoever he was, strode off into the eastward plains. He didn't try to challenge the farmer, just left the boy in a bloody heap."

I scowled, gazing at the stump of the severed ear. "Where is his family?"

"He has none." She set down her cloth, brought forth a strip of moss that had been dipped in lemon balm, and placed it in the boy's mouth. "Chew that, my son, but don't swallow," she whispered. Turning back to me, she explained, "He's an orphan child."

The words struck me like a hammer in my chest. *Orphan child.* All those years in that miserable village, I'd believed myself an orphan. They were years of loneliness and longing, ending in one moment of terror I could never forget. Dinatius attacking . . . flames roaring . . . my very skin burning. His last, agonized cries before he died—and my own, before I went blind.

Without thinking, I touched the ribbed scars on my cheek. Looking down at the boy, I knew that he, too, would bear scars all his life, the worst of them invisible. Just then he turned his head toward me. His eyes seemed to focus, and I felt the weight of his gaze.

I shifted uneasily. As much as I yearned to say something comforting to him, another part of me resisted. He was in my mother's care, not mine. And the truth was . . . I wanted him to stay that way. It was all too close, too raw. I turned away.

But I found myself facing Rhia, who was also watching the boy. She nudged my side. "He's interested in you, Merlin."

"Why should he be?" I retorted. "Mother's taking care of him."

"Only for the time being," Elen herself interjected. She stroked the boy's tangle of curls. "His ear's been cleaned and dressed, and should heal well enough. It's the inner wounds that worry me more. The ones I can't touch."

"Has he spoken yet?" asked Rhia.

"Not a word." She kept running her hand through his sandy hair. "I don't even know his name."

At that, the boy coughed, and spat out the moss. Thickly, he said, "Lleu. Me name's . . . Lleu."

Our mother brightened. "Well then, Lleu, I'm glad to know you. My name is Elen."

He started to speak again, but she shushed him. "Not yet, my son. Not too fast. You've had a wicked day today."

"Mother," I said urgently. "More wickedness is afoot! We came here to warn you."

"About that man? The one you said escaped from prison?"

I nodded.

"Why should he want to harm me?"

"Because it's Stangmar."

At once, the ruddy color drained from her cheeks. She sank down on the wooden planks of the stage, looking almost as drawn as Lleu. In time she moistened her lips. "He's . . . free?"

"Yes," I declared.

"And looking for you," Rhia added. "He's bent on . . ."

Elen closed her eyes. "Not on harming me. No, he wouldn't."

"He would!" I insisted, leaning closer. "He most surely would."

Slowly, she shook her head.

"Elen!" called a deep voice.

I whirled around to see a tall, weathered man pushing his way through the crowd of onlookers. Cairpré! As he slid past Ionn, he patted the stallion's back. Ionn, in return, nipped at the scarf of gray wool wrapped around the poet's neck.

His dark, observant eyes, crowned with bushy tufts of graying hair, fell upon me. "Merlin! And Rhia, too! I only wish our meeting could have been at a gladder moment."

"Cairpré," I began, "we have news."

"Not now," he said, waving his hand. "First we must move the boy out of the cold. This stage is no place to spend the night." His gaze took in Elen. "Are you all right, my dear? You look stricken."

"Yes, yes," she said weakly.

The bard offered his hand. "What is it?"

"Later," she answered, pushing his hand aside. "Did you find a hut for the boy?"

"And for us, as well. I've already brought your warm vest and your other things. There's enough space for Rhia and Merlin, too." He beckoned. "Now come down off there."

She peered at Lleu's round face. "Are you able to walk yet? Or shall I carry you?"

He groaned, fidgeted, and slowly sat up. Gingerly, he reached to touch the side of his head. Before he could, she caught his hand. "Not yet, my son. Wait till the morning."

Fear kindled anew in his eyes, but when she put her arm around his shoulder, he calmed a little. With care, she helped him off the stage. As they came down, the villagers parted, though their whisperings continued.

Elen looked at Cairpré. "Does this hut have a hearth?"

"Not much of one, but it will serve. As the bards say, *When truly in need, my goat is a steed.*"

Ionn released a loud snort, flicking his tail against his massive thigh. The poet rubbed his chin and smiled wryly. "My apologies, old friend."

With that, he started to lead us across the common. Retrieving my mother's bowl, cloth, and pouch of herbs, I followed, as did Rhia. Ionn trotted heavily behind, his hooves pounding on the dirt.

8

LOOK FOR ME
WANDERING

The hut, which had recently been used by the village goats, smelled of dung and fur. It held not even a single shaft of straw for bedding. And its hearth was nothing more than some charred river stones arranged in a circle in the center of the dirt floor. But after we lit the fire, using a few sticks that had been stacked by the wall, and swept the floor of debris, the hut seemed somewhat more comfortable. For whatever reason, Lleu continued to watch me closely, a fact I tried my best to ignore. The greater his interest, the greater my unease.

For supper we sat around the crackling hearth, sharing Cairpré's meager rations. They were all the more meager since he had only expected to provide food for two people, not five. (Fortunately, Scullyrumpus remained soundly asleep inside Rhia's pocket, or we would have been joined by a ravenous—and fussy—sixth.) No one seemed very hungry, though, so a few strips of dried honeyroot and some oat-cakes, washed down with rill water, sufficed. We ate in silence.

In time, my mother coaxed Lleu to lie down on the floor. As she started to pull away, though, he grasped at her robe, his face tightened with fear. She nodded, gently stroked his curls, and began to sing, swaying in time to the verses. Her warm, rich voice filled the thatched hut. I found myself relaxing, along with the boy, for when I was small, she had often sung me to sleep with this very song.

> *Look for me wandering*
> *Oft through the mist;*
> *Look for me ambling*
> *'Tween grain and grist;*
> *Look for me harkening*
> *Ere any cry;*
> *Seek for me slumbering*
> *'Twixt earth and sky.*
>
> *Hush now and wander ye,*
> *Oceans to sail.*
> *Go now and gather ye,*
> *Gold leaf and grail.*
> *Know now the mystery,*
> *All in between:*
> *Find now the treasury—*
> *Silent unseen.*
> *May ye go wandering*
> *'Tween dark and light;*
>
> *May ye go hurtling*
> *Higher than height;*
> *May ye go rambling*
> *Far as ye can;*
> *Lo, to find everything*
> *Where ye began.*
>
> *Hush now and slumber ye,*
> *Never a fear.*
> *Always I'll cradle ye,*
> *Ever so near.*
> *Travel the endless trail,*
> *Far may ye roam:*

Always I'll welcome ye—
Ever your home.

By the time the last tremulous notes faded away, the boy had closed his eyes, curling into a ball on his side. Watching him slumber, Rhia fingered her belt of woven vines. "I wish I could help him with the Orb, using its power the way it was meant to be used."

Cairpré drew together his eyebrows, tufted like a pair of clouds. "Right now, I doubt even that could do him much good. He has known great terror—more than anyone, young or old, should ever have to know."

I faced the poet. "There is more terror to come, I fear."

He frowned. "How so?"

For a moment, I watched Elen tuck a tattered cloak around the boy, doing her best to cover him fully. As she rejoined us, Rhia tossed a few clumps of goat dung on the snapping flames. Then, in hushed tones, I began to describe my vision from the night before. Everyone listened carefully, asking questions only rarely. Cairpré seemed confused by Dagda's reference to the rarest seed of all—though no more confused than I. When at last I finished, the words *when all is truly gained, all is truly lost* hung in the smoky air of the hut.

Then, my throat constricted, I repeated the story of Stangmar's escape. Cairpré's eyes opened wide, while my mother sat motionless, her palm against her brow. After I finished, no one spoke for some time. The only sound was the boy's hoarse breathing and the sizzling fire of the hearth.

It was my mother, her face half in shadow, who was the first to talk again. "I remember a man different from the Stangmar you describe," she said quietly. "A young man, awkward at times and gallant at others, who voyaged all the way to far Britannia to woo me, so great was his love. Long before Rhita Gawr seduced him, and twisted him, he was a man of ideals—flawed, yes, and vulnerable, but a man who tried to show bravery, compassion, and kindness."

"Not Stangmar!" I countered, my temples throbbing. "It's not possible."

Elen smiled sadly at me. "You never knew him, the way he was.

Why, he even gave me the Galator—his precious pendant, the prize of his realm—just to show his feelings for me."

"Then he tried to murder me, his own son," I hissed, "just to appease Rhita Gawr!"

With a forlorn sigh, she said, "I'm not defending what he has become." She rested her head on Cairpré's shoulder, her fingers entwining with his own. "Nor am I saying that his love was nearly as deep, or as true, as the love I've found since."

Seated so close together, their faces warmed by firelight, the two of them seemed to be melting into each other. Seeing them I couldn't help but think of Hallia, traveling northward now in search of help for our cause. How I missed her!

Cairpré loosened his woolen scarf and mused aloud. "The Galator . . . ah, but we could use its help right now! No matter that its powers remain a mystery. They must have been vast to have inspired so many glorious ballads of old."

I recalled the pendant's flash of glowing green. And how it had vanished forever under a mountain of lava. "It's tragic the Galator was lost."

"And far more tragic," my mother added, "that the man who gave it to me was lost." She leaned forward, peering at me. "The man I knew then, I tell you, is not the man you know now."

I grimaced. "The man I know now is out to kill you."

Rhia nodded. "It's true, Mother. You must be careful."

"And what am I supposed to do?" she demanded, her eyes glowing as bright as the fire's coals. "Stay hidden in this crumbling mud hut? Oh no, my children, I'm not going to hide like a burrowing hare."

"Mother," I protested, "you must listen. He's a madman. A killer."

"Maybe so. But I still can't believe he would do me any harm. Not until he tells me, or one of you, that's what he intends!"

I shook my head. "So where will you go?"

"Wherever I choose."

"Won't you at least stay in this isolated village, where he won't think to look for you, for the next two weeks? Then we can find some better way to protect you, after whatever comes to pass on the longest night."

"Won't you please?" echoed Rhia.

She studied us for a tense moment. At last she announced, "I shall stay here two more days, no longer. And not because I want to do it, but because my children care so much to beseech me so."

"But—"

Cairpré silenced me with his hand. "She has a will of hardened oak, your mother. *At times to bend, though never to rend.* It's best not even to try to change her mind. Believe me, that much I've learned."

Elen smirked at him. "Are you saying I'm stubborn?"

"Oh, no. Merely obstinate, inflexible, and absolutely unshakable."

Her blue eyes narrowed. "So you agree, then, I should stay here longer?"

"Elen," he replied, his brow wrinkling deeply, "I agree that here is the safest place. But I know you too well, and love you too much, to ask you to do more than to try your best to stay safe. Commanding you is as good as commanding the waves of the sea, or the clouds of the sky."

Slowly, her face relaxed. She looked at him with deep affection. "You, my poet, have given me something Stangmar never could—a gift much more precious than the Galator."

"A gift we share," he replied.

The fire collapsed on itself, sending a burst of glowing sparks into the air. In the flickering light, the earthen walls of the hut seemed aglow themselves; ripples of yellow and orange flowed over them like luminous waves. I glanced over at Lleu's sleeping form, his maimed ear darkened by shadow. He looked so small, yet sturdy and brave beyond his years. Watching him slumber so serenely, after a day of such terror, I couldn't help but feel a rush of sympathy for him. May he never have to live through another day like this!

Cairpré leaned closer to the fire, poking it with a stick. More sparks flew, lighting up his high brow and most of the rest of his face, except for his deep-set eyes. The effect was to make him look more like a statue of stone, boldly carved, than a man of flesh. Tossing the stick into the flames, he drew his knees to his chest and turned to me.

"One thing Dagda told you wasn't quite correct."

"No?" I asked, amazed at the audacity of my old tutor.

"I'm thinking of the moment when he referred to ancient times, the days when Fincayrans were still a community of races. Before we fell into the divisiveness that exists today—the sort of thing Stangmar took advantage of, and certainly worsened, but didn't invent."

"What's not correct about that?" I asked, unsure where he was going.

The poet's tangled eyebrows, brightened by the firelight, lifted in unison. "You said he called those times *the days now forgotten.*"

"Well they are, aren't they?"

"Not entirely, Merlin. The bards, at least, remember a little of those days."

Wistfully, he gazed into the flames. "And wondrous days they were! Every time a home, or a library, or an orchard was built, the labors—as well as the fruits—were shared. All creatures roamed freely; hierarchies didn't exist. Mer people frolicked openly on the seas, and wolves strode on the same trails as deer and men. Some animals ate others, of course, and almost everyone ate plants, but never more than they needed to survive, and always with an enduring sense of gratitude. Oh, if only I could recite for you *The Eagle's Paean to the Mouse,* or that old ballad *Wounded Dove, Take Thou My Wings!*"

The fire burned lower, deepening the shadows of his eyes. "There were great theatrical events in those days, with performances by members of every race—from the most powerful wind sister, whose arms could reach from one coast of this island to another, to the most delicate light flyer, whose appearance would be more fleeting than a moonbeam."

"The trees also remember," Rhia declared, her leafy garb shimmering in the light from the hearth. "Arbassa—and the only other tree as old, the ancient elm, Helomna—both have told me stories of those days. Anyone older than a sapling could walk, they said, slapping or sliding their roots on the ground. Sometimes a whole forest would march together: *Like a mountain on the move, like a tide upon the land.*" She beamed at me. "Can you imagine anything more glorious?"

"Just one thing," I answered. "Bringing back those days."

"It's possible, you know," said Cairpré. "Really possible. As long as anyone still remembers. Just think of it! To see the return of Fincayra's days of glory!" His brow creased. "First, though, we'll have to survive Rhita Gawr's attack."

I tried to swallow, but found my throat too dry. "Do you think there is any way we can?"

The bard took some time to stir the fire before answering. At last he faced me again. "We live in a land where whole forests have moved. Yes, like the tides! In such a land, my friend, anything could come to pass. Anything."

He drew a slow breath. "I must return home." With a glance at Elen, he added, "Just long enough to probe my library, I promise." His voice dropped to a whisper. "There's something else Dagda said. . . . If I can locate the piece I'm thinking of, it might help."

Grimly, I nodded. "I, too, must leave in the morning. Whatever the chances of getting people to join forces—well, I have to try."

"Merlin," implored my mother, "you will be careful? As careful as you begged me to be a moment ago?" Seeing my nod, she reached for a thick vest, woven from the stalks of dried astral flowers, and thrust it at me. "Take this with you."

"You'll need that yourself."

Her eyes showed an ironic gleam. "You'll be traveling more than I."

"Are you sure? It's your favorite vest."

"That's right. Made by Charlonna, healer of the Mellwyn-bri-Meath, and given to me as a token of our friendship. So you may take all the more comfort in its warmth, since it holds within it the magic of the deer people."

I brightened, and she gave me a tender smile. "Now both Hallia and I will embrace you whenever you wear it."

My head turned to Rhia. "Come with me, won't you? Just for a while. I have an idea for you, a way you could help."

"How could I help?" she asked, shaking her curls. "Unless you'd like my Orb to keep you warm."

My expression hardened. "I need *you,* my good sister. With or without the Orb."

She patted her sleeve, just below the pocket where Scullyrumpus lay sleeping. "I can't, Merlin. I need to return to the Druma, where I belong. Besides, you can't ask me to come without telling me your idea."

"I just did. And I'll tell you when the time is right."

She scowled at me. "Oh, all right. Not for long, though." Under her breath, she muttered, "Scully's going to love this."

"Thanks," I said. "You won't regret it."

"No, but you will."

Elen reached over and took her daughter's hand. "I wish I had another vest for you."

"It's all right," Rhia replied cheerily. "Merlin's going to let me use his whenever I want." She glanced my way. "Right?"

"Right," I grumbled, handing her the vest. "Here. Use it as your blanket tonight."

"In that case," interjected Cairpré, "you'll be needing this, as well." He unraveled his thick gray scarf and threw it in my lap. "And Rhia, you should take my mare, Coella. My journey home is less than a day's walk, so you'll need a horse more than I." With a wink, he added, "Unless you want to make Merlin give you Ionn, that is."

Rhia waved her hand dismissively. "Not yet, anyway." Then she looked at me, her expression serious again. "When do we leave?"

"At dawn," I replied. "Then we ride. For all of Fincayra, we ride."

"Time for some sleep, then, Brother."

We stretched ourselves out on the dirt floor. I lay on my back between Rhia and Lleu. For an extra touch of warmth, I draped the woolen scarf across my chest. Absently, I watched the smoke rising thickly from the smoldering fire, climbing through a hole in the thatching and into the dark skies above. All the while, I listened to the slow, regular breathing of Lleu, until with time, my own breathing took on the same rhythm.

9

KİNDLİNG

Some hours later I awoke with a shiver. So cold! Darkness filled the hut, along with the odors of goat dung and smoky clothes. Shivering again, I could see with my second sight that the scarf had slid off my chest. Yet that wasn't the real problem: The fire had gone out completely.

I rose, flexed my stiff fingers, and crawled over to the hearth, trying not to disturb anyone. Carefully, I poked the fire's remnants with a twig, hoping to find at least one ember. But there was only charcoal, dusted with ash, and some unburned bits of goat dung.

Drat, I told myself. Now I'd need to start a new fire from scratch! I thought of using the incantation of the fire-bringer, but that magic always caused a loud eruption along with the flames—certain to wake everyone. And even more than warmth, my friends needed their rest.

Holding my chilled hands under my armpits, I looked around the hut for more fuel. There! Next to the wall sat a few sticks about the thickness of my staff. I crept across the dirt floor to fetch them, trying hard to avoid the splayed arms and legs of my sleeping companions. But what about some kindling? The sticks wouldn't ignite without it.

Nevertheless, I tried. Retrieving Cairpré's iron stones from the ground next to the hearth, I worked as quietly as possible to produce some sparks. In this I succeeded, though in making the sticks catch fire I failed miserably. After several minutes of fruitless effort, I was colder than I'd been when I first awoke. My fingers felt numb. In disgust, I gave up, resigned to shivering through the rest of the night.

Just then something nudged me from behind. I whirled around to see Lleu, holding out his hand to me. Clutched within his small fingers was a mass of dry bark shavings. The kindling I needed!

Viewing this young lad, so self-sufficient and also so generous, I did something I'd not let myself do before. I smiled at him.

Tentatively, the corner of his mouth twisted slightly. It was gone in an instant. But I knew he had smiled back.

Then, wordlessly, he crawled forward, his bare feet scraping on the floor. He placed the kindling in the center of the charred stones, quickly arranging a pile that left enough room for air. I struck the iron, and a lone spark flew out, landing near the base of the shavings. In unison, ever so gently, we blew on the spark, coaxing it to life.

A pulsing glow appeared, along with a thin trail of smoke. Again we blew upon it. All at once, a flame appeared, licking at the edges of the shavings. We arranged the sticks on top, and before long they started crackling and sputtering, throwing off sparks of their own.

In silence, we warmed our hands before the swelling flame. Then, after a time, we turned to each other. I gave an approving nod; so did Lleu. Around us, the hut rippled with firelight, as waves of orange flowed across the walls. And a new warmth touched us both.

After a time, we crawled back to our places on the floor. As he settled himself on the dirt, I did the same. For a while I watched the new column of rising smoke. Since the air was still cold, I reached for the scarf beside me. The touch of its thick wool in my hand gave me an idea.

I sat up and leaned over Lleu. He watched me uncertainly. I could see, in the firelight, the dried blood that encrusted the hair around his sliced ear. Gently, I offered him the scarf, knowing that Cairpré would be as pleased as myself if the boy wore it.

He hesitated for a moment. At last, he reached out and took the scarf, the hint of another shy smile on his face. Then he did something I hadn't expected. Instead of looping the scarf around his neck, or stretching it across his chest, he wrapped it around his feet, covering his bare toes.

With a final nod of thanks, he curled himself into a ball. Before long, he fell asleep. As did I.

PART TWO

10

AWAKEПIПG

As the first hint of gray light touched the sky, not so much erasing the night as thinning it, Rhia and I set off. We passed through the warped posts of the village gate, our breath, like our horses', forming frosty clouds in the night air. The cold slapped my face and stiffened my limbs; my fingers felt as hard and lifeless as the ground itself. Meanwhile, worries crowded my mind. Only when I thought of Lleu, and the fire we'd built together, did I smile inwardly.

Rhia, like me, seemed lost in thought. Huddled in Mother's vest, she sat astride the mare Coella, whose ears swiveled apprehensively. Meanwhile, I rode Ionn, listening to his hooves smacking the turf, cracking the slabs of ice that might later in the day become puddles. I glanced over at Rhia, glad that she'd wanted to keep wearing the vest. Touched by the vague predawn light, it glowed with the yellow hues of astral flowers. And with the green eyes of Scullyrumpus, who had nestled deep in its folds.

As we passed through a small copse of oak, ash, and hawthorn, the sun arose, touching the tops of the leafless trees with golden hues. Rhia's face, uncharacteristically stern, turned to me. I could tell that she was missing her home in Druma Wood, where winter touched the land so lightly. And I could also feel her unasked questions about my plans.

Plans. That was much too strong a word. I had only an idea, and not a lot of confidence that it would work. Or that Rhia would even agree to it. I felt grateful, at least, that I still had a few more hours to think it through, since Rhia had asked only that I explain myself by nightfall. But the passage of time did nothing to calm my queasy stomach.

For the rest of the day, we rode north together across the frosted plains. We spoke little, though Scullyrumpus' unwavering scowl told me his thoughts quite plainly. Throughout the day, the horses' pace, like the dreary clouds overhead, never changed. Why rush, when I myself wasn't sure where we were going?

In time, a colorless sunset brightened the clouds to the west. We approached a still-flowing rivulet, bubbling out of a thick stand of trees. Pointing to a tilting oak tree by the forest's edge, I declared, "There's our camp for the night."

"Wondyful, just wondyful," grumbled the voice from Rhia's shoulder. "And no food for supper, I suresure."

Rhia silenced him with a wave. "I've got some oatcakes, you glutton. And maybe some rivertang berries if you stay quiet." She shot me a glance. "Merlin has some talking to do."

"Goodgood," chattered Scullyrumpus. "Clumsy man talking helps me sleeping."

Without bothering to tether the horses, we sat by the roots of the oak, which clasped the turf like bony fingers. From one of her pockets, Rhia pulled out a handful of oatcakes, plus a few dried berries, purple and tart. I took some, as did Scullyrumpus with a smack of his lips. Reaching for a rounded stone, I broke away the fingers of ice that were stretching across the rivulet. As I dunked Rhia's flask, filling it to the top, the frigid water drenched my hand.

"We could use some of your raspberry syrup right now," I lamented.

She chuckled at the thought, her eyes alight. Despite everything, I felt glad to be in her company. For one more night, at least.

"Well," I began. "Let's—"

"Night night, talky man," said Scullyrumpus, sliding into Rhia's sleeve pocket with an oatcake in each paw. "Be sure jabber all night now. And don't fallyfall in river, hek-heka, hee-hee-hee-ho."

Watching his ears disappear into the pocket, I shook my head. "He's such good company."

Rhia swallowed one of her berries. "He makes me laugh now and then. That's worth something."

"About as much as a sour stomach, if you ask me."

She reached over to me, rustling her thick vest, and tapped my leg. "So tell me this idea of yours."

Drawing a deep breath, I began again. "Think about our problem for a minute. There isn't nearly enough time to alert every creature on Fincayra. So that means I've got to decide which ones would be most helpful in turning back Rhita Gawr, and go after them. I'm thinking of trying the canyon eagles first."

Rolling a berry between her fingers, she pondered the notion. "Makes sense. Go on."

I studied her for a long moment. "Rhia, there are some creatures you know better than I—who trust you, as I do."

She tensed, backing up against a burly root. "You're not wanting me to . . . No, Merlin. I'd like to help you gather everyone, but I really can't."

"Why not?"

"Because," she blurted out, "it can't be done!"

"We don't know that."

"I do!" She turned away, staring into the gloomy forest behind the old oak. "At least it can't be done by me. I belong in the Druma, you know that. With the trees, my friends."

I laid my hand on the oak's deeply rutted bark. "They might listen to you, Rhia. They might even stir from that slumber that's kept them rooted for so many centuries."

"Unlikely," she scoffed. "Even the Druma's trees, which are more awake than most, can't lift their roots out of the ground anymore. They've slept so long they've forgotten how."

"What about the walkers?" I pressed. "I met one just last year, near the Haunted Marsh."

"A *nynniaw pennent?* A real one? You never told me!" Her gray-blue eyes widened for an instant. Then, just as quickly, her excitement faded. "You know how rare they are. I've heard only five or six are left on this whole island. And besides, they look just like any other tree. Even their name means *always there, never found.*"

My hand moved down the ridges of the trunk, then dropped to her shoulder. "You could find them, Rhia. I know you could! And if you can reach them, they might know how to awaken the other trees." I bent closer, gazing at her intently. "Think of it! A forest on the move, as you described last night! If Rhita Gawr's army ever saw such a thing . . ."

My words trailed off, but my gaze never slackened. "Remember? *Like a mountain on the move, like a tide upon the land.*"

Running a hand through her curls, she stared at me, unconvinced. "It's fine to imagine. But . . ."

"What?"

"Oh, I'm just not good at this kind of thing."

"Come on now. You confronted Stangmar in his own castle, didn't you?"

"Yes, and hated every minute of it."

"And you came with me into the dragon's lair, didn't you? It wasn't our friend Gwynnia we faced there, but her father, three times bigger and a thousand times more wrathful."

Her face softened enough to show a spare grin. "That was the day you took a bite out of your own boot."

"*Mmmm,*" I said, pretending to chew on something impossibly tough. "Bring me," *chomp, chomp,* "some more salt."

Her grin widened. "Not needed! There's enough already from your sweaty feet."

At that, we both laughed, so hard that Scullyrumpus poked out his head, watching us in surprise. Seeing one of Rhia's oatcakes resting unguarded on a root, he leaped down, snatched the morsel, and plunged back into the pocket before anyone could object.

As we quieted, she looked at me long and hard. "You're mad, Brother. Utterly mad."

I nodded.

"And the whole idea is ridiculous. Not to mention dangerous, with both Stangmar and that sword-armed character roaming about."

I nodded again.

She swallowed. "All right, I'll do it." Scowling at me, she added, "How do you ever talk me into these things?"

"The same way you talked me into flying on that vine."

Her fingers drummed on the tilting trunk of the oak, already lined with dusky shadows. "Tell me what else you're thinking. While I'm off trying to rouse the trees, what other allies do you hope to win?"

"Well, the canyon eagles, as I said. They're tricky to find, as you know, but I helped them long ago and I'm hoping they haven't forgotten."

"Who else?"

"The giants, as many as possible. Shim's already taken on that task. But we'll also need some help from the dwarves, fierce fighters that they are."

"That won't be easy." She popped her remaining berry into her mouth. "Your last encounter with Urnalda was about as tart as this berry."

My hand ran along the carved handle of my staff, resting beside me on the roots. "I know, believe me. But she's more than just the dwarves' leader, right? She's an enchantress, a powerful one, with her own ability to see the future. It's possible she already knows the dangers we're facing. And if she could be persuaded—well, one angry dwarf is worth a dozen of Rhita Gawr's warrior goblins."

"Wait, now. You can bet Rhita Gawr will have some help from the goblins, his old allies. But most of his army will be spirits, deathless beings. That's what Dagda told you. How do you expect to fight them?"

For several seconds, I listened to the slapping of the rivulet, bounding past the rims of ice along its edges. "I don't know," I said at last. "I really don't know. We'll just have to do our best."

Rhia chewed silently—not on any food, but on her lip. "We'll need to contact the wind sisters somehow. I wish I knew how to reach our old friend Aylah."

"You never find the wind," I corrected. "It finds you. Now, someone I *might* be able to reach is the Grand Elusa. She'll surely fight for Fincayra! With her size and power—not to mention that appetite of hers, fitting for a giant spider—she's the most dangerous creature ever to walk on this island." I paused. "Except for a dragon."

My throat constricted as I thought of Hallia, traveling northward in search of Gwynnia's lair. Would she find it in time? Would the dragon be there . . . and willing to help?

"We'll need men and women," Rhia said decisively. "Every person we can find. And my friends the wood elves might agree to join us, though they're as elusive as shadows."

My own shadow, barely visible on the darkening ground, shook its head vigorously.

"All right, all right," I said. "None of her elves are as elusive as you." The shaking ceased.

I swung my head back to Rhia. "The marsh ghouls, too."

She frowned. "Not them. They're savage fighters, all right, but they can't be trusted."

"You weren't there when I met them—and helped them. Maybe they'll remember, and want to repay their debt."

Her frown only deepened. "They're at the bottom of our list. Only the living stones would be worse prospects. Ha! You won't even get a living stone to talk with you, let alone join with you."

"But I did, Rhia! Don't you remember? That night when the living stone tried to swallow me? We did speak, and I remember it still— that deep, rumbling voice. There's life in those ancient boulders, and great wisdom, too. I can reach them, I'm sure I can."

"Myself, I'd rather try to wake the trees. If it's really possible."

"Let's find out," I suggested, nodding toward the oak.

She eyed me uncertainly for a moment, then laid her hand, fingers splayed wide, upon the rutted bark of the trunk. Closing her eyes, she started to whisper in the deep, breathy tones of the oak's language. *Hooo washhhaaa washhhaaa lowww, hooo washhhaaa lowww wayanooo.* Again she repeated the chant, and again.

In the root running under my thigh, I felt a very slight twitch— almost a movement, though not quite. Had I just imagined it? I stretched out my own hand, touching the trunk alongside Rhia. Slowly, I began to feel a faint, distant warmth under my palm, radiating out from the heartwood. *Hooo washhhaaa washhhaaa lowww, hooo naaayalaaa washhhaaa lowww.*

Another root stirred, quivering ever so slightly. It tensed, like an arm about to move. At the same time, a branch above our heads started swaying, slapping against the trunk. A dead leaf shook loose and floated downward, landing in Rhia's abundant curls. Her eyes opened, full of wonder, as the heartwood's warmth swelled a little stronger.

"It's working," she whispered excitedly. "Can you feel it?"

"See if you can get it to lift its roots out of the ground!"

At the instant I spoke, though, the tree fell still again. Beneath my palm, the warmth seemed to recede, as swiftly as it had appeared. Rhia and I chanted, louder this time, over and over and over again. The warmth, though, continued to diminish, draining out of the fibers of wood like water from a broken flask. A few seconds later, all I could feel was rugged, lined bark under my hand.

Not willing to give up, we tried chanting again. We kept pressing our palms against the tree, so hard that the veins bulged on the backs of our hands. Nothing stirred, however. No movement. No warmth. No life.

At length, we drew back. Rhia cast me a solemn glance. Shaking her head, she dislodged the frayed leaf, which drifted down to the ground, settling by her feet. "It won't be easy," she said dismally.

"Right," I replied. "Yet . . . you truly started something there. Who can tell? Maybe you'll find another way—a new word or tone that could make all the difference."

The edges of her mouth curled slightly. "You really think so?"

"It's possible, you know."

She leaned her head back, gazing up into the arching branches of the oak. "Maybe, maybe not."

At that instant, a tiny speck of light, no bigger than an apple seed, flickered in one of the grooves of the trunk. It flew outward, glittering brightly, humming in the air. A light flyer! I had seen only one of these delicate creatures before, and had never forgotten its beauty.

The glowing speck circled once around our heads, then fluttered toward me. I caught my breath as it landed, as lightly as a mote of dust, upon the tip of my nose. There it stayed, wings whirring softly, for a few seconds. I couldn't shake the feeling that, even as I watched it, the luminous little fellow was watching me even more closely. Then, with a new flash of light, it lifted off, caught a current of air, and disappeared into the trees.

Rhia, watching the light flyer depart, imitated the hum of its wings. "It reminds me of a shooting star, but so much smaller." She grinned. "And it surely seemed to like that pointed nose of yours."

Gently, I touched the spot where the creature had settled so briefly. "Perhaps . . . we've just won over our first ally."

She almost grinned. "It's possible, you know."

Suddenly Ionn snorted. The stallion, who had been grazing on some willow shoots by the rivulet, lifted his head and turned toward the blackened plains. Following his gaze, I spied an upright figure emerging from the shadows.

I leaped to my feet, staring hard. It couldn't be! Yet, as the figure came closer, padding quickly across the ground, I knew that it was, indeed, the person it appeared to be. The person I least expected to meet on this night, in this place.

"Lleu," I said in amazement, as the young boy trotted up to us. He came to a stop, breathing heavily, by the edge of the rivulet. Kneeling, he plunged his whole face into the water, took several swallows, then stood again. He wiped his dripping chin and cheeks on his sleeve, careful not to touch the stub of his missing ear.

Awestruck, I asked, "You . . . ran here? Followed us?"

He gave a nod, spraying some droplets on the woolen scarf I'd given him the night before, which now encircled his neck. "Sure, I follows ye," he said matter-of-factly, as if a day-long run weren't anything unusual.

I glanced over at Rhia, whose expression showed her own disbelief. Slowly, I knelt, so that Lleu's face and mine nearly touched. "Tell me, lad," I whispered. "Why?"

He tugged on the scarf. "This be yers. An' ye left this morn afore I could give it back to ye."

I couldn't keep myself from smiling. "No, Lleu. I left it because I gave it to you, just as my friend gave it to me." Somehow I felt sure that, while he had told himself he should try to return the scarf, his real motivations lay deeper. Why was he so drawn to me? Could he tell, in some instinctive way, that my childhood and his weren't so different?

Gently, I patted his shoulder. "How is that ear feeling?"

He winced at the mention of his wound. Then, squaring his shoulders, he answered, "Not too bad, master. It be throbbin' still, an' I can't touch it, but me hearin's jest fine." His brow creased fearfully. "The worser part be the dream I had las' night." He shuddered, and looked away briefly. "But ye helped me git over that."

"Actually, as I remember, it was you who helped me. And you may call me Merlin."

His eyes shone, even in the dim light. Then his small mouth pinched. "I seed some others runnin', master Merlin. Child'n, jest like me. They was runnin' fast—away from somebody or somethin', I'm sure. Don't know what, an' I didn't wait to find out." He gulped. "But I was wonderin' if it's . . . maybe the . . ."

"Same attacker?" Feeling his fear, I bit my lip. "No, no, it couldn't be."

He stared up at me, unconvinced. "He's still around, though. An' if he's still around, he could be huntin' down others."

I wrapped my hand around his. "Not you, though. You're safe now. I promise."

Uncertainly, he nodded.

"Here," I said, picking up my own uneaten oatcakes and handing them to him. "Not much supper after your long day, but we'll do better in the morning."

"Thank ye, master Merlin." He stuffed the oatcakes into his mouth and started chewing.

I watched him until he finished. "You can stay with us tonight, Lleu, and nothing bad is going to happen to you. That's certain. But tomorrow, I'm afraid, we'll have to part ways again." Seeing his face fall, I explained, "Rhia goes her way, and I go . . . mine. Traveling with either of us would be far too dangerous, for you or anyone else."

He looked at me bravely, though his jaw quivered.

"Don't worry, now. We won't leave you on your own, though I can tell you know how to take care of yourself. Before we part, we'll get you to a village, or a friendly farm."

Placing my arm around his shoulder, I walked him over to a flat, mossy spot behind the oak. "Here's where we'll be sleeping." As he reached into his pocket, I added, "No need for any kindling tonight, lad. We're ready for sleep, and I'm sure you are, too." I didn't tell him my real reason for not having a fire: It might attract unwanted visitors.

With a lengthy yawn, he nodded. Then he removed the scarf,

wadded it up, and lay it on the moss as a pillow. A few moments later, he was curled into a ball, slumbering.

For a while Rhia and I stood over him, this boy who seemed so used to spending the night on the cold ground. Meanwhile, the darkness around us deepened. The ridges of the oak's trunk could no longer be seen; the trees in the forest beyond melted into a single mass of blackness, much like the sky. There wouldn't be any stars tonight. With a sigh, I wondered whose dreams would prove more frightening, Lleu's or my own.

And yet . . . something about the sight of him nudged my anxieties aside. The simple goodness of his heart touched me. Lying there, his face so careworn, he made me think of the young king whose sword I carried, and whose burden I'd promised to share. In a land far away, a land that one day, I'd heard foretold, would be called Merlin's Isle.

All that, however, was in another world, another time. It was the world I lived in now, the world of Rhia and Hallia and Shim, that inspired my deepest loyalties. That was the place I loved, and would do everything in my power to protect.

11
ELLYRÍAṆṆA'S HAṆD

That night, once again, I dreamed of Trouble's feather. This time, though, I wasn't riding on it but watching from afar. The feather, banded with silver and brown, drifted down from the sunlit clouds. Gracefully it spun and skipped, carried by the currents. Each time one gust would fade, another would swell, so that the feather continued to ride aloft, floating freely through the air.

All at once, the feather started to change. Swiftly it grew larger, swelling in length and breadth, until it was no longer a feather but an entire wing. Another wing appeared beside the first, as much alike as a perfect reflection. The wings looked now very much like my lost friend, Trouble, except that they bore nothing between them—nothing but air.

Bearing an invisible body, the wings started to beat rhythmically. Higher they flew, far above the land, until finally their ascent peaked. Then downward they plunged, heedless of any obstacles, slicing through the clouds like a spear.

Slowly, very slowly, a body started to form between the wings. My own body! Now I beat the wings; now I rode the air. The wind blew strongly in my face, making my eyes water. But I didn't care, for I felt wholly alive. Part feathers and part freedom.

A gale suddenly blew, slamming into me with the force of a huge hand. Everywhere the wind screamed, racing through the clouds, tearing them asunder. Out of control, I spun helplessly through the air. At last, I struck a sandy shore. Rolling across dunes and over brightly colored shells, I fell into the mist-shrouded sea and vanished under the waves.

I awoke. Darkness pressed close, and the branches of the old oak rattled in the night breeze. Sitting up, I instinctively reached for my satchel and felt for the feather within. It was there, soft and flexible. And real. I wiped my brow, streaked with perspiration, with the sleeve of my tunic. All the while, a blur of images still crowded my mind: one wing appearing, then another; feathers glinting in the sunlight; my own body sailing through the sky. Then—a wild wind raging, and the sea swallowing me completely.

What could it mean? Nothing good, that was certain. And why did that sandy shore seem so familiar? Had I seen it before, perhaps in another dream?

The oak creaked loudly, its limbs twisting. While Lleu remained soundly asleep on the bed of moss, Rhia stirred. She sat up, wide awake, her face darkened by something other than night.

"Did you have a dream, too?" I extended my hand toward her.

"No, not a dream," she answered, wrapping her forefinger around my own. "Just a . . . feeling. Like something horrible, truly horrible, is about to happen."

I drew a slow breath of the cold night air. "My dream was about wings, Rhia. Wings without a body, then with one. Wings found, then lost in the sea. I have no idea what it means."

She slid closer to me. "Where in the sea? Any particular place?"

"I couldn't say, except . . ." I gazed up at the shrouded sky beyond the tracery of branches. "Except that it was a shore, a beach, with— yes! The Shore of the Speaking Shells, the spot where I first landed on my raft. That's right, I'm sure of it."

Pensively, she twisted some of her curls with her fingers. "Why there, I wonder?" Suddenly, she stiffened. "Merlin, do you hear that?"

A low, droning sound reached us, as haunting as the creaking branches but more mournful. I listened, trying to make out its source, but with no success. All I could tell was that it was coming through the deep blackness of the forest, from some distance away. And that, whatever its source, the sound was full of sorrow.

"Come," I said, taking my staff in one hand and Rhia's arm in the other. "Let's follow it."

"What if Lleu wakes up and finds us gone?"

I chewed my lip. "We'll just have to hope that he won't. Besides, we won't be gone long."

As I stepped toward the thick stand of trees, avoiding the oak's tangled roots, she hesitated. "It's even darker in there than it is right here. Shouldn't I try to make the Orb glow? We could use it as a lantern."

"And announce ourselves to whatever is making that sound? No, best to keep invisible. Come now. My second sight can guide us easily."

"Can guide *you*, that is. I'll be knocking into trunks and stubbing my toes on roots while you prance along."

I grinned wickedly. "Now you'll see what it's like for me when you go running ahead, the way you did on our way to Caer Aranon."

"Running?" She pretended to be insulted. "That was just strolling."

"Then stroll with me now."

Taking her hand, I plunged into the ferns bordering the trees. We stepped over a pair of fallen ash trees, and entered the new layer of darkness within the tangle of limbs. My second sight did indeed work well in the gloom, and I could see even my own frosted breath. More important, I could see the path of the rivulet, which coursed along despite the patches of ice. Its bank, largely open, made the easiest route through the woods, though overhanging branches still jabbed our shoulders or clutched our hair. I felt grateful that, despite his bumpy ride, Scullyrumpus stayed quietly snuggled in his pouch on Rhia's sleeve.

The sound grew steadily louder. In time, I realized it was not one voice, but several. And they were the voices of men and women. They were chanting something, a deeply rueful song. Yet I still couldn't make out any of the words.

As we followed the rivulet, it merged into a larger stream. Water slapped against the bank, often coating the ground with a thin layer of ice. In such places my foot often slipped sideways, splashing into water almost as cold as ice itself. Several times I had to stop and empty my boot before my toes went numb. To my dismay, Rhia never seemed to have such accidents. I tried not to notice her gloating expression. At least, I told myself, Scullyrumpus wasn't watching.

At last, the trees grew sparser. The banks of the stream widened, stretching into a meadow of frosted grass on both sides. A moment later, as we worked our way around a jagged boulder, I suddenly saw the source of the chanting. I halted, grasping Rhia's hand.

Not far ahead, huddled together by the stream, stood seven or eight people. They wore dark robes, and delicately woven shawls of mourning, signifying the loss of someone they loved. An array of candles flickered by their feet. Behind them rose a little mound of freshly turned soil—the grave of someone small.

As we stood in silence, the words of their song swept over us like a river of tears:

> *A candle lit, a candle doused,*
> *a sunset in the morning:*
> *How brief the life, the love it housed,*
> *that dies while still aborning.*

> *Upon the waters of the world,*
> *the everlasting river,*
> *A candle floats on leaf unfurled,*
> *its fragile flame aquiver.*

> *O candlelight! Burn on and on*
> *until your wick is through.*
> *Restore the spark so early gone,*
> *the flame we hardly knew.*

> *From where appears such potent light,*
> *illumes the lives of men?*
> *And where departs the flame so bright*
> *that never glows again?*

> *A life is gone, its future lost,*
> *now faded like the moon.*

No greater pain, no higher cost:
the candle doused too soon.

O candlelight! Burn on and on
until your wick is through.
Restore the spark so early gone,
the flame we hardly knew.

The chant concluded, though its mournful tones seemed to hover among the leafless branches, echoing through the trees. One by one, each of the people bent down and lifted a quivering candle from the ground. Gently, they placed the glowing candles upon the wide, rounded leaves of the dowthwater plant that grows year-round among the roots of hawthorn trees. They set, with great care, the candles upon the stream, allowing the water to bear them away like a procession of torchlit funeral barges.

Again their voices lifted, chanting once more these words:

A candle lit, a candle doused,
a sunset in the morning:
How brief the life, the love it housed,
that dies while still aborning.

The last words died, disappearing like the flames of the guttering candles soon to be submerged in icy water. Somberly, the people began to depart. One elder man, his head rimmed with a circle of white hair, lingered after the rest had gone. Quietly, he gazed at the candles floating down the stream.

I approached, Rhia at my side. When we were a few paces away, the old man started, and stepped back in fear. His face, tinged with candlelight, studied us anxiously.

"We bring no harm," I declared, raising my staff. "We're merely travelers passing through."

The elder shook his head slowly. "Aye well, this day has seen enough harm already."

Rhia moved a small step closer. Motioning toward the little mound, she asked, "Who has died?"

"A girl," he said distantly. "So young and all ablossom with life. Her name was Ellyrianna."

"Ellyrianna," she echoed. "Such a beautiful name."

"Aye, but her laugh rang out more beautiful still."

"Was she your child?"

The man watched the floating candles for a moment. "Aye, and nay. She belonged to everyone in our village. She slept and ate and labored and laughed with us, though parents she had none."

My throat tightened. "She was an orphan?"

"Aye." He paused, seeing one of the candles sputter and sink into the stream. "And why she was murdered in this way, no one can tell."

"Murdered?" I asked. "Who did it? Do you know?"

The old man turned to me with vacant eyes. "No one knew his name. He was a warrior, a monstrous warrior, with sword blades instead of arms."

Together, Rhia and I sucked in our breath. The elder appeared not to notice, and continued, his tone as grave as the villagers' chant. "He tried to cut off her hand, he did. Ellyrianna's hand!" He blew a long, tormented breath. "We tried to save her, but aye, she bled to death most horribly."

"That's terrible!" moaned Rhia. "How could anyone do such a thing? Especially to a child."

"Such things," I corrected, grinding my staff into the soil. "Who is this warrior? And why is he attacking orphans?" I moved to the fellow's side. "Did he say where he was going next?"

He squinted, thinking, as light flickered across his wrinkled face. "He did say something about Caer Darloch, the next village to the north. Whether he was coming from there or going there, I don't know."

"And did he say anything else?"

Slowly, the old man bobbed his head. "He said that this girl's death was just the beginning. Aye, the beginning! And that many more children will soon lose their limbs—or their lives. Unless . . ."

"What?"

"Unless the one called Merlin faces him in combat alone."

12

DECİSİOⁿ

We returned to our camp, numbed from both the cold of night and from the old man's news. The first thing I did was to check on Lleu, and I sighed gladly to see him sound asleep on the moss, just where we'd left him. Noticing his scarf beside him, I gathered it up and carefully wrapped it around his bare feet. Then, hearing Rhia's teeth chattering, I put caution aside and asked her to warm us with her Orb. She gratefully agreed.

For the rest of the night, we sat on the gnarled roots of the leaning oak, debating what to do. The shadowy form of the tree, lit by the Orb's orange glow, hung over our heads. But a darker shadow loomed over all: our rapidly dwindling time.

"Blood of Dagda," I cursed, jabbing at the tree trunk with a stick. "We had too much to do already. And now this!"

Rhia shifted her weight on the oak's burly root. "Who is this sword-armed assassin?" she demanded, for perhaps the twentieth time. "And why children—orphan children?"

"Great seasons, Rhia! I've no better idea now than I did an hour ago."

She lifted her arms, stretching her back stiffly. "I know, I know, but the questions keep circling in my head." Peering at me across the crackling flames, she added, "One of the strangest questions of all is why he wants *you*."

"Don't you think I know that?" I snapped in frustration. "It's as mysterious as why he appeared now, on top of everything else."

She continued to watch me intently. "Do you think—this is crazy, I know—it might have something to do with the fact you once thought yourself an orphan?"

"How could it?" I flexed my fingers before the glowing sphere, trying to work out the stiffness. "Just because I spent those years not knowing Elen was our mother, or Stangmar our . . ." I halted, choking on the word. "Just because of that, why would he start these terrible attacks? No, no, it doesn't make sense. Sword Arms, whoever he is, has a deeper motivation. A larger purpose. I can feel it, Rhia."

Suddenly a new thought struck me. "Is it possible, do you think, he's really part of the greater wickedness? Part of Rhita Gawr's plan?"

"How so?"

"Well, maybe Rhita Gawr knows that I've been warned about what's to come. He could have sent this warrior to distract me, to keep me from assembling a force to stop him."

Rhia's eyebrows, tinted by the Orb, lifted. "If that's his goal, he's already succeeding. Winter's longest night is only twelve days away. And we've just spent most of the night talking about this, with nothing to show for it."

"True." I ground my teeth. "You agree, though, it's more than just a coincidence that Sword Arms is striking right now?"

"Sure, I'll grant you that. But why orphans?"

I glanced over at Lleu, curled into a ball, his head resting on a thick tuft of moss. Orange light rippled over his face and tattered tunic. "Maybe . . . Rhia, I have it! When Lleu told us about those children running, fleeing from whatever, he didn't call them orphans. Remember? He called them *children*."

She stared at me blankly.

"And when the old man told us about what the warrior threatened, he said many more children will die. Not orphans—children."

Rhia fingered her curls, her face bewildered. "What's your point?"

I leaned closer and grasped her thigh. "Don't you see? Orphans are really just children. But unprotected children! The easiest ones to catch. Or harm."

Her eyes grew round. "So you think Sword Arms is really after any children he can find?"

"Yes! And if he doesn't soon get what he wants—the chance to fight me—he's going to broaden his attacks. He'll stop maiming, and start killing outright. He'll hunt down any child he can get."

"But why, Merlin? It doesn't make sense."

I started to answer, when Lleu rolled over in his sleep, whimpering painfully. In the wavering light of the Orb, his severed ear looked grotesque, a lump of blackened tissue. In my memory, I heard him telling me bravely that he could still hear all right, that the worst part was his dreams. He was far too young to know such terror!

As I watched, he whimpered again, this time more shrilly, like a trapped animal. I shivered, yet I knew his fate could have been worse: the fate of Ellyrianna. Or of others to come.

Both my hands closed into fists. I turned back to Rhia, and announced, "I've made a decision."

"You're . . . going to face him?"

"I'm going to do whatever it takes to save the children of this land!"

"But wait." She shook her head vigorously. "What about the longest night? All you need to do to stop Rhita Gawr?"

I clasped the hilt of my sword. "I must stop this murderer first."

"This is crazy, Merlin! As bad as he is, he's not nearly as bad as Rhita Gawr! One is killing children, yes. But the other is going to destroy everything—every creature who lives on this island. There's no comparison!"

She reached for the Orb, clasping it in her hand, and lifted it toward my face. I could feel its warmth against my neck and chin. "Look at me," she commanded, peering closely at my face. "Tell me the truth, now. Why are you doing this? Is it just because you feel so much for those poor orphans?"

"It's much more than that!" I slapped my hand on top of the sphere, pushing it aside. Rays of orange light sliced between my fingers, striping our faces and the ragged bark of the tree. "These are children, Rhia. Suffering and dying right here, right now. And the worth of every child is untold—beyond any jewel, any treasure. Every child could be a poet, a healer . . . or a wizard."

She swallowed. "I know, Merlin. But I'm talking about losing our homeland forever."

"So am I!" My voice deepened, and my words echoed in the night air. "If this warrior succeeds, it could wound Fincayra deeply. At its heart."

I released the Orb and took hold of her hand. "If you ruin a nation's children, you ruin its future. What will it matter to win at the circle of stones, to push back Rhita Gawr and his army—if so many children have been maimed and killed that our future is forever spoiled? If every day is as tortured as little Lleu's dreams?"

Rhia gazed at me awhile, then nodded grimly. "If you destroy enough children . . . it's like robbing a forest of its seeds."

"Right. Which is why I must go after him. Stop him. And I'm sure I can do it in time to get to the circle of stones by the longest night."

"But who will spread the alarm?" she demanded. "Who will rally the people of Fincayra?"

In silence, I watched her.

She started. "No, Merlin! You don't think . . ."

"I do, Rhia. You can spread the word. You can rally the people."

"But . . . to most of them, I'm just a stranger."

"Not to the wood elves, or your friends the river sprites. And don't forget the canyon eagles, who taught you how to speak their language! And what about the glyn-maters, hidden away in their secret caverns?"

Groaning, she rubbed the side of her head. "They know me, sure. But will they *listen* to me?"

"That . . . no one can say." I slid myself over to the root where she sat, so that our shoulders touched. "I can tell you this, though. Even to those who don't know you, you'll be more than just a stranger. You'll be Rhia, woman of the enchanted trees! You carry the Orb of Fire on your belt, and the pointed ears of every Fincayran man and woman on your face. And you also carry the word of Dagda himself."

She stared into the sphere, her brow deeply creased. Beneath her eyes, her skin glowed, as if it were itself aflame.

I slid my arm around her waist. "And you bear one thing more, something you can always depend on. My love for you. Yes, and my belief in you, too."

Very slowly, she turned away from the Orb and toward me. "I think," she began, "I should try the canyon eagles first."

I heaved a sigh. "Giants' bones, but you're brave."

"Not brave," she replied. "Just full of madness." She cocked her head mischievously. "After all, I'm related to you."

I chuckled. "Of that I'm glad."

"I'll remember you said that, Brother."

Smiling, I glanced to the east. Across the frosted plains, the sky was beginning to lighten subtly. Bands of pink and crimson showed along the horizon, tinting the undersides of the heavy clouds. "It will be dawn soon. Should I go find the makings of breakfast?"

Before she could answer, a furry head popped out of the pocket on her sleeve. After a prolonged yawn, he squeaked, "Breakyfast? Did somebody saysay breakyfast?"

"Yes," I answered curtly. "And if you want some, you can help get it."

Startled, the little beast shook his head, flapping his ears against his face. He gave Rhia a puzzled look. "Grumpy man, he is! Always like this in morning, yesyes?"

She tickled the side of his nose. "He didn't get much sleep, that's all. But do as he says, would you? Find a few turnips, or some winterroot, and breakfast will come all the sooner."

His lips twitched hungrily. Without another squeak, he scrambled out of the pocket and down her arm. Barely had his paws touched the ground before he raced off into the ferns bordering the thick forest behind us.

"You certainly know how to wake him up," I observed.

Rhia's amused expression faded. "I only wish I knew as much about how to wake up the trees."

Retrieving my staff, I stood. "If anyone can find the way, it will be you." I placed my foot on one of the oak's roots. "Now, if you'll build us a tripod and find something to use for a pot, I'll get a fire going and start collecting ingredients."

"An' I'll be helpin'," declared Lleu, walking toward us. "What do ye need?"

I grinned at him. "Some kindling. Know where we might find some?"

13

THE VISITOR

Half an hour later, a thick stew of turnip, late season watercress, moss sprouts, and pwyll nuts boiled over our fire at the forest's edge. Seasoned with a dash of acorn powder (contributed by Lleu), and served in cupped shards of elm bark, the stew tasted surprisingly satisfying. And it was warming, as well, enough so that Rhia removed her thick vest and hooked it on a branch of the tilting oak. As we ate, the first rays of dawn crowned the topmost limbs, bathing them in amber, while a raven cawed roughly in the distance. The dried grass of the plains, stretching as far as we could see to the east, gleamed the color of rust.

As Rhia passed around the dregs from the hardwood burl that had served as our cooking pot, she looked toward the horses. Coella was contentedly grazing on the ferns, while Ionn stood apart, drumming his hoof on the hardened ground. "Ionn senses something," she remarked. "Do you think he knows our plans have changed?"

"Possibly." I took a last sip of stew, and tossed my cup of bark aside. "That horse has a special way of knowing things."

At that, Ionn shook his mane and snorted loudly. I stood, as did Rhia and Lleu. Scullyrumpus, sensing trouble, licked his paws anxiously. Suddenly Lleu gasped and pointed to the edge of the forest, still in shadow.

A lone figure, wearing a hooded cloak, had emerged from the trees. He drew steadily nearer, walking with large, quick strides. Although his shoulders were hunched, he was still quite tall. Beneath his cloak, he seemed powerful, as well as dangerous, like a wounded wolf on the prowl.

Ionn stamped the ground, then trotted over to me. I stroked his nose, but he whinnied nervously. One look in his great brown eyes revealed something most unusual for the great stallion: fear. Again I studied the figure, large under the cloak, drawing steadily nearer. Who was this, that Ionn would react so strangely?

I could discern, under the hood, a man with a thick black beard. The hairs sprouted, it seemed, from a face as stern as chiseled stone. He glared at us with intense black eyes, his jaw etched in a permanent frown. As he reached the other side of the rivulet flowing out of the forest, the man halted. Sharply, he threw back his hood, so we could not mistake his identity.

Yet I already knew him well. Here, standing before me, was the person I most despised, the person whose name had brought nothing but agony to the land he once ruled. Stangmar.

I grabbed the hilt of my sword. Boldly, I stepped forward to meet him.

"So," growled the deep voice. "You would slay me without a thought?"

My teeth ground together. "No, that would reduce me to your equal."

Stangmar's massive hand curled into a fist. "You destroyed all I once had, boy. All! I have a long line of ancestors, too many to name, who ruled this isle before me. Yet none of them was ever toppled by his own son."

"None of them ever tried to murder his own son!"

He merely glared at me. After a moment, he spoke again, his voice grim. "Our wretched history does not concern me now. I seek not you, but someone else."

Behind me, I heard Rhia draw a sharp breath.

"How did you find us?" I demanded.

"The stallion's tracks, of course! Think you I don't know my own horse? He still bears that slice in his forehoof from our first battle."

Ionn neighed, stamping the turf forcefully. I glanced over my shoulder at him; the look in his eyes had changed to defiance.

"You, boy, have stood in my way at every turn," Stangmar said icily. "You have stolen my very realm! My castle, my soldiers, my servants. But you shall not stand in my way this time." His voice snarled like an angry beast. "Tell me where Elen is now."

I held myself as straight as my hemlock staff. "You shall not harm her."

"Tell me where she is!"

"Never."

Stangmar's whole frame quaked with rage. Then, drawing a prolonged breath, he seemed to gain control of himself. "She left me, boy. Left me without a word, or a letter, before I had any chance to—"

He pounded his fist into his palm, as his wrath suddenly returned. "Why should I tell you this? I must find her, that's all you need to know! And I am certain you know where she is." He slammed his foot on the rivulet's bank, cracking off a slab of ice. "Now tell me."

"So you can kill her?" I shot back. "She knows perfectly well what you would have done to her if she hadn't left. The same as you tried to do to me!"

He released a low growl. A spark from our cooking fire landed on the shoulder of his cloak and faded swiftly away. "Hear me out! I don't want to harm her. I never wanted that."

"Oh, no," I scoffed.

"I speak the truth!" he bellowed. "I only want . . . to speak to her. To tell her something."

This was more than I could bear. "You only want to murder her!"

Vigorously, he shook his head. "You don't understand, boy. I . . . well, I . . ." Awkwardly, he waved one of his powerful arms, as if trying to seize the words he needed. "You see, I . . . love her."

Dumbstruck, I rocked back on my heels. "You expect me to believe such madness?"

"No," he grumbled, his voice quiet, almost tender. "I had just hoped you might listen. You—who look so very much like I did at your age."

I stiffened, my mind reeling at the very notion that I shared anything at all with this man. "Leave us," I spat. "And cease your searching. You shall never find Elen. Never."

His face hardened again. "That we shall see, boy." A hint of a smirk touched his lips. "Just as you shall see how Rhita Gawr deals with his foes."

My scarred cheeks throbbed. In my mind echoed Dagda's warning: *To prevail on winter's longest night, you will need to defeat your greatest foe, nothing less.* That meant Rhita Gawr, to be sure. Yet Stangmar filled me somehow with deeper wrath.

Rhia stepped toward him, standing shoulder to shoulder with me. Forcefully, she declared, "He's right. You'll never find her."

"Oh?" scoffed Stangmar. "And who are you, vine-clad girl, to tell me what I shall or shall not do?"

Resolutely, she studied him for several seconds. "I am her daughter," she said at last. "Her daughter—and yours."

For an instant, his harsh face softened ever so slightly. He returned her gaze, eyeing her with more curiosity than scorn. Despite myself, I found myself thinking he looked almost feeling, almost handsome. His clenched fist slowly relaxed, and dropped to his side.

"The daughter we . . . lost?" he asked stiffly. "Long ago, in the forest?"

"Yes, the daughter you named Rhiannon." Seeing his look of disbelief, she went on. "The trees raised me, took care of me. But down inside I never forgot about my true parents, and always wondered if I'd see you again."

From her belt, she took the Orb of Fire. As she held it before her, a glimmer of orange sparked within its depths. Lit by the globe in her hand, as well as the glow of the rising sun, her face radiated. It seemed to shine from another source, as well, a source that could not be seen.

"Once, you possessed this Orb," she said softly. "You called it one of your Treasures. Did you learn how to tap its powers?"

Stangmar, still watching her intently, said nothing.

"It can heal a broken spirit," she went on, stepping a little closer. I shot her a worried glance, but she ignored me. "Here now, take it. Use it for yourself."

Hesitantly, his fingers stirred, as if they were deciding what to do. Then his hand lifted, and his whole arm. He reached toward the glowing sphere.

"Please," she implored. "Use it to restore the man you once were."

Suddenly, Stangmar's face went rigid again. His mouth pinched with pride. With a sharp swipe of his hand, he struck the Orb, sending it hurtling over the fire coals. It struck the weathered trunk of the oak and burst into thousands of shards. A flash of orange light exploded, hovered in the air for an instant, then faded away into nothingness.

Utterly speechless, Rhia stared at the shards, sprinkled across the oak's burly roots. Lleu darted to her side, as did Scullyrumpus. They stood in silence, gawking at the remains of the Orb of Fire.

I pounded my staff on the ground. "You destroyed it!"

"Just as you, boy, destroyed my realm! I curse the day that woman ever brought you back to this isle."

With that, he took a stride toward Ionn. The great stallion's tail swished sharply, and his ears angled back. He reared, chopping at the air with his hooves, before galloping some distance away. Shaking his mane, he stood with his head high, black coat glistening in the early morning sun.

"All right, then," Stangmar grumbled. "The horse shall be yours." His frown deepened. "But the final victory shall be mine."

From his pocket, he hurled something into the coals of the fire. A sudden burst of smoke, thick and dark, erupted. Like a heavy blanket, it enveloped us, choking our throats and searing our eyes, tongues, and nostrils. Coughing violently, tears pouring down our cheeks, we stumbled away from the smoke.

At length, our coughs subsided. The smoke dissipated, and we started to breathe normally again. Ionn whinnied and trotted over to my side. He butted me with his nose, and I stroked his long jaw. Then I looked around. Stangmar had vanished—along with Coella.

"She's gone," I fumed. "The mare is gone."

"She's not all that's gone." Somberly, Rhia kicked at a few shards, all that was left of the Orb. Hoarsely, she whispered, "I never did learn how to use it."

I gave her a hug, hoping to comfort her. "It's not your fault."

"It is," she said sadly. "I should never have shown it to him." Thoughtfully, she pursed her lips. "Even so, do you know what's strange? I've dropped it before, even fallen on it once or twice. But it never broke, or even cracked. It's almost like . . . well, like it was ready to break just now."

I touched the place on her belt where the globe had ridden for so long. "Wish I could bring it back for you," I confessed. "But if there's any magic that can do that, I don't know it."

She swallowed. "For a moment there, I really thought he'd use it to heal himself."

I squeezed my staff. "To heal that man would take more magic than the Orb ever had."

Scullyrumpus trudged over to the shards, chattering to himself in disbelief. For a moment he pawed through the pieces, working his way among the twisted roots. Finally, he quit, apparently convinced that the treasure had truly been destroyed. Ears drooping, he returned to Rhia and climbed up to her shoulder. Gently, he wrapped himself around her neck, embracing her like a collar of fur.

"We've got to warn Mother," I declared. "She has to stay where we left her, in that little village. It's about the last place Stangmar would think to look for her."

"You heard her, though," Rhia countered. "She'll be leaving there tomorrow."

"Then we'll have to get word to her today." I scratched my chin. "And there's another problem. Stangmar might try to follow you or me, so it shouldn't be one of us who warns her."

In unison, we turned toward Lleu. I sank to my knees to face him. "Could you do it, lad? Could you run back to the village today?"

Uneasily, he tugged on his sandy hair. "I could do it, master Merlin, if ye needs it done." His gaze fell. "Truly though, I don't really wants to."

"Please," I implored. "It's to help Elen, the good woman who took care of you."

Slowly, he nodded.

"Now, you must get there before nightfall. And you must tell her to stay in that same village until we come for her. All right?"

"Yes, master Merlin."

I gave him a hug, patting his small back. "Thanks, lad. Now have yourself a drink from the rivulet before you set off."

As he stepped over to the bank, I rose and fetched the woolen scarf from the moss where he'd slept. "Oh, Lleu," I called. "Don't forget this."

He looked up from the water's edge, his face dripping wet. Seeing the scarf, he beamed. He padded back over to me, and stood still as I wrapped it around his small neck.

"There," I pronounced, giving him another hug. "On your way now. Oh—and Lleu."

"Yes, master Merlin?"

I gazed at his muddy brown eyes. "You be careful."

He lingered a few more seconds, his tongue working inside his mouth as if he longed to say something. But no words came. Hesitantly, he turned and started running south across the stubbly grass of the plains.

For a while I watched him, then felt Rhia push something under my arm. It was the vest, its woven astral flowers aglow in the sunlight.

"You'll be needing that," she declared.

"So will you," I objected. "You should keep it."

She shook her head. "No, no, Mother gave it to you. And besides, it's only fair, since I'll be taking your horse."

My eyebrows jumped in surprise.

She glanced over at Ionn, who was walking toward the old oak. The muscles of his legs and back gleamed darkly, rippling as he moved. "That's right, isn't it?"

"Of course," I agreed. "You'll have more ground to cover, and more need for speed." With a grin, I added, "It just always amazes me when *you* have my ideas before I do."

She grinned back. "They're usually your best ideas, though."

"Too true."

She took my hand. "Where will you start to look for that warrior?"

"In that village to the north, the one the old fellow mentioned. What was it? Yes—Caer Darloch." I inhaled the crisp morning air and blew out a frosted breath. "If that Sword Arms character is truly searching for me, it won't be long until I find him. I only hope it's before he's harmed anyone else."

Rhia curled her forefinger around my own. "Find him, Merlin. Do what you must to stop him. Then meet me at the circle of stones. Don't fail me, all right?"

"I won't fail," I promised. Fixing her with my gaze, I declared, "Nor will you." One last time, I studied her face—so sensitive and aware and yet, at the same time, so bold and unpredictable. "Ride well, now. Ride as if you had wings."

14

SΠOWFALL

Snow came suddenly. Even as Rhia and I parted, the sun vanished behind a thick mesh of clouds, and the first flakes began falling. Large and unwieldy, they drifted down relentlessly, coating the upper limbs of the oak and filling the deep grooves of its trunk. In a moment's time, the tree's twisted roots became nothing more than ridges of white upon the ground.

I tramped northward, keeping just outside the edge of the forest, in the hope that less snow would accumulate at the base of the trees. I knew from experience the difficulties—and dangers—of trekking through drifts out on the open plains. Though I seemed to be heading into the worst of the storm, I worried about Lleu, traveling south across unprotected grassland. Would he lose his bearings in all that whiteness? How long would his bare feet last in an onslaught of snow?

Just ahead of me, a hemlock bough snapped, releasing a cloud of shimmering white crystals and dumping a mound on the ground. As I stepped across, my boots crunched on the frozen mass. And my thoughts turned to another set of worries: where to find this sword-armed warrior. Clearly, he expected me to seek him out, which was why he'd announced his challenge to the old man—and, no doubt, to others. What if, by the time I reached Caer Darloch, he'd already left?

Or maybe he hadn't intended to stop there at all, just to pass by on his way to the rising plateaus farther north, home to Urnalda and her dwarves.

The mere thought of Urnalda chilled me deeper than the frosted air. As much as I wanted the dwarves to join Fincayra's ranks at the circle of stones, I hoped that Rhia wouldn't have to deal with their treacherous enchantress. She would have more than enough difficulties already in trying to win over the canyon eagles and the others!

Snowflakes continued pouring down as I reached the end of the trees. The instant I left their cover and started tramping across the exposed plains, a biting wind struck, piercing even my thickly padded vest. Before me, the land had already transformed from rusty brown dappled with gray to a uniform blanket of white. Drifts gathered, lifting above the ground like a succession of frozen waves.

The wind howled fiercely, freezing my fingers to my staff. Meanwhile, the frosty clouds of my breath froze the skin of my cheeks as well as the stubbly hairs on my chin. I wished, as I had often before, that I could grow a beard. Yes, a great thick one that could shield my face from such a storm.

How could I battle anyone in such conditions? No matter. I would find that warrior, that murderer of children, wherever he was. And put an end to his brutal attacks. Forever.

Spying a gnarled apple tree, so old that several of its snow-covered branches drooped down to the ground, I decided to seek a moment's shelter from the wind. As I approached, I noticed a small glint of rusty red on a higher branch—an apple, shriveled and dry, but possibly edible. Climbing under the boughs, I knocked it loose with my staff, sat down, and took a small bite.

Tough it was, and bored out by worms. But a hint of tart apple flavor burst in my mouth, reminding me of the fragrant spring that now seemed so far away. Apple blossoms, new green leaves, fresh blue gentians, tiny strawberries exploding with sweetness . . . How long had it been? Legs crossed, I gnawed on the fruit, wondering whether springtime would ever come again to this landscape.

For now, the world was filling up with snow. When I finished the meager apple, I discarded the core. It landed on the head of my shadow, barely visible on the ground through the shadows of the interlaced boughs. Easily miffed as ever, my shadow gathered itself and flung the core back at me, barely missing my nose.

"Oh, do behave," I scolded. "My nose may be large, but it's not a target."

The shadow placed its hands on its hips, rocking its head back and forth as it scolded me in return.

"All right, then, I apologize." I shook my own head. "Sometimes, though, I wonder how I ever endure you! Really. You can be as testy as, well, as . . ." I caught myself, grinning guiltily. "As me."

As the shadow shook with justifiable mirth, I reached for my leather satchel. From its pouch I pulled out the feather from Trouble's wing. Twirling it slowly between my thumb and forefinger, I tried to imagine what his life was like in the Otherworld of the spirits. Surely he soared and swooped and dived for hours in that world of mist, as he had once loved to do in this world. Did he fly at Dagda's side, perhaps, or wherever the winds chanced to take him? And who did he screech at, in his regular fits of rage or passion, now that I was no longer by his side?

Giants' bones, how I missed him.

Wistfully, I put the feather back in the pouch. Then, despite the howling wind, I ducked under the branches and stepped out into the snow. Grateful more than ever for my mother's vest, I pushed through a mounting drift. For a brief moment, I paused, gazing back at the tree, knowing someone must have planted it long ago. That had been an act of faith: in the future, in the children who would one day reap its harvest. Grimly, I slid my staff under my belt and set off.

Tucking my hands under my armpits for warmth, I trudged through the gathering snow. My best chance to find the village, I knew, was to stay alert for any signs of water—a stream, a tarn, or a branch of the River Unceasing. Guessing at the sun's position behind the clouds wasn't easy, but I did my best to keep myself on a northerly bearing. Otherwise, in this swirling storm, I could easily spend the rest of the day roving in circles.

Snow matted my hair and slid down the back of my neck into my tunic, but I paid no heed. What mattered now was finding Sword Arms. Before long, my toes grew stiff and numb from the cold. Slender icicles started to dangle from the hair over my ears. Still, I pressed on.

Suddenly I stepped into a hip-deep hole. Face first, I toppled forward, taking a mouthful of snow. Flailing about to extract myself, I noticed a subtle line of depression at the edge of the deeper snow. A stream! I had, unwittingly, stepped right off the bank.

As I clambered back onto the higher ground, wiping the snow off my face, I began following the path of the stream. After a while it grew noticeably wider, so that the snow didn't fill the whole channel. At the same time, the storm itself began to slacken. The flakes became sparser, and the wind blew less fiercely.

Then I smelled smoke. Whether it came from a single cooking fire or a multitude of hearths, I had no idea. But I pushed onward, staying with the route of the stream. In time I noticed a faint gray haze in the distance. As the snow lightened further, I spied the outline of a thatched roof. Then another, and another. It was, indeed, a village.

It consisted of more than a score of homes, sturdier and tidier than the huts of Caer Aranon. I saw pens for sheep, goats, and chickens, some of which were already venturing out of their shelters and gamboling in the snow. Many of the houses had porches and window boxes, and a few offered swinging seats for relaxation. Beyond doubt, this was one of the prosperous farming communities at the southern border of the dwarves' realm. But was it Caer Darloch?

I approached the common, a wide square between several of the largest houses, including one that held a blacksmith's forge. Suddenly I heard a sound that struck me with dread. A wailing child! I spun around to find the source. There, to my relief, stood a mother on her porch, taking off her child's leggings, which were soaking wet from snow. The child, shrieking miserably, looked red faced and teary, but otherwise quite unharmed.

At that moment, a gruff voice addressed me. "What's yer business, stranger?"

Turning around, I faced a stocky, dark-haired man with a ruddy complexion. In one hand, he held a spear—though he held it upright, like a staff. Seeing its gleaming tip, I felt relieved it wasn't pointed at me. Not yet, at any rate.

"Well?" he barked, eyeing me suspiciously.

"Is this Caer Darloch?" I asked.

"First tell me yer business."

"My business is yours, as well," I replied, brushing some snow off the sleeve of my tunic. "I need to know if you've seen any signs of a warrior with no arms, but sword blades instead."

The man raised his dark eyebrows. His face twisted. For an instant he looked as if he were going to be ill. Then, all at once, he released a huge guffaw. He began laughing raucously.

"A warrior, ye say? Without arms? Hoohooha-ha-ha!" He slapped his thigh. "Oh, ho-ho-hee, that's a precious one, hoho."

I scowled at him, wiping some snow off my tunic collar. "It's no laughing matter. He has swords *instead* of arms. He's a murderer, a maimer of children."

Again the burly fellow slapped himself in mirth. "A great lot o' ha-ha-harm he can do widdout any arms! Hahaha, hoohoo."

"I speak truth!"

"Then yer truth, haha, heehee, is precious funny."

"Not at all!" I countered, my rage rising. "Don't you understand? Every orphan—every child—is in danger! Have you no heart, man?"

"Ya, ya," he replied with a chortle. "An' I also have arms." He fell again into hysterics. "Hoho, that's precious. Arms, heart, hoohoohoo."

My patience gone, I pointed at the head of his spear, carved from black obsidian. "No doubt you'll think it funny, too, when Rhita Gawr attacks this village and skewers you with that very spear."

The man's face grew suddenly stern. "Now yer no longer funny." He lowered the spear, pointing it squarely at my chest. "An' no longer welcome."

"Who are you to turn me away?" I demanded. "I need to speak with your village elders, whoever is in charge. Someone with a grain of sense in his head."

His arms flexed as he squeezed the spear. "I am Lydd, guardian o' Caer Darloch." He jabbed the spear, grazing my tunic. "An' I am tellin' ye to leave."

Despite the fact that my fraying garb and snow-matted hair made me look more like a vagabond than a wizard, I replied, "And I am the one called Merlin! I command you to take me to your elders."

His face flushed. "Merlin, is it? Ye think ye can pass yerself off as a mighty wizard just by stealin' his name? Why, stories have it the real Merlin can dispatch a troop o' goblins with naught more than a flick o' the wrist!" He pushed the spear point closer until it pressed against my ribs. "Why, yer just a beggar, an insultin' jester. Be gone, I say! Or yer blood'll paint the snows o' this common."

Grinding my teeth, I stared straight at him. "Not my blood, but yours."

With a flick of my wrist, I sent a bolt of blue fire into the head of his spear. He shouted, leaped backward, and dropped the weapon. Aghast, he watched as the obsidian point melted completely away, sizzling on the snow. A moment later, all that remained was a splotch of black on the white-coated ground.

He lifted his head, his eyes filled now with terror. "So ye really are . . ."

"Merlin. Now tell me. Are there any orphan children about?"

He opened his mouth, then closed it tight. He started to back away, one step, then another. I raised my hand to stop him—and he turned and bolted off, his boots pounding in the snow.

"Come back!" I called.

He kept running, disappearing behind the blacksmith's house. In frustration, I looked down at my shadow. "Drat! He may be a terrible guardian, but I'm even worse as a wizard."

The shape on the snow waved its arms at me.

"Try again?" I sucked in my breath, then nodded slowly. "Yes, yes, you're right. I'll look for someone else. And hope to fare better this time."

Seeing no one else about, I walked across the common to one of the larger houses. As I ascended its porch steps, I heard someone's feet scurrying inside. A child called out: "It's a stranger, Mama! Looks like a beggar." Grimacing, I rapped on the door. No one answered. Again I tried, with no more success. Angrily, I stamped my boot on the porch and left.

At the next house, the door at least opened—before it slammed in my face. Seething with frustration, I strode back to the common. I paced around, wondering which house to try next.

A sudden, shrill scream pierced the air, stopping me in my tracks.

Another child with wet leggings? But no, there was something different, painfully different, about this cry. Again it came, from somewhere behind the thatched shed in the goats' pen. Grabbing the hilt of my sword, I dashed toward the pen and leaped over the snow-covered railing.

I rounded the corner of the shed. There, on the straw beneath the overhanging roof, huddled a small, disheveled boy, squealing piteously. Standing with one foot on the child's forearm, ready to slice off his hand, was a massive, square-shouldered figure. Beneath those shoulders, where arms should have been, hung a pair of wide, gleaming swords.

15

SLAYER

"Halt!" I commanded. "Release that boy!"

With a flash of light on his deathly blades, the warrior kicked his prey aside, spraying straw in all directions. The small boy crawled, whimpering, deeper into the shed, trying to hide behind one of the goats. At the same time, his attacker whirled around. Seeing me, he stepped boldly into the center of the pen, his boot prints blackening the fresh-fallen snow. He faced me squarely, looking the very essence of brutality. He stood a full head taller than most men, with plated armor on his broad shoulders and chest. A mask, fitted with the skull of a man, covered his face. And at his sides hung a pair of heavy, double-edged swords.

"So," he bellowed, "the cowardly whelp of a wizard hides no more!"

"You are the coward," I shot back. "You who hunts down innocent children."

He glowered at me, his weapons twitching. "I have my reasons. Sweet death of Dagda, I do."

My hand, starting to draw my own sword, hesitated. Something about the warrior's voice struck me strangely. Had I heard it somewhere before? Or dreamed it, perhaps? That must be it: another one of my dreams come hauntingly true.

"What is your name?" I demanded, planting my feet as best I could on the slippery snow. "And why should I not strike you down here and now?"

The massive man took another stride toward me. "Call me Slayer," came the voice from behind the skull. "For that is how you shall know me."

With a roar, he rushed at me, swiping both his blades at my chest. I had barely enough time to draw my sword, which rang in the air. Suddenly, with a flash of metal, the angle of his blades changed. They were coming at my knees! Just a fraction of an instant before they sliced into me, I leaped backward, barely avoiding them.

Seeing me land off balance, he charged at me with surprising speed. His hefty shoulder crashed into my side, sending me sprawling into the railing. Snow and bits of straw flew across the pen. I rolled away as his blades bit into the wooden rail, which splintered from the force.

Quickly, I pulled my staff out of my belt. Now I held two weapons, as he did. Again he bore down on me, this time swinging for my head. I ducked as his blades passed over, so close I felt the *whoosh* of air just above my ear. Both of his swords slammed into the top of my staff. Though the reverberations from the blow jangled me down to my ankles, the staff held firm, sending off a blaze of blue sparks. Taken aback, he retreated a step, which gave me time to move away.

Aha, I thought. This staff is made from more than wood. Just as I am made from more than muscle and bone! Magic—that's the way to quash him. And while my staff's magic remained unpredictable, even for me, I possessed plenty more magic that I could control. And use!

Spinning on my heels, I flung a powerful spell at his swords. *Grow heavy. Too heavy to lift.* At once, streaks of black flowed down from his shoulders, wrapping around his blades like dark webs. In an instant both swords were swathed completely in black.

Slayer staggered, as if struck by some invisible blow. He started to raise his weapons again, but faltered, straining mightily to hold them aloft. At last, he doubled over from the weight, as his blades crashed to the ground. Outraged, he roared aloud, straining to lift them. But they wouldn't budge.

I started to gloat—when I felt a strange sensation in the hand holding my own sword. To my shock, black threads poured out of the hilt, encircling the entire blade. Suddenly it felt heavy, too heavy to hold. Despite my efforts, it slammed down in the snow. Hard as I tried, I could not lift it again.

The same spell! He's thrown it at me! Or had I just aimed my own spell poorly? In either case, all our blades were now useless.

Urgently, I recited the counterspell, crafted to unwind the enchantment's power. It took several seconds, owing to its complexity in both words and tones. And I took extra care to aim it exclusively at my own sword. At the instant I finished, the dark web withdrew, melting back into the hilt. My sword moved freely again. I lifted it, swinging it over my head with a shout.

An equally fierce shout came from my foe. He, too, had used the counter spell! I felt a rush of awe, tinged with fear, that he knew such intricate magic. Who could he be, to possess such power?

Just then he hurled himself at me again, slashing his weapons wildly. I had no time to think. All I could do was block his strikes with my upraised staff. Sparks sizzled in the air.

He beat at me ceaselessly, giving me no chance to return the attack. My arms ached from fending off his blows. Harder he pressed, and harder. All at once I realized his plan: He was backing me into the shed! In a few seconds I would be cornered, unable to maneuver. The shed's wall loomed on one side, the railing on the other.

I must get out of here! Another enchantment? Yes—one that would buy me a little time. Enough to devise a plan of my own! My mind whirled, even as my elbow jammed against the wooden wall.

Dodging a thrust, I threw myself to the ground. As soon as my hands hit the ground, I knew what to do. Lunging forward, not just with my feet but also with my hands, I felt new power coursing through my limbs. With a surge of strength, I leaped as high as I could. Slayer's blades sliced through the air, barely missing the tan-coated back of the stag who bounded over the railing to safety.

Sleek and strong, I ran across the common, my hooves pounding over the snow. Finally, I turned my antlered head around. I expected to see my attacker staring at me, bewildered, from behind the goats' pen.

Instead, a blur of brown came rushing at me. Another stag! How could that be? I jumped out of the way, but not before a sharp point of his antlers ripped into my flank. A wrenching pain twisted through my hindquarters. Blood streamed down my leg. With great effort, I bounded away.

Across the whitened ground we tore, my pursuer gaining on me with every stride. I veered sharply, leaping onto the porch of one of the houses, but the stag followed me. Hooves clattering, we ran down its length. Despite the deepening pain in my leg, I managed to jump just high enough to clear the row of snow-filled flower boxes on the far end.

When I landed again on the common, my injured leg buckled under me. My belly skidded over the cold snow. But I willed myself to stand again, scrambling out of the way just as the other stag plowed through the spot. Off I raced, swerving into the blacksmith's forge. I careened, and my flashing hooves knocked over the bellows. Down it crashed, sending up clouds of soot and ash. My eyes burned, my leg throbbed, but I dashed through the dark clouds and out again into the snow.

As I hurtled across the common, the other stag drew close enough that I could hear his heaving breaths. His antlers grazed my wounded leg again. Around one house and behind another I ran, trying my best to evade him. But none of my maneuvers worked. I was tiring rapidly. I needed something to hide behind, even for a moment. Seeing an old wooden wagon, tilting from a broken wheel, I dashed toward it and threw all of my strength into a desperate leap. If only I could clear it—

But no! My foreleg struck the wagon's side, pitching me out of control. I slammed with a thud into the wooden bed, splintering the planks under my weight. Spinning helplessly, I slid through the snow. When I came to rest at last, I was no longer a stag, but a man. My left thigh ached terribly; my legging was torn and bloody.

The other stag bounded around the wreckage of the wagon. As I watched in horror, he metamorphosed, changing into the sword-armed warrior. So he, too, knew the magic of the deer! Chortling with satisfaction, he stepped toward me, raising his gleaming swords to slay me at last.

I tried to stand, but collapsed weakly. My sword and staff, left behind in the goats' pen, could not help me now. Desperately, I wriggled backward through the snow, even as Slayer's shadow fell over my own.

My shadow? Perhaps it could do something. But no, I needed something stronger than that. Much stronger. Something as powerful as the wind itself. Yes! That was it. Even as the deadly blades flashed in the air above my chest, I hurriedly whispered the incantation to summon a windstorm, taught to me by Aylah herself. And I finished with the plea: *Blow him far from here, O tempest. Far away from here!*

A sudden gust shrieked through the village, blowing over chairs and tools and water jugs. Doors flew open; a pair of wooden shutters pulled off from a window and sailed away. Cloaks and sticks and snowflakes swirled in the air, lifting off like so many flocks of birds.

"No!" bellowed the warrior as the wind threw him backward, then carried him up into the air. "Nooooo!"

He flailed and struggled, cursing at the unseen enemy that had borne him aloft. Then, as he flew over the nearest row of houses, a new gust whipped through the village. Ferociously it blew—in the opposite direction! Despite my efforts to cling to the corner post of someone's porch, I myself was lifted high above the ground. In the swirl of debris, I caught a glimpse of my sword and staff, also airborne.

Through the air I tumbled, rolling and spinning, helpless to stop myself. Winds screamed above and below me. They would cease, I knew, only when they had finally run their course: This spell had a life of its own. How, I wondered, could Slayer have known the incantation? His own magic was strong indeed. Far too strong to be used for such evil! Yet how could I possibly stop him when his powers so fully rivaled my own?

Turning over and over, I sailed through the air, unable even to grasp my wounded leg. I whirled past the edge of the village, then over trees bare of leaves, and fields whitened from snow. Weak and disoriented, I didn't notice the winds starting to fade. Nor did I notice the rocky plateau drawing closer and closer beneath me.

With a resounding thud, I hit the ground. Over the flat stones I rolled, at last coming to a halt. Yet the world continued spinning, as it grew steadily darker. Before I lost consciousness, though, I felt something hard and pointed jab my ribs. It might have been a rock—or the head of a spear.

16

THE QUESTION

I awoke.

Darkness shrouded me, though not the darkness of night. Cold, hard stone pressed against my back. Was this the rocky plateau where I'd landed? No, no. The air smelled . . . different somehow. Dank and stale, with the slightest hint of something I knew I'd smelled before. What, though?

Fingers spread wide, I touched the flat stone beneath me. To my surprise, I felt the subtle grooves and ridges made by stone chisels, expertly wielded. So this was a tunnel, or a room underground! Reaching out with my second sight, I detected a wall rising steeply beside me. And another, on the opposite side. On each, a clasp of wrought iron had been placed to hold a torch, now extinguished—but at a height too low for a man or a woman.

All at once, I knew the smell: beard hairs, dense and tangled. And I knew this place, this underground realm, and those who had made it. Dwarves!

I sat up, half dazed. Suddenly I realized my leg didn't hurt anymore. How could that be? My hand kneaded the muscles of my thigh. No pain whatsoever. And no scar! My leggings were no longer torn, having been mended with heavy, rough thread.

At that instant, the torches sizzled, sputtered, and flared into bright light, illuminating the entire room. Alas, I saw no sign of my missing staff or sword. Like my gaze, my shadow swept around the room searching for any sign of them. But the surrounding walls were utterly bare, broken only by a single, cast-iron door opposite me. It had been etched with intricate designs of dwarves laboring to carve stone, set jewels, and shape metal. Just then I heard the sound of boots clomping toward the door's other side.

The heavy latch lifted. As the door swung open, a pair of stout dwarves marched in. Each of them stood to one side of the passage, crossing their burly arms that had been painted with strange symbols. Although they stood only as high as the middle of my chest, they would prove more than a match for most men. They stared at me with eyes like molten iron. Behind their beards, thick and black, their jaws clenched firmly. An assortment of weapons dangled from their bodies, including jeweled daggers, double-sided axes, and sturdy, oaken bows with quivers full of arrows. With their feet firmly planted, they seemed as solid as the stone floor beneath me.

Then through the doorway strode a bizarre, yet regal, figure, wearing a purple robe adorned with silver runes and geometric designs. In one hand she held a wooden staff, weathered and blackened with age. In her other, she bore the remains of some sort of fruit pastry, which she crammed into her mouth and chewed avidly. Her brow glistened with a finely wrought band of jewels, mostly sapphires, though her unruly red hair sat like a thornbush on her head. Urnalda, enchantress of the dwarves, stood before me, her earrings of dangling shells clinking as she chewed.

Seeing her again made my stomach churn. I tried to disguise my dread, standing on the stone floor to greet her. But as I started to bow, she cuffed my ear with the tip of her staff.

Swallowing her pastry, she declared, "You be unhappy to see me." Her sharp voice echoed among the walls of the chamber.

I rubbed my tender ear, striving to remain polite. "I am grateful to you for healing my leg."

"That be true." She shook her head, clinking her shell earrings. "Yet still you be unhappy to see me."

I glared at her. "We didn't part on the happiest terms, last time we met."

She snorted angrily, and the two dwarves at the door reached for their axe handles. My shadow, sensing trouble, shrank down on the floor by my feet. But Urnalda raised her hand, saying, "Not yet. I still be feeling gracious toward our guest, the renowned wizard Merlin."

"You mean you want something from me," I snapped.

The guards, who had released their weapons, reached for them again. They turned their bearded faces to the enchantress, awaiting her command. Urnalda, though, seemed unperturbed. She nodded her adorned head, jostling her earrings.

"You be wiser, Merlin, at least a little." A crooked grin creased the pale skin of her face. "But be you wise enough to win back your wizard's staff? And your precious sword? That be not so clear."

"My staff and sword?" I thundered. "You have them?"

"Mayhaps, wizard, mayhaps. Yet before Urnalda decides whether to help you, it be up to you to help Urnalda."

Behind her, one of the guards grunted in approval. The enchantress whirled around instantly, jabbing a stubby finger at him. "I not be asking your opinion!" she spat.

His red eyes opened wide. "M-m-my apologies, Urnalda."

"Good." She shook her finger at him menacingly. "Be certain it does not happen again."

"Yes, Urnalda," he replied, standing rigidly at attention. As soon as she turned around again to face me, though, the guard glanced at his companion and gave him a sly wink.

Immediately, the enchantress spun around, her purple robe swishing on the stones. She took a step toward the dwarf, who backed up against the iron door. "So now! You mock me, do you?"

"N-n-no, Urnalda," he replied. This time, judging from the beads of perspiration on his brow, he was truly afraid. "By-m-m-my beard, I wasn't."

She hunched forward, her wild red hairs quivering with rage. "Then by your beard, you be a liar."

Before he could object, she raised her hand and snapped her fingers. A scarlet flash lit the underground chamber, obscuring everything, even the torches. As the red light faded, a change in the dwarf's appearance was clear: His tangled black beard had vanished. In its place sprouted a mass of bright pink feathers, delicately curling like the plumes of an exotic bird.

The guard, still unaware of the change, stood motionless. His companion, however, started to guffaw—until Urnalda silenced him with a glare. Anxiously, the transformed dwarf reached up to stroke his beard. Feeling feathers instead of hair, he released a terrible howl. He plucked a long pink feather, took one look at it, and bolted out the door. He ran down the passageway, his wailing cries reverberating among the stone walls.

With a sidelong look at the other guard, who was shivering to hold back his laughter, Urnalda turned her squat frame around to face me. Her cheeks, normally pale gray, were still flush with anger. As she studied me, her eyes narrowed. "Be you wanting your precious sword and staff?"

"I need them, yes. And now! For we have much work to do, you and I."

The crooked grin returned to her face. "We? Now it be you who wants something."

"That's right," I declared. "All Fincayra is in trouble."

"Fincayra?" She sniffed, adjusting the jeweled band on her brow. "And why be that any concern for the dwarves, the people of Urnalda?"

I started to speak, when she raised her stout hand. "I be uninterested in your tales of woe, Merlin. I only be interested in my people."

"But—"

"Hush!" she commanded. "And be not so foolish as to try any of your enchantments on me." Her voice lowered a notch. "You be faring poorly enough against your sword-armed adversary. And you be faring far worse against Urnalda. Besides," she added with a throaty chuckle, "I still be holding my staff."

I started. "You know about Slayer?"

"Hush!"

"He could be part of the plot against—"

"Hush, young wizard!" She leaned forward, her earrings vibrating as she stared up at me. "Here be my terms. Answer my question, and I return your possessions. Fail, and . . . well, that be my decision."

"You must listen," I protested.

She jammed the base of her staff onto the stone underfoot, sending up a spray of dust and pebbles. "No! You be mistaken. I shall speak, and you shall listen."

With effort, I held my tongue.

"Good, then. Here be my question." She drew in her breath to say whatever it was, then suddenly caught herself. Turning to the guard, she waved her hand at him. "Stand outside the door. And be not eavesdropping, or I be changing your beard hairs into slithery worms!"

The dwarf anxiously touched his beard. He bustled out the doorway and into the tunnel, marching at least a dozen paces before coming to a halt. Apparently satisfied, the enchantress faced me once more. She cleared her throat, then began speaking in a raspy whisper.

"My question be this: For several weeks now, my visions of the future be strangely clouded. That never be happening before, not to Urnalda, so brave, so wise." She paused, choosing her words. "I be unable to see anything—anything at all—past the night we call Dundealgal's Eve, the longest night of the year."

Her pale brow contorted. "Except . . . snakes. Ghostly snakes, who be hissing and spitting at each other. They be coming often in my visions." Disdainfully, she spat on her hands and rubbed them together briskly. "But Urnalda cares not about the snakes. Urnalda cares about seeing nothing else!" She grimaced, trembling with rage. "This be unacceptable. An enchantress without visions!"

I nodded grimly. "And your question is why it's happened?"

She ground her staff into the stone floor. "That be my question."

"And if I answer it, you will return my staff and sword?"

"Those be my terms."

"The answer," I said flatly, "has nothing to do with you or your powers. You are still as strong as ever. It has to do, instead, with the future."

Unmistakably, a look of relief washed over her face. Then her expression darkened. She asked, her voice no longer a whisper, "What be this future?"

"I only know what I learned from a vision, several nights ago. Dagda came to me, spoke to me."

Urnalda's back straightened. "The greatest of the spirits spoke to you? A wizard so young he is yet to grow a beard?"

"Yes. About the future."

She scrutinized me, and I could tell she was trying to judge the truth of what I'd said. After a few seconds, she gave a nod. "Go on."

"He said that, on winter's longest night, the Otherworld of the spirits and the world of Fincayra will come perilously close. A passageway of some sort will open between them, at the stone circle, the Dance of the Giants." I drew a ragged breath. "And through that passageway, Rhita Gawr and all his forces will come pouring out, bent on crushing every mortal life in their path—unless you and I and the rest of Fincayra are there to stop them."

For a long period, she gazed at one of the torches, hissing and sputtering in its clasp on the wall. "Did he say anything more?"

"Some things I didn't understand, yes, about lost wings and other notions. But the point of it all was a warning, not just to me or the race of men and women, but to all the people of this land." Hopefully, I reached out my hands to her. "Won't you join me, Urnalda? Help save the world we share?"

Swinging her staff, she slapped away my hands. "Join you and the race of men? Fight alongside the very same warriors who be trying not long ago to destroy my people?" Her voice grew shrill. "Have you no memory of what your ruler Stangmar, whose blood be running through your own veins, did to the dwarves?"

"It's our only hope," I pleaded.

"*Your* only hope! The people of Urnalda be surviving now very well indeed."

Her face relaxed for a moment, and took on a look of deep longing. "One day, our people will be truly free from harm, enough to stop building more tunnels and defenses. Then we be constructing a great stone amphitheater, open to the air and sky. The amphitheater of Urnalda's people! I be wanting this for more years than you be living, Merlin! A place where I be able to view all my people at once, a place for my weekly addresses, and dramatic plays in my honor."

Suddenly she snapped out of her reverie. She stamped angrily on the floor, sending a rumble through the stones of the chamber. It seemed to shake the very bedrock, vibrating for several seconds before fading away. "Go talk to the giants, those hairy-footed dunces, about fighting alongside you! They be dangerous, and almost as terrible to the dwarves as men. But they be stupid, very stupid, so mayhaps you be more successful."

Scowling, I struck the flat of my hand against the stone wall. "It's you, Urnalda, who are stupid! And stubborn—as immovable as these very stones. Do you really think you can evade Rhita Gawr after he's taken the lands above? Why, your underground realm will be as easily broken as a butterfly's wing in his hand."

The eyes of the enchantress blazed as bright as the torches. "I never be joining forces with the race of men. Never."

Holding back my wrath, I decided to try one last time. "Please. I know you care deeply about your people's well-being. I've heard many stories about how much you have done for them in your rule. For their sake, you must reconsider."

"You flatter me, wizard," she spat back. "You be knowing nothing about my rule. My dwarves be forbidden to speak of such things to your race."

"No, I speak honestly. My friend Shim, a true giant who lived for a time among your people, has told me many stories. And he—"

"Is a traitor and a spy!" She squeezed her staff so hard that thin trails of smoke started rising from the runes on the shaft. "Of all the giants, he be the worst. Masquerading as one of Urnalda's people! If he ever sets foot again in my realm, he will be killed immediately." She grimaced at me. "We be ready for him, oh yes, if he be so foolish to return."

"You're wrong about him," I fumed. "And wrong about what's best for your people! Can't you understand? I'm trying to warn you about the gravest danger we've ever known."

Urnalda merely glared at me. "You be better off, Merlin, worrying about other dangers. Yes, like your sword-armed friend." Her eyes gleamed strangely. "He be closer, much closer, than you know."

Before I could ask what she meant, she clapped her stout palms together. The stones beneath my feet started to quiver, then shake violently. Dust rose out of the cracks. I jumped aside, just as the floor split open in a narrow chasm. To my astonishment, my staff and sword rose out of the depths, passing through the opening, floating upward to meet me. I reached for them instantly, not willing to give the enchantress any chance to change her mind.

As I sheathed my sword, I growled at her. "You may be stubborn, but at least you honor your word."

"Better than most of your race," she retorted. "Honor! That will be the subject of my first address to all my people one day, when my great amphitheater be built." She furrowed her brow. "Whenever that may be."

Her stubby fingers drummed the wood of her staff. "You be a fool, Merlin, but you, too, be honorable. You answered my question, as I be hoping. Even if you be insulting me, as well! That be my reason for healing your wounds, though you be nearly dead from bleeding. And so weak it took Urnalda many days to coax back your strength."

I blanched. "Many days?" Bending nearer, I demanded, "How much time is left before the longest night?"

"Seven days, young wizard, come the next sunset. Then we be finding out the truth of your vision."

17

SEEDS

Several hours later, the band of dwarves escorting me through the maze of underground tunnels came to an abrupt halt. Their low, rhythmic chant, which they had kept up from the moment Urnalda sent us off, also stopped. My passionate cursings, though, continued: Why did I have to waste so much time marching? Why couldn't she have set me free through the closest doorway, as I'd pleaded?

Even now, we faced not a door but a dark slab of stone. The wavering torchlight revealed a complex pattern of runes swirling across its surface—runes that held, I knew, the symbols of enchantment. Without a word, two of the stout, bearded fellows shoved me roughly toward the slab. My staff caught on a rim of rock across the floor, and I stumbled forward. Throwing my arm across my face, I braced myself to smash into the stone.

But I didn't fall into it. Instead, I fell *through* it, landing on my face on hard-packed ground.

Rolling over, I spit out some stems and frosted bits of leaves. The first sunlight I'd felt in days warmed the back of my neck, though the air still felt wintry. With a mixture of anger and admiration, I gazed at the apparently solid boulder out of which I'd just tumbled. Urnalda's skills were, indeed, extraordinary. Virtually no one would perceive the doorway buried in that boulder, let alone find some way to open it.

No one but Rhita Gawr. He would, no doubt, make quick work of all her secret entrances and clever defenses. And he'd be just as merciless with her as she planned to be with Shim.

What had she meant, exactly, when she vowed that she'd be ready for the giant if he ever returned? Some sort of trap awaited him—that much was certain. But what kind? An enormous pit? A slew of specially treated spears? I shook my head. If only Urnalda had paid more attention to my warning than to her rage against men and giants, then everyone, including her own people, would be better off.

Casting a glance around, I spotted some low, flat hills, sprinkled with a few twisted trees, on the horizon. Snow streaked the hills, alternating with patches of dark brown, making them look like a row of striped cakes. At once, I knew my location.

Urnalda had released me near the far reaches of the eastern plains—the extreme edge of her realm. That explained the long march! Whether she had done that so I could be nearer to the circle of stones, and the battle to come, I didn't know. But I suspected she just wanted to get me as far away as possible before setting me free.

The position of the sun confirmed my fears about the time. Late afternoon had already arrived; I'd lost the better part of a day just getting here. The snow-striped hills gleamed in the golden light. Yet I saw no beauty in that scene.

Barely one week remained, and I'd accomplished nothing. Nothing at all! I hadn't defeated Slayer, nor found any way to stop his attacks. And he could have killed more children during the time I'd been with the dwarves! I could only hope that Rhia was faring better in her task of gathering support for Fincayra's cause. Where, I wondered, was she now?

As I scanned the distant hills, my thoughts turned to someone else: Hallia. I yearned to see her again, to bound by her side again. Only a few months ago, we'd roamed together on this very terrain, following the ancient trails of her people. As usual, we'd kept entirely to ourselves, but for a brief visit to my friends, the aging gardeners T'eilean and Garlatha.

That was an idea. I'd go there now, to their cottage in the hills. They could give me no help in my quest, that I knew. But they could provide something else, something they had given me many times before—a brief respite from my troubles. A moment of quiet, in the company of friends. And a chance to think about what to do next.

I started trudging toward the hills, blowing frosty breaths, my shadow moving despondently at my side. It knew, as did I, that my problems, and Fincayra's, worsened by the hour. With each step, my staff's tip stabbed the hardened ground, impaling dead leaves and crusted dirt.

In time, the land started rising to meet the snowy hills. A falcon soared overhead, screeching in its high, whistling voice, but otherwise the world seemed empty of life. Hollows where, in spring, water splashed down over mossy stones and dew-soaked rushes, lay dry and hard. A young hawthorn that would, in a different season, explode with pink and white blossoms, stood as bare as my own staff.

Just ahead I spied a spur of one of the hills, split by a deep cleft. My pace quickened, for I knew it well. Now, within the cleft, I could see the gray stone hut that seemed to sprout out of the very soil of the hillside, the home of my friends T'eilean and Garlatha.

I approached the hut, dark in the shadow of the embracing hill. Then I glimpsed, beside it, a trace of green. The closer I came, the brighter the green appeared. Surprised, I concentrated my vision to make certain—but no, the color was there. Lavishly there.

Rows of trees, every bit as leafy as Rhia's gown, stood on both sides of the hut. Their branches hung low, laden with ripening fruits. As I drew nearer, I could make out luscious golden pears, and some purple plums as big as my fist, as well as cherries, apples, and my favorite, the spiral-shaped fruit of the larkon tree. Beneath the fragrant boughs ran hedges of berries, overflowing with blackberries, strawberries, and brambleberries. Even the rare llyrberry, capable of healing torn muscles—and, it was said, broken dreams—grew in abundance. Trailing vines, including two or three heavy with grapes, clung to the walls of the house; a cluster of light blue flowers draped over the doorway.

I chewed my lip, bewildered. It was one thing to see this garden still blooming in autumn, as I had with Hallia. But now, in the midst of winter? Even the great gardening prowess of my friends couldn't turn back the cycle of the seasons.

All of a sudden, I understood. Just as Rhia had been entrusted with one of the Treasures of Fincayra, so had this couple. They cared for the legendary Flowering Harp, whose magical strings could coax any land to life, any plant to flower.

How fitting, I thought, that so much life remained within their garden wall! For T'eilean and Garlatha themselves, despite their great age, seemed never to lose their vitality. This showed in their passion for gardening, as well as their passion for arguing ferociously, the kind of arguing only possible for people who have lived together many years. I recalled, with fondness, how Garlatha often teased her husband that she could see right through him, but still enjoy the view.

Stepping through the wall's wooden gate, I felt a rush of warm air, as if I had stepped right into springtime. I undid the buttons of my vest, smelling the sweet fragrances. Dragonflies, honeybees, and green-backed beetles hovered around the blossoms, their wings humming.

Up to the door I strode. Just as I started to knock on it, though, I heard a groaning sound from somewhere behind the hut. Swiftly, I dashed around to the other side. When I rounded the corner, I halted, my shadow stretching behind me as if it were pulling away, trying to evade what confronted us.

There lay T'eilean, his white hair falling loosely about his shoulders, leaning against the trunk of an old cherry tree. His right hand clutched his chest, pinching the folds of his heavy brown tunic. But for the dark pupils of his eyes, and the webbing of wrinkles that surrounded them, his face was completely pale. Kneeling by his side, Garlatha stroked his brow, her own face much the same.

In unison, their heads swiveled toward me. Garlatha, her eyes brightening, exclaimed, "Oh, it's you, Merlin! If ever we needed your healing powers, it's now."

Weakly, the old man shook his head. "Not even a wizard . . . can help me now, my duck."

I stepped forward, kneeling next to Garlatha. "Tell me what happened."

With her starkly veined hand, she pointed at the russet sack made of homespun cloth that lay open among the cherry tree's roots. "T'eilean was out here, gathering seeds from the fallen fruit, as we always do, to plant them come spring—when he suddenly collapsed."

She ran her hand through her husband's white mane. "It was all I could do to get him over here where he could sit up."

"My chest," said T'eilean with a groan. "Hurting . . . badly. Squeezing me. Can hardly—*oooh,* good Dagda! Hardly breathe."

I lay my hand below his, flat against the ribs. Focusing my mind, I tried to sense each of his organs in turn. Liver, then stomach; left lung, then right; intestines, and heart. A twisting bolt of pain shot through my hand and up my arm, making me jerk backward. Wincing, I gazed at him.

"It's your heart," I said, my voice shaking. "T'eilean, it feels, well, very deep. I don't know if it's something I can heal."

He swallowed, working his tongue. "It's not. I can . . . feel it."

"Don't be so sure now," reproached Garlatha. "When you're most sure, you're most wrong."

Her mate smiled weakly. "Have you only just learned that . . . my duck? After sixty-nine years of marriage?"

"Seventy," his spouse corrected.

"Whatever it's been," I declared, "I'm not giving up on you yet. Let me try to find a way." Replacing my hand on his ribs, I started to probe more deeply.

"You never did give up . . . easily," T'eilean said crustily. "I remember when . . . you first came through here, on the way to . . . take on Stangmar and all his soldiers at once. Why, you hardly . . . stayed long enough to taste . . . a larkon fruit."

Sensing the layers of torn tissues within his heart, I felt a wave of nausea. Still, I did my best to keep my composure, to sound relaxed and confident. "I remember that fruit. Like a bite of sunshine, it was, purple sunshine. Best fruit I've ever tasted."

"Or ever will," said Garlatha flatly. "That fruit holds so much more inside its skin than you'd ever guess."

"Like those seeds over there," I observed, still trying to work my way down through the tissues. "The same is true for them."

"Yes," she agreed. "Or like children. I'm always amazed by all they hold inside."

Even as I probed deeper in the old man's heart, her words made me shudder.

T'eilean groaned, loud and long. At the same time, another wave of nausea washed through me, this time so powerfully that I needed to lean back against the knotted trunk of the tree to steady myself. Trembling, I lifted my hand from his chest.

"It's just too deep." Glancing down at my shadow, I saw it nodding its head somberly. "Something is broken, or ripped, in there. But I just don't know how to heal it."

The old man's eyes flicked toward the hut. "Same as . . . the harp," he muttered.

"The Flowering Harp?" I turned to Garlatha, who was clutching her husband's hand. "Is it broken?"

"It is," she whispered, never taking her eyes off her mate. "This morning, without any warning, it fell off its peg, where it's rested safely for so long. Such a clatter and clang it made! When we went to fetch it, all the strings but one had snapped. And when T'eilean reached down to lift the instrument, that last string broke. It curled itself up to the soundbox, making a cry like a tortured, wailing babe."

A tear slid slowly over the folds of Garlatha's wrinkled cheek. At first I thought she was thinking of the harp, and perhaps of her garden, that would no longer feel its magic. Then, seeing her quivering hand stroking T'eilean's, I knew better.

"It's not so much," he said to her, "that I don't . . . want to die." His face contorted as another spasm of pain coursed through him. "I just don't . . . want to leave you . . . alone." The dark eyes shone as he added, "Who will be left . . . to quarrel with you?"

She nodded solemnly. "Our life together is like a precious bulb, holding whatever we need to last the seasons."

"No, no, not really," he countered. "More like a windblown seed . . . that can land . . . anywhere, and survive."

I thought of Hallia, now so far away, who wore around her wrist the string of another broken instrument. "It seems to me," I offered, "that your life together is more like something else."

Surprised, Garlatha glanced over at me. "What's that?"

"A pair of trees, grown so closely together that their branches have intertwined. They are still independent trees, you see, standing on their own roots. But now they are more than that, as well—a new being altogether. For they support each other, shelter each other, and hold each other every day."

For a long interval, both of the elders stared at me. Finally, Garlatha broke the silence. With a breaking voice, she asked, "But how does one tree go on living without the other?"

I shook my head, looking up into the boughs of the cherry tree, speckled with dark red fruit.

"Do you remember," asked T'eilean, "on that day . . . you first came here, you told us a tale from another land, about two people . . . who had lived a long life together? When it came time . . . for one of them to die, the gods . . ."

"Turned them both into trees!" exclaimed Garlatha. "Can you, Merlin? Can you do that for us?"

"Please," asked her husband, wriggling higher against the trunk. "That . . . is my desire . . . also."

I raised my hand. "Wait now. I'm not sure I can do such a thing. And even if I could, I'm not sure you really want that."

"Oh, but we do," implored the old woman. "More than you can imagine." She looked into T'eilean's eyes. "Much more."

"It would be risky," I protested, my tone grave. "Transformations like that involve your spirits as well as your bodies. It could end up damaging both, maybe severely."

"Please," they begged in unison.

"No, no. I really shouldn't."

"Please, Merlin."

I gazed at them for some time, feeling the strength of their desire. At last, I nodded. They deserved the chance to choose their own risks—and their own fates.

Slowly, I stood up. Taking hold of my staff, I moved back a few paces, careful not to trip over a hedge bulging with blackberries. Drawing a deep breath, I concentrated all my strength. At the same time, with hopeful looks, T'eilean and Garlatha gripped each other's hands more tightly than ever. After a moment, I began reciting to myself the various chants that could, I knew, release the magic that filled every seed, that powered every spring: the magic of Changing.

A new warmth flowed through my body, from my innermost chest right down to my fingertips. The wind stirred, rustling the tree's branches and causing a few cherries to fall to the ground. Leaves and twigs and scattered seeds lifted into the air, circling around me and the white-haired couple, shining with a light that came not from the lowering sun.

A flash of white light exploded. I stumbled backward from the force of it, falling in a heap. When I looked again at the spot where my friends had been, I saw that they had disappeared. Vanished entirely.

In puzzlement, I looked around me. Nothing else had changed. The trees stood as before, as did the gray stone hut. Even the sack of seeds lay on the ground, undisturbed.

My mind reeled. What had I done? Something had gone wrong— terribly wrong. I had meant to transform them, not . . . Groping for some sort of answer, I crawled to the base of the cherry tree, studying the ground where my friends had been only seconds before. There was no sign of them, no hint of an explanation, except for the one possibility too terrible to grasp.

I had eliminated them. Body, spirit, everything.

Overcome with grief, I clambered to my feet. Dazedly, I picked up the russet bag of seeds, along with my staff, and began to shuffle to the front of the hut. I couldn't speak, nor think, nor feel. I was numb. The garden that had, not long ago, seemed so full of life, now felt utterly empty.

As I came around to the other side, I moved somberly along the wall toward the swinging gate. When I reached it, I started to go through, when something made me turn around for a last look at the hut. As soon as I did, I dropped the seed bag in astonishment.

For there, before the entrance, stood a pair of majestic larkon trees, their boughs dappled with fruit. Their leafy branches wrapped around each other securely. And I knew, as I studied them, that they would stand together for a wondrously long time.

My gaze fell to the open sack of seeds. Many of them had spilled onto the garden's rich soil. Some were as tiny as specks of dirt, others much larger than the special one in my satchel. They glinted at me, aflame in the last golden light of the day.

Seeds, Garlatha had said, were like children, holding all the hopes and possibilities of the future. All at once, an idea struck me. I knew, in that instant, how to stop the sword-armed warrior from doing more harm. I had barely enough time, but still, it might be done. With a final glance at the spreading pair of trees, I strode out of the garden.

18

GATHERING

As the garden gate swung closed behind me, I entered winter again. A frigid gust of wind swept off the bare hillside above the hut, slapping my face and chilling me instantly. I felt as if I'd plunged into a mountain tarn, its water as cold as the surrounding snowfields. My hands stiffened, as did my toes. And no more luscious aromas tickled my nostrils. Instead, all I could smell was cold dirt, cold grass, and cold air.

Breathing frosty breaths, I buttoned my mother's vest with my numbing fingers. On the ground, my shadow looked as thin as a frozen sapling. Its long body seemed to shiver as I stepped away from the gate.

High above, the scudding clouds shone deep red and purple, as did the wings of a lone sparrow swooping past. The swollen sun dropped lower in the sky, almost ready to disappear behind the wide stretch of plains. *Seven days, come the next sunset.* Those words of Urnalda rang in my ears, hastening my heartbeat as before.

Now, though, I had a plan. Rather than trying to defeat the sword-armed warrior, which seemed impossible—or waste valuable time searching for him again—I would change my tactics. Instead of battling Slayer, I would throw all my zeal into keeping him from doing any more harm.

I glanced over my shoulder at the verdant garden of my friends, and the sack of seeds on the ground. Just as they had gathered all those seeds, so would I gather all the unprotected children! Yes, I'd find as many as I could and remove them from danger—whether they were orphaned or otherwise separated from their families. That way, at least Fincayra's most vulnerable children could escape Slayer's attacks. There couldn't be more than a few dozen of them on this island—a manageable number to gather. And if I could somehow do it within a week, I'd still be able to join Rhia before the longest night.

But how? I started pacing back and forth on the hillside, my mind churning. On the frozen ground, my shadow paced as well, its form growing longer as the sun drew closer to the horizon.

To be sure, I'd need some help. There simply wasn't enough time left for one person to assemble all the unprotected children of the land. Now more than ever, I wished that I'd mastered the power of Leaping!

Stamping hard as I paced to keep myself warm, my mind turned to another problem: where to take the children after I'd gathered them. It should be someplace far removed, where they would remain out of danger. Someplace where even Slayer, with all his power, couldn't find them. I ground my teeth, even as they chattered. My plan was really no plan at all! Unless I could find someplace to hide them, the children would be just as endangered as before.

Pacing up the slope, I watched the scudding clouds overhead. Bathed in such deep colors, they looked almost solid, like islands of soil and stone. They seemed so unreachable, floating on high, so entirely separate from the rest of the world.

I halted, leaning against my staff. Unreachable. Separate. Removed. Those were the qualities of islands—and of one island in particular.

The Forgotten Island.

I exhaled, blowing a white puff of air on my staff, frosting the image of a butterfly that had been etched into the wood. To get there, I knew, I'd have to break through the thick web of spells that sepa-rated the island from the rest of Fincayra. That would not be easy. Yet that very obstacle, if I could somehow surmount it, would give true protection to the children.

Still, I wondered what we'd find once we arrived there. I really knew almost nothing about the place. Once, long ago, a wise spirit named Gwri of the Golden Hair had said a wreath of golden mistletoe, the emblem of the Otherworld, grew on the island. She had, alas, revealed nothing more. But if mistletoe, the golden bough, bloomed there, the land must at least be habitable.

I shook my head. These were problems for later. Besides, I still hadn't solved my original problem—how to find the children, and somehow gather them, in the days that remained. Unless I found help, and soon, nothing else would matter.

Deep in thought, I stared at the ground, following the line of my shadow. With the sun nearly on the horizon, the dark form now stretched most of the way up the hillside, looking much like a slender giant. In a flash, I knew both the person who could help, and the best way to reach him.

"Shadow!" I called. "I need you."

On the crimson-colored hill, my shadow's head tilted skeptically.

"Hear me now," I beseeched, using my most dramatic tones. "Your homeland, and mine, are in grave danger, as you know well. So are those innocent young ones, who have no one but themselves to rely upon. I have a plan to protect them, but it can only work with your help."

As I'd hoped, the shadow's head lifted and its chest seemed to swell with pride.

"You must go find Shim. Now, stop shaking your head! He's up north, with the giants of Varigal. And it's up to you to locate him. Stop that shaking, I say! I need you to convince him to seek out all the orphan children he can find, as well as any other children wandering around unguarded. He must bring them to me at the Shore of the Speaking Shells, by the dunes where the great river enters the sea. You know the spot. Since I'll need the better part of three days to walk there, let's meet three days from now."

Though its head shaking ceased, the shadow placed its hands on its hips obstinately. I could feel, even in the bitter wind, the icy stare it was sending me.

"Please, now. Your help could make all the difference."

The obstinate pose didn't change.

"Please," I implored.

The shadow stepped a few paces away, then turned back to face me.

"What?" I exclaimed. "You want *what?* No, no, I can't do that! Out of the question."

Sternly, the shadow folded its arms.

"Outrageous," I declared. "Completely outrageous."

The shadow simply glared at me, as I glared back.

The sun sank lower, dimming the light as well as my shadow. I knew that only a few more minutes remained when I could see the dark form and talk with it. Following sunset, I would have to wait until dawn to continue. After all, I didn't even know where it spent its nights! Some mornings I half expected to find it hadn't returned, though that had never happened yet.

"Oh, all right then," I growled. "Your condition is unjust. Undignified. And unacceptable!" I glared at the insolent shadow. "But I agree to it anyway. Find Shim, and help him collect the children—including Lleu, back at that village. If you do that, I will . . ."

The words seemed to vanish like the white vapors of my breath. I glanced over my shoulder at the setting sun, then turned back to the shadow. "I will grant you a full week off every year, to go wherever you choose and do whatever mischief you like."

Gloatingly, the long head nodded. Then my shadow strode down from the hillside and past me on the frozen turf. Breaking into a loping run, it headed northwest with surprising speed, fading swiftly with the sun.

19

THE MIND
OF THE MIST

As I trekked to the southern shore for my meeting with Shim, I passed many leafless trees creaking in the wind, and several frozen ponds—but precious few living creatures moving about. Once I watched a fox, bushy tail erect, padding across a snowy field; once I spotted a pair of tiny light flyers darting behind a boulder. But that was all. Near the ford of the River Unceasing, I found some strange tracks, deep ruts gouged like claw marks in the soil, heading toward the east. I had no idea what they could be, nor time to find out.

Under the swelling moon, I kept walking late into the night. All the while, I pondered my plan. Could Shim gather the children in time? And assuming he succeeded, how would we get to the Forgotten Island? We could probably build some sort of vessel to cross the water, though that wouldn't be easy. Then, of course, we'd still have to pass through the barrier of spells. Yet I preferred all these uncertainties to the thought of Slayer's attacks continuing—and to the thought of battling him again myself.

On the second day of my trek, I veered south, following the River Unceasing. Even in winter, its waters pounded and sprayed. Sometimes I glimpsed vague movements within the spray, and wondered if I'd seen river sprites on the move, but I couldn't be certain. As I

moved southward, the cold grew less bitter and snow vanished from
the banks. Yet winter's grip never loosened on the land. Even as I
passed through the floodplains, where the river widened into marshes
that teemed with animals and birds in other seasons, I saw nothing but
a snake sliding over a web of dried vines on the ground.

Just before I reached the coast, I caught sight of Druma Wood to
the west. Viewing its vibrant greens again, I felt a yearning, as sweet
as hemlock, to live among those trees with my dearest friends again.
Yet that, I felt certain somehow, was impossible.

In the pale light of early afternoon, I approached the row of dunes
lining the southern shore. I'd reached my destination, almost a day
ahead of Shim. If, that is, he was coming. I could only wait and wonder how all this would end.

I started climbing the highest of the dunes, my boots and staff sinking into the sand. Like the shell of a great turtle, the dune rose steeply
at first, then more gradually toward the top. Marching higher, I heard
the surf crashing against the other side. The barest whiff of salt
enlivened the air. I disturbed a black cormorant who flapped angrily
and flew, neck outstretched, to a neighboring mound.

At last I reached the top. Breathing hard, I sat down to empty my
boots of sand. Beside me rested a large, tightly curled shell, its purple
point jutting upward like a spiraling spear. Turning toward the water,
I saw nothing but a rolling wall of mist, so dense that it obscured the
waves beyond. This was the mist that encircled all the lands of Fincayra. The mist that made the storied threads that were woven, Hallia's people believed, into the Carpet Caerlochlann. The mist that
moved according to its own mysterious mind.

Hidden though they were, the waves announced themselves. For a
long moment, I listened to them heave and slosh, slap and pound.
With its own unending rhythm, the sea itself was breathing, drawing
watery breaths as it had for ages upon ages. Somewhere out there, I
knew, swam the glistening bodies of the legendary people of the mer.
So elusive were they that in all my travels, I had only seen them
twice, and even then for just an instant. Yet their voices had long
called to me silently, fascinating me.

Mer people . . . they seemed somehow near, even now, when the
mist obscured their watery realm. Perhaps there was some truth to the

tale that my own grandmother—Olwen, wife of the powerful wizard Tuatha—had emerged from the sea, forever binding her people to the race of men and women.

What, I brooded, would Tuatha do? Surely he could have found some way to transport the children to the island. Absently, I tapped the wood of my staff, which had long ago been touched by his power. A gentle scent of hemlock wafted to me, mixing with the briny breeze.

Slowly, the wall of mist before me shifted, forming strange shapes within its depths. None of them could I recognize, yet all of them felt disturbing, as if they had been stolen from my most hideous dreams. Then, for a flicker, I glimpsed an eye, dark and mysterious. Watching me—I felt sure of it! Tuatha? I stared at the eye, even as it melted away. No, it couldn't be him. Dagda, perhaps. Or perhaps . . . Rhita Gawr.

The heavy, arched brow was the last part of the eye to fade. As I watched, it coalesced, transforming into a fluid, shimmering wing. It stretched across the shore, fluttering as if buffeted by the winds of flight. Then it, too, dissolved, disappearing into the shifting clouds.

Beneath the wall of mist, I noticed something strange lying upon the sand. It appeared to be a kind of rope, running the full length of the beach—but a rope made from kelp, eelgrass, gull feathers, and other gifts from the sea. Rolled together by the gently lapping waves, and pushed higher and higher on the sand as the tide lifted, it had been left behind when the high water finally receded.

Sadly, I smiled. It was, truly, a lover's braid, woven by the ocean itself and given to the land. It made me think of the woman whose auburn hair I loved to braid, and whose own gifts came from someplace as deep as the sea.

Something tugged on my tunic, near my waist. To my amusement, a small crab, mottled brown, was scaling me like a mountain. Carefully, I lifted him by the back, but his largest claw pinched the cloth tightly. I tugged, and he finally let go, though his wriggling made me drop him. He fell onto the hilt of my sword with a *ping*. The sound swelled for an instant, ringing like a distant chime, then faded into the sound of the surf.

I thought of Slayer, and his own deadly blades. What was it about him that had seemed so oddly familiar? It might have been his stance, or his voice. Yet that didn't seem possible. Someone of his power, and wickedness, I'd surely remember.

As I pondered, the mist seemed to harden, flattening as if it were a sheet of metal. Like an enormous sword, it rose right off the base of the dunes, slicing a crisp line between sand and surf. I wondered how Slayer had come by his power. It rattled me that his abilities so closely mirrored my own. I gave weight to his sword; he did the same to mine. I transformed myself into a deer, or called upon the wind; he followed suit. It was terribly hard to fight someone like that. Impossible, really—as if I were dueling against myself.

Dueling against myself. A new idea struck me, one that sent a jolt down my spine. Was it possible, even remotely, that my adversary had no real power of his own? That his magic came not from himself—but from me? Listening to the waves surging behind the sheer wall of mist, I considered this radical notion. It might just be possible that, in unleashing my skills in battle, I was somehow empowering my own enemy!

My gaze moved down to the base of the dune, where a glistening pool of seawater, as slender as a snake, wound its way through the rounded stones and brightly colored shells. Pink, yellow, and lavender the shells glowed. Like the spiraling one beside me, all of them had once made their home somewhere beyond the mist, beneath the waves. All of them had been brutally torn away from that home, removed from the world they knew, and finally hurled ashore. Just as I had been, on this very spot.

It seemed so long ago, that day I washed ashore! Brackish water soured my mouth. I had no parentage that I knew, no identity that I believed. Yet, despite all that, I remember having felt a tender spark of hope. A belief that somehow I would find what I yearned for, if only I searched long and hard enough.

I sighed, wishing I felt that same spark today. Instead, I felt a growing sense of doom. And a deep ache, worse than usual, in the tender spot between my shoulder blades.

On an impulse, I grasped the pointed top of the purple shell beside me. Pulling hard, I extracted it from the dune, spraying my tunic with sand in the process. With care, I lifted it higher and pressed its open end to my ear. A rushing, coursing sound came pouring forth. And with it, something more.

"Fffllllyyyyy," spoke the shell in its breathy voice. "Fffllllyyy fffaaaaarrr."

I nearly dropped it on the sand. "Fly? But how?" Cautiously, I replaced it on my ear.

"Fffllllyyyyy," repeated the shell, its voice rushing to me as a wave rolls to shore.

Unsettled, I lowered it. Maybe I'd only imagined its voice, twisted into words the sound of the sea. But no, I knew better. This was a place, as I'd learned before, where the shells might speak, whether or not the listener could understand. I gently replaced the shell in its sandy lair, puzzling over its choice of words.

The mist softened, and began to shift yet again. The metallic sheen vanished, replaced by rolling billows. Then the vaporous wall withdrew, revealing much more of the beach. Before me lay a wide stretch of fine, golden sand, dotted with shafts of driftwood, starfish, crab parts, sea kelp, and colorful shells, including whelks, conchs, mussels, and ribbed scallops. Wet from spray, the shells gleamed like precious metals—gold, iron, silver, and bronze. Past the beach lapped the shallow waters of the surf, the thin leading edge of the ocean beyond.

At that moment, a lone seabird broke through the mist. It was a brown cormorant, its long neck curved like an enormous worm. Landing in the shallows with a splash, it padded around, squawking noisily. A few seconds later, another bird soared out of the vapors. This one, a blue-tinged heron, splashed down, ambled onto the beach, and stood regally looking out to sea. Another cormorant joined them, then a pair of brightly painted ducks, followed by a ragged-looking crane with black feathers all askew. Still more birds arrived, swimming and preening and wading together.

As more and more birds descended from the sky, crowding the beach, their sound overwhelmed even the ceaseless sloshing of the waves. They chattered and piped continuously, flapping their wings great and small, stamping through the shallows and tide pools, smacking their beaks with gusto. Whenever several flew together, I could feel the rush of air from their wings, their own gentle wind. Fascinated, I watched them, for I'd never seen the massing of such a huge number of birds.

A rush of wind blew across my cheeks. Expecting to see a new group of flyers, I looked up. But there were no birds there. Only air. The wind blew again, warmer than before, almost like a living breath. With it came a particular smell, the faintest scent of cinnamon. It was a scent I well remembered.

"Aylah!" I called to the wind sister who had once carried both Rhia and me across the whole length of Fincayra. "Aylah, it's you."

"Ahhh yes, Emrys Merlin, I have come." Her whispering voice swept around me like a whirlwind, fluttering the sleeves of my tunic. "And with you I shall stay for a while, though the wind never stays very long."

Suddenly an idea struck me. "Aylah, sometime tomorrow, some children will arrive here. And I must take them away, so they'll be safe." I paused, as a large wave splashed onto the beach, raising a great cacophony from the birds. "Could you help me, Aylah? Could you carry them across the water to the Forgotten Island?"

The warm air flowed over my face, surrounding me with the aroma of cinnamon. "I cannot stay until tomorrow, Emrys Merlin, for very soon I must go to other seas and other shores."

"But I need your help!"

"I cannot stay, Emrys Merlin, I cannot." She spun around me, whirling in the air. "And you will need more help than mine if you wish to voyage to that island. Many others have tried, ahhh yes, but none have ever succeeded."

I struck the sand with my fist. "I *must* succeed."

"Then you must try, Emrys Merlin, you must try."

Pleadingly, I asked again: "Can't you help us?"

For several seconds, the cloak of warm air encircled me. "I cannot help in the way you ask, for tomorrow I shall be far, far from here. My sisters and I are gathering, as the wishlahaylagons have done for years beyond count, at the place we call *the wellspring of the wind.* Yet I shall return, Emrys Merlin, on another day, and perhaps I can help you then."

"I need your help right now," I beseeched.

"You have other friends, ahhh yes, who might be able to help. And now farewell, Emrys Merlin, farewell."

With that, she brushed my cheek lightly. At the same time, the smell of cinnamon faded, and the warmth around me disappeared. Aylah had gone, and with her, my fleeting moment of hope. Suddenly I winced. I'd forgotten to tell her about the longest night! Even if she couldn't help me save the children, she and her sisters might have helped at the battle. Damn! What an idiot I was to miss such a chance!

I hunched forward on the dune, staring at the congregating water birds. After some time, my thoughts returned to the children. What had Aylah meant when she'd spoken of other friends? My friends were scattered all across Fincayra, with plenty of difficulties of their own. They couldn't possibly help me right now. Still, would she have said that unless she knew something?

At that instant, a shadow fell over me from behind. The shadow of a man! I spun around.

"Cairpré!" I leaped to my feet to embrace my old mentor.

He threw back the hood of his heavy cloak, and returned the hug. After a moment, he stepped back to study me in his inscrutable way.

"You look as worn out as I feel, Merlin." His mouth twisted wryly. "Recall the lines from my last ode? *So ready for rest: Alas! Now the test.*"

"Yes, the test," I replied grimly. "You always have the fitting couplet."

"Only because I've written so many, my boy." He looked at me wistfully. "And yet the poetry never gets any easier to write. Especially endings! They can be impossibly difficult. My greatest challenge."

He paused. "Except for your mother, that is." He fingered my astral vest. "She's worth it, though, wouldn't you say?"

I managed a grin. "How did you ever find me here?"

"Shim. He's stomping around the countryside, at a rapid pace even for a giant, bearing a great load of passengers."

"So he got my message," I said, feeling relieved that at least one part of my plan was working.

"Yes," Cairpré replied, his eyes alight. "And he is carrying them in a rather, well, unusual way."

"Tell me."

"No, no, I'll let it come as a surprise." He placed his arm around my shoulder. "I do have something else to tell you, though. Something important. Come sit with me—away from that throng of birds, where it's quieter. You'll want to listen carefully."

20

FIN'S BALLAD

Together, Cairpré and I strode down the sand to the lee of the dune, facing away from the sea. As we dropped lower, the noise from the water birds' shrieking and honking lessened, though we continued to hear their clamor along with the sloshing waves. We sat in a small gully at the base of the dune, near a stand of trees drowned by one of the River Unceasing's spring floods. Their whitened trunks, stripped of most of their bark, stood like gigantic arrows shot into the ground. Beyond the dead trees stretched the floodplains, a quilt of dry grass and hardened mud.

"Cairpré," I announced, "I have a plan to save the children, a place where they'll be safe."

"Good, my boy. *May whimsical fate not destroy but create.*"

"I just have to figure out—"

"Later, Merlin. You must hear what I've found."

The gravity of his tone caught my attention. "All right, then. What is it?"

He leaned closer. "It's an ancient ballad, so obscure I'd forgotten about it completely. Until you spoke about your vision, that is." Urgently, he took my hand. "It's written by the bard Fin Gaillion!"

I shook my head. "Who?"

He frowned, scratching the tip of his nose—a look I'd seen occasionally during our tutorial sessions over the years, and which I knew meant something akin to *you blockhead*. More slowly this time, he said, "Fin Gaillion, seer of the western shores."

Blankly, I stared at him.

Cairpré ground his teeth impatiently. "He was a prophet, a seer. Famous—at least to some of us. He wandered the coast centuries ago, putting his prophecies to verse. Unfortunately, most of his predictions are about as clear as the misty shores where he wrote them. But every so often, he gives quite a vivid glimpse of the future." Under his breath, he added, "Though it may be a glimpse we'd rather not have."

"What does this ballad say?"

He closed his eyes, concentrating on the words, as his fingers drummed against his thigh. At length, he recited:

> *On solstice that summons*
> *The year's longest night,*
> *Fincayra shall suffer*
> *The Otherworld's might.*
> *For spirit and mortal,*
> *True sighted and blind,*
> *There cometh a battle*
> *Of ultimate kind.*
>
> *At Dance of the Giants*
> *A gate doth appear*
> *On worlds out of balance,*
> *Now riven by fear.*
> *When dawn's light caresses*
> *The circle of stones,*
> *The fate of Fincayra*
> *Shall truly be known.*
>
> *If land long forgotten*
> *Returns to its shore,*
> *And ancient opponents*
> *Stand allies once more,*

> *Then all through the heavens*
> *Grand music may sound:*
> *The balance restored;*
> *The hidden wings found.*

> *Yet tidings, more likely,*
> *Are vilely reversed—*
> *All hope torn asunder,*
> *The Treasures all cursed.*
> *Then over the heavens*
> *A shroud shall descend:*
> *The longest of evenings,*
> *The uttermost end.*

His eyes reopened, watching me with concern. "The stakes could not be higher, my boy."

I nodded. "You heard him mention wings? Just as Dagda did. I just don't understand how that fits in."

The poet rubbed his hands together, trying to warm them. "Nor do I. The part that puzzles me most, though, is that earlier reference: *If land long forgotten returns to its shore.*" Turning, he gazed at the bone-white trees. To himself, he muttered, "It couldn't possibly mean the Forgotten Island."

I drew a sharp breath. "That's where I'm taking the children!"

His face showed, in rapid succession, surprise, doubt, and horror. "You can't do that, Merlin! Don't you remember? Ages ago that place was part of Fincayra, then Dagda cut it off completely, pushing it out to sea and surrounding it with spells."

"I know all that. And if I can just figure out how to get there, the children will be safe. Out of that wicked warrior's reach forever!"

Vigorously, he shook his gray mane. "Impossible. First of all, how do you plan to get there?"

"Well, I . . . we could, um . . ."

"I see," he said gravely.

Suddenly, an idea burst into my mind. I leaped up, dashed over to the stand of dead trees, and slapped my open hand against one of the whitened trunks. "We'll build a raft! Yes, a great raft, using these trees. Shim will help me. It will work, I know it!"

My old mentor, far from sharing my enthusiasm, watched me with heightened concern. "The ocean is the least of it, my boy! The spells—don't forget the spells. No one, not even your grandfather Tuatha, has ever made it past them. And most of those who tried never returned."

Angrily, I swung my arm. It collided with a small branch, snapping it in two and spraying me with shards. "I must find a way. For the children, I must!"

The ridges on his brow seemed as deeply engraved as those on the sand dune behind him. "Can't you battle this warrior?"

"Battle him, yes. But I can't defeat him." I stepped closer, my face grim. "He takes my own powers somehow, and hurls them right back at me. That's right! So the children's best hope is to get as far away as possible."

"They—and you—may well die trying."

"Their chances are worse if I don't try." Folding my legs, I sat beside him again on the sand. "Cairpré, you could help me. Tell me what you know about those spells."

He bit his lip. "Virtually nothing. Just that something terrible rises up out of the sea whenever someone gets too close to the island. Don't you see, my boy? Whatever Dagda's reasons, he wanted no one to go back to that place. Ever."

I blew a long breath. "What could have happened there? Do you really think it had to do with the lost wings?"

"That's my guess," he said with a shrug, "though no one knows. Why, everything about the island is a mystery! We don't even know if it ever had a name of its own."

"So it truly is forgotten. Even its name."

"That's right," he said somberly. "It's as if the whole place, even the memory of it, was destroyed. And if Fin's ballad is right, the same fate awaits Fincayra."

"Wait now," I protested. "As bad as the ballad sounds, it still leaves room for hope. We might yet avoid that *uttermost end*."

The dark pupils of his eyes seemed to grow distant. "There is more, I'm afraid. You haven't heard the final stanza."

His voice wavering, he recited the ballad's concluding lines.

> *Beware, you that joineth*
> *To rescue the cause:*
> *Your sacrifice dearest*
> *Holds ruinous flaws.*
> *For times may occur,*
> *So laden with cost,*
> *When all truly gained*
> *Is yet truly lost.*

"Those words again!" Grasping a handful of sand, I poured it onto the side of my boot, watching the grains tumble over the edge and onto the ground. "How can what is gained also be lost?"

Cairpré drew his bushy brows together. "Hard to know. It's only after *sacrifice dearest,* I fear, that we'll finally understand."

For quite some time we sat in silence, hearing only our thoughts and the ongoing cries of the water birds on the other side of the dune. The ballad, once spoken, seemed etched upon my mind. Over and over I repeated some lines, though with no better understanding.

At last, the poet spoke again. "Let's have a fire, Merlin. And a spot of food." He nudged his leather satchel. "I've brought the makings."

"Yes," I replied. "We need our strength if we're going to prevail."

He paused in opening the satchel to smile at me fondly. "My boy, you are persistence personified."

"No, no. I'm just hunger personified."

With a flourish, he pulled out the contents of his satchel: plenty of oatmeal for porridge, some dried bilberries, a large slab of honeycomb, a flask filled with apple cider, one vial of ground nutmeg, a cooking pot, and a pair of wooden spoons. Quickly, we set about collecting driftwood and dry grass to build a fire, the first I'd seen since the torches of the dwarves' underground realm. Soon crackling flames arose, warming our chilled hands. For a moment, I thought of Lleu, coaxing our own fire to life back in the village.

"Did you return to the village after you went home?" I asked, as Cairpré stirred the nutmeg into the simmering pot. "And was Elen there? And Lleu?"

"Yes on all counts," he replied. "Little Lleu brought her your message. She's staying there, as you demanded, though she's not very pleased about it." He gave the pot a final stir. "There now. Break off a generous piece of honeycomb and grab your spoon."

In short order, we were eating porridge from the pot. Simple though it was, it seemed like a grand repast. The aromas of apple, oats, and honey filled our nostrils as well as the air beneath the dune; the porridge warmed our bodies thoroughly.

The poet studied me as he blew on his spoon. "In a way, it's really a blessing that Stangmar has reappeared."

I nearly dropped my spoon. "How so?"

"Because otherwise your mother couldn't resist going to the circle of stones, not to fight, but to be near you and Rhia. Much as she detests being confined to that squalid little settlement, she's probably quite safe there, and she'll be spared all the horror of the battle." He gazed wistfully into the fire. *"O gentle soul, thy innocence stole."*

I threw another piece of driftwood onto the flames. "It's Stangmar's legacy, though, that's made it so difficult to win the allies we need! I tried with Urnalda, and she practically spat blood at me." The fire, as if in emphasis, crackled loudly. "I doubt Rhia's having any better luck with the canyon eagles and the others."

Somber again, Cairpré said, "If you don't return in time from this misadventure at the island, she may be there all alone."

"I'll be there. Whatever happens, I'll be there." Quizzically, I examined him. "You won't be there yourself?"

"Me?" He shook his gray head. "I'm a man of words, not weapons. As bad as I am fighting with the ending lines of a ballad, I'd be far worse fighting any living foe! No, the last thing you need is an old bungler like me on the battlefield."

He gazed at me intensely across the flames. "I shall be with you and Rhia in every other way, though. Yes, and so will that woman with the sapphire eyes."

"I know," I whispered. "You'll be staying with Elen, then? Keeping her company through all this?"

His gaze never wavered. "You can count on that, Merlin. As long as she'll have me, I'll stay by her side. I know no treasure even half so precious as a single day with her."

Thoughtfully, I pursed my lips. "In the ballad, where it spoke of the Treasures of Fincayra, what did that mean?"

"Nothing good," he answered. "Fin was implying that the Treasures are somehow linked to the future of Fincayra. So if the Treasures are cursed, Rhita Gawr is likely to prevail." He ran his fingers through the sand of the dune. "That seems unlikely, though. And besides, only the Caller of Dreams has been destroyed."

"What?" I grabbed his tunic sleeve, imagining the graceful horn in his keeping. Often called the Horn of Good Tidings, it held the power to bring a person's most cherished dream to life. "It's been destroyed?"

"That's right. It cracked somehow, inexplicably, a few days ago. I was combing through my books, looking for the ballad. Suddenly, from its place on a neighboring shelf, it gave out a mournful wail and split in two." He frowned. "There's no way to repair it."

"That's what happened," I exclaimed, "to the Flowering Harp! Destroyed, with no explanation."

He looked at me, aghast. "Truly?"

"Yes! And Rhia's Orb is gone, too, though in that case the curse came in the form of Stangmar."

His body went rigid. He seemed lost in thought for a moment, then exclaimed: "No, no, it can't be related! Why should the fate of the Treasures be connected to the fate of Fincayra?"

I reached over and touched his knee. "Because, my friend, it's not their fates that are connected but their *lives.* They were hewn from the same wondrous fibers, by the same great forces. It's the magic of this land that gave birth to the Treasures to begin with. It's the magic of this land that has empowered them always."

Slowly, Cairpré nodded, his brow aglow from the firelight. "You're right, Merlin. I see it now." With his boot, he pushed an ember back into the flames. "And while I am gladdened that my student has become my teacher, I only wish it hadn't happened when we're about to lose everything."

"We haven't lost it yet," I declared. "Listen, now. Do you recall that night, that terrible night, when you and I first met?"

He watched me, saying nothing.

"Well, on that night, you said something I've never forgotten."

Seeing the grim line of his mouth relax ever so slightly, I continued. "You told me that you couldn't say whether I really belonged in Fincayra, whether it was truly my home. The only one who could ever know that, you said, was me. Well, I'm telling you now that it is my home! It will *always* be my home, no matter what fate might befall it—or me."

I squeezed his knee, my sightless eyes watering. "I love this land, Cairpré. So much I'll give everything I have to save it."

The poet swallowed hard, then spoke. "Then, my boy, it is truly your home."

21
AİRBORΠE BODİES

Late that afternoon, Cairpré departed our sheltered niche at the base of the dune. He stood stiffly, knees cracking, and brushed some of the sand off his tunic. With an air of grim resolve, he studied me, the light from the lowering sun turning his hair silvery bronze.

"Good luck to you, my boy. You have revived my spirits, a major feat in its own right. True evidence of the strength of your powers!" His fingers wrapped tightly around my arm, and his voice dropped to a whisper. "Perhaps you will be the one to find the way to the island."

"That I will," I declared, jamming my staff into the sand. "And then I'll do my best to turn back Rhita Gawr."

His steady gaze faltered. "No power, I fear, is strong enough for that. He'll be terribly vicious—whether he takes the form of a man, a wild boar, or something else entirely." Slowly, he filled his lungs with the briny air. "Even so, your bravery has inspired my own. While I won't be joining you myself at the circle of stones, I will do my very best to urge others more capable of fighting to be there."

"Thank you, my friend." I cocked my head. "Don't even think about trying the dwarves, now. With Urnalda's state of mind, any man or giant who enters her realm is just asking to be killed."

The poet smiled wryly. "Worry not. I'll try something easier, such as the great man-eating spider of the Misted Hills."

"Elusa? Finding her is just as dangerous."

His eyes narrowed. "Everything now is dangerous." Pensively, he worked his tongue. "I should say something before we part, I know. Something profound, or at least poetic, something befitting a bard." He sighed. "Can't think of anything, though. I told you I wasn't very good with endings."

Doing his best to smile, he released my arm. Then he drew up the hood of his heavy cloak, throwing his face into shadow, all but the very tip of his nose. Turning, he strode through the stand of dead trees, a dark shape amidst their white trunks. He continued over the floodplains, his boots crunching on the hardened turf and brittle grass.

Standing in the lee of the dune, I watched him go, wondering whether we would ever meet again. When his cloaked figure finally disappeared, I started gathering driftwood, enough to keep the fire burning through the night. The winter's sun would soon be gone, and with it whatever meager warmth came from its rays.

As the blue overhead deepened into purple, the color of wild grapes, I ate the remains of our porridge and honeycomb. In time, darkness flowed across the land like the tide of a shadowy sea. My thoughts turned to the dead trees, and I contemplated how to bind them together in a seaworthy craft. Strands of kelp might work. Or some of the dried vines I'd seen while crossing the floodplains.

The size of the raft, of course, would depend on the number of children it would need to carry. If Shim did well, despite so little time, he might be able to find thirty, maybe thirty-five. Even for a large raft, that would be a full load. Yet the thought of saving that many lives—that many seeds—made me all the more determined to try.

A new realization hit me: If I succeeded in protecting those children from Slayer, perhaps they would also be safe from Rhita Gawr! Might the curtain of spells that hid the island be enough to keep its shores, and anyone there, out of the warlord's grasp, even if he did prevail on winter's longest night?

The moon, deep red, rose into the darkened sky, resembling a swollen, angry eye. Behind the row of dunes, the water birds that had settled on the shore grew quieter. I listened to their occasional cries, and the surging waves, for quite some time, ever mindful that only four days remained before the longest night. At last, I drifted into a fitful sleep.

Not long after dawn's first rosy rays touched the top of my dune, I awoke. Though I couldn't be sure, I thought I heard a rhythmic rumbling in the distance. Grabbing my staff, I scurried up the sandy slope. When I reached the ridge, I realized that the congregation of sea birds had swollen to enormous size. Thousands of them milled and chattered, filling the entire beach and shallows right up to the edge of the rolling wall of mist. I saw pelicans and gulls, cormorants and kitiwakes, long-legged cranes and gray-necked swans, as well as ducks, herons, gannets, and many more kinds I could not name. Some marched around squawking or honking; some flapped their wings or danced vigorously; some stood aloof on one leg, paying no heed to the tumult surrounding them.

As the morning light swelled, so did the birds' raucous noisemaking. At the same time, the distant rumbling also grew louder, enough that some of the birds at the edges of the crowd started to take notice. In groups of three or four, they lifted off and circled through the folds of mist, wings spread wide, trumpeting loudly to their companions. Not until the ground actually started to shake, however, did most of them take to the air. Then, by the hundreds, they took off, wings whooshing in unison.

I stood atop the dune, drenched in golden light, watching the awesome scene unfold. Higher and higher rose the mass of birds, a great spiral of airborne bodies darkening the sky. Rhia's dreamlike words, spoken at the stargazing stone, came back to me: *Imagine taking time to rise above the lands below, your spirit along with your body.*

Now, viewing these winged creatures ascending into the sky, I understood her words in a whole new way. Here was freedom, true freedom, as pure as I'd felt in my dreams of flying—but more tangible, more real. I still longed for the speed and directness of Leaping, of course, but physical flight offered something more than that: a fullness of feeling, a grandness of motion, an endless soaring of the senses.

The spiraling cloud of birds angled eastward and began pouring toward the rising sun. I watched them depart, fading into the shredding light. Their tumultuous cries, too, began to fade, blending into a single melancholy chord that echoed across the shore.

As trails of mist arose, obscuring the last of them, I felt I was watching not a vast flock of birds, but my beloved homeland itself, slipping away. Fincayra was vanishing, no less than these creatures. Its colorful scenes and richly varied sounds were disappearing, no less than their own.

An instant later, they were gone. I stood above the beach, so recently charged with life, now utterly empty. Everything was quiet, but for the pulsing of the sea—and the rhythmic rumble, steadily growing. Spinning around, I gazed past the dead trees to the wide floodplain beyond.

Before long a great, shaggy head appeared on the horizon. With each new rumbling step that rocked the ground, the head grew larger. Soon I spied the red flames of Shim's eyes above his bulbous nose, along with his immense neck, brawny shoulders, and massive chest. In his hands, he held a wide-brimmed hat made from woven branches, while on his chest hung a vest infinitely bigger than my own.

Leaning on my staff for balance, I peered at him closely. My brow knitted, for I could see no children. None at all! A feeling of dread swelled in my chest. Something had gone wrong with the plan. Seriously wrong.

I gasped, seeing a subtle movement inside the bowl of the hat. Heads—tiny heads! Lots and lots of them, more than I would ever have predicted. Why, there must have been at least seventy or eighty! Shim had, indeed, done his job well.

Then my wave of relief vanished. There were too many children for one raft! I looked over at the straight trunks of the whitened trees, counting them. Fifteen, sixteen, seventeen. Enough, perhaps, to build a very large vessel, one that might just hold everyone. Could I control it, though? Guide it through the spells?

My attention turned back to Shim. As he came nearer, his feet slamming against the ground, I could make out the faces of some of his passengers. There were bright-eyed ones, eager ones, doubtful ones, and several very sleepy ones. One little girl, wearing her hair in two braids that stuck out sideways from her head, sat on the shoulders of a boy with a chin so slender, he reminded me vaguely of Hallia. Both of them were pointing at the sky, in the direction of the departing birds, probably still visible from their higher vantage point.

I searched the sea of faces for Lleu, but with no success. Perhaps he was standing behind someone else, or even sleeping down inside the bowl. Still, I did recognize one lad who was wriggling out of the hat onto Shim's thumb: the boy whose life I'd managed to spare in the goat pen of Caer Darloch. Another girl was seated on the brim of the hat, grasping one of the branches beside her for support. Sunlight streaming through her long brown hair, she watched the coils of mist rising from the shore, her face full of awe.

In a few more thunderous strides, Shim reached the dunes. I barely kept my balance as powerful tremors coursed through the sand. Just before the dead trees, he stopped, planting his bare feet on the ground. As always, his sheer size amazed me. His ankle, thick with hair, reached nearly halfway up the dune.

"Well done, Shim!" I called up to him.

Beneath his gargantuan nose, the giant's lips parted. "You asks me to do some crazily things befores, Merlin, but this is the crazilyest."

He released a bellowing yawn, the force of which knocked over several of the children in the hat. "I is so sleepily, after walkings for two nights, trying to find all the orphanly kids! Some in villages, some in mountains, some by roads . . . It wasn't easily! And somelytimes they is scrapping with each others, pulling out hairs and ripping clothes. Then, for mostly of the night, they wants me to sings, and tells them stories. Now . . . I really needs to rest. Sleepily, definitely, absolutely."

Many of the children, some of whom were giggling hysterically from being blown over by Shim's yawn, piped up. Their voices rang across the dunes, as discordant as the departed sea birds.

"No sleeping, master Shim! We want some more bumpy rides."

"Sing some more, Shimmy! Sing us your longest song, pleeease?"

"Hey! Hey! How'd you getta be so big 'n' fatlike? Didja eat a whole big mount'n fer brekkyfast?"

"Heeyah, after that mount'n, now ya need ta drink up the sea ta wash it all down. Yah! Then you'd make a great big waterfall, hee-heeyah, hee-heeyah."

At that, a deeper voice called from the rear of the hat. "Now children, we don't need—"

"It's all right, don't worry! The waterfall won't spray you."

Gales of wild laughter followed. But my attention was focused on the source of the deeper voice. My mother! So she had come, too!

In the midst of the joyous chaos surrounding her, Elen looked at me with a sparkle of genuine amusement in her eyes. Shim, for his part, stifled another yawn and started to lower the hat. Carefully, he placed it on the sandy shore, between the braid of kelp that marked high tide and the base of the dunes.

"Oh please, please, master Shim," cried the girl with the two horizontal braids. No older than three, she was now seated on the brim of the hat, her legs swinging freely. "Don't put us down yet! Fly us, like them birdies was flyin' before."

Shim bent down to her, so that his lumpy nose pressed against the sand beneath the brim. "Don't you be worriedly, little one. I'll gives you another ride somelytime soon."

She gazed at him, wide-eyed. "Really will you, master Shim?"

"Of course, you sweetly girl."

She crawled across the meshed willow branches of the brim until her face was right next to Shim's. Timidly, she leaned forward, then planted a kiss on his massive cheek. The giant's face, always ruddy, reddened more deeply. And for the first time in quite a while, he smiled, his wide lips wrapping around his face.

By the time I trotted down to them, other children had already started scrambling over the edge of the hat. Oblivious to the chill air, several of the older ones started climbing up the dunes, rolling in the sand, or running off to explore the beach. A few stayed around to help me with the smaller children, coaxing them to jump into our waiting arms, or carrying them if they were too cold to walk. Shim grabbed by their feet a pair of boys who had been hitting each other, holding them upside down for a moment while they squealed and squirmed in protest. Finally, when they'd calmed a bit, he laid them down on the sand.

At the same time, my shadow emerged from the darkness behind Shim's vest. With an unmistakable air of smugness, it slid down the seam, through a buttonhole, and leaped to the ground. I was about to remind it that its vacation, while earned, hadn't begun yet, when my attention was diverted by a lanky girl, about ten years old. She was boldly climbing out of the gap between Shim's ear and his temple! Catching hold of a lock of his hair as if it were a rope, she swung from it and dropped to the ground before taking off down the beach.

"That girl Medba reminds me of your sister."

I spun around to face my mother. Her hair was tangled, her blue robe soiled, and she looked almost as sleepy as Shim. But her face glowed bright as she tousled the hair of the young boy beside her.

"Lleu!" I exclaimed, giving his woolen scarf a playful tug.

He looked up at me, his lone ear catching the sunlight through his curls. "I be much glad to see ye, master Merlin."

"And I you, my friend."

He beamed at me, showing the gap where his front teeth would someday appear.

I turned back to Elen of the Sapphire Eyes. "So," I said through my grin, "you couldn't resist a chance to escape from that village?"

"Certainly not," she declared, her own mouth curling in a grin. "But much as I dearly loved the place, somebody *had* to help Shim take care of all these children."

Glancing at the figures scampering down the beach, splashing in the tide pools, kicking sand at each other, and jumping in and out of the hat, I had to agree. "I'm sure Shim was glad to see you! As am I."

We embraced, and I felt her patting my back through the astral vest she had given me. As we separated, she scrutinized me carefully, her brow wrinkling with concern. "You've had some troubles, haven't you?"

"Oh," I said as casually as possible, "a few here and there. Right now, though, my challenge is how to build a vessel big enough to hold everyone."

"Why not ask Rhia? She's always brimming with ideas." Her eyes swept over the dune, then back to me. "Where is she, anyway?"

"She's . . . ah, gone a different way. Riding Ionn, which you know she loves to do."

My mother scowled. "She's not riding for pleasure."

"No," I admitted, feeling the weight of her gaze. "She's fine, though. Believe me."

She shook her head sadly. "I don't believe you, Merlin. None of us are fine, what with all that's happened."

"Wait, now." I waved my staff at the children spreading out along the beach. "*They* are. And what's more important, for a brief moment, at least, they're safe. Free from the threat of that sword-armed scourge, who is probably still searching for me near the place we last fought, far away from here."

"Still, my son, he's bound to find out where we are. Then the children—and you—will be in danger again."

"Eventually, yes. But I have a plan that, if it works, would keep them safe forever. I just need to . . ."

Suddenly, I felt something tug on my satchel. I whirled around to find Lleu withdrawing his hand, a guilty grin on his face.

"No harm, master Merlin. I jest be . . . well, curious. 'Bout yer bag."

"You mean, what's in it?"

"Well, yes, master Merlin."

I couldn't help but feel amused, since sneaking a peek into someone's satchel was just the kind of thing I'd have done at his age. Elen's expression, too, had softened; no doubt she was thinking something similar. With dramatic tones, I proclaimed, "Behold, young man, I shall grant your wish! View now the world famous, roundly acclaimed, triply enchanted . . . magic feather."

"Magic feather?" he repeated skeptically.

Delicately, I lifted the satchel's leather flap, holding my breath in mock anticipation. Silently, I summoned the required powers, bidding them to follow my will. As the air above the satchel started to quiver, Lleu gasped. Slowly, very slowly, Trouble's feather rose upward. The boy drew back, standing next to Elen, his back pressed against her thigh, while the feather floated higher.

Lleu stared in amazement as the feather rose higher, drifting lazily toward him. Like a fluffy butterfly it floated, spinning past his chest, over his shoulder, and along the length of his arm. It hovered, twirling, before his face. Suddenly it darted closer, tickling his nostrils.

The boy laughed, swatting the feather away. He tried to catch it, even as the feather spun behind my mother. Eagerly, he swung around to reach it. As he did so, he knocked his head into her side, bashing the scabbed remains of his ear.

He yowled in pain, covering his wound with his hand. Elen bent down and stroked his head with compassion, whispering softly as she did so. But he continued to whimper painfully.

"Oh, Lleu, I'm so sorry," I offered, steering the feather back into my pouch. "That was a foolish, clumsy idea."

After a moment, he turned to me, a thin trickle of blood running down from his ear. "Nay, master Merlin," he said weakly. "I likes yer idea, very much. I be the clumsy 'un, bangin' me noggin like that."

I started to speak, when Shim kneeled beside us, flattening a spur of the dune and a jumble of firewood with his great knee. He looked down on us glumly. "I is sorry, Merlin, but I has some badly news."

I groaned. "What now?"

The giant's face contorted, twisting his oversized nose. "Hardly as I tried, I couldn't convince any other giants to comes to the battle. Not even Jingba, my oldest friend. When I tells him about Rhita Gawr and all, he just laughs at me and says I is full of exaggeratinglyness."

The report made me wince. "That's terrible! Without at least some of the giants, we won't stand a chance."

"I is sorry, verily sorry. Maybily I will tries them again, after I takes the nap I is longingly for." He stretched his jaws with another yawn. "And if that doesn't works, I tries the dwarves! If I can just finds Urnalda, maybily I can convince her to helps."

"No, Shim," I declared, recalling her death threat. "You mustn't! She has set a—"

"There you are, you cowardly runt of a wizard!" boomed a voice from atop the dune.

I spun around, though I already knew who was hailing me. Yes, and with every particle of my body! It was the person I least wanted to see, the person I had no idea how to fight. Slayer.

22

ATTACK

The warrior stood atop the dune, poised for battle. Sunlight glinted off his breastplate, and from the deadly sword blades attached to his shoulders. From behind his skull mask, his coarse laughter roared. Then, with the edge of one of his swords, he lifted the mask slightly—not enough to reveal his face, but enough to spit on the sand at his feet.

"You fled me before, runt wizard! This time, by the spirits, you won't escape."

"It's you who won't escape," I flung back, jabbing my staff into the sand of the beach. Looking up the slope at Slayer, my mind raced. He was here! Somehow he must have discovered my plan—and now that plan was ruined. No, worse! Now that the children were gathered all in one place, they were in far greater danger than before. I'd done this madman a favor. And I couldn't possibly stop him if he turned all my own magic against me.

"Come prove your brave words," he shot back. "Come up here and fight to the death."

By my side, Lleu shrank back into my mother's arms. He trembled all over; the blood drained from his face. He released the urgent, heartrending pule of a cornered animal.

Farther down the beach and in the shallows, other children stopped splashing in the tide pools, forming shapes in the sand, collecting colorful shells, or swinging from the brim of Shim's hat. As one, they turned to find out what was wrong. Several of them, seeing the terrible warrior with the face of a skull, froze in their tracks, standing as rigid as barnacles on sea-splattered rocks. Others started running away, kicking wet sand in all directions. A few even plunged into the rolling wall of mist that lined the shore, obscuring the sea beyond.

"Well?" boomed my foe. "Are you no braver than that squealing boy beside you?"

Shim gave a thunderous growl. He rose from the kneeling position, blocking out the sun with his massive frame. "You is the unbravely one," he bellowed, his voice blowing the remaining leaves off a linden tree at the base of the dune. "I'll squashes you like a tinyly bug."

"No, wait," I commanded, lifting my staff. "He has strange magic, Shim. Powerfully strange. Leave him to me—while you round up the children. Get them all safely away, however you can."

"No, Merlin," implored my mother. "Don't fight him."

"I must. Now go, both of you! Get the children."

The giant frowned. "I surely hopes you knows what you is doing, Merlin."

"So do I," seconded my mother, shielding Lleu with the folds of her robe.

Waving them away, I turned back to Slayer. "You are a coward!" I called, trying to gain some time for them to gather the children. "Why don't you show your face behind that mask?"

He seemed to hesitate, then slowly raised his bladed arms above his head. He stood there, a terrible silhouette against the sky, light glinting along the edges of his swords. "For you, runt wizard, this is my true face. The face of death."

With that, he stormed down from the crest of the dune. Slashing his blades, he ran straight at me, cursing as his boots dug into the sand. Now I had no choice but to fight him. In just a few seconds, he'd reach me.

How, though, to fight? All my wiles were turned back on me. Then an idea suddenly struck. If I resisted using any magic, then he couldn't throw my power back! Yet . . . that meant I must rely on brute strength alone. And that was a battle he surely would win.

Just before he reached me, I flung my staff aside and hurled myself bodily at his legs. The force of my charge sent him sprawling over me. Both of us tumbled down to the beach, throwing sand in the air.

No sooner did I scramble to my feet than he did the same. Roaring like a wrathful boar, he lunged at me, slicing with his swords. Rather than draw my own blade, I waited until the last possible instant, then stepped aside. Slayer plunged past me, rolling into a tide pool. Seawater, kelp, and gull feathers sprayed us both. Rising again, he stumbled, landing on a large, orange conch shell, crushing it to bits under his weight.

Immediately, he charged again. With a stream of curses, he slashed his blades, barely missing my chest as I feinted one way and dodged the other. Huffing for breath, I faced him once more. Sooner or later, I knew, one of his swords would strike its target. I glanced over my shoulder to see Shim far down the beach, herding all the children behind the dunes. His pounding footsteps, like their cries, were swiftly retreating. Before long they, at least, would be out of danger.

Again he charged, flailing his deadly arms. Once more I escaped, leaping aside and turning a somersault on the sand. This time, though, when I stood and faced him, he made no move to attack.

"You're even more afraid than I recall," he snarled, panting hoarsely. "Why do you run from me? No magic left?"

"Plenty," I retorted, slowly circling him on the beach. "I just don't need it to fight you."

"Then fight me, whelp!"

He lunged again. Just as I spun away, though, he halted himself. Seeing this, I tried to stop—but my foot caught on a twisted piece of driftwood. I tumbled onto the wet sand, rolling over on my back. Right above me stood Slayer, chortling in satisfaction. Behind him, a steep-sided dune rose off the beach like a sheer cliff, casting its dark shadow on both of us.

"No time to fight now, you runt wizard." He raised both of his blades, ready to skewer me. "Just to die."

He planted his feet. I saw the muscles under his breastplate flex. The twin swords lifted high, their gruesome edges flashing in the sun.

"No!" cried another voice. Elen! Hurling herself on the sand at

Slayer's feet, she placed herself between us. She threw back her head and glared up at him fearlessly. "Don't you dare harm my son."

Slayer guffawed. "Only after I deal with you, woman!" Under his breath, he added, "How very fitting."

He started to bring down his swords. As bright as streaks of light, they shone against the darkened dune behind him. In that brief instant, I knew I had no choice but to call on my magical powers. No other way to stop him! But I also knew that any magic would be thrust back at me—or worse, at Elen. My mind reeled. There must be another way!

The swords swept through the air. I saw them plunging toward my mother. My rage at last boiled over, and I was about to form a fireball in my hand.

Just then, the blurred figure of a man leaped off the top of the dune. With a ferocious shout, the man, wearing a hooded cloak, smashed into Slayer, knocking him to the ground. Bellowing with rage, Slayer struck out, stabbing the cloaked figure with his swords. He slashed at the man's chest, arms, and legs in a brutal frenzy. Blood splattered the beach.

All of a sudden the sky darkened. I looked up to see Shim's immense form stepping over the dune from behind. His bare foot slammed down onto the sand. Before Slayer could move, the giant's huge hand reached down and grasped him by the middle, pinning his murderous blades to his sides. Although the warrior struggled so hard to break free that his armor seemed ready to burst, he couldn't budge. Shim lifted him higher, glowering at him with enormous eyes. Then the giant roared angrily, with such force that the great wall of mist shuddered, thinned, and pulled some ways back from the shore. Shim reared back and hurled the warrior straight through the mist and far out to sea—so far that we heard no splash.

The hulking form bent over me. "Is you alrightly, Merlin?"

"Thanks to you, old friend." I clambered to my feet. "You and . . ."

My words faded away. I saw Elen, her back to me, kneeling over the heroic figure. Although her back obscured the man's face, I recognized the cloak. It belonged to Cairpré! My insides wrenched at the sight. Cairpré, my mentor, my friend—lying there on the sand, dying.

I stumbled over to join my mother, who was holding his hand, sobbing quietly. Then my heart froze. The hood of the cloak had fallen back, revealing his face. It wasn't Cairpré after all! Instead of the face I knew so well, I viewed a thick black beard, a jutting jaw, and eyes as dark as my own. No, there could be no doubt. It was Stangmar.

Though blood soaked his chest, staining the sand, he lifted his head slightly, uttering a single word: "Elen."

She turned to him, still holding his limp hand. "I am here. With you."

"Elen," he repeated, his voice raspy. "I had to find you. Had to . . . tell you."

She leaned closer. "Tell me what?"

He squinted, as if his eyes were having trouble focusing. "I have done wrong . . . so much wrong. To this world, to so many, but most of all . . . to you."

"Please," she said softly, "don't try to speak."

For an instant, his eyes flashed angrily, a reminder of the ruthless king he once was. "I must speak! Before . . ." Again he tried lifting his head, but it fell back to the wet sand. Weakly, he closed his fingers around hers. "Elen . . ."

"Yes?"

"Please . . . forgive me."

She brought his hand to her lips and kissed it. Her soulful eyes gazed at his. "I forgive you."

A new quietness seemed to flow over his face, moving like one of the waves sweeping through the shallows. His mouth softened; his brow relaxed. Then, slowly, his head turned to me. I could see, by his eyes, that he was seeking my forgiveness, as well. But whether from weakness or from stubbornness, he could not bring himself to ask.

Nor could I bring myself to answer.

For a long moment, we stared wordlessly at each other. A sudden spasm shot through him, arching his back. With a final groan, he swung his head back to Elen, fixing his eyes on her. Then he closed them forever.

23

†HE VESSEL

Gently, Elen laid Stangmar's hand upon his bloody chest. With tear-stained cheeks, she peered at me. Her tone full of grief, as well as rebuke, she said, "You could have forgiven him."

My boots twisted uneasily in the sand. "No," I replied. "Not after everything he did."

She merely gazed at me sorrowfully.

I turned away, heading down the beach. My boots dragged across numerous shells, bright with colors, but I paid no heed. In the distance, I could see Shim's woven hat, its lower edge lapped by waves. Already, some of the children had returned. A few stood gawking at the corpse of Stangmar; others climbed the dunes or waded in the shallows.

Moving past them, I trudged along the shoreline. Noticing my shadow alongside me, I snapped, "Where were you in that battle? Some help you were!"

The shadow stopped walking, separating its feet from my own. I could almost feel its glare.

"No," I declared, "I am not going to apologize. Sure, you do just fine on the easier tasks, like finding a giant. But when it comes down to something really risky, involving life or death, where are you?"

The shadow gave me a defiant shake of its head.

"All right, then," I ranted. "You just do that. Go away, as far as you like. And I hope you never come back!"

The dark shape on the sand waved its arms wildly. Then it turned and stalked off down the beach.

I watched it move away, certain it would return before long, ready to behave better. My stomach churned. What if it didn't, though? I glanced down at the empty sand by my feet, feeling strangely bereft. I almost called to the shadow before it disappeared among the dunes, but no words came.

"You is angrily, Merlin. I can tells."

I looked up to see Shim's oversized nose dangling over me. "Yes, I am. At that sword-armed menace, at Stangmar, at my shadow . . ." I paused, swallowing. "And most of all, at myself."

"Better to be angrily at that swordly warrior," advised the giant. Gingerly, he licked the palm of his great hand. "If he wasn't so cuttingly sharp, I'd have squeezeded him into stewballs." After another lick, he added, "But I guesses he doesn't bother you for a whiles, since I throws him so far out to seas."

"You did well, Shim. Even if he survived, you certainly got rid of him for now."

"I wishes I'd gotten rid of him for everly! He's muchly dangerous. Even with his bladely arms, I wagers he can still swims. He might come back here to kills you and the tinyly childrens in another couple of dailys."

"By then we'll be gone," I declared, cutting him off. "You see, Shim, I have a plan." My gaze slid to the highest of the dunes, where I had watched the rising spiral of sea birds at dawn. Behind the dune, the very tops of the dead trees protruded slightly, looking like white hairs growing out of the sand. "If it works, that plan will keep the children out of Slayer's reach—and maybe also Rhita Gawr's—forever. But I'll need your help to do it."

The giant straightened, wobbling slightly as he yawned. "I gets the feeling I won't be gettings my nap for a whiles."

"Just a little while," I assured him.

I turned to the wall of mist, behind which the waves sloshed and pounded without end, and chewed my lip thoughtfully. The mystery of Slayer's identity still tormented me. And why did he say, just when he was about to strike Elen, that her death would be truly fitting?

Shim bent lower again. "What is you thinkings, Merlin?"

"Oh, I was just wishing I'd removed his mask before you threw him out to sea."

"Me toos," came the reply, followed by another enormous yawn. "Now tells me this plan, before I falls asleepily."

And so I did. Taking Shim over to the trees, I explained that we needed a raft large enough to hold all the children—eighty-three, according to his count—plus Elen and myself. He seemed skeptical, especially when I told him that I planned to guide the vessel, by my own magic, through a deadly barrier of spells. Even so, he set right to the task. Wrapping his arms around the trunk of the nearest tree, he uprooted it with a single great heave, showering us both with sand and broken branches.

For the next several hours, the two of us labored, hauling trees, removing their roots and branches, and arranging the trunks side by side on the beach. Sand and flecks of bark got in my mouth, eyes, and hair. Yet despite all the grit and the aches in my back and upper arms, the raft began to take shape. The trunks fit together nicely when placed so that the thicker end of one lay next to the thinner end of another. And by working some of the larger limbs into any gaps, I made the fit even tighter. I felt increasingly convinced that our vessel would indeed hold us all—and be ready to sail by the next morning.

As we worked, we were flanked by a large group of children who sat on the dunes watching our progress. Lleu did more than watch, however, as did the athletic girl, Medba, and a few of the older youths. They helped me trim the branches, whacking at them with shafts of driftwood, and also hauled off the debris. When the trimming was done, I asked them to round up some onlookers for another task. Before long, I had two teams, one led by Lleu and one by Medba, scouring the beach for the supple strands of kelp that I needed to bind the logs together.

By late afternoon, the job was nearly done. As bronze hues dappled the dunes, and shadows started to lengthen, I stretched my stiff back and surveyed the vessel. It looked quite seaworthy, thanks to the sturdiness of the logs. All that remained was to secure them with kelp—and push off.

Tempted though I was to finish everything now, before sunset, I knew that another, less satisfying, task took precedence: burying Stangmar. I'd promised my mother we would do it by nightfall, and the light was steadily dimming. Besides, I could see from her solemn pacing along the beach that she was ready. The raft's completion would have to wait until tomorrow.

Calling Lleu to my side, I asked him to build a bonfire for warmth, using all the scraps from the trees, as well as any driftwood he could find. Clearly delighted, he jogged off, kindling in hand. I then turned to Medba and asked her to take her team and dig up as many mussels as they could find in the wet sand by the shallows. Roasted mussels, she agreed, would make a fine meal. Then she told me something else: In the bowl of the giant's hat were generous supplies of oatcakes, bread loaves, dried fruit, and caskets of cider, contributed by some villagers while Shim was gathering the children. I told her to break out some of the cider, but to save the rest for later.

My attention turned to the burial. Again I asked for Shim's help, and with a single swipe of his hand, he dug a deep hole in the sand at the base of the dune where Stangmar had leaped to our aid. As my mother and I lowered the heavy, bloodstained body into the ground, I struggled with another, far greater weight—my own tortured feelings. How could he have expected me to forgive him? And yet, for all the pain she'd experienced, my mother had done so. Why, then, couldn't I?

As I bent over Stangmar's grave, smoothing the last sand over the spot, Shim's enormous finger tapped me on the back. The force of the blow knocked me flat. I rolled over, spluttering sand, and gazed up at him.

"I is leaving now, Merlin." He pointed his arm, as hefty as one of the trees he had uprooted for the raft, toward the east. "I shall sees you, though, soon. In just three more dailys at the circle of stones."

"Stay the night, Shim," I urged, using my sleeve to wipe some more sand off my tongue. "You can leave in the morning when we do."

"No," he replied with a cavernous yawn. "There's something I is wantings to do for a long time." His wide mouth twisted in a strange smile. "A verily long time."

Assuming he meant his long-awaited chance to sleep, uninterrupted by children crawling all over him, I nodded. "Good luck to you, my friend."

"Samely to you." He looked doubtfully at the nearly finished raft. "You is still full of madness, Merlin."

"Always will be," I replied with a grin. "Now, don't forget your hat over there on the beach."

Shim's massive head swayed from side to side. "The childrens love playing with it so much." He paused, watching a group of fifteen or twenty taking turns leaping off the brim into the shallows, splashing and shouting boisterously. "I is happily leaving it heres."

My grin broadened. "They're going to miss you when you're gone."

"Aw, I already says good-byes to mostly of them." He gave me a wink, and lowered his voice to a gale-force whisper. "Anyways, I is leaving verily sneakingly. So quietly nobodies will notice."

My eyebrows lifted, but he turned to go. He stepped over the dune, and his footsteps started thundering across the floodplains. Several dozen children, seeing him go, raced to the tops of the dunes, waving their arms and calling after him. They stayed there, shouting merrily, until the echoes of his lumbering strides had long vanished.

As I stood, brushing some of the sand off my knees, a sudden thought made me gasp. What if Shim's goal was not to find a quiet spot to sleep, but to go to the dwarves' realm in search of Urnalda? Hours earlier, he'd mentioned trying to win her support—and my warning had been interrupted. He'd be walking right into her death trap!

In a frenzy, I ran to the top of the nearest dune, stumbling in my haste. Breathlessly, I stood on the ridge, hoping to catch a glimpse of him, to warn him somehow. But I saw only a wide stretch of dried grasses and bog holes, tinted a dusky purple by the setting sun.

Grinding my teeth, I kicked at the sand. If there was ever a time to fly, this was it! No—this was truly a time for Leaping. That way I could travel to Shim in an instant, warn him, and be back here before anyone even knew I'd gone. Yet that was utterly impossible.

I shook my head glumly. Tomorrow's voyage with the children, now that it was upon us, seemed almost as difficult. I turned around, studying the beach shot with shafts of crimson and purple. Girls and boys were everywhere, hurling stones at the shallows, digging themselves into the sand, frolicking on Shim's hat. Two boys had started to scuffle near the raft, and my mother was pulling them apart. Several children had gathered around Lleu's bonfire, which was burning vigorously, sending up a tower of orange flames against the dark blue wall of mist beyond the shallows. No one on the beach, I knew, understood the risks of tomorrow's journey.

But I did. And now, on its very eve, I felt a deepening pang of uncertainty. Perhaps the better course was to remain right here. It was likely Slayer had drowned. Or if he hadn't, he'd surely need some time to recover before he could attack again. Could I take that risk, though? And what about the risk of Rhita Gawr himself attacking these children, if his invasion succeeded?

I gazed at the wall of mist, which was transforming into another shape: a high, steep-sided mound. The island, perhaps? The dangers of going there couldn't be any worse than the dangers of staying. And they might well be less. Even assuming some trouble at the barrier of spells, the voyage shouldn't take us more than a day. Then, with the children safe, I'd have two days left to run as a deer to the battle with Rhita Gawr. Enough time—barely.

Brimming with doubts, I strode down the dune to the bonfire. I spied my mother, and veered toward her. She was seated cross-legged on the sand, watching not the fire but the place where we had laid Stangmar to rest. As I joined her, I followed the line of her gaze. Sparks floated upward, dancing brightly, never quite reaching the grave before they were extinguished.

I cleared my throat, and she turned to me. We studied each other, our faces lit by the wavering flames, for some time. I felt certain that she, like me, was thinking about the man who had affected our lives so profoundly, and yet who remained, even in death, such a mystery.

The small girl with protruding braids, whose name I'd learned was Cuwenna, pranced over, chewing on a roasted mussel. She flopped down on the sand between my thighs. "Do you mind, master Merlin? I'm cold."

I couldn't help but grin. "No, Cuwenna, I don't mind. You can stay right here as long as you please."

"Thank ye, master Merlin."

Even as I patted her shoulder, some instinct made me turn away from the fire, toward the long line of dunes. Suddenly I glimpsed a vague shape on the farthest dune, the one closest to the water's edge. The shape seemed to be moving toward us, but so slowly that it might have been just a stray curl of mist. Yet something told me this was not mist, but a man.

A man who was creeping stealthily, like a cat stalking its prey. The light from the fire reflected dully on something metallic by his side.

My heart slammed against my ribs. Slayer! But how? I must have underestimated his strength—and his hunger for revenge. He had returned!

Frantically, I scanned the beach, looking for anywhere the children could conceivably hide. But there was no shelter anywhere, other than the sea itself. If only we'd finished work on the raft! Then we could sail off before he arrived. If only—

Wait! There was a way, a vessel we might sail. It might work. . . .

Hurriedly, I scooped up Cuwenna and called to everyone, "Come now, all of you! Follow me." Seeing my mother's look of puzzlement, I said urgently, "He's coming back." To Lleu I cried: "Come! Bring everyone. We're going to the hat!"

Down the beach we dashed, every last one of us, tripping over ourselves on the soggy sand, to the great hat. The waters of high tide licked the willow branches around its base. I couldn't tell if it would hold together on the water, nor if it would even float. But it was our only chance. Slayer, most likely, had seen us leave the fire; he could be running along the base of the dunes right now, closing in on us fast.

"Shove, everyone!" I shouted, leaning my shoulder against the hat's tightly woven branches. Children large and small did the same, as did Elen. Voices grunted and groaned, feet dug into the sand, but the massive object wouldn't budge.

"Again!" I shouted. "All together!"

Backs and legs strained. One of the smaller children started sobbing. Then, at last, the whole hat jolted. It scraped along the sand, sliding over a rock-rimmed tide pool and into the shallows, toward the roving wall of mist that separated us from the sea.

To my relief, the hat floated, its mesh of branches bobbing on the water. Like a troop of ants climbing into their mounded home, the children scaled the sides, slithered through gaps on the brim, and dropped down into the bowl. Older children helped younger ones: Medba lifted a frail-looking boy onto her back, hauled him to safety, then jumped back down to the water for another load. Meanwhile, I saw Lleu carrying little Cuwenna up to the brim.

As more children climbed inside, I pushed the vessel into deeper water so we wouldn't run aground. At last, all were aboard. Shreds of mist wrapped around my arms as I gave a final shove and leaped onto the hat. I scrambled higher, grabbing hold of the knobby branches.

Suddenly I heard heavy boots pounding across the sand. I was right—it was Slayer! Now he plunged into the shallows, his skull mask askew, leggings torn, and armor coated with wet sand. He waded swiftly toward us, slashing the air with his murderous blades.

"Come back here, you coward! Come back and fight!"

Clinging to the side of the hat, I pleaded to the deep, ever-churning powers of the sea. *Deliver us, please. Take us away from this shore!*

Waves continued to surge, slapping the vessel, but with no greater strength than before. Slayer drew nearer, and nearer. I could see his chin protruding from under his mask, and hear the whistling of his blades. Then, without warning, heavy mist closed over the hat, cutting us off from the shore—and from Slayer. I could see no sign of him through the impenetrable vapors, though I could still hear his cursing. As the mist thickened, that sound gave way to a slow, ceaseless rumbling, fathoms deep.

The sea had accepted us.

PART THREE

24

†HE VERY DEP†HS
OF †HE SEA

Darkness spread over the evening sea, and over our vessel.

The great hat bobbed and swayed on the water, while the children, my mother, and I perched on its brim like a mass of gulls on a rocky ledge. Some, including me, dangled our legs over the edge of the brim. Others lay on their backs upon the knobby mesh of branches; still others sought shelter from the briny breeze by climbing down into the recesses of the bowl. I looked past all the anxious, awestruck faces and into the folds of mist surrounding us. Even probing with my second sight, I saw nothing but vapors swirling darkly—vast, impenetrable, and as mysterious as the sea itself.

Waves slapped against the sides of the hat, making the tight weave of branches creak incessantly. I peered into a gap where some rebellious branches had pulled loose, exposing the interlocking layers of willow, ash, and hawthorn. A complex splicing of vines supported every bend and wrapped around every joint, while something like spider's silk reinforced the knots. Spruce resin, carefully applied, gave the outer branches an eerie gleam, as well as extra resilience. I shook my head, wondering how the burly fingers of giants could have crafted something so intricate as this hat.

For a timeless moment, I watched the dark waves. They surged and withdrew, surged and withdrew, in a pulsing rhythm I could feel as clearly as that of my own heart. The waves hissed and sloshed, seeming almost to speak, sounding out their watery words, pondering meanings both deeper and wider than I could imagine.

Then, from somewhere inside myself I felt a vague stirring, the same indescribable yearning I'd always felt in the presence of the sea. Whether it was the lingering touch of my mer ancestry, or a half-remembered dream from my childhood, I couldn't be sure. Yet it told me that, for now at least, we were safe, cradled by the whispering waves. And I knew, without knowing how, that the currents were bearing us westward, along the coast—in the direction of the Forgotten Island.

Someone nudged my shoulder. I lifted my head to find myself looking into eyes as blue as the sky after a summer rain. Elen smiled at me gently.

Brushing some salty spray off her cheek, she sat down next to me, her legs dangling alongside mine. For a while we simply sat there, our hair blowing in the misty breeze, as the hat sailed along. Neither of us spoke a word, listening only to the sounds of lapping water and creaking branches.

At last, gazing not at me but into the darkening mist, she spoke. "Where are you taking us, my son?"

"The sea, not me, is taking us. With Dagda's blessing, we should land by midmorning."

"Land where?"

I listened to the continuous slapping of the waves. "The Forgotten Island."

She tensed for an instant, then relaxed. Turning, she faced me squarely. "I have faith in you, my son."

"So do I, master Merlin."

I spun my head to see Lleu crouching beside me, his curls fluttering in the wind.

"Come join us, lad." I slid closer to Elen. "There's a space right here."

Moving with care so not to bump into me with his head, he sat down on the brim. Mist flowed over his bare feet, slipping between his toes. Giving me a wry grin, he said, "I've never went ridin' on a hat afore."

I chuckled. "Nor have I."

"Makes me want to see everythin', ye know? The whole wide world, an' all the seas in between."

"One day you will, I'll wager." I patted his thigh. "You're already quite the adventurer."

"Not likes you, master Merlin."

"Oh, I'm sure you've already done some things I haven't." Glancing at his blackened stub of an ear, I wanted to add, *and survived some things I haven't.* "Before you're done, you'll go to all the places you like."

"Maybe so," he replied, the wry gleam returning. "But I won't knows how to make a feather go flyin' around, ticklin' yer nose."

Both my mother and I laughed. "You might well do that, too," I said. Feeling my stomach churn, I waved toward the bowl of the hat. "Do you think there's enough food down there for me to have some supper?"

Lleu nodded vigorously. "Twenty suppers, if ye likes." He drew up his legs and started to crawl over to the bowl. Trying not to knock into any other children—not easy with all the swaying—he called, "I'll bring ye a loaf or two o' bread, an' maybe—"

"Hey there, ye one-eared oaf!" An older boy with muscular arms and a jutting chin grabbed him roughly by the arm. "Watch where yer goin'! Ye crunched me knuckles wid yer knee." He brandished a fist. "Methinks I'll do jest the same to yer face."

Lleu tried to wriggle free, but couldn't escape. "Sorry, Hervydd," he blustered. "I didn't see ye."

"Aye?" The bigger boy gave him a brutal shake. "Then maybe ye'll see this." He raised his fist. "Or maybe I should give that ol' ear some more flattenin'."

"No, no!" squealed Lleu, doing his best to cover the tender side of his head.

Hervydd smirked, clearly enjoying his power. He drew back the fist—when I seized him by the wrist. He struggled briefly, then seeing who was holding him, fell still. Even so, he glared at me angrily for spoiling his fun.

My temples pounding, I commanded, "Let him go."

"Aw, I wasn't really gonna hurt 'im none."

"Let him go," I repeated through clenched teeth.

The boy complied, shoving Lleu down hard against the spiky branches. Hearing Lleu's whimper, I glowered. Hervydd merely watched me with a sassy grin.

My wrath swelled, out of sympathy for Lleu . . . and also something more. This bully, so rough and unrepentant, reminded me of Dinatius, that scourge of my childhood. Dinatius had treated me just the same way when I was no older than Lleu. And whenever Elen had tried to stop him, he'd shown the same insolence as Hervydd was showing now.

"No one aboard this vessel treats someone like that," I said sternly.

"What're ye goin' to do?" he shot back. "Throw me overboard?"

My fingers squeezed his wrist more tightly. Now that was a tempting idea! Of course, I wouldn't really do that—but I still wanted to punish him somehow. Maybe I could use the idea to frighten him a bit.

"Well," he said sassily, "ye gonna do it?"

"That's what you deserve," I retorted.

"Wait, master Merlin." Lleu touched my forearm. "Don't fling him in the sea."

I looked down at him, scowling. "Why shouldn't I?"

"Because . . . well, he's not so bad, really."

"No?" Viewing Lleu's earnest face, my mood softened slightly, though my grip did not. Hervydd, meanwhile, watched Lleu with a mixture of surprise and suspicion.

"I did step on top o' his hand," Lleu explained. "An' I figures, well, we're all together here, for a whiles anyway. So we might jest as well try to get along."

My eyebrows lifted. "You're a rare one, lad."

Finally, I let go of Hervydd. "And you're a lucky one. If Lleu here hadn't spoken up, I might well have thrown you overboard." I bent low, so my face nearly touched his. "But only after I turned you into a sea urchin, or maybe a jellyfish."

Seeing his skepticism, I decided to emphasize the point. I took one of the hairs hanging over my brow and gave a sharp tug. Then, holding it in the palm of my hand, I uttered a simple spell. The hair sizzled, curled, and abruptly vanished. In its place lay the wet, formless body of a jellyfish. I held it, fingering its slimy mass, before flinging it over the edge into the waves.

For the first time, Hervydd's face showed traces of fear. His eyes widened, and he started to back away, crawling across the brim.

I stroked my chin, pretending to muse aloud. "Or maybe a shard of driftwood? No, no, too little character. What about a handful of sea scum, floating on the water like a rotten fish? Yes, that's just the thing."

Hervydd retreated even faster, scurrying over to the far side of the hat.

Again Lleu tapped my arm. In a whisper barely audible above the slapping waves, he asked, "Ye'd really've done that to him?"

"No," I answered with a wink. "But he doesn't need to know that, does he?"

I placed my arm around his shoulder, when a sudden lurch sent us both sprawling on the woven branches. Children shrieked, tumbling across the brim, thudding into one another. One boy pitched headlong into the bowl. My mother flew backward, knocked into me, then grasped a bowed branch just in time to keep from falling into the sea. Others weren't so lucky: I heard several cries that ended in splashes.

The hat, while continuing to rock with the waves, seemed to have stopped moving over the water. Winds blew harshly, shredding the mist. The whole vessel began listing to one side, as if it were sinking.

"We've run aground!" shouted Medba, adroitly seizing my staff, which was about to roll off the brim.

"Everyone into the bowl!" I roared above the din. "Right now!"

Turning to Medba, I took the staff with a grateful nod. "Go see if you can help anyone who fell over. But be careful! I'll try to get us out of this."

Before I could blink, she was off, sliding through a gap and scuttling down the side with the agility of a spider. I crawled to the edge and peered down into the darkness. Meanwhile, the hat tilted even more sharply. Leaning as far as I could without falling over, I searched the waves for some sign of whatever we had struck.

Nothing but water.

The hat tilted further, creaking ominously. I jammed my staff into a space between some branches, making a sturdy post rising up from the brim. Hooking my legs around the shaft, I hung my entire chest over the edge. Splashing waves drenched my face, stinging my sightless eyes, but my second sight continued to probe the depths.

Something stirred beneath the surface. Long and thin, like a strand of kelp. But no, it moved too purposefully for kelp. Then, along its side, I glimpsed a row of quivering suction cups, glowing with their own greenish light. A tentacle! I could tell by its immense length and girth that it belonged to something big—far bigger than our vessel.

Stretching out my arm, I sent a stream of water, concentrated to strike as hard as a spear, at the tentacle. Seawater sprayed in all directions. But the tentacle swiftly recoiled, pulling itself out of reach. At the same time, other serpentine limbs lifted out of the waves, entwining themselves with the branches. Glowing strangely, they pulled on the hat, tearing at the webbing, dragging us downward. The vessel listed precariously. From within the bowl, I heard frightened screams.

Drawing on all the power within me, I called to the great hat. *Rise, now. Rise, O vessel of willow and vine!* An errant pelican swooped past, brushing my back with its wing tip. Again I called, urging the hat with all the force I could muster. *Rise now, up from the sea!*

More spray drenched me, chilling blood and bone. Suddenly I felt the vessel starting to vibrate. The vibrations grew swiftly stronger, loosening the grip of my legs on the staff. With a wrenching effort, I pulled myself back up onto the brim.

At that instant, the quaking hat began to turn, spinning slowly in a circle. The rotations came faster, and faster still. Buffeted by gusts of spray, I clung to the staff, trying to keep my balance. Then, without warning, the spinning ceased.

A loud, extended slurping noise erupted from the water beneath us. The noise swelled steadily, ending with a sudden *pop*. At the same time, the entire hat lifted out of the water, creaking and snapping like a grove of trees writhing in a storm.

Peering over the edge, I saw great streams of water cascading off the sides of the hat, pouring back into the sea. Our vessel hung in the air, just above the surface. More than a dozen tentacles stretched out of the depths, glistening with green light that rippled across the tops of the waves. The tentacles flexed, tugging, but the hat didn't budge.

Weakened though I was from the strain of the spell, I threw whatever I could into keeping our position firm, muttering a new round of chants.

A strange, raucous cry arose from the sea—half bellow, half hiss, and full of fury. The tentacles slowly unwound themselves from the branches, releasing us at last. In unison, the supple limbs slid back under the waves. Their menacing glow lingered briefly, hovering just beneath the surface, then also disappeared.

Exhausted, I rolled onto my back. As my breathing calmed, I listened to waves pulsing beneath the hat, the sound of a tranquil sea. Below, in the bowl, the children's voices had quieted. I could hear some of them climbing out to the brim again. Then I heard another sound, one that slapped me like a frigid wave.

"Help me," came a thin, wailing voice from somewhere below, near the surface of the water. "Someone please . . . help me."

Summoning my strength, I crawled back to the edge of the brim. Anxiously, I scanned the dark waves. I saw no one—until I looked not at the water, but at the side of the hat itself. Clinging to the sopping branches, huddled and frail, was the figure of a small girl.

Cuwenna!

Swiftly, I slid through an opening between the layered boughs and clambered down to her. Prying her shivering body off the branches, I gathered her in one arm, holding her tight. With great care, I carried her back up the side, pushing her through the opening in the brim before following after. I peeled off my mother's vest, still warm even though it was soaked with spray, and wrapped it around her tiny body.

She looked up at me, her eyes bloodshot but radiant. "Thanks, master Merlin," she whispered.

I touched her nose gently with my finger. "You're welcome, little one. Next time you want to go swimming, though, tell me first."

Through her shivers, she nearly smiled.

I carried her down into the bowl, gave her a drink of apple cider, then tucked her into a quiet corner where she could sleep. Returning to the surface, I released the hat from my spell—a process that took longer than expected. The reason had nothing to do with my chants, and everything to do with Medba's insistence on first climbing down to the bottom of the hat. Though she claimed she wanted to make sure there was no serious damage to the weave of branches, I suspected she really just wanted to experience hanging upside down over the water. After she returned, her hair dripping wet, I released the spell. The great hat dropped into the sea with a resounding splash. Waves lapped against the sides, bearing us westward once again.

For the rest of the evening, I sat on the brim, my knees drawn up to my chest for warmth. Though the thick mist hid the rising moon from view, I watched as silvery beams scattered through the vapors. And I promised myself, however long this night might last, to stay alert for any trouble—whether from another creature of the depths, or from the barrier of spells that lay between us and our destination.

I listened, beyond the rhythmic slapping of the waves, to the voice of my mother down inside the bowl of the hat. To any children not already asleep, she told one of her favorite tales, about the winged horse Pegasus. It was one I knew well, for she had often sent me to sleep as a child with its vivid images: great hooves trotting through the sky, starlit wings beating steadily, and a graceful form leaping from one constellation to the next.

The story, I knew, came from that other world across the water, the place where my destiny seemed determined to call me. Yet as I heard Elen tell it on this particular night, under the shimmering blanket of mist that surrounded us, it seemed to be a story that belonged to Fincayra. Just as I, in my heart of hearts, belonged to Fincayra.

In time, the rocking waves did their work, and my mother's audience succumbed to slumber. Moments later, she climbed back onto the brim. She sat beside me, her warm shoulder touching my own. From the pocket of her robe she pulled a small loaf of grainy bread.

"If I remember right," she said, "you never got that supper you wanted."

"Thanks," I replied, tearing off a bite of crust. I chewed avidly, savoring the flavors of roasted oats and rich molasses. "I'm almost as grateful for this as I am for hearing you tell Pegasus again. You're a powerful storyteller."

Elen shook her head, making her flowing hair sparkle with moonlight. "No, it's you who is powerful, my son. What you did to free us from that beast was marvelous."

"Not really," I said with a sigh. "All it took was a bit of elementary Leaping, nothing like what Tuatha could do. Now there was a true mage! He knew the art well—so well he could send himself anywhere he chose, and get there an instant later."

As usual, she read my unspoken thoughts. "Which is how you'd like to get us to the Forgotten Island."

I nodded, staring into the mist, as a swelling breeze flapped the sleeves of my tunic. I wondered what sort of spells Dagda had placed around the island. And whether I could possibly unravel them without knowing why he had put them there.

"The truth is," I said with a sigh, "I really know so little."

"You have great powers, Merlin. I've seen them in you from the very start." Pensively, she observed me. "As did your father."

I bristled at the mention of him.

She touched my cheek, turning my face toward hers. "You don't know everything, but you needn't torment yourself about that. Neither did Tuatha. Not even the healer from Galilee, someone you've heard me tell many stories about, knew everything."

"But do I know enough? That's the real question." I forced back the lump in my throat. "Enough to do all I need to do? For all those children down there, and for everyone else besides?"

She drew a slow breath. "Do you know what Tuatha said to me once about you?"

Halfheartedly, I replied, "That I would be a wizard one day."

"Not just a wizard." Gently, she lowered her hand, placing it flat against my back, behind my heart. "A wizard whose powers would spring from the very deepest sources, so deep you could change the course of the world forever."

Hesitantly, I nodded. "Maybe so, but which world did he mean? Mortal Earth, where I'm supposed to go one day to deliver this sword?" My fingers wrapped around the scabbard. "Or our Fincayra, the world I long to save right here and now?"

She gazed at me with that look that seemed to see under my skin. "That I don't know. What I can tell you, though, is this. Your grandfather said that one day your powers will have grown so strong that you will stir the very depths of the sea."

We sat together a while longer, feeling the cold wind off the waves. When she spoke again, it was to bid me good night. "I'm going down to check on the children now. Then I'd like a little sleep myself." With a thin smile, she added, "I hope you'll be doing the same, Merlin."

I merely nodded.

After watching her go, I stretched my second sight outward. I followed the folds of mist, which thinned only rarely to reveal a hint of coastline or an edge of rounded moon. Now and then I gazed at the mesh of woven branches, streaked with silver, beneath me. My thoughts lapped, like the waves, against the memories of my dearest friends. Rhia . . . How had she fared with the trees, and the others? And Shim—was he heading into Urnalda's trap? I wondered about Cairpré, probably searching for some way to rejoin Elen. Nothing would stop him, I knew, not even a wall of deadly spells. And I understood his feelings all the more since I felt that way about someone else. If only I could be with her again soon . . .

Despite my vow to stay alert, my head sagged lower. When at last I awoke, it was already too late.

25

†HE ΠEW DAY

I awoke to the crash of an enormous wave against the vessel's side. Water splashed the brim of the hat, soaking me completely and rolling me over with its force. Much of the wave sloshed down into the bowl, causing loud commotion from those below. Grasping my staff, I managed to stand.

A pale, golden light was filtering through the parting shreds of mist, sparkling on the churning crests. The light of dawn. In that first instant, I saw two things at once, both lit by the new morning light: a line of waves just ahead, rising strangely high—and beyond, a rugged little island with sheer cliffs of dark rock. Atop the island sat a jagged hill, glowing like a sunlit crown.

Glancing to the rear, I could see, through the haze, the outline of Fincayra's western shore. Its own sheer cliffs rose steeply out of the frothing surf. I turned back to the crown of land ahead. So we were, indeed, approaching the Forgotten Island!

But first—the waves. Less like a wall than like a jagged row of teeth, the line of waves rose vertically out of the sea. Between the tall spires of water, parallel rays of light lifted into the sky, arching high over the island, shielding it on all sides as well as from above. The bars of light shimmered ominously, quaking in the air. All the while they hummed a single, eerie tone. Wherever they touched the ocean itself, wild waves crashed furiously. Some of those waves, like the one that had struck us, rushed outward, colliding with anything that happened to stray into their path.

At that moment, another wave hit. Even larger than the first one, it slammed into our vessel like a gigantic hand. Children screamed as bodies rammed against one another inside the bowl. I tumbled over backward, crashing on the mesh of branches. My staff flew out of my hand and plunged into the sea.

The hat tilted at a crazy angle, hurling me to the edge of the brim. Somehow I caught myself on a protruding knot of vines. Struggling to pull myself up again, I heard sharp creaking from the timbers nearby. Hastily, I crawled over to investigate. I could see that several layers of branches had snapped completely, while others were rapidly working loose. All at once, my section of the brim shuddered violently. Great seasons, it was breaking! Before I could do anything, the whole section sheared off and collapsed into the sea.

I spun down into the whipping waves. Seconds later I surfaced, gagging from all the water I'd swallowed. Right before me rose one of the shimmering bars of light, humming like a colossal swarm of bees. At its base, the water boiled violently. The great hat, I could see, had veered toward the spot. Already, it was pitching in the froth of the maelstrom.

Turn back! I willed the vessel. *Turn back before—*

A wrenching groan arose from the hat as two powerful waves smashed it from opposite sides. A gaping hole opened just above the base, spewing twisted branches. Water started flooding in. I heard the children's shrieks above the din.

With all my strength, I swam toward the collapsing craft. Another wave toppled over on me, thrusting me downward. Frigid water poured into my lungs. Gasping, I regained the surface—just in time to witness the final destruction of our vessel. Vines unraveled, waving in the air like angry snakes. Branches tore apart, sending countless shards into the air.

One whole section slammed into a column of light and instantly burst into flames, showering the churning waters with sparks and fiery embers. Blazing resins, glowing orange, bubbled out of the joints and dribbled down into the sea. Great columns of steam rose upward, hissing noisily, wherever fire and water met.

All around me, little heads bobbed and limbs flailed, grasping for floating bits of wood. "Elen!" I shouted. "Lleu! Cuwenna!" But I couldn't find them. Beyond the roaring and crashing of waves, and the ominous hum in the background, the sound that pierced me most deeply were the terrified screams—screams I knew I'd caused myself.

Spotting a boy sinking nearby, I reached out to help him. His sand-colored curls floated on the water like a mesh of yellowing kelp. Grabbing hold of his locks, I lifted his head. It was Lleu! Sputtering, he hugged my neck in panic, squeezing like a noose—so tight I couldn't breathe.

As I twisted to break free, both of us sank beneath the surface. The boy released me, flailing wildly. I grabbed the shoulder of his tunic and hauled him upward, kicking furiously. But the surface seemed so far away, my arms so much heavier than before. My lungs ached for air! I struggled to swim, but felt myself sinking rather than rising. I couldn't lift Lleu's body, nor even my own.

My mind started darkening. From somewhere, I dimly heard my mother's words: *One day you will stir the very depths of the sea.* What bitter irony! The words rang in my memory, laughing raucously.

Stir the very depths . . . From somewhere else, somewhere deeper, another memory arose. It was not a memory of thought, nor of the mind at all. Rather, this was a memory of the blood.

"Mer!" I heard myself crying aloud, emptying my last shreds of breath into the surging sea.

Vaguely, I felt something brush my chin. Then my hands, chest, and thighs. Bubbles! All around me, by the thousands, so tiny I couldn't see them but only feel them. The bubbles surrounded me like a net, pressing against my body, supporting my weight. Gently, they caressed me, held me, then guided me upward. At last, I broke through the surface.

The sea had answered my call.

Beside me, Lleu bobbed in the water, held by his own net of bubbles. He gasped for air, coughing, as did I. Yet I felt no more terror, only an uncanny sense of well-being. Reaching for his outstretched arm, I drew him close, holding him as securely as the surrounding waters held us both. Despite the churning currents, we floated on the surface, along with everyone else from our vessel.

Suddenly, I caught sight of a sleek, glistening form rising above the water. Not far away, an enormous fish tail broke the surface with a shimmering veil of spray. Then another tail appeared, and beside it, a silver-scaled torso. More shapes, glowing pink and green, purple and yellow, burst into view.

All at once, a new wave lifted out of the sea. Higher it rose, streaming water off its colorful crest. In a flash I realized that it wasn't a wave at all, but a bridge. A luminous, living bridge.

Merfolk—dozens and dozens of them—had interlocked their tails and fins, arms and heads, to form an enormous, radiant archway. Vaulting out of the depths, the bridge of bodies swelled higher. Finally it reached completely over the wall of waves, all the way to the shore of the Forgotten Island. Like a rainbow rising out of the ocean, whose colors came from sea instead of sky, the archway gleamed in the light of the rising sun.

Voices, deep and fluid, poured forth as the mer people started to sing. Some sounded as ancient as the ocean, others as new and fragile as a single drop of spray. Their voices combined in a complex, interwoven chant, with sounds that reminded me of whales breaching, seabirds wailing, waves colliding, and so much more. Beneath it all ran a great, rolling rhythm, echoing like an undertone of time.

Carrying Lleu in my arms, I started to climb. My sopping boots stepped first upon a purple fin; then a long, muscular back; then a pair of linked arms. With every step, I spoke words of thanks, for my gratitude ran as deep as the sea. After me followed the children, one by one. They looked thoroughly bedraggled, but amazed and relieved to be alive. Despite their wet shivers, their arms swayed playfully. Last of all came my mother, her face shining with awe, holding my staff in her hand.

And so I led them all, at last, out of the waves and into a new day.

26

A GOLDEN CROWN

The mer people continued chanting as we stepped off the glistening bridge and onto a cove of black sand that ran beneath the island's rugged cliffs. As soon as I came ashore, I set down Lleu, who smiled up at me, his face aglow. Together, his small hand within mine, we turned around to view the awesome spectacle.

The mer people's bridge, luminous in the morning light, arched high over the terrible barrier of waves that ringed the island. Across the bridge, in single file, strode our companions—more than eighty boys and girls, followed by my mother. As they stepped ashore, one by one, they joined us on the beach, gazing back at the swelling waves threaded with mist and spray. Cuwenna, wearing my vest as if it were a great yellow cloak, plopped down by my feet, shaking her small head in wonder.

Tasting the salt on my lips, I studied the channel that separated the Forgotten Island from the western shore of Fincayra. Through the middle of the channel ran the churning wall of waves, studded with bars of light, that had kept anyone from setting foot on this spot for countless ages. Suddenly, as I watched, the entire barrier collapsed in on itself. The wall of waves tumbled into the surface of the sea, sending up great towers of spray, as the glowing bars of light melted into the waters. They had only receded, I felt sure, waiting for the next voyager who dared to try this passage. Moments later, the sunlit sea, rippled with golden-tipped waves, looked deceptively calm.

Then, as my mother finally set foot on the sand, the mer people's bridge also collapsed. A thunderous splash echoed across the channel, punctuated by the din of hundreds of tails and arms slapping the water. In a few brief seconds, the merfolk vanished beneath the surface. For a while, after the other sounds had faded away, the soulful notes of their chant hung in the air. Finally that, too, disappeared.

We stood, dripping seawater in the warming rays of the rising sun, looking out to sea in silence. Even the smallest of the children seemed transfixed. We knew that we had been saved by a miracle. A miracle from the deepest heart of the sea.

I glanced down again at Lleu. He watched me with his thoughtful eyes, then slowly curled his mouth into a grin. "You saved me," he said, brushing a trickle of brine off his cheek.

"No," I gently replied. "The sea saved us both."

He tilted his head, thinking. "So the sea's magic is stronger than yers?"

"Much stronger, lad."

My mother strode over, her countenance serene. She glanced again out to sea, shook her head, and turned back to me. "They're gone," she whispered.

I nodded, feeling the wet locks of hair slap my brow. "Not completely, though."

She sighed. "Yes, we'll always hear their voices." After a long pause, she added, "I counted all the children. They're here, every last one." She winked at the boy by my side. "Including you."

"An' you, too, Mama Elen." Angling his face upward, he looked at her probingly. "Is it . . . all right I calls ye that?"

She smiled down at him. "Yes, Lleu, quite all right."

He brightened, then bent to retrieve a speckled brown conch shell. My mother watched him for a moment, then handed me my staff. "I found this, or perhaps it found me. It kept me afloat until the bridge appeared."

Gladly, I wrapped my hand around the shaft. The smell of wet hemlock wafted over me, as did another scent, one I couldn't quite identify. It smelled of magic, powerful magic, unlike any I'd encountered before. It might have come from the mer people. Or perhaps . . . from the island itself.

Spinning around, I scanned the cliff rising from the back of the cove. It rose sharply, like a shark's fin jutting out of the sea. Its craggy face, with no trace of shrubs or grasses, showed not even the slightest softening from wind or water, as if it had just been severed from another wall of rock. Above the cliff, set back some distance, I spied the upper rim of the crown-shaped hill I had seen from afar. The hilltop looked strange somehow—unnatural. Yet I couldn't put my finger on why.

No plants, no green, anywhere. Not even any sign of the golden mistletoe that my friend Gwri had long ago promised grew on this isle.

With a sudden pang, I wondered how the children would fare here after I left. They were safe now from Slayer, that was assured. But if the island held no fresh water and no firewood, they couldn't long survive. For food, they could always dig for mussels and clams, and find stalks of kelp, but that alone wouldn't be enough. Even if my mother chose to stay and help them for a while, as I suspected she would, they would need lots more supplies than this beach could provide.

My gaze followed the narrow stretch of black sand. Most of the children had already started inventing games and challenges for themselves. Thanks to the sun, and the lack of wind, only a few seemed cold. Several, including Lleu, were busily erecting towers out of colorful shells. One red-haired girl had built a glistening bridge from wet sand, and was pretending to walk an orange starfish across its span.

Other children, meanwhile, waded in the shallows, splashing and cavorting. Still others reached their bare arms into tide pools, trying to catch the tiny fish living there. A knot of boys had just run a race across the cove, and were panting heavily, slapping each other boisterously. Several older girls, led by Medba, performed somersaults and headstands on the sand, while Cuwenna walked hand in hand with my mother, stopping frequently to examine a snail, crab claw, or sea cucumber carried ashore by the tide.

I turned back to the cliff towering over us. Somehow I must get to the top. The only way to judge whether this island was livable was to explore up there. Pacing back and forth on the sand, I examined the sheer face from several angles. It looked impossibly steep.

At last, I spotted a jagged, diagonal cleft running almost to the top: a possible climbing route. Cautiously, I tapped the rock face with my staff. Several chunks broke off—not a good sign. Nevertheless, I had to try. Thrusting my staff into my belt, I called to my mother that I'd return soon. She knew better than to try to dissuade me, but I couldn't miss the concern in her eyes.

I started to climb. The rock wall was slick with spray, making it difficult to find a reliable grip. Worse, the stone sometimes crumbled without warning, pulling apart in my hands. Even so, I managed to climb gradually, wedging my body into the cleft for support as I moved higher. When I reached three times my height above the cove, I paused to rest my bruised fingers and shake some of the chips of rock out of my hair. I pretended not to notice Elen's pacing below the cliff.

A moment later, I continued, working my way higher. Every so often my knee or foot would slip on the wet rock, or a hold would break off, but I managed to keep myself from falling. At length, my head bumped against a flat lip of stone that protruded slightly from the wall. There seemed no way around it. Judging from my height above the sand, I felt sure I was very close to the top. Wrapping one hand, then the other, around the edge, I put as much weight as I dared on the outcropping. A few shards broke loose, but it held. Gingerly, I threw one leg over and started pulling myself up.

My heart raced, less from the strain than from eagerness. At last, I'd learn the truth about this island—whether it held anything that resembled food. And, less likely, anything that justified those old myths about wings.

Rolling onto the flat stone, I gasped. Before me lay nothing but wreckage and ruin. The crown-shaped hill was, in fact, the remains of an enormous mound. Ripped apart, its contents scattered everywhere, the mound now resembled some sort of immense, violated grave.

All across the steep, grassless slopes, mixed together with the dirt, broken timbers, and huge blocks of granite, lay an endless array of iron cauldrons, brightly painted masks, silver-handled drinking vessels, sounding horns, and shards of pottery. I could see bejeweled

swords, several of which had been snapped in two, plus the pieces of
an ox's yoke. Strewn among the wreckage were broken bowls,
beaded necklaces, shoe ornaments, neck rings, golden belt covers,
numerous crushed shields, armored plates, and daggers darkened
with rust. Smashed statues lay among the debris, along with at least
two upturned wagons—and more than a few twisted skeletons, some
still draped with armor.

I stepped closer, avoiding the fragment of a skull, and lay my hand
on the side of a block of stone more than twice my height. By the
deep scoring on the granite, I could tell that it had served as the lintel
stone of an entryway. To what, though? An underground fortress, perhaps. Or a community of some kind, where many people once lived,
together with all their prized possessions.

A community that had been utterly destroyed.

Studying the block of granite, I noticed something. Its shape
resembled the sarsen stones that people in ancient times placed at the
entrances of burial mounds! Imbued with magic of their own, sarsen
stones acted as sentries to guard the spirits of whoever lay buried
within the barrows. Was it conceivable that this whole hill had been a
burial mound? No, that was absurd. The largest barrow I'd ever seen
or heard described was less than one hundredth this size.

I slid my fingers along the stone, leaving tracks in the dirt that had
settled on its face. To my surprise, I felt some subtle depressions. I
blew away the dirt—and found rows of carved runes, as intricate as
spiders' webs. I bent closer and read aloud:

> Enter ye and worship here:
> Lords divine dwell deep entombed.
> Ever more their lives revered,
> Never cursed with mortal doom.

My gaze fastened on a single word: *entombed*. So this had been a
barrow after all! And yet, given its size, it could easily have served
other purposes, as well.

I pursed my lips, wondering. *Lords divine . . . their lives revered.*
Perhaps this place was also some sort of sacred monument. A place
for worship. But of whom?

Lords divine surely sounded like they were gods. Perhaps this was a monument to Dagda and his chieftains. But no, great spirit though he was, Dagda wasn't the kind to encourage, or even allow, such heavy-handed worship. He was far too humble. And besides, if the old legends were indeed true, it was he who destroyed this place and set it forever apart. Surely he wouldn't have done that to a monument in his own honor.

I turned again to the skull fragment lying on the ground. With the toe of my boot, I nudged it. The sun, rising high overhead, glinted on part of the bone, giving it an eerie gleam.

All at once, a new puzzle occurred to me: If the beings this monument glorified were indeed gods, and thereby immortal, why had they been entombed? *Never cursed with mortal doom,* claimed the inscription. Yet . . . either they were truly divine and only their mortal forms had been buried here, or they weren't really gods at all.

Pulling my staff from my belt, I started to climb up the side of the mound. As I ascended, I searched for any more clues that might help explain the origins of this place. Surely the answer lay around here somewhere! At one point I paused to glance behind me, following the line of my footprints, the only ones to mark this slope. Below me, I viewed the edge of the cliff I had scaled, and beyond, a wide expanse of whitecaps that stretched all the way to Fincayra's western shore.

I continued tramping up the slope, stepping over broken pottery, a cauldron full of dirt, and a crumbling thigh bone. Frowning, I imagined what my shadow would be doing if it were here right now: creeping cautiously ahead of me, shrinking to avoid any skeletons. Bravery was not one of its virtues. Nor was dependability. Even so, I had to admit that I felt strangely alone without its company.

At last I reached the top of the mound. As I approached the gap between two great piles of earth, rock, and splintered wood, the ground under my boots shifted. I edged closer to the gap, and found myself staring down into a steep-walled pit. It seemed almost bottomless. It was perfectly rectangular, except for a long, narrow passage that bisected it on a north-south axis. Protruding from the walls were numerous timbers and jutting stones, all that remained of the chambers—several floors of them—that had once filled the pit. Around the edges, mostly covered by debris, stood several more sarsen stones, along with scattered uprights and capstones that might have lined the entries. But I still didn't know what it all meant.

Then, near the edge of the pit, I noticed the first living plant I'd seen since arriving on this island. Its leaves, quivering in the breeze off the sea, were not green, but glittering gold. Mistletoe! Cautiously, testing my weight on the loose earth, I drew nearer. It was, indeed, the golden bough, emblem of the spirit world. Strangely, it lay not on the soil, but wrapped around a shiny black stone.

Something crunched under my boot. I leaped backward, sending a tremor through the unstable soil, which caused a blue-painted shield to slide over the edge of the pit. In disbelief, I listened to the long silence before the shield finally hit bottom.

I stooped down, looking for whatever had struck my boot. More bones—this time the remains of someone's hand. Bleached white by time, the hand wore an emerald ring upon one of its lifeless fingers. Lightly, I touched the bones, wondering who had moved them, and for what purposes.

In a few more steps, I reached the mistletoe. I halted in surprise. The black stone around which it curled was actually the head of a statue! Painstakingly carved from black obsidian, the life-size statue depicted a man—who now lay facedown in the dirt. Even so, he carried an unmistakable air of power and wealth. He stood regally, wearing flowing robes, a mantle studded with rubies and flecks of copper, and a belt made from spun gold. I could see, even from the back, that he wore a wide, thick beard, the kind I dreamed of growing myself one day.

Something about this man seemed appealing. Familiar, almost. Crowned by the shimmering wreath of mistletoe, he seemed both strong and frail, dignified and humiliated. Then I noticed a strange, chipped point emerging from his back, almost like a spear shaft between his shoulder blades.

I reached down and touched the point. As I pricked my finger on its edge, I felt a subtle throb between my own shoulders. Instantly, I understood. These had been wings! Sure enough, when I scraped away the soil by the statue's side, I found several jagged fragments, carved with graceful feathers. Fitting some together, I knew beyond any doubt that I was holding the remnant of wings.

Lost wings.

On an impulse, I grasped the statue's shoulders and heaved. The figure rolled over, crushing the fragments of wings underneath. Seeing the man's face, I caught my breath. Not because it scowled at me, with stern brow and dangerous eye, but because it was a face I recognized. This was the face of Stangmar. The face of my father.

Horrified, I peered at the visage. Was it merely a coincidence, someone who resembled him uncannily? Or was it really one of his ancient forebears?

My ancient forebears.

I dropped to my knees. With a quivering hand, I touched the jaw, shaped so much like my own. My fingers moved down the beaklike nose, and across the wide brow that wore the mistletoe. This was, I knew, the face of my ancestor. My father. Myself.

Even the statue's stance, its posture, looked so much like Stangmar. Such a man of opposites! He showed no mercy for anyone who dared oppose him, yet gave his own life to save Elen's. He ruled with such wrath and brutality, yet showed, at the last, such tenderness. He tried to kill me—his own son—yet sought my forgiveness.

I clenched my teeth. No, I could never give him that. Not after everything he did. To Elen. To all the people of this land. And to me.

Angrily, I struck my fist against the statue's shoulder, making the figure rock from side to side. The golden wreath fell off, landing with a puff of dirt on the ground. I scowled down at the man I saw in this statue. A man who gave me nothing in my whole life, except a heaviness in my heart.

A man who ruled this land ruthlessly.

A man who became the twisted tool of Rhita Gawr.

A man who hurt anyone who came too close to him . . . because, perhaps, of his own hurt.

A man who burned with rage at his father—a feeling I knew all too well.

A man who, also like me, always felt a gnawing pain between his shoulders.

A man who, for all his faults, never stopped loving Elen.

A man who might have loved me, too, if only . . .

I stared at the statue. A man who fell, facedown in the dirt, and yet still wore a glowing crown.

Moistening my dry lips, I thought of his dying words to the woman who loved him. I remembered the hopeful look on his face when he turned to me for the very last time. And I recalled the willingness of Lleu, so very young, to see the bully who had tried to hurt him as someone who deserved a second chance. *We're all together here,* he had said.

Tenderly, I touched the statue's brow. Then, so quietly it was more a breath than a whisper, I uttered a simple sentence. "My father . . . I forgive you."

Nothing changed. Nothing, at any rate, that could be seen or touched or measured. And yet I felt something new, a strange feeling—of being lighter somehow. It began to fill me, expand within me, flow through my every vein. The feeling seemed delicate, even ethereal, and yet I knew somehow that it would last.

27

FLOWП AПD FALLEП

I sat atop the ruined mound, hearing the waves slamming against the bases of the surrounding cliffs. Beyond, sea and sky melted into a single swath of blue, stretching on, it seemed, forever.

All at once, I noticed some movement on the wreath of mistletoe lying on the dirt beside me. Looking closer, I realized that the movement came not from the golden wreath itself, but from the open circle inside it. I gasped—for there, on the bare soil within the circle, an image was starting to form. An image with vibrant reds and purples and yellows, swirling around rapidly, a dazzling whirlpool of colors.

Amazed, I bent nearer. All of a sudden, the colors stopped whirling and began to coalesce. Now, within the wreath, a detailed scene took shape. I could see creatures, birds of some kind, beating great white wings, flying above a place where sheer cliffs dropped into the sea. Although I could hear nothing of the scene, I could easily imagine the roar and hiss of the pounding surf.

In some ways, the place I was viewing resembled the shore of this very island. Yet that, of course, couldn't be: The land grew lush and green, and no mound topped the cliffs. Besides, I could tell that it wasn't an island on its own, but part of the rugged coast of Fincayra.

Then I saw something that made my mouth fall open. The white-winged birds weren't birds at all—but men and women! They were swooping and diving among the cliffs, clearly enjoying the thrill of flight. Some flew hand in hand; others burst from the clouds and shot straight down, veering upward just before plunging into the glittering sea. All of them flew with playful freedom, thanks to the glorious white wings that sprouted from their backs.

Watching them soar and glide and swoop, I thought of Rhia. How she would love to see this! No . . . to *do* this.

Suddenly the scene melted into another whirlpool, spinning faster and faster, until the spiraling colors re-formed into an entirely new scene. The place was the same, but now a bustling town had appeared above the cliffs. The winged people lived there, but not alone. They lived and worked alongside many others: dwarves, elves, sprites, and more than a few giants. I even glimpsed a group of tiny bright dots that might have been a flock of light flyers. Full of wonder, I stared. Truly, this scene could only have happened long ago!

Something else struck me. The winged people were busily performing numerous tasks—carrying water, assembling furniture, repairing roofs, planting fruit trees and crops, and more. Yet they seemed to be doing these things not for themselves, but for the other races. Everywhere, they were doing helpful deeds, as if they were guardians of some sort, watching over all the rest. Though they had the bodies of Fincayran men and women, right down to the pointed ears, they reminded me more of angels.

Another whirlpool of colors, and the scene shifted again. I viewed the same town above the cliffs, but much had changed. The winged people seemed more distant somehow, flying in the azure sky above the others, rather than laboring alongside them. From on high, they were shouting something—commands, I felt sure. And though the races below bent their backs obediently, I could tell they didn't like it. Several dwarves shouted back; a female giant raised an angry fist.

In the middle of the town, a huge structure was rising. At first I thought it resembled a castle, a fortress facing out to sea. Then I realized that it required less stone and timber than dirt, in great quantities. This structure was a mound! A single, gigantic mound. I sucked in my breath. Could it be the same?

As I watched, one winged man, wearing flowing purple robes, flew down to a knot of dwarves. He hovered above them, his face contorted. To my shock, he drew from his side a hefty whip. Snapping it behind him, he brought it down right on—

Everything swirled as the scene changed. The town had disappeared, pushed aside by the mound, which had swelled to twice its former size. Beneath its gargantuan shadow, a throng of winged people gathered, arranged for some sort of ceremony. A dwarf, his arms bound, stumbled to the fore, falling to his knees before one winged man who stood upon a platform of sarsen stones. The winged man, wearing a silver sash that fell almost to his feet, raised his arms in what seemed to be a ritual invocation. Without warning, two winged people drew bejeweled swords and slew the dwarf. His blood splattered the stones.

I shuddered at this spectacle. What had brought the dwarf to such a ghastly end? Had he committed some horrendous crime? But no, all my instincts told me otherwise. I had witnessed a blood sacrifice! And not to some gods, but to some people who *saw* themselves as gods. Yes, as *lords divine.*

I could not tear my gaze away from the mistletoe. All at once, the scene darkened. Huge, lumbering clouds gathered overhead, seared by lightning. Then the mound and everything around it started shaking, so violently that crevasses opened in the land, spewing dirt into the air. The winged people fled, in panic, to the skies—when an enormous shape started to emerge from the clouds, ready to descend on them. Amidst all the chaos, I couldn't quite tell what it was, though one flash of lightning revealed a shadow falling over the mound, a shadow that looked like a single enormous hand.

Suddenly, as I watched, I heard a voice—not with my ears but with my mind. It was a voice I knew well: resonant, wise, and steeped in sorrow. I knew, in a flash, that I was hearing the words of Dagda:

"Heed my words, thou who hast flown and fallen! Thou hast spurned my trust, ignored my warnings. Yea, thou hast stained thy very wings with blood! And so thy gifts shall be taken, thy precious barrow destroyed, the land beneath it forgotten."

The voice paused, its words echoing through my mind as they had echoed in the air on that fateful day. *"Now, with this very hand that gave thee wings long ago, I shall tear this land away from all other land, just as thou hast torn thy people away from all other people. So it shall remain, unchanged, like the ache that lies deeper than thy bones. For this land stands cursed and condemned."*

The scene abruptly ended, swept up in a swirl of colors, darker and redder than before. In time, the colors faded, then vanished completely. All that remained within the wreath of golden leaves was soil, dry and bare.

I stared at the empty wreath, then gazed around me at the windswept slope, littered with the wreckage of that day. Weapons, jewelry, and enchanted stones lay everywhere. Yet none of those things had been enough to save that people—my people—from their fate. I winced, thinking of the arrogance that allowed them to create a place of worship in their own honor. That allowed them to lose so much, both for themselves and for Fincayra.

I scooped up a handful of soil, squeezing it through my fingers. No green plants had grown here since that day, nor ever would. *Cursed and condemned.* This land could never bloom with life again.

Unless . . .

Slowly, I reached into my leather satchel, still damp from its plunge into the sea. From it I pulled my seed, whose brown surface still pulsed to its own rhythm. Seeing it gleam in the sunlight, I thought of how long I'd carried it, always wondering where it should be planted. And I knew that, while I couldn't do anything to change the miserable past of this place, I could still do one small thing to change its future.

"Hear me now, magical seed," I proclaimed, my voice fluttering in the wind off the waves. "I offer you to the soil of this desolate land. Give it life! Let it flourish, as it must have flourished long, long ago."

With care, I placed the seed on the bare ground in the center of the wreath of mistletoe. The instant I pulled back my hand, the seed suddenly quivered, trembling feverishly. It started wriggling, working its way down into the soil. As it dropped lower, dirt folded over it, as if the land itself were clasping it tightly. A few seconds later, it was gone.

I waited, hoping something might happen. But no movement stirred the soil; no green shoot emerged inside the golden circle. Still, I felt somehow certain I'd done the right thing.

Then, to my surprise, I heard Dagda's resonant voice again. These were, I felt sure, the final words he had spoken on that darkened day:

"And one thing more I shall say: Only if, in times to come, thy people shall voyage here, and truly learn what thou hast wrought, may this land be freed at last from its curse." He paused, and my heart swelled, hoping that I had, in fact, truly learned . . . and that the curse of this place had finally ended. Then he concluded: *"And yet those voyagers of the future, though they may stand upon this very soil, shall never leave the forgotten isle again."*

Never leave again!

My mind reeled. Was I, along with Elen and the children, doomed to stay here forever? Or until we perished from hunger and thirst? No! I had to find some way to leave—both to get supplies for the others, and to travel to the circle of stones.

I looked upward, checking the position of the sun. Mid-afternoon already! In barely more than two days, the gateway between the worlds would open. And Rhita Gawr's invasion would begin.

My jaw set, I turned to the distant coastline across the water. I would find my way back there. And no curse, no barrier, could possibly stop me.

A movement on the ground halted my thoughts. A shadow! It spread across the fallen statue, and the wreath of mistletoe. I felt a surge of relief. My shadow had finally returned.

Only then did I notice its odd shape. It seemed both broader and taller than it should for this time of day. That was when I realized that, instead of arms, this shadow bore a pair of deadly blades.

28

LAND LONG
FORGOTTEN

"No more escapes for you, whelp!"

I leaped up, my heart slamming against my ribs. Slayer!·

The warrior stood before me, his feet planted amidst the ruins of the mound. He gave a sharp kick to the axle of the upturned wagon, sending one of the wheels careening down the slope and over the edge of a cliff. Then he took a step toward me, laughing coarsely through his skull mask, which dripped water off its whitened cheekbones. More water ran from his breastplate, his boots, and his massive, double-edged blades.

Speechless, I stared at him. How did he get here? The mere sight of him, standing on the same island as my mother and the children, stunned me. After all I'd done to escape him!

Behind his mask, he growled. "Haven't you learned by now, runt wizard? I'm always closer than you know."

Closer than you know. The same words Urnalda had used to describe him.

"I've been swimming too much, thanks to you," he grumbled. "None of your fish-men friends wanted to help me. But I found others in the sea who would, by the sweet breath of death I did."

So that was how he got here! I had called to the sea for help in crossing over, and so had he. Just as he'd done with every other power I tried to use against him, he'd hurled this one back in my face! Even as my temples throbbed with rage, I felt again there was something familiar about him. But I just couldn't pinpoint what it was.

He glowered at me, his sword blades flashing in the sun. I clasped my staff in one hand and drew my sword with the other. As always, the great blade rang in the air for a moment, calling like a distant chime. I had barely enough time to heft it before Slayer charged, slashing the air with his arms.

I leaped aside, swiping my staff as he dived at the spot where I'd been standing. The knotted top slammed into his back, throwing him into a huge capstone. The chunk of granite wobbled, fell on its side, and slid into the deep pit with a spray of soil. He spun sideways from the impact, but somehow kept his balance, his legs churning in the loose dirt. With a wrathful roar, he threw himself at me again.

To parry his assault, I swung both my sword and staff upward. They collided with his blades in midair, clanging and showering us with sparks. He pulled back and slashed with one blade, while I countered with my own. He whirled on one foot and stabbed at me; I knocked him aside with the staff. Across the wreckage and scattered treasures we fought, trading blows.

At one point he pressed me so hard that I was retreating swiftly, trying my best to block his thrusts. Suddenly I stumbled on a gold-rimmed cauldron, sprawling backward onto a pile of shattered plates, bowls, and drinking vessels. Slayer advanced, moving too fast for me. No time to regain my feet! As his twin blades sliced downward, I caught the lip of a bowl with the toe of my boot and kicked as hard as I could. The pottery flew straight into his face, smashing into bits on his mask. I rolled aside, as his swords went askew.

Upright again, I returned the attack. I swung my sword wildly, driving him back up the slope until he reached the top of the mound. The deep pit loomed just behind him. As he dodged one of my blows, he stepped back too far, dangling his leg over the cavernous hole. For an instant, he hovered there, about to tumble over the edge. Dirt and bits of rock broke off from the wall of the pit, clattering down into the depths.

I rushed at him. To my dismay, he plunged both of his blades into the ground by his boot, gaining new leverage. Even as I reached the spot where he stood, he hunched over and threw his shoulder into me. We collided, rolling through the dirt together until we struck a statue of three winged women, which burst into shards.

Over and over we rolled, locked together for a terrible moment. One of his blades sliced into the flesh of my shoulder before we separated. I struggled to stand again, crushing the thigh of a skeleton under my boot. Opposite me, Slayer rose to his feet, panting as hard as I.

"First blood," he taunted. "More to come!"

Unwilling to let go of my weapons, even for an instant, I couldn't reach my hand to touch my wounded shoulder. But I could feel it throbbing. Blood oozed down my left arm, soaking my tunic to the elbow. My staff felt heavier by the second.

A glimmer of light to one side caught my attention. It was an arc of silver lifting over the horizon. The rising moon! Glancing at the sky, I realized that we had fought through the afternoon and past sunset. Already dusk was spreading its cloak of shadows over the ruins of the island. Drenched with perspiration, I shivered from the cold night air.

Suddenly I thought of Elen—down there somewhere, under one of the cliffs that ringed us. She'd be frantic with worry by now, unable to reach me up here, unaware of what had happened. That was probably for the best: She'd fling herself bodily at Slayer if she saw him. Better for now that she and the children remained away from all this.

Flailing his murderous arms, my foe charged again. I blocked one swipe, parried another, and ducked to avoid yet another. Sparks jumped into the air, illuminating the darkened mound. Slayer tried to work me back toward the edge of the pit, but I slid behind a carved amethyst table that had been turned on its side. Using the table for cover, I dashed away from the edge, gaining more space to maneuver.

My relief, though, was short-lived. My shoulder ached terribly. And with each blow to my staff, my whole arm felt increasingly weak. Before long I wouldn't be able to lift the staff at all, and in a little more time, I wouldn't even be able to grasp it. Slayer knew he was wearing me down, and aimed his most savage thrusts at my weakened side.

As the nearly full moon lifted above the island, tinting the ruined barrow with ghostly light, Slayer and I continued battling. Now I braced the top of the staff against my hip, trying to hold it out like a spear. But my shoulder grew steadily weaker. Finally, with a wrenching moan, I let the staff drop. Now I had only one weapon, and one good arm.

Through the rest of the night we fought, stiff from our wounds as well as the cold. Slayer's swings grew sloppier—he was as tired as I. He stumbled often, and his torn leggings flapped whenever he moved. Yet his drive to kill me never slackened. He pressed the attack for hour after hour.

My night vision, better than his, gave me a slight advantage. I could see weapons better, and anticipate moves an instant faster. Still, that hardly made up for having only one blade to his two. I was constantly fighting off his blows, rarely striking ones of my own. How I longed to use my magic against him!

When the moon finally dropped behind the horizon, I was barely able to stand. Slowly, the eastern sky began to lighten. Swaths of crimson and scarlet rose into the sky, pushing back the darkness. The sea itself looked frothy red, like a wicked brew on the boil.

Slashing his blades, the warrior backed me down the mound, right to the edge of a cliff. Though it wasn't the one I had climbed, it was just as steep. Behind me and far below, I could hear the surf pounding against the wall of rock. To plunge over that edge would surely mean death—a fact he clearly understood.

One of his blades whizzed over my head, screaming in the air. Dodging, I tripped on a broken harp protruding from the debris. Tumbling on my side, I dropped my sword and skidded almost to the edge. My fingers clawed the dirt, trying to hold myself back. At the last fraction of a second, I managed to stop myself.

I started to sit up, when a sword point jabbed at my chest. Slayer stood over me, swaying from exhaustion, his skull mask streaked with scarlet from the dawning sun. "So," he rasped, "time to kill . . . a runt wizard." He panted hoarsely, then added, "I've waited a very . . . long time for this."

Despite the sword poking my ribs, I tried to sit erect. "Who are you? What have I ever done to you?"

"More than you can imagine," came the gruff reply.

I caught my breath. For the voice—yes, without doubt, the voice—rang so familiar that I could almost place it. Almost, but not quite.

"I don't believe you," I shot back.

From the warrior's throat came a long, low growl. "Well then, you whelp, maybe you'll believe this."

Keeping one sword at my chest, he lifted the other to the chin of his skull mask. With a flick, he threw the whole mask off his head. He glared at me, his gray eyes aflame.

Dinatius. I slumped back to the ground in shock. The same Dinatius who tried, long ago, to kill both my mother and me. The same Dinatius who perished, or so I'd thought, in the terrible blaze I brought down on us both. I cringed at the memory: Dinatius trapped, his brawny arms crushed under the weight of a tree, shrieking in agony as his skin and muscles burned. That blaze cost me my eyes— and Dinatius, I now realized, his arms. Great seasons!

"You recognize me, then? I'm glad. You should know who finally vanquished you." He rubbed the two blades together, as if readying himself for a feast. "Dinatius is your conqueror! I, and my powerful friend."

"Friend?" I sputtered. The wind off the sea whistled, blowing cold against my back. "Who is that?"

He started to pace back and forth in front of me, like a hungry wolf whose prey was cornered at last. All the while, his eyes gleamed in triumph and he kept jabbing the sword point at my chest. "Can't you guess, whelp? Or does he need to stand here in the shape of a wild boar?"

I blanched. Rhita Gawr! Just as I feared, he must have wanted to distract me from rousing the people of Fincayra. So he recruited the help of Dinatius, giving him arms of deadly steel, and the power to turn my own magic against me. No doubt Rhita Gawr also thought of the idea of attacking children. He had trapped me—and even worse, the instrument of the trap was my own creation! If I hadn't harmed Dinatius so badly in that fit of rage long ago, he'd never have joined with Rhita Gawr. Now many more lives, and the life of my homeland itself, would be lost.

"Dinatius," I beseeched, "don't you see how Rhita Gawr has used you for his pawn? He gave you swords, not real arms as you had before, so you could serve him. All he offered was—"

"Revenge!" roared my adversary, so loud that his voice could have shaken the far coastline across the channel. "He offered that, whelp, and I took it." His cheeks, covered with brown stubble, flushed. At the same time his pacing accelerated—as did his jabs, which pushed me almost over the edge of the cliff. "None of your clever words for me, you beggar's plague."

"I just want you to understand! It was a terrible thing I did to you. Terrible! And I've long regretted it. But now we must—"

"Now we must settle things!" he roared, pacing even faster. He strode from the lip of the cliff on one side of me, over to the other side. "You will die for what you did, runt wizard. Right now."

With that, he bellowed angrily and thrust his blade at my heart, throwing all his weight into the assault. At the same instant, the rock directly beneath him, lining the edge of the cliff, crumbled. I felt his weapon nick my skin, then slash upward as he flailed wildly. His bellow turned into a shriek as he plunged downward in a jumble of rock and flying dirt.

Finally, the choking cloud of soot cleared. I saw that the rock slide had left a chute, steep but passable, down to the shoreline—a stretch of sand much slimmer than the cove where I'd left Elen and the others. Below me, half buried under all the debris, lay Dinatius. Swiftly, I grabbed my sword and slid down on my backside, braking myself with my boots. More dirt sprayed into the air, pelting my face. Finally, I reached the bottom and scrambled over to him.

I glowered at him, much as he'd done at me. Judging from the contorted position of his legs, they were both broken. A heavy slab of rock lay on his ribs, and blood flowed from a gash on his forehead. Still, he looked at me with undiminished wrath, and spat some dirt at my feet. One of his bladed arms slashed the air, barely missing my wounded shoulder.

I lifted my sword. The blade flashed in the morning light. Even above the hammering surf all around us, I could hear the pounding of my temples. Here he lay, my great tormentor! Servant of Rhita Gawr! Only moments ago, he tried to kill me. Just as he had killed that poor girl Ellyrianna. And would do to many others if he had the chance.

A wave crashed against the shore, spraying us both with sea froth and torn fronds of kelp. Blinking the salt from my eyes, I prepared to bring down my sword. Then, as a drop of seawater rolled down my cheek, touching my ridged scars, I hesitated, recalling the blaze that had burned us both. Maimed us both.

My hand squeezed the hilt. This was it, my chance to end it all. And yet . . . where indeed would it end?

"Come on, whelp," he snarled. "Kill me if you can."

I studied his twisted form. "Oh yes, I can," I declared. "Easily."

Slowly, I lowered my sword and slid it into the scabbard. "But I won't."

Dinatius glared at me in disbelief. "None of your games, runt."

"It's no game," I answered calmly, feeling a fresh wind off the sea. I cast a glance at the cliff behind me, and the ruined mound above, thinking of all the bitterness and suffering that this place represented. Suffering fostered by my own ancestors.

I turned back to Dinatius. To him, to the island itself, and to the roaring sea that surrounded us, I proclaimed: "No, I won't slay you. Too much blood has stained this soil already."

All at once, the sand under my boots began to tremble. I heard a distant thunder, which gathered steadily, swelling into a deafening rumble. The whole island shook, knocking me to my knees on the sand. At the same time, the surrounding surf grew strangely calm, as if awaiting something. All the way across the channel to the opposite shore, the waves ceased rolling, and the water became as still as a vast sheet of ice.

The island, though, continued to shake—so violently my legs slid out from under me. Several chunks of rock broke loose from the cliff, bounced over the sand, and splashed beside me in the shallows. It was all I could do to try to keep my head up. Dinatius, for his part, slashed at the ground with his free arm, moaning painfully, until he finally fell limp.

A moment later, the quaking slowed dramatically, while the rumble grew much quieter. A brisk wind kicked up, ruffling my torn tunic. Shakily, I managed to stand, though my boots continued to vibrate. Bewildered as to what was happening, I turned again out to sea. What I saw nearly made my legs buckle again.

The island was moving! It was sliding across the sea, like a lone leaf blowing across a tarn. Wind rushed against my face, whistling in my ears. A thin stream of water surged along the shoreline, racing past us, but beyond its edge the ocean remained calm. Meanwhile, Fincayra's western shore, lined with dark cliffs identical to the one rising above us now, was drawing swiftly nearer.

For a timeless moment I gaped at the sight. The Forgotten Island was returning to the mainland! The opposite shore would collide with the very place where Dinatius and I were now. And, at this speed, it would happen in just a few more minutes.

I rushed over to the unconscious warrior and braced my good shoulder against the rock on his chest. Digging my feet into the quaking sand, I heaved with all my remaining strength. The slab slid off, rolling to a stop. I glanced at the channel, which was narrowing rapidly.

I kneeled by Dinatius' side. Where the strength came from, I don't know, but I somehow managed to lift him onto my back. Staggering under his weight, as well as the ongoing vibrations, I carried him to the chute that had opened after his fall. Steep as it was, I crawled slowly up it, trying all the while to balance his limp body. My knees and thighs ached; my wounded arm felt like a dead branch. Yet I persisted—and clawed my way higher.

Huffing from exhaustion, I finally reached the top. I rolled on my side, pitching off my cargo. For several seconds, I lay on the shaking ground, too weak to move. Suddenly, a grinding crunch erupted, drowning out all other sounds. At the same instant, I was hurled back toward the chute I had just climbed. I threw my arms over my face, sure I was going to plunge back over the cliff.

But there was no cliff. In the eerie silence that had descended, I lowered my arms, and saw the truth. The stretch of shoreline where we had been only moments before had vanished. So had the channel dividing the lands.

Weakly, I stood. The shorelines had merged! Not seamlessly, of course. Rock heaps and narrow chasms remained, marking the border. Still, there could be no doubt of what had occurred. This place was now a promontory, jutting out to sea. The banished island had rejoined Fincayra at last.

If land long forgotten returns to its shore. The line from Fin's ballad, so puzzling when Cairpré recited it, now held meaning.

How, though, had it happened? I gazed up at the mound, littered with the remains of its treasures. Unsteadily, I clambered up the slope, my boots sinking into the soil. The glitter of golden leaves caught my attention, and I worked my way over to the wreath of mistletoe. I peered inside its circle, where I had planted the pulsing seed, hoping to see some sign of change. Nothing but bare soil.

Still puzzling over what had caused the island to move, my gaze shifted to the toppled statue, whose wings had been shattered so long ago. And I remembered Dagda's final words: *Only if, in times to come, thy people shall voyage here, and truly learn what thou hast wrought, may this land be freed at last from its curse . . . And those voyagers shall never leave this isle again.*

As the words echoed in my mind, I tramped back down to Dinatius, his body broken but alive. Was it possible that, by sparing his life, I had shown that I'd learned the truth of the winged people's mistakes? And that my gesture of mercy had been enough to end this island's curse of separation? Only Dagda himself knew the answer to that. In any case, his words had indeed proved true. For when it came time to leave this place, I wouldn't be leaving an island at all, but a lost promontory that had finally come home.

29

A STAR WITHIN A CIRCLE

The sun rose higher, sparkling on the cracked stones, broken weapons, and half-buried jewelry strewn across the mound. To the west, golden-tipped waves formed roving lines that merged, at last, with the distant wall of mist, which in turn merged with the azure sky. Surf pounded and hissed at the base of the cliffs, which stood sheer and black but for the outcroppings that ran down them like thick, yellowish cream. But now those cliffs ringed the mound on just three sides. To the east I saw no more sea, just brown fields rising into hills spackled with snow.

At my feet lay the body of Dinatius. He may have been broken and unconscious, yet he remained a danger to us all. I'd spared his life, yes. But I wasn't about to leave him any more opportunities for harm.

I spied a length of red cord, fitted with silver tassels on each end, draped over a sarsen stone. Just the thing! Quickly, I wrapped it around the warrior's body, taking extra care to press the flats of his blades tight against his sides. Weak from exhaustion and loss of blood, it strained me just to roll him over to secure the knots. I couldn't possibly lift him again; keeping on my feet was difficult enough. Moments later, he was bound. Though I'd have to watch him to make sure he didn't cut through the cord, it was the best I could do.

A sudden fear gripped me. Were Elen and the others all right? Even if their cove hadn't collided with the shore, the impact could have toppled a cliff wall. Children could have been injured—or worse. Anxiously, I scanned the area, searching for the lip of rock that protruded above their beach.

Then I saw where it should have been. The whole section had collapsed, leaving a deep gouge at the edge of the mound. Without even pausing to grab my staff, I stumbled toward the spot. My foot caught on the handle of a dagger and I crumpled, rolling in the loose soil. The gash in my shoulder, blackened with dirt, ached painfully.

Panting, I pushed myself to my feet—when a small, curly head poked above the edge. Lleu! He clambered up the slope, followed by my mother, whose blue robe was splattered with sand. A few seconds later, all three of us embraced, swaying in the wind off the water.

In time, Lleu's arms released me. He fingered the scab on the side of his head as he gazed in awe at the scattered treasures surrounding us—and at the motionless body of his assailant. Meanwhile, Elen's sapphire eyes probed my face, then turned to my wounded shoulder.

"This is deep, Merlin." She tried to clean the gash, using her seawater-soaked sleeve. "Kneel down so I can try to mend you. Oh, what I'd give for a sprig of lemon balm!"

"No, Mother. Clean it, please, but that's all. I've—*ehh!* that hurts—got to go . . ."

"You're going nowhere, my son, until I've dressed this. Why look, it's bleeding again." She chewed her lip. "And then you'll need some rest."

"Can't." Weakly, I shook my head. "Just two days left before the battle! That's barely enough time, even if I run like a deer."

"How can you even talk about running?"

With the firm touch of a practiced healer, she pressed down on my good shoulder. My weakened legs buckled, and I collapsed to my knees on the dirt. Reluctantly, I gave in, telling myself I'd leave right after she finished. Even as she coaxed me to lie flat on my back, she peppered me with questions about the ruins, the island, and of course,

Dinatius. I did my best to answer, though not before she assured me that the rock slide above the cove, which had opened the passageway for Lleu and herself, had injured no one.

I remember hearing her ask Lleu to fetch some moist kelp and a flask of seawater. I remember listening to the incessant pounding of waves, slamming constantly into the cliffs. And I remember glimpsing the shape of a lone kittiwake, swooping in the early morning light. Then I lost consciousness.

When I awoke, I felt another jolt of fear. Time was running out! To my relief, the sun's position showed it was only midmorning. I hadn't lost more than an hour.

I sat up, rustling the warm yellow vest I was wearing. The astral vest! My mother must have put it on me again. I worked my shoulder—stiff, but much stronger than before. And I felt hungry, more hungry than I'd felt in days.

"So, my son, you've awakened."

Seeing Elen approaching, her robe fluttering, I pushed myself to my feet. Lleu strode behind her, carrying something on a flat piece of driftwood. "I'm feeling much better," I announced. "Thanks to you."

She nodded gladly, though her brow remained lined with worry. "Here, we brought you something to eat." From the driftwood she took a rolled kelp frond, stuffed thick with something juicy. "Mussels and sea grass," she explained. "The children have been living off it."

Lleu grunted. "Looks like nose drippings, don't it? But it tastes passable."

Without hesitation, I took a large bite of the roll. Tangy flavors of the sea filled my mouth, though the mussels required a great deal of chewing. Fortunately, Lleu offered me another kelp frond, this one holding a melting piece of ice, which I could suck to wash down the mouthful. For several minutes, I ate greedily. All the while, my mother watched me with concern.

"How are the children?" I asked through my last mouthful.

Her expression brightened. "They are, well, children. And very good at it! They're all well, though a few are sneezing more than I'd like."

"And Lleu, how about you?"

"Me?" Gingerly, he touched his scab. "I'm all right. Sleepin' better."

"So much better, it's hard to believe." Elen tousled his curls. "He's made of strong stuff, this boy."

"Very strong," I agreed.

Lleu beamed at me, his round face alight. "Like ye, master Merlin."

I wiped my chin, then tilted my head toward the spot up the slope where I'd left Dinatius. "What about . . . him?"

"Still unconscious," my mother replied grimly. "I made myself set the bones of his legs. I should tell you, though, it took all my will not to break them again."

"I understand, believe me." Reaching beneath my vest, I felt the soft compress of seaweed she'd placed over the gash. "I'm grateful to those healing hands of yours."

"They did very little, really." Her eyes glinted with a mixture of puzzlement and pride. "Once I cleaned them, your sinews practically bound *themselves* together. Yes, and right as I watched! I've never seen anything like it, Merlin."

"Your skill at work, that's all."

"No, your magic at work." She peered at me. "It's that strong."

Stiffly, I moved the shoulder. "Nothing would have happened if you hadn't made me stay for a bit. And really, you did remarkably well for just an hour's time."

She winced slightly. "It's not been just an hour. It's been a day."

"A day!"

She nodded. "You passed out, right here, when I started working on you. That was yesterday morning."

"A whole day!" I turned toward the snowy hills on the eastern horizon. Only a few hours remained. How could I ever get to the other end of Fincayra before sundown? Rhia would be there, waiting, I felt sure—along with anyone else she'd convinced to come. I couldn't let her down. Couldn't! Yet . . . what could I do now? It was hopeless!

Elen touched my forearm. "I'm sorry, my son."

I said nothing, but kept peering at the horizon. The gateway between the worlds . . . the fight to save our homeland . . . the final confrontation with Rhita Gawr . . .

Lleu tugged on my legging. Angling his round face upward, he asked, "Why is you so sad?"

Elen answered for me, patting the boy's shoulder. "Because there's no way now for him to do what he feels he must."

Lleu scrunched his nose doubtfully. "But you said—when you told us that story about the seven labors of Herc . . . ah, whatever his name was—there's always a way."

"This time," she said somberly, "there isn't."

My jaw clenched, and I growled in frustration. *There's always a way.* But what could it be? A cold gust of wind slapped my face, piercing even the vest's layers of woven flowers. I folded my arms, trying to keep warm. Suddenly I caught my breath. Perhaps . . .

Raising my arms high above my head, I looked up into the cloudless sky. "Aylah!" I cried, my voice wavering in the wind. "Ayylahhhhh."

I felt no new presence, not even the faintest smell of cinnamon.

"Aylah! Come to me, O sister of the wild wind. Wherever you are, come to me! I need your help."

Still nothing.

Stretching my arms higher, and every one of my fingers, I tried once more. "Aylah, please! Carry me to the circle of stones, before this day ends."

Not even another bitter gust answered my call. Dejected, I lowered my arms. My gaze met Elen's. With a sigh, I said, "It's useless."

She gave a slow nod. "If only you could fly, like the people of old. Or use Leaping, like the mage you will surely become."

"Or maybe . . . ," I replied, my chest swelling with the strength of a new idea, "like the mage I am *now.*"

She studied me, her expression moving swiftly from surprise to belief. "Why, of course! If you can cause an island to return to its shore . . ."

I slammed my fist into my open palm. "Yes! There's at least a chance."

"Takes me with ye," pleaded Lleu. "If ye be goin' anywheres, I want to come."

I gave his woolen scarf an affectionate tug. "No, my friend. This trip's too dangerous. If my powers go awry, I could end up at the bottom of the sea, or under a pile of rocks somewhere. And if they actually work—well, the perils will be just as great."

"I don't care, master Merlin." His eyes narrowed. "Takes me."

"Sorry, Lleu." I glanced at Elen. "I'll need you to stay here, to take care of her."

"That will be hard," she declared, "since I'm coming, too. Now that we're back on the mainland, and without any more Slayer to worry about, the children will be fine. They're quite good at fending for themselves. As to the littlest ones, I could ask Medba to watch over—"

"No!" I proclaimed, grinding the heel of my boot into the soil. "Neither of you will come." I squeezed my mother's arm. "Please. You must trust me on this."

She drew a long, hesitant breath. In a faint voice, she said, "I do trust you, my son. Even as I fear for you."

"Much as I fear for you, and everyone else in this land. Which is why I must do this." With a wave at Dinatius, lying on the dirt, I added, "He's the one person I will bring along. That way, wherever I end up, he'll be with me—not with you."

Glumly, she nodded, as did the small boy at her side.

"I'll see you again," I declared, not entirely believing my own words. "Both of you."

With that, I turned and started pacing across the slope. As I reached Dinatius, he moaned and stirred slightly, rolling his head on the soil. For an instant I paused, watching him, then bent to retrieve my staff. Grasping the cold wood of the shaft, I jammed its tip into the ground. The wind pressed against my back, whistling in my ears. But I stood firm, just as I intended to stand before Rhita Gawr.

For some time I remained there, as rigid as the staff itself, pondering the highest of the magical arts—the power of Leaping oneself. I couldn't be sure I was really ready. My gaze wandered to the upper rim of the mound, and I felt a sudden urge to climb up there and check the wreath of mistletoe for any signs of life from my magical seed. But I resisted, knowing I needed to concentrate on the one task that mattered.

Leaping. All the way to the circle of stones.

The gusts swelled, causing me to clasp the staff even more tightly. My hand, I realized, was wrapped around the mark of Leaping itself, burned deep into the hemlock: a star within a circle. Much time had passed since Gwri of the Golden Hair gave me that mark—and also predicted that a bough of mistletoe awaited me here. Yet the moment of our meeting glowed as bright in my memory as the shimmering circle of light that always surrounded her. She had told me then that the true magic of Leaping lay in the hidden connections that bound all things to one another, even things as diverse as air, sea, mist, soil, and every person's hand. For all those things and more have a part in what she called *the great and glorious song of the stars.*

I thought of the great stone pillars, so far from this spot, where I needed to go. Once they had witnessed the Dance of the Giants, and in just a few more hours they would witness the meeting of two worlds. Dagda's warning echoed in my mind: Fincayra's only hope lay in enough of its people, from many different races, coming together at the circle of stones. But in the time since Dagda had spoken, I hadn't been able to do anything at all to help that happen. Rhita Gawr, through his puppet Dinatius, had seen to that.

And yet . . . one chance remained. Yes, and her name was Rhia. I looked eastward, toward the distant hills, certain she was on her way, right now, to the circle. Even if she hadn't found a single ally, she would come. Alone, if necessary.

Who else could I count on? Not Shim, who might well have fallen prey to Urnalda's schemes. Not Hallia, who could still be searching the dragon lands in the far north. Not Cairpré, who, like my mother, would be elsewhere. And not my shadow. That I regretted especially, for as rudely and impertinently as it often behaved, it was still part of me. I dearly wished I hadn't driven it away.

I sagged a little, leaning against my staff, as I thought about Hallia. *Like honey on a leaf.* The phrase, which rang so true on that day in Druma Wood, seemed hollow now. Not because Hallia and I loved each other any less, or no longer yearned to run together as deer, but because the ground had shifted beneath our bounding hooves. Our whole world, our whole future, was now uncertain. But no! We could never live apart from each other, just as we could never live apart from our homeland.

Our Fincayra.

Planting my boots securely, and making sure that one of them was touching Dinatius, I gazed up at the crystalline sky. It was time to go. Slowly, I opened my heart, my mind, my spirit to the magic of Leaping. I summoned its powers, calling to all the places where it lay hidden—the embracing air, the bottomless sea, the mist ever swirling, the wondrous soil, and my own living hands.

At first, I felt nothing beyond the chill of the ocean wind, which blew my hair and flapped my vest. Then, gradually, from some strange quarter, I felt a hint of warmth. It wasn't in the air, nor outside me at all. Rather, it swelled within my veins and pores and very bones, filling me like a drinking horn. Steadily it gathered in force, a wave of warmth that flowed through my whole body.

Send us there, I beseeched. *Send us to the circle of stones.*

A sizzling flash of light exploded in the air, encircling us like a blazing cloud. An instant later, it vanished—as did we.

30

FIRST TREMORS

The blazing cloud faded, shooting glowing sparks and fiery trails into the air. At my feet lay Dinatius, still unconscious, though he continued to moan and twitch within the cord that bound him. Bare ground still supported us. But this ground felt different, flatter as well as harder. As the fiery cloud dissipated, I could see that the ruins of the ancient mound, strewn with broken weapons and forgotten treasures, had disappeared.

Instead, a ring of mammoth stones surrounded us. The stones, which rimmed the top of a rounded hill, stood in a stately circle—some upright, others leaning to the side, and still others supporting huge crosspieces. The circle of stones!

Triumphantly, I rammed my staff into the ground. I'd done it. I'd traveled by Leaping!

In the gaps between the stones, I caught glimpses of the surrounding hills, patched with snow and stands of leafless trees. But there were no trees on this hillside. Nothing stood here but pillars of stone—with one exception. A lone, moss-covered boulder rested near the edge of the circle, looking like a small, shaggy mountain.

Then I noticed something odd. While snow crusted much of the ground outside the circle, even dappling the pillars themselves, not a single flake of snow lay within the ring itself. And something else: The color of the ground seemed unusual, not quite right. Lighter somehow. Yes, that was it. The soil itself, and the few brittle blades of grass, seemed subtly whitened, as if they'd been infused with mist. Bending low, I lay my open hand on the turf. It felt strangely warm.

I scratched my nose, thinking. It could, I supposed, have been caused by my Leaping, which required a great concentration of power. And yet I couldn't quite shake the feeling that it was something more, something ominous.

I glanced at the sun, shining high overhead. Under its rays, the air felt chilly, but not unbearably cold. In just a few more hours, it would set—for the last time, perhaps, on the Fincayra I knew.

My gaze moved to the encircling stones. Rough-hewn and immense, they seemed part of the land, and equally old, pillars of time as well as of rock. And they seemed quiet. Intensely quiet. Almost as if they were waiting, and watching.

Where was Rhia? I scanned the distant hills, searching for any sign of her. Nothing. And no trace of anyone else, either. Not a single canyon eagle perched on the pillars; not a single man or woman stood beside me in the circle. No living things at all. My stomach churned. Was it possible, in Fincayra's time of gravest need, that no one would come to help?

Stiffly, I worked my left shoulder. Though rapidly healing, it still felt weak. Too weak, I feared, to help much in battle. I hefted my staff, swinging it savagely over my head as I'd done in my fight against Dinatius.

Suddenly a spear whizzed through the air, passing just over my head. At the same time, I heard a chorus of raucous cries. From behind several pillars raced at least twenty warrior goblins, fully armed with daggers, swords, and spiked clubs. They charged straight at me, their thin eyes glinting under their pointed helmets.

Roaring and snarling like ferocious beasts, they rushed forward. Their three-fingered hands grasped their weapons tightly, while countless scars marked the gray-green skin of their arms. I knew from past encounters with warrior goblins that some of those scars came not from battles, but from the ritual slicing of their skin that they performed afterward, using their own blades. And I knew, as well, that each scar represented one more foe they had slain.

Instinctively, I stretched out my arm toward them. Howling winds erupted from my fingers, blasting them so fiercely, they couldn't advance. Several lost their footing; others were forced back out of the circle. One of them stumbled backward into another member of the band, causing them both to fall down. Before the first one could rise again, the goblin he'd knocked over smashed him brutally in the head with his club, leaving him senseless.

The winds, though, could not stop the goblins' advance for long. They spread out rapidly to attack me from several sides. Many hurled poison-tipped spears. Halting the winds, I drew my sword, hearing its resonant ring once more. I darted around the circle, rushing any goblin who ventured too close. One I slammed in the chest with the head of my staff. The blow, though struck by my weak arm, tore off his breastplate and sent him sprawling.

"Diiie!" cried another, attacking from behind. His broadsword slashed my legging, grazing my thigh. I whirled around, sweeping my own sword. The blade bit deep into his brawny arm. He roared in pain, dropping his weapon. I kicked him hard in the abdomen, knocking him backward into a pair of attackers. All three fell together in a tangle of limbs.

My left shoulder began to throb. I was still holding my own, but I knew that couldn't last for long. The warrior goblins were too numerous, and I was tiring quickly.

Two of them hurled themselves at me from opposite sides. I stepped back, and they smashed into each other with the force of falling trees. Swiftly, I drubbed them in the heads with my staff. At the same time, I sensed something coming at me from the rear, and spun around.

Six warriors, arms interlocked, were charging as a group. I struck the ground with my heel, even as I uttered the command to ignite a scarlet ball of flames on the spot. Then I kicked hard, flinging the blazing sphere into the assailants. But my aim went awry. The fireball brushed the shoulders of two of them, making them roar all the louder, but did no further harm. It merely sailed past and struck a stone pillar, exploding into sparks.

The line of warrior goblins bore down on me. In seconds, we would collide. Glancing behind, I saw several more attacking, swords

and spears upraised. Panting heavily, I knew that I couldn't defeat all
of them at once. At the edge of my vision I saw one especially brawny
goblin, wearing purple armbands, charging at me. He bellowed
fiercely, thrusting his spear point at my ribs.

Just then, a sharp tremor rocked the stone circle. The jolt knocked
me to the ground, sending rumbling reverberations through my whole
body. Likewise, the brawny warrior goblin lost his balance and slid
sideways, barely brushing me with his spear. The interlocked group
reeled as the ground shook beneath them, falling over one another in
a writhing mass. All around the ring, goblins tumbled.

Before anyone could get up again, another tremor struck. And
another, louder and stronger still. Then came another, more powerful
yet. The rumbling quakes came faster and faster. The warrior goblins,
struggling to stand, raged and cursed and beat on one another with
frustration—as well as growing terror. For they knew, as did I, the one
force on Fincayra that could shake the ground that way.

"Shim!" I cried in a lull between the great footsteps. "We're here in
the circle!"

Thanks to my staff, I clambered to my feet. That lasted only briefly,
because one of the leaning pillars, shaken loose by the incessant
pounding, smashed to the ground just a few paces away. I fell back in
a heap, landing on top of Dinatius, slicing my forearm on the tip of
one of his blades. But I was lucky compared to the goblins: Judging
from the agonized shrieks, at least three of them had been crushed
beneath the falling stone.

At that very moment, the enormous, wild-haired form of Shim
reached the top of the hill. He bent down over the circle of stones,
lowering his massive hand to the ground. To my astonishment, when
he opened his palm, out leaped a host of squat, muscular figures, each
of them armed with double-sided battle-axes.

Dwarves! Some carried barbed pikes and stone-tipped spears as
well; a few also bore a dagger between their clenched teeth. They
wore light but sturdy chain-mail vests, and wide belts above leather
leggings. Their beards, whether black or red or gray, had been
trimmed to a sharp point, ready for battle.

Instantly, the dwarves set upon the confused warrior goblins. At the
same time, more dwarves lowered themselves skillfully from Shim's

arm or slid down the edge of his baggy vest. Even though the largest of them stood only half as tall as their enemies, they were ferocious fighters, agile as the wind, and completely fearless. They hacked away ruthlessly at the goblins, who fought back with equal fury, all the more because the tide had turned against them. For his part, Shim plucked several terrified warrior goblins between his thumb and fore-finger, then flung them off into the distance like rotten pieces of fruit.

Even as I rejoiced at the dwarves' arrival, it struck me that one of their number was missing. Nowhere could I see Urnalda.

Shrieks and cries of warfare, together with the clanging of axes and spears against broadswords, echoed within the ring of stones. Gore marred the snowless ground, while blood stained the pillars. Within a few minutes, the last of the warrior goblins fled or fell, ending the skirmish.

A deep-chested roar rose from the dwarves. They waved axes and pikes in the air, triumphant in victory. Soon, though, the cheering ceased, as the battle's losses came clear. Several dwarves had been badly wounded, and at least half a dozen lay dead on the hard soil. Immediately, the survivors began the gruesome work of tending to those in need.

Shim kneeled at the base of the hill, resting his mighty chin on one of the stone crosspieces. His grin widened, showing a row of mis-shapen teeth under his bulging nose. Smugly, he gave me a wink. Only then did I notice the short, bejeweled figure with unruly red hair who sat perched on top of his nose. Urnalda! She watched me, arms folded across her gold-embroidered black robe, clutching her staff with one hand. She looked equal parts regal, frightening—and simply comical.

To get closer, I climbed on top of the moss-draped boulder near the edge of the circle. "So," I called up to them, "you two made peace. I'm glad, as well as grateful."

"Peace be not the right word," retorted Urnalda. "Instead, we made *pieces.*" She slapped her thigh at her joke, cackling with delight so that her blue shell earrings danced up and down, tinkling.

Puzzled, I stared up at her. "I don't understand. Pieces of what?"

"Of stone, that be what!" Her laughter broke out again. One of the earrings flew off, but she waved a finger and halted its fall, then made it travel back through the air and hook itself again on her ear. "Shim

and I be friends now, Merlin. You be remembering the little, er, surprise I had waiting for him? Well, it be a pit, a giant-sized pit."

More puzzled than ever, I tapped my staff against the boulder.
"This is how you made friends?"

Shim nodded. "But the pit is not giantly enough, harr harr! I falls
into it, and breaks through into some more underly tunnels. Manily
more. Then I tries to get out, and breaks lotsly more rock everly-
where. By the times I escapes, there's a hugely hole in the land."

"My amphitheater!" crowed the enchantress, waving her arms.
"Now Urnalda be waiting no longer to give weekly addresses to my
people, to view plays in my honor, and all the rest. So kindhearted
Urnalda be offering pardon to Shim for his crimes of spying." Her
voice suddenly lowered to a growl. "Unless I be learning that he says
or does anything I not be liking."

The giant grinned ever so slightly. "I is muchly grateful to her."

Without warning, the boulder shifted under my feet. I toppled off,
scraping my back on the rough surface as I fell. At the same time, a
spear hissed directly through the spot where I'd been standing. Even
as I hit the ground, I saw who had thrown it: the brawny goblin with
the purple armbands. He stood at the far side of the circle, bleeding
from a gash in his ribs. Cursing vehemently at having missed his target, he slipped between two standing stones and started running down
the hill, pursued by several dwarves.

Slowly, I stood. With a knowing nod, I placed my open hand upon
the shaggy moss covering the boulder. I could feel, beneath the moistness of the moss, the slightest quiver, gentler than a butterfly's fluttering wing. "Thank you, living stone, for saving my life."

From deep within the mass of rock, I felt an ancient, throbbing voice.
It was a voice I had heard once before, years ago, a voice I could never
forget. For it spoke out of the vastness of time, from the strength and
experience of stone. Its words came slow, hard, and unadorned.

*You are welcome, young man. You have never been far from my
thoughts, since the day you entered me and spoke your two-legged
notions.*

I sighed softly. "Yes, I know, I resisted you that day. You wanted
me to harden into stone, but I couldn't do it. I want too much to live,
and change, as a man."

Change! bellowed the voice, flowing into my hand like a torrent of sound. *It is I who knows the truth about change—I who have bubbled within the belly of a star, risen aflame, circled the universe in a particle of dust, then built a new world over numberless eons. Not in many wizards' lifetimes could you learn what I have learned, or see what I have seen.*

"I know, great stone. And yet I hope that somehow, if we survive this day, I could come and learn from you."

The boulder rocked slightly, grinding into the soil. *For that you will need patience, young man, not one of your strengths. And yet you are the first of your kind to speak with me, and the only living creature ever to resist my powers. So it is possible you could learn, with time.*

Gratefully, I nodded. "Who told you of our plight, that you came here today?"

Just above my hand, the stone's surface quavered. From under one of the drooping clusters of moss, a tiny, glowing speck emerged. The light flyer fluttered toward me, hovered before my face, and landed gently on the tip of my nose—just as it had done once before, at the old oak tree that Rhia had tried to awaken.

"Thank you," I whispered.

The delicate creature whirred its wings softly. Suddenly it flew off, flashing brightly. It circled one of the pillars, then veered westward, invisible against the lowering sun.

"Less than an hour be left before Dundealgal's Eve," declared Urnalda from her throne atop Shim's nose. Shielding her eyes against the sun, she surveyed the hills beyond the circle of stones. "Yet no one be joining us."

"They will come," I assured her, though my uncertain tone betrayed my thoughts.

She grimaced. "These goblins be just a few mortal allies of Rhita Gawr. We be needing more, many more, to turn back a full invasion." Nervously, she spat on her hands, then rubbed them together. "I still be seeing no visions past tonight, Merlin. This be most worrisome! No visions at all, except for those ghostly snakes who be hissing at me in my dreams."

Her pale brow wrinkled. "Tonight, I be fearing, will prove our very last."

31

THE DOORWAY

As Urnalda spoke her fateful words, I scanned the perimeter of the ring. The dwarves had nearly finished their work of tending to the wounded. Now they were carefully removing the last of their slain from the circle, to be buried facedown with their weaponry at their sides, as was the custom among dwarves. The bodies of the warrior goblins had already been cleared away, though I doubted they'd been treated with much dignity. The bound form of Dinatius had been left undisturbed in the middle of the ring. Though still unconscious, he seemed to be stirring more actively than before.

All of a sudden I felt new movement under my boots. This was no tremor caused by a giant, however. It felt more like a vibration, slow and distant but steadily quickening. With every second, it grew stronger.

The dwarves inside the circle leaped about in confusion, calling to their leader, while those standing outside didn't seem to feel any shaking at all. Shim, too, felt the vibrations. His bulbous nose twisted in puzzlement, almost knocking off Urnalda. She cursed, slapped him hard, then crawled off, placing herself in the middle of the crosspiece where his chin had been resting. Right away, she started shouting orders to her troops, moving them to the stones at the edge.

The vibrations grew more intense. Shim grunted, then stood up again, adding his own quaking to the ground. As the dwarves pulled back, only Dinatius, the living stone, and I remained within the ring.

Accelerating more, the vibrations produced a low, eerie hum. It came not from the ground itself, but from somewhere far deeper, as well as someplace higher. The air within the circle grew dense, pressured, sparking with tension. I realized, in a flash, what we were feeling—two worlds veering perilously close to each other. How had Dagda put it? *So close, in truth, that their terrains will nearly touch.*

I sensed another change. The misty whiteness of the ground, which I'd noticed upon arriving, was deepening—and accelerating. Even as I watched, the turf grew steadily lighter, melting from brown to gray, with patches of milky white. Then I gasped. In the lightest patches, I saw traces of movement! Streaking shadows, gathering forms . . . the forces of Rhita Gawr! They were close, very close, to passing through the doorway.

I checked the sun. Already dipping close to the horizon! Only minutes remained. Swiftly, I climbed back onto the living stone for a better view of the surrounding hills. Stretching my second sight to the limit, I searched for any sign of Rhia or other allies. But I saw only a few skeletal trees, their outlines swiftly darkening.

No more defenders of Fincayra. Not even Rhia. I shuddered, knowing that only death or severe injury would have kept my sister from this place. And I shuddered again to think of what awaited us all after Rhita Gawr's forces poured into our world.

At that instant, I heard a distant screech, barely audible above the hum of the vibrating ground. I looked up, just in time to see a tiny black dot soaring out of the pink-tinted sky. Downward it spiraled, growing steadily larger. Another screech ripped the air, echoing among the hills so many times that they seemed to be shouting in reply. Soon massive wings gleamed in the reddening light, as did the creature's broad tail, hooked beak, and powerful talons. A canyon eagle!

Not far behind, swooping downward, came others, flying singly or in pairs. Before long, the sky was dotted with their arching wings. Diving in parallel paths, the eagles streaked toward the circle of stones. As the leader landed on one of the pillars, clasping it firmly with his outstretched talons, he faced me and gave a majestic flap of his wings.

I bowed in greeting, my ears ringing with the eagles' cries.

The living stone quivered beneath me. *They remember you, young man. They remember how you fought for them when no one else dared.*

I nodded, but my mood remained grim. For while these winged warriors were powerful allies indeed, they were not enough. No, not nearly enough.

Then, as the rest of the eagles settled on the pillars, I noticed something else in the sky. Birds—more of them. Many more! Birds of all shapes and sizes were arriving, blackening the air with their bodies. They reminded me of the ones I'd seen massing along the Shore of the Speaking Shells, and I wondered if those birds had been gathering for this very moment. As the enormous flock neared, I recognized cranes, owls, pelicans, terns, swallows, cormorants, and hawks—though I knew the hawk I most longed to see again, the one whose feather rested in my satchel even now, was not among them.

Another form, larger than a bird, approached from the northern sky. Its jagged wings, long neck, and massive head cut a shape I couldn't possibly mistake. The shape of a dragon. Gwynnia! Beyond doubt, Fincayra's last dragon had joined our cause. A thin trail of smoke poured out of her nostrils, but I couldn't tell whether she had, indeed, learned to breathe fire. Nor, alas, could I tell where Hallia might be, for she was not riding on the dragon's back.

Over the hills, now bathed in lavender and pink, the shadows of Gwynnia and the assorted birds sped. I watched the shadows rise and fall with the contours of the land, darkening the slopes as they had the sky. I caught my breath. Not all those shapes on the land were shadows!

Emerging from behind the hill adjacent to ours, a proud black stallion came galloping. Ionn! And on his back, Rhia! In the last rays of the sun, which sat like a great red shield on the horizon, her leafy suit glittered like a gown of rubies.

Onward she rode, charging up the slope, the hooves of her steed pounding the turf like a drum. Dust flew, often obscuring her face. But I saw written on her features the wholehearted determination that I'd always known she possessed.

"Rhia!" I shouted, waving to her from atop the boulder.

She waved back, even as her other arm beckoned to others behind her, still shielded by the adjacent hill. At the same time, Scullyrumpus, his long ears flapping, lifted himself higher on her shoulder. In his shrill voice, he piped: "Yaaaaa-hee! Scullyrumpus Eiber y Findalair is herehere at laaaaast!"

"Look there, Merlin," boomed Shim's great voice from above me. "Manily more is coming!"

From behind the hill a host of creatures poured, beasts of every color and size and description. They came striding and lumbering, crawling and flying, slithering and trotting across the soil, ascending the slope to the ring of stones. There were bears, wolves, wildcats, straight-backed centaurs, water nymphs, frilled lizards, stags and does, large-eyed squirrels, foxes, hedgehogs, butterflies aplenty, mice, snakes, shrews, a dense swarm of bees, glyn-maters who ate only one meal every six hundred years, horses, fauns, wood elves, and at least one white unicorn.

I saw a pair of wydyrr serpents, transparent except for their flickering tongues and the tips of their tails; a jellibog, who rolled limply along the ground, leaving a shimmering trail of green slime; and the legendary frog-footed people from the northern coast of the Lost Lands. I spotted a troop of deer people, their narrow faces held high—but no Hallia among them. Then, to my delight, I saw the huge, hulking spider known by all as the Grand Elusa. Hungry as always, she was grinding something between her massive jaws, perhaps the remains of a warrior goblin who had escaped from the dwarves' onslaught.

Also marching in the crowd were men and women, hundreds of them. Near the front strode a tall, gray-maned man. Surprised, I peered closer. It was, indeed, Cairpré! So he couldn't stay away after all! He strode near the front, his white tunic glowing in the light of sunset, leading a contingent singing a rhythmic ballad.

Many more people I recognized, as well. There was Honn, the bare-chested laborer who once sheltered me on my way to destroy the Shrouded Castle. And there—Pluton, the master baker, who helped me find the true name of my magical sword. Even Bumbelwy, the dour jester who finally learned to make a dragon laugh, had come.

Then, behind the marchers, came the most stirring sight of all. Trees, scores upon scores of them, advanced steadily. They slapped the ground with their splayed roots, sending up billowing clouds of dust. With their boughs, they rowed the air, creaking and groaning in unison. Oaks and ashes, hawthorns and pines, cedars and rowans swept steadily across the hills.

Like a mountain on the move, like a tide upon the land. I smiled to myself, knowing that Rhia had found the way, at last, to awaken the trees.

Several giants came lumbering behind the moving forest, their towering forms lit by the setting sun. They seemed to be herding the trees, keeping them together, just as shepherds might do with a flock of sheep. One giant wore a nose ring made from a waterwheel; another carried a crown of stones on her streaming yellow hair; still another waved an immense hand at Shim, who returned the gesture. I noticed that they walked more lightly than Shim, placing their hairy feet with care, perhaps to keep from shaking the ground enough to entangle the trees' roots and branches.

I glanced down at the ground within the pillars. Almost entirely white! Strange shapes shifted and coalesced beneath its surface. Meanwhile, the air grew warmer—and heavier, stiflingly so. Even above the din from the approaching Fincayrans, I could hear the vibrating hum from two worlds about to collide.

Looking up again, I saw the edge of the rising moon as it lifted over the distant hills. Suddenly, a mass of dark, wispy shapes moved across its face, dimming its silvery light. At first I thought they were clouds. But as they drew nearer, flying across the darkening sky, I spotted eerie, flickering eyes within the vaporous forms. And I knew that we were being joined by marsh ghouls.

Amazed, I stared at them. Only the depth of our troubles—and perhaps the memory of how I'd saved them from slavery—could have caused them to leave their treasured isolation. But who had told them of our plight? Had Rhia somehow found time to plunge deep into the remotest swamps and coax them into coming?

With a start, I noticed a lone figure being pulled along by some marsh ghouls in the lead. While its shape resembled the others, it was darker and more sharply defined. No, it wasn't one of them at all. It was a shadow. *My own shadow.* So it had finally returned, and brought with it the marsh ghouls. Great seasons!

Rhia, astride her steed, galloped into the circle of stones. At the same instant, a new sound erupted from the ground below: voices, thousands of them, roaring in unison. The stallion reared, beating the air with his hooves, his black coat glistening with the last scarlet rays of the sun.

Gently, Rhia stroked his neck until he grew calmer. Despite the swelling chorus, she managed to guide him over to the boulder where I stood. Her gaze met mine—just as the sun went down.

Winter's longest night had begun.

32

WINTER'S
LONGEST NIGHT

As soon as the sun descended, the air within the ring of stones grew denser—almost impossible to breathe. Sparks ignited at the bases of the pillars, sizzling and crackling as they floated upward in the heat. From my vantage point atop the moss-draped boulder near the edge of the circle, I thought the ground itself might soon burst into flames.

A steadily swelling roar poured from the shapeless figures moving just beneath the surface. Already the ground had turned completely white, looking thinner than a newly frozen sheet of ice. The full moon began to rise over the far hills. It resembled a ghostly reflection of the white ring, sailing on high.

Meanwhile, more Fincayrans joined us, lining the full perimeter, crowding up against the pillars. Soon the entire ring, and most of the hillside below, teemed with countless bodies of every imaginable description. As I'd done so often before, I scanned the crowd for Hallia. With no success.

Rhia, sitting astride Ionn, called to me above the growing din: "Merlin! Shouldn't we leave the circle?"

"No," I replied, planting my staff firmly on the shaggy surface of the living stone. "This is our world, and we stand here to protect it."

She nodded, her face grim. High above us, Shim's massive head bobbed in agreement. From their perches on the surrounding pillars, the canyon eagles screeched their emphatic support. Ionn, too, whinnied defiantly. And beneath me, I felt the living stone shift, grinding its bulk even more deeply into the soil.

Anxiously, I wondered what our foes would look like. Just how they would come. And whether the very ground would melt away as they passed into our world.

"Beware!" cried Urnalda, waving her stubby arms from atop her stone crosspiece. "There be snakes!"

She pointed to the center of the ring. Not far from the unconscious figure of Dinatius, whose tightly bound body was vibrating along with the ground beneath him, two wispy spirals of mist were rising slowly skyward. Ever so gradually, the pair of spirals lengthened, until they stood almost as tall as the surrounding pillars. At the same time, they grew thicker, especially at the top, where triangular heads began to form. Bright silver eyes appeared, along with hoods that arched menacingly over their slanted brows. As the wraithlike shapes writhed in the air, their surfaces hardened into scaly skin, coldly shimmering in the light of the moon.

Both of the ghostly serpents faced each other, opened their jaws, and started hissing savagely. Ionn whinnied and shook his mane, though Rhia kept him from bolting. Her companion, Scullyrumpus, scampered across her shoulder, wrapping his furry paws around her neck. His eyes grew as round as moons themselves, and he shuddered, flapping his ears against his head.

Like the roaring beneath the circle, the snakes' hissing grew louder. Then, in the open space between their wide mouths, a vague shape began to form. It looked, at first, like a glistening silver thread that stretched between their heads. The thread split along its middle, while bowing upward and downward, until it formed the outline of an egg. The egg grew rounder and rounder, a misty circle within the circle of stones.

All the while, the serpents hissed angrily at each other. Hovering over the ground, the circle started to spin—slowly at first, then faster and faster. In seconds it became a round blur, and then a sphere. Louder roared the tumult of voices; brighter glowed the sphere. Yet more than brightness, or even roundness, this sphere seemed to possess a kind of *depth*.

All at once I realized that it was not really a sphere—but a hole. A hole leading down to the world below. At the instant it became fully formed, the serpents withdrew, fading back into vapors that finally vanished.

But the hole remained, suspended in the air just above the ground. Suddenly, from out of its center, a terrible apparition emerged. It slid outward, expanding as it stretched its jagged wings to fly. Shining silver against the night sky, it had the scaly body of a dragon, with a fearsome, barbed tail, and the head of a giant frog with menacing spikes protruding from its brow. From its forelegs hung vicious, curved claws, long and sharp enough to impale several men and women with a single swipe.

Many of the Fincayrans crowding around the circle gasped in horror as this monster from the spirit world flapped its wings and rose into the sky. Even worse, though, were the silvery shapes that came after it: ogres with bulging, filmy eyes, and arms that reached down to their feet; serpentine wraiths that kindled fire as they slithered over the ground; and enormous lizards that strode about on their hind legs, with pulsing necks and snapping jaws filled with row upon row of daggerlike teeth. Like the winged monster, they had ghostly, silver-toned bodies, sturdy enough to strike painful blows, yet wispy enough to seem made partly of mist.

Next, from the tunnel to the Otherworld, came ghostly figures of a different kind—one I knew all too well in mortal form. Warrior goblins! By the scores, by the hundreds, by the thousands it seemed, these spirit goblins poured out of the hole, brandishing deadly swords.

The furious battle began. Silvery warriors rushed at the defenders, slashing and thrusting with blades, claws, and teeth. Fincayrans who were seasoned fighters—such as dwarves, wolves, bears, men and women—returned the blows in equal measure. The fighting raged, both inside the circle and across the whole expanse of hillside.

Rhia, her hair streaming, rode from one fray to another, rescuing those in trouble, jabbing at invaders with a spear she had found. Shim and the other giants hurled handfuls of attackers into the distant hills.

Canyon eagles and marsh ghouls attacked from the air, shrieking vengefully. Gwynnia swooped down on the huge lizards, scorching them with her first breaths of fire, then trained her wrath on the winged monster, pursuing it across the sky.

No one battled more savagely than the trees. They waded right into groups of warrior goblins, swinging their mighty limbs like battle-axes. Foes broke off their branches and slashed at their trunks, but the trees kept on fighting, striking powerful blows with their roots. Several trees even toppled themselves to pin down invaders. Leaves and chips of bark showered the terrain.

Swinging my sword wildly, I fought off attackers trying to dislodge me from the boulder. At the same time, I hurled fireballs this way and that, anywhere I spotted someone needing help. When I glimpsed two deer people about to be mauled by a warrior goblin, I let loose a searing blast that engulfed the goblin's sword in flames. Just then I caught sight of an ogre about to pounce from one of the pillars on top of Rhia, who was riding right beneath him. I threw a fireball that struck the pillar and exploded into arcs of flame, knocking the ogre backward.

Everywhere I turned, however, Fincayrans were taking a terrible beating. I witnessed, too late to help, as many brave fighters lost their lives. One huge bear continued slamming her paws at the invaders even with half a dozen swords lodged in her legs and back. Finally, she fell, her burly frame crushing three warrior goblins as she crashed to the ground.

Seeing the bear go down, I seethed with fury. Then I watched the worst of it: The goblins got up again. The bear did not.

Great seasons! How could I have ever thought mortal creatures could prevail over deathless spirits? How could Dagda? All we could do, at best, was defend ourselves. And that couldn't last indefinitely. Not against such numbers. Even my magic couldn't turn back a whole invasion. My fireballs only won us time, not victory.

The hard truth could not be denied. I'd urged my friends to join in a battle we couldn't possibly win! And yet I knew, as well, that this was a battle we would have fought in any case. A battle for our homeland.

Suddenly I caught a glimpse of my friend Cairpré, at the other side of the circle. He was in trouble! Standing over someone who had been wounded, he was trying valiantly to keep a band of warrior goblins from killing them both. By sheer fury he was holding them off, though his only weapon was the broken branch of a tree. But he was flagging. Blood spattered his chest, and he staggered weakly. A goblin was about to hurl a lance at him from atop a slanting pillar.

With a vengeful cry, I vaulted off the living stone. Flinging fireballs into Cairpré's assailants, I rushed at them. One flaming missile struck the assailant on the pillar, but not before he released his lance with an angry roar. In a few seconds, I drove the others away, and ran to my friend's side.

Too late. Cairpré slumped to the ground, blood soaking his once-white tunic. The spear protruded from the base of his ribs. Immediately I set to work extracting it, though he writhed in anguish as I pulled it free. Finally, I cast the weapon aside.

Then, as I propped his gray head on my lap, I saw the face of the person he'd been so gallantly defending. Hallia! Her thigh had been cut, and her forehead bruised, but all the same, she lived. I held out my hand to her, my heart pounding with both relief and dread. She took it, sliding closer to me. Without a word, we turned back to the wounded bard.

As soon as I felt the weakness of his pulse, I knew that his life was rapidly fading. Concentrating my thoughts, I tried my best to ignore the fray around us. Carefully, gently, I probed within his wounded chest. Organs, muscles, and tissues cried out to me, all at once, yet I lacked time even to begin mending them. At least I could stop some of the bleeding! With all my will, I tried to stem the flow of blood.

"Merlin," he said, his voice dry and scraping. "It's too late for me. But Hallia . . ."

"Will be fine," she completed, taking his hand and holding it against her cheek. "Thanks to you."

The poet smiled painfully. He started to speak, but a ragged cough interrupted him. When the spasm receded, his head slumped back heavily on my lap.

"You shouldn't have come," I declared, brushing the shaggy hair away from his eyes.

Desperately, I searched my mind for some way to help. "I could try to take your spirit into myself—as I did once for Rhia, remember?

Then I'd have time to work on your body. It might work, old friend! Let me try."

He squinted, studying me thoughtfully. It was a look I knew well from our years together, the look of a mentor who was also much more.

"No," he answered hoarsely. "This is . . . my time." He closed his eyes tight, then reopened them. "Do you remember that old couplet? *The leaf, still green, must someday fall. Such gr—*" A new spurt of coughing cut him short.

When he quieted, I said the rest: *"Such grief, and joy, to live at all."*

Again, he forced a smile. "So you did finally learn . . . a few lines of poetry, eh?"

"Not nearly enough," I replied. "Cairpré, are you sure? It could work."

"I'm sure, Merlin." His bushy eyebrows drew together, as a different sort of pain struck his face. "I wish I could say good-bye . . . to Elen."

Somberly, I nodded. "She'd tell you that you could never really say good-bye."

"Yes," he said with a wistful grin, "and be endlessly . . . stubborn about it, too." He turned his head and gazed up at the full moon, radiant in the night sky. For a long moment, none of us spoke, as the sounds of brutal combat raged around us.

"What are you thinking about?" I asked at last. "Not composing a verse?"

"You know me well," he replied, shifting his gaze to me. "I was searching for the right word to rhyme . . ." His limp hand found its way into my own. "With *friend.*"

A sob rose out of my chest, and I couldn't keep it from escaping.

"You are a true mage, my boy . . . full of greatness." He blinked, trying to focus on my face. "And your greatness flows not from your power, which is vast . . . but from your compassionate heart."

I slammed my fist against the stone pillar behind us. "What kind of mage am I if I can't do anything to save my friend—or my homeland?"

"Fincayra's not lost . . . yet."

Glancing at the battleground surrounding us, I knew better. Everywhere, Fincayra's defenders lay dead or dying; cries of anguish raked my ears. The spirit warriors, especially the goblins, kept hacking away ruthlessly, without any signs of tiring. And despite their heroism, the Fincayrans were faltering. But for the marsh ghouls, who were deathless themselves, most of those who had stood on this hillside at sunset would surely be dead by morning. Or if they somehow survived the onslaught, Rhita Gawr's forces would kill or enslave them before long.

Feeling Cairpré's head and neck suddenly stiffen in my lap, I looked down at him again. His eyes seemed dull, his breathing forced.

"Merlin . . . ," he rasped weakly, then stopped, working his tongue. "I hope . . . oh, never mind. I never was very good . . . at endings."

His eyes closed, and remained that way. The battle raged all around us, but I heard nothing except the echo of the poet's final couplet. *The leaf, still green, must someday fall.*

Then, from beside a towering pillar next to us, I heard another voice. One that made my scarred cheeks burn. It was, I knew, the voice of Rhita Gawr.

33

A DISTANT HORN

"Such a shame, tut tut, to lose a friend," said Rhita Gawr, his voice oozing mock concern. "Ah well, just part of life, I suppose."

Angrily, I leaped to my feet and faced the tall, broad-shouldered man who had spoken. Even amidst the tumult of battle, he seemed exquisitely calm and composed. He wore a light blue tunic, unstained by so much as a single fleck of dirt, which rippled elegantly in the moonlight. His hair, as black as my own, lay perfectly parted and combed. Even his eyebrows looked immaculately groomed. Only his eyes, as vacant as the void, and the wrathful turn of his mouth, revealed his true nature.

"You know nothing of life," I snapped, glaring at him.

Casually, he licked the tips of two of his fingers. "Mortal life, yes," he answered in gloating tones. He stroked the hairs of one eyebrow, flattening them with his moist fingers. "But what is that compared to the life of an immortal spirit?"

I straightened myself. "Everything."

Still stroking his eyebrow, he spoke with renewed sympathy. "How sad, my dear wizard, you haven't learned the difference yet. Sad for you. And also sad for your friends." He gestured at the body of Cairpré at my feet, and then at the mounting slaughter surrounding us. On every side, mangled forms lay draped over the encircling stones or sprawled upon the bloody ground. "The friends you caused to lose their lives tonight."

My scarred cheeks throbbed. "That's not true. All these people are here not for me, but for Fincayra."

"Ah, but of course. How clumsy of me to forget! Fincayra . . . wasn't that the name of a place? A world that once existed?"

My reply caught in my throat. For I couldn't dispute the truth of his words. Right beside me, a pine tree, toppled against a pillar, was being torn to bits by swarming lizards; a pair of brawny dwarves had just been skewered by a spirit goblin's lance; and my old friend and mentor lay dead on the ground. With every passing second, the numbers of slain and wounded swelled—and the chances for our world to survive diminished.

Rhita Gawr sniggered. "Your pitiful little army," he said with a casual wave, "has already lost." His hollow eyes glowered at me. "And so have you." He raised his arm and pointed menacingly at me. "A lightning bolt should do it. Yes, one strong enough to obliterate even your ashes."

"No!" protested Hallia, dropping Cairpré's lifeless hand. "Don't kill him, please." She stood and limped to my side, her whole body trembling. I tried to push her back behind me, but she refused to move.

Feigning a look of sorrow, the warlord of the Otherworld leaned his head against the great pillar beside him. "Ah, doe woman, you make things so complicated. I've been looking forward to the chance to kill your friend here for quite some time, you see. And since my sword-armed soldier didn't manage to do it, I really must."

Calmly, he started buffing his fingernails against his tunic. "But if you insist, like a good little maiden, I shall kill you first. That way he will have the pleasure of causing your death, too."

"You are a coward," I declared.

His expression darkened. "And you are a fool. One soon to die."

The tip of his forefinger began to glow red, as the bolt of lightning gathered, about to burst forth. While combat continued to swirl around us, for a fleeting moment I saw nothing but Rhita Gawr: the swelling light of his finger, the wicked void of his eyes. His finger twitched, ready to release the blast.

Suddenly, a silver-hued shape shot out of the night sky. Plummeting downward, it whistled sharply just before it slammed full force into Rhita Gawr's arm. His lightning bolt exploded with a resounding blast, but went askew, slamming into the pack of lizards chewing on the fallen tree. Scarlet flames engulfed them. The warlord roared angrily, clutching his arm through his torn tunic.

As fast as it had arrived, the shape disappeared into the silvery beams of moonlight on high. Not before I glimpsed its outline, though. Just as I'd heard its whistle, and recognized its boldness. My friend Trouble had returned! He must have followed Rhita Gawr out of the Otherworld, then circled silently overhead until the moment we needed him. The moment I needed him. How like the hawk I knew so well!

Hallia and I stared up at the sky—as did Rhita Gawr himself, boiling with rage. Though all of us were searching for the hawk, we saw instead something strange. So unaccountably strange that I stumbled backward in disbelief, knocking into the slanted pillar behind me.

Flying toward us, bright under the glowing moon, came seventy or eighty figures. They floated steadily nearer, their bodies bobbing with the gusts of air, like a flock of ungainly birds. But these were no birds, nor any creatures with wings. These were children.

The children. Steadying myself against the block of stone, I watched them approach. Swiftly, they sailed toward our hilltop, arms and legs outstretched, tattered clothing flapping against their bodies. Flying! But without wings. How?

In the lead, his face aglow in the moonlight, I saw a small boy. Lleu! The woolen scarf that had once belonged to Cairpré trailed behind him, fluttering in the night. To one side, I saw Medba—flying upside down, her hair blowing crazily. To the other, I found little Cuwenna, holding the hand of someone much larger: Elen. I glanced down at the corpse of the bard at my feet, shuddering at what grim tidings awaited her.

Then my whole body stiffened, as I thought of what awaited the children. They were flying into a gruesome battle. No, into certain death! Whatever allowed them to soar this way, I felt sure, couldn't also spare them from being killed once they landed.

As the flying children neared the circle of stones, one combatant after another looked skyward. The fighting slowed, then finally halted, as puzzled warriors—mortal and immortal alike—paused to view the uncanny sight. All across the hillside, a collective hush fell over the battlers. Even Rhita Gawr kept staring at the sky, seemingly unsure what to make of this.

At that moment, I caught the slightest scent of cinnamon on the air. A gust of warm wind brushed against my cheek. And I understood, in a flash, how the children were able to fly.

"Aylah," I whispered anxiously, not wanting Rhita Gawr to hear. "Why did you bring them? They'll all be killed!"

The wind sister swirled about me, ruffling the sleeves of my tunic. "It was you, Emrys Merlin, who called to me, from the land long forgotten. Do you not recall?"

I winced. "Yes, yes," I whispered. "I sought your help to get here. But—"

"And when I arrived at that place, Emrys Merlin, you had already gone. The boy named Lleu begged me to carry him to you. As did the others, including the one you call Mother. I could not refuse them, ahhh no, for I could tell they spoke solely out of loyalty and love."

"They will die!" I exclaimed, shouting in distress. "Every last one of them will die!"

My outburst echoed over the hushed hillside, startling the combatants. One warrior goblin in the center of the ring turned to another and asked in a bewildered voice: "We'll all die?" The second goblin repeated the words, as did another, and another. Like ripples flowing over a tarn, the phrase swept across the circle and down the hillside. *We'll all die,* went the refrain. *Every last one of us will die.*

"Fools!" roared Rhita Gawr, sensing the swelling discord among his troops. "You can't die. Only mere mortals can die!"

But his words were lost in the rising chorus of voices coming now from the spirit warriors:

"Flying children—how can they do it?"

"Great powers, that's how. Curse the bloody day! What else can they do?"

"No tellin'! But they spell the end of our conquest, I feels it."

"More likely the end of us!"

Rhita Gawr clapped his hands to his head, mussing his perfectly combed hair. "Nonsense, you fools! Whatever powers those children have, it's nothing compared to mine!"

Just then, Lleu veered downward, leading his companions to land on the hillside next to ours. One by one, they settled on that slope unmarred by battle, their feet touching the ground with grace that mystified the onlooking crowd. Indeed, they landed as gently as windblown seeds, yet they lacked wings or anything else to support them. The anxious mutterings of the warrior goblins grew louder.

Lleu stretched out his hands to the sides. Medba took one, and a gangly boy wearing leather sandals took the other. Quickly, the rest of the children joined hands, forming a long line. Then, as one, they started marching down the hillside, advancing toward our embattled slope.

Seeing them approach, the spirit warriors grew increasingly agitated. They seemed completely unable to comprehend these strange attackers striding boldly into their midst—attackers who bore no armaments at all.

"Look there. They've got no weapons!"

"Just their magic, that's enough."

"Don't be a fool, they must have weapons! Hidden, like their wings, I'll wager."

"And powerful enough to . . . well, I'm not waitin' to find out!"

Singly, or in small groups, the warrior goblins started retreating. Several dropped their swords and fled up the hill to the circle of stones, plunging into the tunnel to the Otherworld. More followed, and still more, heedless of the furious commands of Rhita Gawr to stay and fight. Newly heartened, Fincayrans of all kinds—dwarves and giants, four-leggeds and two-leggeds, light flyers and marsh ghouls—started pursuing the spirit warriors. In the span of minutes, the invasion had turned into a rout.

Amidst the chaos, Rhita Gawr remained inside the ring, stomping about and ranting hysterically at his troops. "Come back here, you cowardly slugs! Plague-ridden fools! Now, I say. How dare you retreat before I give the command? Stay here and fight, you craven, fainthearted, bone-brained idiots!"

For minutes on end, he cursed venomously and spat orders, flinging lightning bolts that exploded on the pillars, shooting towers of flames into the air. Any of his own warriors who strayed into his path he pummeled without mercy, threatening to torture them into eternity if they didn't obey. Nevertheless, the ranks of his deserters swelled; wave after wave threw themselves into the tunnel. His soldiers fought against themselves for the chance to escape.

At last, the defeated warlord stood alone before the gaping hole he had opened between the worlds. Soot and bloodstains splotched his tunic, and his hair looked completely disheveled. He glared at his surroundings, aghast, his moonlit figure glowing against the black hole behind him.

Catching sight of me across the ring, he clenched both of his fists and shook them. "Scourge! Worthless wizard. You did this!" He raised his already-glowing hand and pointed straight at me. The air around his extended finger crackled, and I knew a lightning bolt was about to burst.

At that instant six or seven warrior goblins, hotly pursued by shrieking marsh ghouls, plowed right into him. The lightning bolt shot skyward, illuminating the snow-laced hills. Like a surging wave, the fleeing warriors carried Rhita Gawr backward as they tried desperately to escape. Heedless of their leader's screams, they plunged into the tunnel.

Just before Rhita Gawr reached the hole, Trouble swooped out of the sky and gave him a sharp peck on the forehead. The warlord's wrathful shriek rose into the air, then abruptly ended as he and the others dropped into the darkness.

Trouble veered sharply and flew toward me. He circled once, close enough to my head to brush my ear with the tip of his wing. It felt even softer than the precious feather in my satchel, more like air than body. He whistled triumphantly, and my heart soared alongside him. Once more he circled, then shot straight into the hole, just as it shrank down and vanished completely.

Hallia moved to my side, slipping her arm under my thick vest and around my waist, while I wrapped my own arm around her shoulder. We watched, in silence, as the moon dipped lower and the eastern sky grew gradually lighter. A faint swath of pink, braided with lines of azure blue, appeared on the horizon. Somewhere down the slope, a curlew piped its morning greeting. Not far away, a companion answered, trumpeting its own salute to the day. Fincayra's longest night had ended.

From somewhere on high, a distant horn joined the curlews' song. Deep, graceful notes it blew, rising in ascending steps of exaltation. Then the sound of harps, plucked gently, drifted through the brightening sky. A flute warbled, as did another, along with more songbirds. All these and more joined in the rising chorus that echoed across the slopes.

I recalled the words of Fin's prophetic ballad:

> *If land long forgotten*
> *Returns to its shore,*
> *And ancient opponents*
> *Stand allies once more,*
> *Then all through the heavens*
> *Grand music may sound:*
> *The balance restored;*
> *The hidden wings found.*

Hallia and I embraced all the more tightly. For this moment was ours, and could never be lost.

34

†HE jOİNİNG

For the next several days, the Fincayrans encamped at the circle of stones. Though they had plenty to celebrate, they also had much to mourn. And much to do: It was time to bury the dead, seek out the missing, and bandage the wounded—as well as grieve for those who, like Cairpré, had given their lives.

Still, something more potent than grief filled the crisp wintry air. The surrounding hills no longer echoed with the music of the heavens, but with another kind of music altogether—the sound of widely varied creatures working together in concert. While dwarves still eyed men warily, and foxes still watched sparrows hungrily, something remarkable had happened. The shared experience of marching to the hillside, and the battle itself, had cast aside many old fears and resentments. Now the air atop the hill vibrated with a cooperative chorus of growls, whinnies, whistles, chirps, buzzes, brays, squeals, hisses, and hoots, along with the occasional spoken word.

Women and men built fires on the frosted slope for warmth, using broken branches discarded by the trees, gathered by the children, then chopped to size by the dwarves with their double-sided axes. Badgers, moles, and bears dug graves, while healers of every race tended to those in need, illuminated by the glow of light flyers circling them late into the night. Horses and goats carried loads of firewood or chunks of ice to be melted for drinking water. Giants (except for Shim, who lay down between two hills and took a nap that lasted nearly two days) made regular trips to the eastern seacoast, returning with enormous nets of woven kelp that overflowed with fish, clams, mussels, and a fruity purple reed.

Gwynnia set to work roasting fish with her fiery breath; eagles gathered watercress and eelgrass from the southern streams, along with huge quantities of winter mushrooms, beetroot, and bryllnuts; bees carried bits of honeycomb to anyone who craved some. The spidery form of the Grand Elusa scoured the surrounding hills for any mortal—and thus edible—warrior goblins who might have survived. Meanwhile, for everyone's entertainment, centaurs danced in stately formations, elves and sprites performed acrobatic leaps and tumbles, curlews staged whistling competitions, and larks and nightingales sang for all to hear.

Only a few of Fincayra's defenders didn't stay long. For the solitary unicorns, the crowd in and around the stone circle was too much to bear, and they slipped away to the farthest reaches of the isle. On the first day after the battle, the marsh ghouls also departed, floating off as silently as they had arrived. Before they vanished from sight, however, a great, bellowing cheer arose from their fellow Fincayrans, thundering across the hills.

My shadow, who had been acting more cocky than ever since the sun rose on our victory, seized that moment to leap from my side. It positioned itself against one of the largest pillars and took a series of bows. As long as any cheers continued, so did the bows. Watching its performance, I felt like cringing and laughing at the same time.

When the shadow strutted back to my side, I declared sternly, "You know, you really don't deserve that week off I promised you."

Stunned, the shadow glared at me, hands on its hips. Its edges started to vibrate angrily.

"No," I continued, "you deserve *two* weeks off."

Instantly, the vibrating ceased. The shadow took a single, low bow, doubling up on the ground.

Just then I felt a whirling of air across my face, and the sweet smell of cinnamon. "Aylah," I said, my voice full of gratitude, "you made all the difference."

"Not I," she whispered gently, "but those I carried."

"Yes . . . and now, you're ready to move on?"

"The wind must fly, Emrys Merlin, for I have new worlds to explore." She spun slowly around me, fluttering my tunic. "As do you, Emrys Merlin, as do you."

I scowled. "I've just seen my homeland saved! I don't want to go anywhere else."

The scent of cinnamon grew stronger. "Your homeland may not be your true home, Emrys Merlin, ahhh yes. Just as neither Emrys nor Merlin is your true name."

Suddenly, as she spoke, I remembered Dagda's promise, long ago, that he would one day reveal my true name—my soul's name. The name, as he'd told me, that he could give only after it was truly earned. At the same time, I recalled his grimmer promise that some-day I must return to Britannia on mortal Earth: the land of the young king I would mentor, the land of my heralded destiny.

I thought of that world I'd seen so often in my dreams. The cave, sparkling with crystals, that I would call my own; the boy named Arthur, whose eyes shone with high ideals; the society, full of tragedy as well as hope, where I might leave a lasting mark. So much about that world inspired me, lifted my heart, yet one crucial aspect left me fearful. There was no sign of Hallia in those dreams. Nothing—but for a single lock of her auburn hair.

"I don't want to go," I repeated. "At least not for a very, very long time."

"So be it, Emrys Merlin," answered the soft voice surrounding me. "But when the time comes for you to decide, listen to your innermost wind. Ahhh yes, and follow it, wherever it may carry you."

With a final flutter of my sleeve, she was gone.

I stood there in the center of the teeming ring, pondering her words. Absently, I watched Lleu and a few other children sliding down the foot of a giant seated just outside the circle. So deep in thought was I that I hardly heard Lleu's shrieks of laughter as he slid across the hairy flesh, bounced over an immense ankle, and rolled onto the sloping ground.

Someone's hand touched mine. I knew, even before turning around, it was Hallia. My hand closed on hers, and I gave a wan smile.

"Where did you go, young hawk?" She lifted her slender chin, probing me with her gaze. "Somewhere far away?"

Puzzled, I shook my head. "I've been right here, ever since you left me to visit with your clansfolk."

Releasing my hand, she reached up and stroked my temple. "In here, I mean. Where did you go?"

"To the future. And Hallia . . . I didn't like everything I saw."

Her brown eyes watched me soulfully. In a hushed voice she said, "I've been there, too."

"Am I there?"

She paused awhile. "Only as a wish, a longing—not as you."

I twisted my staff into the turf. "It doesn't have to be that way."

She said nothing.

Slowly, we walked across the ring. For the rest of that afternoon, we worked together as healers, helping bind wounds wherever we could. One young eagle, whose wing had been badly torn, screeched triumphantly when I assured him that he'd soon fly again. The cry, so fierce and vital, reminded me of Trouble, and I wondered when—and whether—I would see the hawk's bright eye again.

To my surprise and delight, we found a spark of life remaining in the bear who had battled so bravely. I did my best to mend her gouges, a job made more difficult by the angry swats she took at my head whenever I touched someplace tender. Hallia, meanwhile, fed her handfuls of the giants' freshly caught fish. And judging from the bear's appetite, she was sure to recover.

Throughout that day, and those that followed, Hallia and I spoke no more about our future. Yet the same doubts continued to hover around us. They filled my mind even when I spent the better part of a day alone with Rhia, following her as she strolled among the assembled trees. She moved as gracefully as a walking tree herself, stroking bark, untangling branches, and conversing in the ancient languages of rowan and oak, cedar and pine. Throughout the day, she (and Scullyrumpus, perched upon her shoulder) peppered me with questions about the strange events at the Forgotten Island, and about the lost wings. I did my best to answer, despite the furry beast's constant grumbling that I should have been more observant—and less clumsy.

One cloudy evening, when the moon showed only as a veiled orb, and shadowy steeds raced overhead, I joined my mother at Cairpré's grave. Together, we sang some of his most cherished ballads, and for a few moments I forgot my own concerns. What sorrow lined her face, dimming even her sapphire eyes! Yet I couldn't do anything to help; her wounds ran too deep for healing salves and poultices. Her only solace, it seemed, came from helping the smallest of the children, several of whom joined her even at the graveside.

Every so often, as I roved about the hillside, I thought about Dinatius. He'd awakened on the morning after the battle, but remained weak and disoriented. He said nothing, ate very little, and couldn't walk because of his broken legs. Still, he was Dinatius—and thus dangerous. So I asked some dwarves to fashion a chain to bind his arms, replacing the worn cord. Broken and defeated, he sat on the ground, his back propped against a stone pillar.

As I looked at him, sitting silent and alone amidst the bustle of the circle, I felt an unexpected touch of sympathy. Sure, he had tried his best to slay me, and nearly succeeded. Yet he, like me, had suffered for years in that wretched village of our childhood; he, like me, had been maimed in that terrible blaze. And while I couldn't forget all the harm he'd brought to others, I also couldn't forget the harm I'd brought to him.

Throughout those days of our encampment, something else was happening, something very strange indeed. It involved not the varied creatures gathered on the slope, nor the towering stones, but the land itself. A mist was rising, spreading over the terrain.

I first noticed the mist in the center of the ring, lapping at my feet. Gradually, it grew thicker, and before long it filled the whole circle and pressed against the surrounding pillars. Eventually, it started rolling down the slope, through the trees, and over the neighboring hills. It even mingled with the flames of the Fincayrans' campfires. Yet for some time I paid it no heed, assuming it would pass.

It didn't.

With each succeeding day, the mist grew more pervasive, spreading like an inland sea. Still, it seemed just a curiosity—until I noticed that, unlike ordinary mist, it seemed to be seeping upward through the ground within the circle. Then, with a shudder, I realized the meaning of these encroaching vapors.

"Hallia," I said, taking her hand and leading her over to the edge of the ring. I pointed beyond the pillars, to the rumpled horizon of hills. "What do you see out there, in the distance?"

She twisted her mouth quizzically. "Why, hills, of course. Lots of them."

I gave a grim nod. "What else?"

"What are you getting at, young hawk? All I see are hills, and some scattered trees."

"And?"

She stomped her foot in frustration. "Nothing! Unless you mean . . ."

"The mist. Yes, that's exactly what I mean." I faced her squarely. "Have you ever seen mist like this before? So thick, so lasting?"

"Hmmm," she said, her brow furrowing, "I suppose I haven't. Not even on the coast. That wall of mist is always there, just offshore, but it never moves inland." Her eyes searched my face. "It's not . . . just some sort of weather?"

Slowly, I shook my head. "No, it's not. Hallia, this mist is coming from the Otherworld."

She started, then kicked at a fluffy spiral near her foot. "You mean it's rising through the gateway Rhita Gawr opened?"

"That's right. You must have seen how it started right here in the circle, then flowed down the hill and beyond." I squeezed her hand. "Dagda warned me, when he came to me that night at the stargazing stone, that terrible things could happen if Rhita Gawr broke the barrier between the worlds."

"Now wait a minute." She gave her flowing hair a skeptical shake. "What's so terrible, really, about some mist from the spirit world covering our hills?"

I drew a long breath. "It's not just covering the land. Don't you see? It's *taking* the land."

She gaped at me, even as curling strands of mist wrapped around our hands, slipping between our fingers.

"My love, I'm certain." I gestured toward the creatures gathered around the ring of pillars. "This is what Dagda meant when he said that sometimes, when all is truly gained, all is truly . . ."

"Lost," she completed, her voice suddenly hoarse.

Together, we sat upon a fallen pillar. Its rough edges seemed softened by the mist rising around its sides. We said nothing, overwhelmed by the weight of this realization, much as the land we loved was being overwhelmed by a new kind of force, one we could not fight.

Hallia tapped the pillar beneath us. "Already this seems part stone, and part mist." She scraped the surface with her finger, pulling away some threadlike vapors. "What does this mean, young hawk, for my people, for our sacred lands? For all those hidden pathways and glades and meadows that you and I ran through together as deer?"

"Drowned in mist," I answered somberly. "Just like everything and everyone else in Fincayra." I swatted at some white tufts clinging to my leggings. "Our homeland is lost, I can feel it. All we fought for, all Cairpré and so many others died for—lost."

We sat in silence for a long time, watching the mist deepen. My doubts about the future returned, but with a different twist. With no more Fincayra, what would become of Hallia? Of us? Perhaps we could live out our days in the Otherworld that was swallowing our homeland. Perhaps my time had truly come to travel to Britannia, with Hallia at my side. Or perhaps . . .

At that moment, I noticed that a visitor had entered our camp. Up the hill he strode, moving briskly through the swelling mist. When he neared the circle, a gust of warm air blew over us. At the same time, birds of all kinds flocked to the stones, perching where they could see him. Many other creatures—centaurs and sprites, butterflies and wolves—followed him into the ring. Even the bear, with bandages on her whole body, hobbled in his wake. The living stone, too, rolled behind him, crunching heavily on the soil.

He was an elderly man, his silvery hair as wispy as the vapors curling about his ankles. One arm dangled uselessly at his side, but his confident stride conveyed an air of strength. As soon as he approached, I recognized him. Yes, even before I gazed again into those deep brown eyes, full of wisdom and compassion and hope.

"Dagda," I said reverently, walking over and kneeling before him.

He touched my shoulder lightly, and his face crinkled in a sad smile. "I am sorry for what you have lost."

I couldn't find the words to reply.

He studied me for a moment, then said in a resonant voice, "All is not as it appears, however."

"I . . . don't understand."

"You shall, in time. Rise now, Merlin. I have brought someone to see you."

As I stood again, he reached down and scooped up a curl of mist. It rested in the palm of his hand, slowly spiraling. Then he blew upon it, very gently. It began to enlarge, growing taller and fuller. A rounded body appeared, then sleek wings with bands of silver and brown, then a proud head with yellow-rimmed eyes and a perilous beak. Trouble!

The bird whistled, glanced at Dagda, and fluttered his wings. He lifted off, landing on my left shoulder with a rush of cold air. Again he whistled, before grasping me tightly with his talons.

Feeling his weight again on my shoulder, I almost smiled, yet my heart remained too heavy. "Thank you," I said quietly. "I've missed him."

"And he you," the elder spirit replied.

I beckoned to Hallia, and also to Rhia, who was standing across the circle. More than anyone else, they knew how much this hawk meant to me. Both kneeled in greeting to Dagda, as I had done, then stroked Trouble's feathered back. The hawk strutted happily on my shoulder, pausing once to tickle Rhia's nose with his wing tip. Scullyrumpus, peering in awe over the edge of Rhia's sleeve pocket, was uncharacteristically silent.

At length, I turned back to Dagda. "Tell me, please, what you meant."

The old man's eyes lowered. "You know now that the veil between the worlds has been torn, the cosmic balance shifted. Nothing can change that."

He splayed his fingers, causing the mist to lap against our legs like waves on the open sea. "And now . . . our worlds will merge. They are joining, even as the Forgotten Island has joined with the mainland. No longer will Fincayra stand apart, a haven between mortal Earth and immortal Otherworld."

"So it *has* been destroyed." I shook my head dismally. "Just as I thought."

The elder raised his hand. "Not destroyed, Merlin. Transformed."

I traded uncertain glances with Hallia and Rhia. "Transformed how?"

"Look more closely," bade Dagda, waving at the vapors flowing over the stones and all the assembled creatures. "Do you notice something else about this mist?"

I scanned our surroundings, increasingly white. "No," I admitted.

"I do," offered Hallia, her face suddenly aglow. She pointed at the fallen pillar where we had been sitting. It looked now almost like a rectangular cloud, not so much covered by mist as infused with it. "Instead of drowning our world, it could be, well . . . *becoming* our world."

"I see!" exclaimed Rhia, bouncing so vigorously that Scullyrumpus' ears flapped against her arm.

"Well, I don't," I said in exasperation.

Dagda reached over and placed his hand upon my shoulder, right next to Trouble's talons. "Now you shall, thanks to all your good work. For the moment has come that I have long awaited."

35

MIRACLES

Dagda's eyes brightened, like stars emerging in a dusky sky. "Fincayrans have united," he declared, loud enough that all the creatures gathered around the stone circle could hear. At once, the entire ring fell silent. Not a single bee buzzed; not a single bird chattered. Even the great bear, swathed in bandages, seemed to hold her breath.

"Fincayra's many threads have bound together into a sturdy rope," proclaimed the elder spirit. "Not only have all of you fought together against a common enemy, you have done something much harder still. You have begun to live together as a single community, sharing your food and labors and dreams. That has not happened since days long past."

He paused, the barest hint of a smile touching his lips. "Those days held gifts for all, none of them more precious than peace. And for the men and women of that time, those days held one gift in particular."

Beside me, Rhia gasped.

Lifting his hand high above his head, Dagda drew a graceful circle in the air. "And so shall it be again."

Rhia gave a shriek, as shrill as one of Trouble's whistles. At the same time, Hallia leaped like a surprised doe. For both of them were experiencing the same thing as I—a deep, sustained pulsing in the middle of the back. This wasn't the old ache between my shoulder blades. Far from it! This was a feeling of exhilaration and contentment combined, what I imagined a seed might feel before erupting at last into sunlight.

My tunic felt suddenly tight around my chest. Before I knew what was happening, I heard a tearing sound. And out through my tunic and vest, as through Rhia's suit of woven vines and Hallia's robe, burst something utterly extraordinary.

Wings.

Awestruck, I spread them wide, closed them tight, then opened them again. Watching their edges glitter in the sunshine, I realized they weren't made from flesh, blood, and bone, as was the rest of my body. No, these wings were made from something more ephemeral, like air, and more luminous, like starlight.

Trouble whistled in delight and leaped into the air. Then came the greater miracle. I joined him!

Pumping my broad, shimmering wings, I rose into the air above the circle of stones. Higher I climbed, and higher. Wind rushed over my face, flattening my hair and sending streams of tears across my temples. Though my glowing feathers quivered with every gust, the powerful wings kept beating rhythmically. I inhaled with every upstroke and exhaled with every downward *whoosh*.

Trouble joined me, coaxing me to climb so steeply I could hardly breathe. Then, together, we veered and plunged straight down, wind coursing over us. Faster we fell, and faster. Grinning, I imagined myself with a long beard, stretched straight out behind me.

Just above the tops of the pillars, we pulled up again. I caught a glimpse of my shadow on the ground. It seemed terribly woozy, ready to give me back all its promised vacation if I would just return to the ground. But I'd never agree to such a bargain. The thrill of flying now flowed through my veins.

"Come join me!" I called to Rhia and Hallia, and they followed me upward. Behind them came more men and women, along with my mother and most of the children. Then birds joined the throng, and the sky was soon filled with eagles, cormorants, owls, and curlews. Even Gwynnia took flight, flapping to catch up with Hallia. In short order, the air above the hillside vibrated with the pulsing of countless wings.

I climbed higher, meeting again with the hawk I knew so well. Around each other we spun, performing twists, turns, and loops. Trouble's acrobatics were much tighter and sharper than mine, but I didn't care. All that mattered was that we were flying together, soaring as one.

Vigorously I pumped my wings, then caught an updraft that carried me higher than ever before. Riding the wind, I felt made of air myself. And I recalled again Rhia's impassioned description of flight: *lifting the spirit along with the body.*

Looking at the landscape far below, I viewed almost the entire isle of Fincayra. My sense of loss rushed back to me, for I could see that the mist, flowing outward from the circle of stones, by now reached all the way across the Rusted Plains to the southern shores and western cliffs. Druma Wood gleamed white, as did the giants' city of Varigal and the remotest lands of the far north. And along every coastline, the ancient mists of the sea were joining with the new, expanding mists of the land.

Yet one aspect of the scene surprised me: Fincayra seemed no less varied than before. Hills retained their old contours, cliffs dropped sharply, and the forests still swayed to the rhythm of the wind. Veering down for a closer look at the western coast, I made out individual boulders and trees, even twisting branches. They were white, and blurry at the edges. But they still existed.

All at once, I understood the meaning of Dagda's words. Fincayra had, indeed, transformed. My old homeland, that place of vivid colors and magnificent seasons, was gone. But a new land survived, one imbued with mist, and tied forever to the Otherworld. Now Fincayra was really something more—an intricate melding of two worlds.

Sailing above the coastline, I felt the air whistle past me, buffeting my luminous wings. Suddenly I noticed a lone hillside that hadn't been covered by mist. Thickly forested, it shone brilliant green, right down to the edge of its cliff-lined shore. By some mysterious power of its own, this verdant headland held back the vapors.

Flying closer, I discovered yet another marvel. The forest was thickening even as I watched! With phenomenal speed, oaks and hemlocks and rowans sprouted, their moss-draped branches lifting skyward, their roots expanding as they thrust into the soil. Hefty vines twirled around swelling trunks; boughs burst into leaves, or cones, or red and purple flowers. Shafted by slanting rays, feathery ferns spread across the stream banks, joined by legions of mushrooms and blossoming gorse. Wafts of sweet resins rose off the hill, tingling my nostrils with their wondrous aromas.

In a flash, I recognized the hillside's contours. This was the promontory that had once been the Forgotten Island! And yet . . . it had been so bare, so devoid of greenery, when I left it.

I banked hard and spiraled downward, until I was gliding just over the tops of the highest trees. There, wrapped around an uplifted rowan branch, I found a single bough of mistletoe, gleaming in the sunlight. The same golden bough where I had planted . . .

The seed! This whole explosion of life was the work of that one remarkable seed. Once planted in the right spot, no soil could resist its magic, no winter could dull its vitality. *The rarest of seeds,* Dagda had prophesied, *shall find a home at last.*

I circled the hillside, watching my shadow sweep across the burgeoning forest below. Just how, I wondered, was this lone spot able to hold the mist at bay? All around, the land grew whiter, yet this one place grew steadily greener.

Another shadow approached mine, rapidly gaining. I looked over my shoulder. Rhia! Her face glowed as bright as a newborn star. And Scullyrumpus, whose furry head protruded from her pocket, seemed just as enthralled.

She flew alongside me, so close our wing tips touched. Together we soared and spun, our bodies moving in perfect unison. Currents carried us higher, then lower, over the misted lands to the east, and back to the forested mound.

We swooped down, marveling at the thriving trees. Rhia angled her wings, banking close enough to an elm to brush its quivering leaves with her outstretched hand. She made a low swishing sound as she passed, and the elm waved its upper limbs in reply. I couldn't help but laugh out loud; now my sister could chat with trees from the air.

I flew with her a while longer, then caught a swell that bore me swiftly higher. Like a bubble rising out of the deepest sea, I floated upward effortlessly, passing through alternating layers of cold and warmth. Soon, from on high, I viewed the whole of Fincayra again. Then I spotted Hallia, sailing above a cluster of clouds.

I pumped my wings to join her—when another sight arrested me. The mist shrouding the western sea had parted, just enough to reveal a shining pathway across the water. In the far distance, at the end of that swath of luminous blue, I could see another island, partly veiled by vapors of its own. Subtly, it sparkled, beckoning to me across the sea.

Although I knew only a little about the island, I could feel its pull, tugging me westward. And I knew well its name: Britannia. As well as another name, which it would one day be called in story and song—Merlin's Isle of Gramarye.

Merlin's Isle. As I said the words to myself, a westerly wind gusted, rustling my feathers gently. I yearned to ride that wind, to fly with it across the sea. Stronger it blew, and stronger, pushing me past the coastline. Suddenly I found myself floating over open ocean; Fincayra was rapidly receding. I caught a fleeting glimpse of Hallia, diving into a cloud. Furiously, I beat my wings, fighting with all my will to return.

At last, I broke free of the wailing wind and crossed back over the coastline. Trembling, my wings flapping heavily, I flew back toward Hallia, our home, and whatever lay ahead.

36

MERLIN'S
CHOICE

Swift as the wind itself, Hallia and I returned to the ring of imposing
stones. With a flutter of shimmering wings, we landed in the center of
the circle, stirring shreds of mist off the ground. I noticed right away
that the air within the ring felt warmer than before, and wondered
whether that was due to Dagda's presence. And I noticed, as well, that
the mist had seeped more deeply into the land. The pillars now
seemed as soft as clouds; even the stray tufts of grass on the ground
had turned from brown to creamy white.

Hallia and I glanced at each other. I sensed the uncertainty in her
eyes, doubly so since I felt the same unease myself.

As I folded my wings against my back, a piercing screech echoed
across the surrounding hills. I looked upward, but I already knew who
had called. As gently as a falling feather, Trouble landed on my
shoulder, clasping me once again with his talons.

Rhia arrived a few seconds later, her face still alight from the exhilaration of flying. Scullyrumpus, looking bedraggled but very pleased,
climbed up the woven vines of her garb to wrap himself like a thick
scarf around her neck.

From across the circle, Dagda approached, followed by a variety of
creatures including the bandaged bear, the mossy living stone, several

sparrows, and a family of raccoons with five chattering infants who tumbled over one another in their excitement. The silver-haired spirit strode over to us, smiling, his feet moving through the mist as if he were wading in the shallows of a summer sea.

"So," he said in his deep voice, "now you have flown."

"Yes," I replied. "And now I understand better what has happened to our world."

Dagda nodded slowly. "While I know you still feel more what Fincayra has lost than what it has gained, all the Otherworld is now yours to explore. You can still inhabit your favorite places on this world—yes, Hallia, all those trails and meadows you know so well—but you are also free to discover many more in the misty lands below."

"Thanks to our wings," said Rhia gratefully.

"That is right, Rhiannon. Because of your wings, you may venture into the Otherworld, even during your mortal lives. For the doorway that was breached shall, in time, open even wider. Spirit creatures of all kinds will voyage here, walking and flying and swimming in this realm, just as you may do in the realms below."

Hallia tapped her foot excitedly, sending up puffs of white vapor. "So my people will still be able to run, as deer, across our sacred lands?"

The elder smiled at her tenderly. "That will never change. But now, when you take the form of men and women, you may do something new. You may soar, as gracefully as hawks, in lands you have yet to discover."

On my shoulder, Trouble puffed out his chest feathers and ruffled his wings proudly.

"What about that place all alive with trees?" asked Rhia. "There wasn't any mist at all there."

"None at all," I echoed. "It almost seemed . . ."

Dagda lifted a silvery eyebrow. "Seemed what?"

"Well, like the whole place was separated somehow from the rest of Fincayra. Just as it was when it was still the Forgotten Island. Only now, it's covered with greenery."

"Quite so." He watched me closely. "You have seen the magic of your seed, Merlin. Planted in the place of its destiny, it has worked wonders untold."

"But how," I pressed, "does that land push back the mist? Why hasn't it been swallowed like everywhere else?"

The corners of his mouth lifted slightly. "Because the place you have renewed will become a world of its own."

I pondered his words. "You mean, a new Fincayra?"

"In a sense, yes. The cosmic balance requires a place that stands apart, a place that remains not wholly of Earth and not wholly of Heaven, but somewhere in between. That kind of world resembles mist itself—not really air and not really water, but something of both, and something else all its own. So when Fincayra has fully joined with the spirit world, this new land shall become that *in between place*."

Hearing the phrase our mother so often used to describe Fincayra, Rhia and I traded glances.

"And that land," continued Dagda, "no longer cursed or forgotten, shall at last have a name of its own." He paused, savoring the word before he uttered it. "Avalon. Its name shall be Avalon. And it shall have a destiny no less wonderful than the seed that gave it new life."

Trouble lifted his talons and paced a little, finding a spot closer to my head. Feeling his soft feathers brush against my cheek, I recalled the wind on my face during our first moments of flight together. And I felt again the freedom, the sheer thrill of it all.

The wise spirit looked directly at me again. "Now, my son, tell me what else you saw."

I worked my tongue, which felt suddenly dry. "I saw another land, one that calls to me." Swinging my face toward Hallia, I drank from the depths of her liquid brown eyes. "But I cannot go there without you."

For what seemed an endless moment, she studied me. At last, her voice cracking, she replied. "And I cannot go there with you, young hawk. My life, my people, are here. All our stories, past and future, are here."

"Come with me," I pleaded.

"Stay with me," she replied.

Several seconds passed. Neither of us spoke, or said a word.

Dagda took a step closer. "The choice is yours, Merlin. You are not required to go. Since Fincayra no longer exists as a world unto itself,

the ancient prohibition against a son or daughter of Earth remaining
here no longer applies."

I swallowed. "What, then, are my choices?"

He spoke slowly, as if each syllable carried the weight of an entire
world. "You, like Rhia and Hallia, have three choices. Hallia has
already made hers clear: to stay here in the Otherworld, a world that
includes more, much more, than can ever be described."

The hawk perched on me whistled enthusiastically, strutting across
my shoulder.

"Or you may go to the new world of Avalon." With a glance toward
Rhia, he added, "I should tell you that your mother, with whom I
spoke just before you returned, has decided to go there. As has your
friend Lleu, the young girl Cuwenna, and several other children."

"That's my choice, too," announced Rhia. Curled around her neck,
Scullyrumpus nodded vigorously, slapping his long ears. Then Rhia
stiffened. "That is," she added, "if . . ."

"Yes," Dagda agreed, laughing. "You may keep your wings." His
gaze swung back to me. "Your wings are yours in either of the first
two choices. But not the third. For that is to return to mortal Earth, to
the land called Britannia."

I looked at Hallia, who would remain here, and then at Rhia, who
would go with my mother to start a new society among the groves of
Avalon. My hand wandered to the hilt of my sword, and the magical
blade started ringing softly in its scabbard.

My heart pounded. How could I possibly make such a choice? If I
chose my destiny, my calling, I would lose the people closest to me—
as well as my wings.

"Be careful," Dagda advised, using his finger to draw the outline of
a misty wing in the air. "Whatever choice you make will be forever."

My gaze moved around the sacred ring, whose pillars glowed with
luminous vapors. There sat the eagles, fluttering their wings on the
highest stones; there stood my mother, with Lleu by her side; and
there, propped against one of the stones, lay Dinatius. Thin trails of
mist wrapped around his bladed arms, softening them. He looked far
more forlorn and embittered than dangerous.

All the while, I listened. To the breathing of those I loved. To my
own beating heart. To the ringing, so quiet and yet so clear, of my

magical sword. And perhaps, though I couldn't be sure, to what Aylah once called my innermost wind.

Slowly, I turned to Dagda. "I know now what I must do."

"And what is that?"

Trembling, I drew a deep breath. "I must follow my destiny."

I faced Hallia, whose round eyes held a mist of their own. "It's what I know is right, my love. But even so . . . I don't really know if I can do it."

With difficulty, she swallowed. "You must, young hawk. You must."

I stroked the back of her hand. "The better part of me will always stay here, with you."

She nodded, brushing her eyes. "We'll still be together."

"Yes," I said. "Like honey on a leaf."

She shook her auburn hair, pulling some strands away from her wing. Then she reached for the hilt of my sword, drew the blade partly out of its scabbard, and cut off a single lock. She pressed it, moistened by her tears, into my hand.

"Take that with you," she said softly, "to the next world."

"I will," was all I could manage to say. Somberly, I tucked the lock of hair into my satchel, next to Trouble's feather.

Turning back to Dagda, I ruffled my radiant wings. "I'd like to ask, if I could, a boon."

His silver eyebrows lifted. "And what might that be?"

"It's about, well, my wings. Since I'll be losing them . . ."

"Yes, my son?"

My hand lifted, pointing at the dejected figure of Dinatius. "I'd like you to give my wings to him."

Hallia and Rhia both sucked in their breath. On my shoulder, Trouble released a dissatisfied squawk and pinched me with his talons.

Dagda's eyes narrowed. "You would have me give your wings to one who served Rhita Gawr?"

"He bears as many wounds as he has inflicted. And one of those wounds, a grave one, he received from me. So you see, by healing him, I'm also healing myself."

The elder's face softened. "You are truly a wizard, my son." He paused, scrutinizing me. "But I shall not grant your request."

"You won't?" I protested.

"No. To have wings, he must earn them. That will take time, in his case much time, if it ever is to happen." His voice lowered. "I will, however, honor your request by doing something else."

Bending low, he swept his hand through the carpet of mist. He seemed to search for just the right thread of vapor before catching a spiraling one in his palm. Slowly, he stepped toward Dinatius, who took no notice of him. With a twist of his hand, Dagda dropped the shred of mist over the young man's head. It floated down, seeping into his body.

"This," pronounced the spirit, "is a gift from Merlin."

All at once, mist gathered thickly around Dinatius, covering all but his head. Then a sudden expression of disbelief came over him. Shaking himself, he looked down at his body, swathed in vapors. With dawning amazement, he worked himself higher against the pillar, until part of his chest rose above the mist. His chains, newly severed, fell to the ground. And below his shoulders, instead of deadly blades, hung two arms. His own arms, made of his own flesh.

Awestruck, he moved them, flexing his restored muscles. He lifted his arms into the air, bent them, and touched his cheeks with his hands. He stared first at Dagda, then at me, unable to speak. But his eyes, wide with wonder, said enough.

With a luminous smile, Dagda strode back through the mist. Gently, he touched my shoulder. "Come walk with me, young wizard."

Quickly retrieving my staff, I started walking alongside him. Across the circle we strode, leaving vaporous footprints on the whitened ground. This time, none of the creatures within the ring followed Dagda, so we were alone—except, of course, for the silver-toned hawk on my shoulder. The elder spirit led me all the way to the westernmost edge of the ring, where two upright pillars rose skyward, separated by a shaft of golden afternoon light. There we stopped, our backs warmed by the sun's rays.

Dagda studied me with affection. "When I came to you in a vision, so many nights ago, I warned you that you would have to confront your greatest foe."

I nodded. "And now I know you didn't mean Rhita Gawr. You meant my harshest rage, my deepest fears, whether they involved my father, my old enemy . . . or my future."

"You have leaped in more ways than one, my son." Pensively, he stroked his lame arm. "And so you shall know, at last, your true name—a name that you have earned, and that will empower you always, though it will never be known by more than a trusted few. For to most people, you shall forever be Merlin."

He inhaled deeply, drawing shreds of mist up his chest and arms. "I give you now your true name: *Olo Eopia*. In the language of the spirit lords, it means *man of many worlds, many times*. And it is a name that may be borne only by one such as you—a man who is complete, as the cosmos is complete."

My eyes brimming, I stood rigid, holding my staff. *Olo Eopia*. Many worlds, many times.

With a profound mixture of love and sorrow, I scanned the faces surrounding me. Dagda, whose gaze warmed me as much as the afternoon sun. Rhia, who was talking with a hemlock at the edge of the circle, spreading and contracting her wings as she spoke. Hallia . . . watching me longingly. Trouble, whose bright eyes never left me, not for an instant. My mother, standing beside Lleu, who nestled in the folds of her robe much as I'd often done as a child. And the tip of Shim's gargantuan nose, all that could be seen of him as he snored contentedly at the base of the hill.

"No matter how long I live," I said to the spirit beside me, "I'll never know another time as wondrous as these years on Fincayra." I sighed heavily. "How can I even start to describe them? Impossible. They're far too dear for words. And so I won't speak of them—at all. No, forever more, I'll think of them as my lost years."

Dagda cocked his head slightly. "So it shall be, then. But the day may come when you change your mind."

Resolutely, I shook my head.

He spoke quietly, his face aglow in the golden light. "You have done much in these years, to be sure. Why, you have learned to see without your eyes, taken the spirit of your sister into yourself, run with the grace of a deer—and now, with your own wings, you have flown."

My shadow, hazy on the misty ground, drew itself up with pride.

"And," continued Dagda, "you have almost learned to tame your shadow. Almost, but not quite."

The hazy form quivered, then shrank down to its normal size.

Turning, the wise spirit waved his arm westward, into the light. He stood very still, peering at something beyond the towering pillars, beyond the distant hills, beyond even the lowering sun. And then he spoke to me, with words I have never forgotten:

"For all the wonders of your time in Fincayra, the wonders ahead shall be greater still. You will soar to heights even higher than wings would allow. You will create more marvels than your magical seed." With a subtle smile, he added, "And yes, you will grow that great, flowing beard you have long dreamed of wearing."

Instinctively, I touched my chin.

"For this I can say with certainty, my son. You yourself are the rarest of seeds, bound at last for your own true home."

He smiled. "And that is why it is right you should have this."

He extended his hand, and there was a sudden flash of glowing green. The Galator! The legendary pendant lay on his palm, its jeweled center gleaming with the radiance of a star.

"B-but," I stammered, "it was lost under a mountain of lava."

"Just where I found it," Dagda replied matter-of-factly. "Here now, put it on." He placed the leather cord around my neck, as Trouble looked on, whistling in approval. Then he tucked the pendant under my tunic, so that it lay directly on my chest, just above my heart.

I patted the green jewel through the cloth. "Tell me, please. What is its true power?"

"To see those you love, Merlin, no matter if they are worlds away. So even after you leave here, you can visit your dearest friends again in that crystal."

Coughing, I cleared my throat. "Do you think . . . somehow, I could ever really come back to this world myself?"

The elder made no answer, though I did detect a curious glimmer in his eyes. Then he nodded in the direction of my companions. "Come now."

Together, we walked back to them. Shreds of mist curled about my boots, as if trying to hold me back. My pace slowed; I wasn't ready for farewells.

Hallia opened her arms to me. We embraced, rocking slowly from side to side. In time, our bodies trembling, we separated.

Gently, I touched the charred bracelet that I'd given her when our days held so few cares. And I spoke the words of the old riddle we'd often shared: *"So where, indeed, does the source of music lie?"*

In a raspy whisper, she replied, *"Is it in the strings themselves? Or in the hands that . . .* oh, young hawk, I can't."

I gave her a tender kiss. "I am with you, even after I've gone."

"I know, my love." She swallowed. "May green meadows find you."

A shadow suddenly fell over me. I looked up to find myself staring at a huge, bulbous nose.

"You is leavings?" asked Shim, the force of his breath scattering the mist under our feet. "For goodly?"

I gave a somber nod.

"Certainly, definitely, absolutely?"

"Yes, old friend."

"I says no!" he thundered, causing hundreds of birds perched on the pillars to take flight. Then, his voice quieter, he said earnestly, "I wants to comes with you."

I chewed my lip. "You can't, I'm afraid."

The giant lifted a tree-sized eyebrow. "Who will watchly out for you, when you is full of madness?"

I reached up and placed my hand flat against his nose. "You will, Shim. I'll still consult with you, in your dreams."

"Really? You can do such wizardly things?"

"If not, I'll learn," I promised. "And when I come to you, I'll bring a big tub of honey with me."

Shim's enormous mouth curled upward. "I'll still miss you muchly, Merlin. You is my firstly friend! But . . . so you can visits more easily, I'll tries to takes lots of naps."

I started to smile, when I felt someone's finger twirling the hair on the back of my head. I spun around to face Rhia. Placing my hand on her leafy shoulder—and being careful not to disturb the furry creature wrapped around her neck—I drank in the sight of her.

Finally, I said, "I'm going to miss flying with you, my sister."

Her blue-gray eyes sparkled. "And I'm going to miss landing on you, my brother."

We hugged each other. As my hand brushed the edge of her wing, I observed, "No more contraptions made from leaves and sticks for you."

"No," she replied with a bell-like laugh. She pulled back, studying my face. "Come to Avalon someday, will you?" With a mischievous grin, she added, "Plenty of vines there for swinging."

Now it was my turn to laugh. "No, no. Not that, please."

Her gaze grew intense. "Come, Merlin. I'll miss you."

With effort, I swallowed. "I'll try. Hard as I can."

Someone tugged on my tunic. I knew, before turning, it was Lleu. Beside him stood my mother. She looked careworn, much older than I remembered.

The boy peered up at me. "Don't go, master Merlin."

"I must, Lleu." Touching his head, I tousled his sandy curls. "You earned those wings, my friend. Enjoy them now."

He frowned. "It'd jest be better if ye'd stay."

Biting my lip, I faced Elen. She said nothing, but I couldn't miss the sorrow in her eyes. "Do you remember," I said softly, "all those years ago, when I left you to find my way here? You said to me, when we parted, that there comes a day for every bird . . ."

"To fly." Slowly, she nodded, making herself stand erect. "Yes, it's true. Every bird must fly." Though her mouth quivered, she gazed at me proudly. "And you, my good wizard, will fly in more ways than I can imagine."

Just then, a feathered wing brushed against my ear. "Trouble," I said, meeting the bird's unwavering gaze. "How can I ever say good-bye to you?"

The hawk's beak clacked sharply, and he gave me a scolding whistle. For a moment he paced back and forth on my shoulder, pinching me with his talons. At last, he settled again. He stretched out his wing, lightly nudging the side of my neck.

I reached up and stroked the edge of his wing. Then, with a final whistle, Trouble took flight, landing on Dagda's own shoulder.

Squarely, I faced the elder spirit. "It is time."

"Yes, Merlin, it is time."

Dagda raised his hand, making a small spiral in the air. Instantly, my shimmering feathers melted away. A blaze of white light seared the ring of stones. All at once, I was soaring, with invisible wings, high over the mist, the hills, and the sunlit sea.

And so I flew, in that moment, into another world—and into my heralded destiny.

EPİLOGUE

*There you have it, the tale I have carried within me all these years—
a tale that connects my life of many worlds, many times.*

*Those days happened long, long ago, yet they feel to me as fresh as
this morning's call of the curlew. All their glory, all their sorrow, all
their moments of longing and hope, remain as bright as my home's
crystalline walls. How I miss that land and those precious faces,
even now!*

*A story, like a feather, should be free, allowed to float wherever the
winds may blow. That, in truth, is why I have chosen to share this tale
at last. May it travel far, though it is but one tiny feather on the
unending winds of time.*

—Olo Eopia

A · Detail · of · Southeastern · FINCAYRA

To · THE · DARK · HILLS ·

be · there
Kreelixes?

Domnu's · Lair ·
— the Galator may lie here

THE
HAUNTED
MARSH

The · Wheel · of · Wye

hidden · caves

This · way · to
THE
RUSTED
PLAINS

The · Legendary
Carpet · Caerlochlann
found · here

The · Region · of ·
THE · SMOKING · CLIFFS

Ancient · home · of · the · Mellwyn-bri-Meath · clan

IAN · SCHOENHERR

MCMXCVIII

A · Detail of · THE HAUNTED MARSH

To EAGLES · CANYON

To THE DARK · HILLS

Beware the Sorceress

The · Mists · of · Time lurk · within · the · Mirror

The · Flaming · Tree

The · Lair of · Domnu

To THE RUSTED PLAINS

Giants' · Pathway

Be · there Queljies?

Ector's · Hiding

Tunnels of · Thorns

Deadly Beetles

Marsh Ghouls be · here?

village

Bally mag's · Cave

To · the Region · of

THE · SMOKING

CLIFFS

The · Troubled · Forest

Heed · well · the · warnings · of · the · trees

IAN · SCHOENHERR · MCMXCIX

T. A. BARRON wrote his first stories as a child under an old ponderosa pine on his family's Colorado ranch. His passion for writing, like his appreciation for nature's patterns and mysteries, never left him. During his years as a Rhodes Scholar at Oxford University, he traveled widely, trekking through places as diverse as east Africa, the Himalayas, rural Japan, Scandinavia, and Uzbekistan—as well as Scotland and Wales, where he grew fascinated by the ancient tales of Merlin. After returning to the United States, he spent several years managing a fast-growing business, but continued to write—and to ponder the legendary wizard who was the mage of Camelot and the mentor of King Arthur. Finally, Barron decided to leave his business and move back to Colorado to write full time. Now he writes novels, nature books, and picture books in the attic of his Colorado home. He also serves on a variety of environmental and educational boards, including The Wilderness Society, which recently awarded him its highest honor for his conservation work, and Princeton University, where he helped to found a program in environmental studies. His favorite pastime is hiking the mountain trails with his wife, Currie, and their five children.